AFTER THE FERRY

C.A. Larmer is a journalist, editor, teacher and indie publisher, and the author of numerous books including the Amazon-bestselling *Murder Mystery Book Club* series and the *Ghostwriter Mysteries*, as well as the non-fiction book about pioneering surveyors in Papua New Guinea, *A Measure of Papua New Guinea* (Focus; 2008).

Christina grew up in Port Moresby, PNG, was educated in Australia, and spent years working in London, Los Angeles and New York. She now lives with her musician husband, two sons and cheeky Blue Heeler in the Byron Bay hinterland of NSW, Australia.

Sign up to her newsletter: www.calarmer.com
Connect online: facebook/CALarmer

ALSO BY C.A. LARMER

The Murder Mystery Book Club
The Murder Mystery Book Club
Danger on the SS Orient
Death Under the Stars
When There Were 9
The Widow on the Honeymoon Cruise
Gone Guest
Peril on the Indian Pacific

The Sleuths of Last Resort Series
Blind Men Don't Dial Zero
Smart Girls Don't Trust Strangers
Good Girls Don't Drink Vodka

The Ghostwriter Mystery Series
Killer Twist (Book 1)
A Plot to Die For (Book 2)
Last Writes (Book 3)
Dying Words (Book 4)
Words Can Kill (Book 5)
A Note Before Dying (Book 6)
Without a Word (Book 7)

The Posthumous Mystery Series
Do Not Go Gentle
Do Not Go Alone

Plus:
An Island Lost

A Measure of Papua New Guinea:
The Arman Larmer Surveys Story

C.A. LARMER

AFTER THE FERRY

LARMER MEDIA

Published by Larmer Media
Northern NSW
Australia

www.calarmer.com

Paperback ISBN: 978-0-9924743-6-2

Cover design by Stuart Eadie
Edited by The Editing Pen
& Elaine Rivers (with heartfelt thanks)

For Nimo and Felix,
my beautiful, beautiful boys

PART ONE

PROLOGUE

Later, much later after they had pulled my battered body from the dark, volcanic sand and I somehow pulled myself back from an even darker place, I began to wonder, *What if?*

What if I had behaved differently on the ferry that day?

What if I had never locked eyes with a Greek stranger across a crowded stern? Or met a pair of Sydney university lads? Or set off on a journey with an old school friend with a chip on one shoulder and a crush of her own?

Instead, for now, it is the mid-1990s and I am filled with the arrogance of youth, the folly of a child, and my only question is of love and whether it is staring me in the face.

If that seems a tad dramatic to you, a little schoolgirlish, then forgive me for I am but a schoolgirl, just a few years out. I am lying with my head on a lumpy backpack, a book resting on my chest, my legs sprawled across a gusty deck, staring into the eyes of a man I do not know and wondering: Is *this* love? And can it be trusted?

I am watching the Greek man, and the two Sydney boys are watching me. Or at least one of them is, but I do not know this yet. I do not know this for some time.

For now, I am focused on a stranger.

We exchanged words a few minutes earlier, my Greek god and I, while waiting for burnt coffees in the bowels of the boat. No more than pleasantries, a flirtatious banter, but the chemistry was electric, the attraction like a smack in the face. And now, as he chews on his Styrofoam cup half a deck away, cheekily eyeing me above the rim, I wonder how the boat can keep moving, how the earth can keep turning, how this extraordinary, unfathomable attraction has not stopped the world in its wake.

He has sleepy brown eyes—almost anthropoidal—and they are boring into mine across the lurching ferry. I feel his pull, his shameless yearning. It matches my own, a yearning I have stowed since I set off on this trip. No, before that. It's the *reason* I set off. The reason I said yes when Monty Brennan asked me to see the world with her. Not because I wanted to see the world—and certainly not with her—but because I wanted more in life. I wanted love, I realise now, and now here it is, staring me in the face.

"Anyone want to go inside?" someone asks. "Get out of this bloody wind?"

"No," I manage. *No.* I want to stay right here, ogling a man I cannot know but who seems so oddly, giddily familiar.

The ferry lurches again, and he looks away. I frown, following his eyes down, beyond the bow, towards a speck on the painfully bright horizon. The speck is too rapidly becoming a smudge and now a rocky outcrop that turns into land as my eyes flit from there to him and back again. He is now standing, discarding his cup. He is reaching for his backpack, he is offering me occasional, sad smiles.

Oh well, his smile says. *It could have been beautiful.*

My frown deepens. *No, no! This cannot be it!*

And then the blasted place is upon us and he is edging his way towards an exit while my heart does a somersault and I go into panic mode.

Where is he going?

Why is he leaving me?

This must all have taken many minutes, but it seems to happen in a flash. At the top of the gangplank he turns, one final glance back, and he offers me a sliver of a smile, a subtle twitch of his head towards the bobbing beyond. It is a silent invitation, as loud as smashed glass in the dark.

My mind goes into overdrive, recalling my recent job as a feature writer at a woman's magazine in Sydney. The endless articles I wrote informing foolish girls how to snag their soul mate. Was I really prepared to ignore my own advice?

"Where are we, exactly?" someone asks. Angus, I realise now, the business student who's been clinging to me like soggy cardboard since we left Rome.

"Trust you to score the hot one," my friend Monty had teased the morning after the night we all met below the Spanish Steps. I was flattered at the time; smug, too, because she was right. Angus *was* the better-looking of the two mates, the one with the broader shoulders, the chiselled jawline, the winning smile. And he had chosen me. Well, that was the vibe he gave off. We hadn't hooked up yet, but everyone knew it was coming. It was as inevitable as the sea.

Angus Tower was enthralling to me at first, with his lofty ambitions—"I'll be a millionaire before I'm twenty-five, just you sit back and watch"—and his dapper way of dressing, all turned-up shirt collars and Polo logos, and certainly more attractive than his ranga mate, Thomas Wilson, whose only claim to fame was an uncanny memory. (He knew all the words to almost every Aussie song and could recite his entire Visa card number from memory, as if that mattered. As if anyone cared.)

I glance at Angus and wonder what I ever saw in him. His smile seems so smarmy now, his stiff collars so ridiculous.

"Says here it's Sa-ree-see Island," says the redhead, Thomas, wielding his battered *Lonely Planet* like the bible it has become. "Nothing but a crusty old convent and a couple of tacky tavernas. We'll keep going on to Santorini. This one sounds like a bore."

How could it be boring with *him* on it?

I glance from Thomas to Angus and then to the back of my Greek god's head. He is fast vanishing. Then I notice the book in my lap—a book I scored early in the trip and have quoted from incessantly since—and I smile because I know I have no choice. It's as clear as Times New Roman.

I get up and grapple for my backpack.

"Hey, Silly Millie, just chill," Monty says to me, barely looking up from beneath a crisp Akubra. Her head is resting on Thomas's dusty lap, his wide-brimmed hat covering her face from the scorching sun. I wonder momentarily if *they* have hooked up. "Thomas is in charge of the schedule, remember? We're heading for Santorini, right, Thomas?"

"Right, Monty," he says, his eyes boring into mine. "You and Millie are exactly where you need to be."

Yet I ignore them both. My heart is thumping, blood is rushing through my ears, and I know in that moment that if I do not follow that man, I will never forgive myself. Yet I also know, even in the haze of youth, that if I *do* follow him, I may have so much more to forgive.

It's a toss-up. It's a gamble. It's a game of chance.

As my hand hovers over my backpack and my eyes dart to the gangplank, I hesitate only briefly, then I make a decision that will change absolutely everything.

What I don't know yet, what I cannot possibly foresee, is that this is a story of choices, two choices, as clear as the glassy Aegean, each one with consequences that will reverberate not just across my life—the life of Millie Malone—but across all the lives around me.

One choice will see me return to Sydney, married to my career, the other will see me married to one of the men on this boat.

One choice will lead to a deep, everlasting love.

The other will lead to murder.

So which way do I go?

PART TWO

Thirteen years later

EVE MAGAZINE
(Sydney)

Millie Malone had mysteriously vanished, and her personal assistant could not have been happier. For two days now there'd been no sighting of the infamous editor, and if it wasn't for her incessantly ringing phone, Brianna Miles would have enjoyed every moment of them.

Still, it was a small price to pay for a break from the menacing Amelia (no one called her 'Millie' now, it didn't suit her, and they wouldn't dare).

And there it was again. *Brrrrring! Brrrring!*

Brianna sighed dramatically, wedged a fake smile to her lips, and answered with a monotonic, "*Eve* magazine, Amelia Malone's phone, Brianna speaking."

"Please tell me she's turned up," came a deep growl from the other end.

Brianna's smile turned genuine. "Good morning, Gerry. I'm sorry, sir, no, she has not come in. Again."

The publisher exhaled, or perhaps it was another growl. "It's bloody deadline week for Christ's sake! What the hell's she playing at?"

"I don't—"

"What about Monty?"

"The art director is not due back from her trip until later this afternoon, sir. She's at a shoot in—"

"I don't give a flying toss where she's at! It's Amelia we need to find for f—" He swallowed the rest of that sentiment and took a calming breath. "What about her place? You check there?"

"Yes, sir, not answering."

"Not the *phone*. Did you think to go over? Make sure she hasn't gassed herself or something?"

Brianna thought about that for a moment. Goodness! It hadn't even occurred to her. Could this week get any better?

"Great idea, sir. I'm onto it."

"Good. And, er, what's your name again?"

"Brianna, sir."

"Right, Brenda, let me know how you go. This is a massive worry. It could be disastrous."

"Oh I agree, sir, we're all very—"

"We're due at a Revlon lunch at one"—he interrupted—"and if she's not found by then, we can kiss the account goodbye." And with that the line went dead.

Brianna's eyes twinkled. It was the longest conversation she'd ever had with *Eve's* formidable publisher Gerry Henderson, and despite the tone, she had thoroughly enjoyed herself. He was a midsized man with an enormous, peppery moustache and a nose so mottled it looked like a pincushion, but that didn't matter a jot. The guy was a publishing dynamo with a direct line to Rupert Murdoch. He oozed charisma, helped in part by the power he wielded over twenty of Australia's top-selling magazines. It brought a constant stream of flirtatious females to his door, from the editors to the marketing department. He was even rumoured to have dallied with a few, despite a chiselled trophy wife at home, but Brianna doubted Amelia had ever had a crack.

She was married to the magazine. One of Murdoch's brides.

Snatching up her faux Gucci handbag, Brianna got to her feet and glanced around. The entire office was staring at her. She thought that she would burst. It was extraordinary the power that had shifted to her shoulders in a matter of days. It was as though she, the measly editorial assistant, held the key to the very survival of *Eve*.

That's when Alex Jones decided to pounce. The deputy editor leapt from her chair and dashed across.

"Gerry hassling you?"

Brianna nodded.

Alex drew her into Amelia's office and closed the glass door. "What are we going to do?"

"He wants me to check out Amelia's house."

"Exactly what I was going to suggest. Just switch your phone to… er…"—she glanced around the office outside—"…to Melissa's. She can cover your calls."

Alex flung the door open and called out. "Mel, you're on phone duty. But if Gerry calls—or Amelia for that matter—put them straight through to me, you hear? No one else."

A young redhead waved from the other end of the office. "What about any calls that come in for Amelia? Do you want to take them too?"

"God, no," Alex replied. "Just take a message. It's not rocket science, Melissa. I'm sure you can handle it." She turned back to Brianna. "Get going, but don't take too long. And if you find our wayward editor, call me, okay? Not Gerry. Me first. I'm in charge now."

Brianna's twinkle flickered out as she leant across to Amelia's phone. She punched in a few numbers, diverting the line to the feature writer, and then picked up her bag again.

Well, what a surprise. It hadn't taken long for her power to be usurped.

~ ~ ~

Amelia's house was a one-hundred-year-old semidetached in the upmarket Sydney suburb of Rose Bay. It had been freshly renovated with an ornate garden planted at the front, but none of that changed the fact that it was a pokey, draughty place. Not even its two-million-dollar price tag could hide that. Brianna had been here several times before, usually in the middle of the day to pick up something Amelia had inadvertently left behind—cover mock-ups, invoices, her dry cleaning would you believe! But she had never been here chasing down the editor herself. It wasn't necessary. Until yesterday, Amelia had not taken so much as a sick day. Rumour had it she hadn't had a day off since she started at the magazine more than a decade ago. She certainly hadn't taken time out to find herself a hubby or have a child. The very notion left Brianna snickering.

Amelia Malone lived and breathed *Eve* magazine, which is why her absence was so oddly compelling.

She rang the doorbell long and hard, then hammered on the door for a good minute before smudging her nose up to the front window. There was no movement inside. She glanced about. Yesterday's mail was still in the letterbox out the front, soggy from the overnight rain, and she didn't bother retrieving it, simply turned on her heel and left, her twinkle now like fireworks, bursting in the dark.

SHEPPERDIN VILLAGE
(Rural New South Wales)

The man with the ginger-coloured beard and the battered Akubra hat waited at the gate of Shepperdin Primary School for his son to emerge. There were women everywhere, as always, but Thomas Wilson kept his distance, sensing their sympathy. Not wanting any of it. No, it wasn't sympathy yet; just curiosity at this stage. The sympathy would come, he knew, when they learned that his wife, Millie, had vanished, followed quickly by accusations from some. He wasn't sure he was ready for that.

Shit. There's that busybody again. Polly, was that her name? The one who bustles about bossing everyone in sight as though she's running a multinational corporation when all she's in charge of is the measly parent-student committee. The P&C they called it, something like that.

He showed up at one meeting, a few years back, offered to cook snags for some fund-raising thing or another. Never again. Several of the single mums hit on him, as slimy as the sausages, causing a ruckus with the missus. She'd been skittish about flirty chicks since they'd first hooked up in the Greek Isles. So he always kept his distance, but he couldn't stay away today, or yesterday for that matter. Silly Millie had seen to that.

In fact, before this week, he hadn't shown up at the school in months. Avoided the place at all costs, with its stern-faced teachers and mothers who wore their superiority with tight smiles. He spotted a few dads, but most just rushed past with their heads down and their shoulders hunched to retrieve their kids and vanish again before anyone could ask them to mow the lawn or drive the kids to another bloody excursion.

He thought of Phil and felt a rush of relief. *High school next year, thank Christ.* At least there they let you off the hook, for the most part. They're just happy if you get the buggers to school at all, preferably not stoned. And with his mother gone, young Phil has been desperate to go to school, as though being around the house was a reminder of all that went before. Of the deathly silence that led to her vanishing.

Screaming he could cope with, accusations, anger. But the silence had been deafening, chilling even.

If only there was a note. Some kind of explanation.

He heard a "Yoo-hoo!" and looked up. *Jesus, Bossy Sox was coming over.*

He turned away, pretending to be engrossed in something along the fence line. Too late, she was upon him, her eyebrows lifting, her head held slightly to one side in that "Do you remember me?" way.

And then she said it: "Hi Tom, do you remember me? I'm Polly Wildermon, a good friend of Amy's."

She was using Millie's new moniker. Well, not *new* exactly. Amelia had shed her childhood nickname 'Millie' a decade or so earlier, when she first settled in Shepperdin with him, choosing the shorter, sharper 'Amy' instead. Tom liked it. It was less fussy, less frivolous. The same reason he'd downshifted from 'Thomas'.

He turned back, now thinking, *You're no friend of my wife's.*

"Is Amy okay, Tom? We haven't seen her for a few days and Toby mentioned something—"

"She's fine, thanks, Polly. Thanks for asking." He tried to offer her a confident smile but was sure he hadn't pulled it off.

"Oh, okay. Great!"

Polly reached out and rubbed one of his shoulders. It felt intrusive, but a few mums were watching and he didn't want to shake her off.

She got the gist, though, and dropped her hand. "Please tell that beautiful wife of yours that we'd *love* to see her at the hall this arvo if she's around. Yolanda's running her hatha yoga class. Be right up her alley."

"Yep, sure."

She smiled, paused, looked like she had more to say but ended with, "Take care of that boy, hey?"

"Of course." *One of us has to.*

Tom spotted his son and watched him, mesmerised for a moment. Phil had a mop of floppy wet-brown curls and twinkling green eyes like his mother and was slapping his palm against his head, grinning at something his mate Zachai was saying. Zac ended with a roar of laughter, then noticed his mum and kept laughing as he ran off to join her while Phil twisted his head around, looking this way and that.

When he locked eyes with his dad, his grin dissolved.

Tom sighed and headed towards him.

SARISI ISLAND
(Greece)

Millie Malone tried not to think of the world she'd just left behind as she strolled across the esplanade, towards the dark, swirling sea. Tried not to think of who she was letting down.

How they would react to her sudden, inexplicable absence.

Instead, she focused on the wharf at Sarisi Bay, where fishermen were but ghostly silhouettes against the grey. She watched as they checked nets, freed buoys, rolled one for the road. Continued watching as they chugged their engines and set off, first one boat, then another, then two more, each slicing through the grey until there was nothing left but the faint scent of their tobacco to prove they had ever existed.

From the esplanade, Millie felt just as ghostly. Just as lost.

Why had she returned after all these years? What did she hope to find? And why had she left in such a blasted hurry, forgetting to pack something warmer than the silly cotton coat she was now donning, its pockets so high she had to bend her elbows to keep her hands contained?

Still, the chill was not entirely unwelcome. It numbed her a little, matching her mood. Beneath the coat, the edge of her black pleated skirt was caught in her leather ankle boots, and she noticed for the first time in hours that her feet had ceased to ache. They were numb too. She made no effort to move, though, simply stared out to sea, surprised by its persistent darkness and the mist that her breath was now making, clouding her view. Something else quickly replaced it.

A memory from a lifetime ago: a man and a woman, laughing as they gulped in the crisp air between two long fingers pushed against swollen lips. Their fingers moved away swiftly as they exhaled, their lips upturned Hollywood-style into the sky, and they watched as the condensation conjured up imaginary cigarette smoke before their eyes.

He pulled her to him then, thrust one arm behind her neck and pushed his fingers to her lips this time.

"Inhale," he demanded, his voice deep, commanding. "Inhale deeply."

She giggled nervously, did as he said and then whispered, "I should probably go."

"Stay" was his reply, his thick fingers now making their way down her chin, her neck, towards her décolletage.

She inhaled. Shivered. "Really," she said, her voice catching. "I'll miss the ferry."

His body stiffened. He did not let go.

A dog's howl snapped the woman's lips shut, and she glanced around, pulling her coat closer to her chest from within, feeling her pounding heart beneath the flimsy fabric. She took a calming breath, released one hand from its warm cubbyhole, and scooped her bag up again. She must get on. She had no time to waste. Everything depended upon it.

But what if I can't find him? Millie thought. And then more terrifyingly, *What if I can? What on earth will I say?*

She jiggled her head a little as if trying to refocus and returned to the cobbled road just as another memory hit her like a slab of concrete: a piercing scream, a smattering of blood. So much blood, so much pain.

Her knees buckled, her legs wobbled, but she steadied herself, swallowing the memory down as she has done every day for almost five thousand days, and kept on walking.

~ ~ ~

From a distance someone was watching. Curious at this point; unconcerned.

Nicholas Xydis was in a good mood. It was his favourite hour,

5:00 a.m., and even the early risers of Sarisi were only just beginning to twist and turn in their beds, one last dream before reality rushes in. He has been up for ten minutes, watching the fishermen depart, dragging on his own rollie, a cup of thick black coffee recharging his batteries. He would be joining them soon, but he was in no hurry. His livelihood did not depend upon it.

In the bedroom beyond, the sheets are rumpled, the mattress dipping and diving where fervent limbs have beaten it out of shape. Catalina had dropped by again. His mood darkened. He liked her well enough but was glad she was somebody else's wife.

He grimaced. At least Theo didn't catch them this time. He knew he was botching everything up, but he couldn't seem to help himself. Couldn't find another way. And so he ploughed on towards certain disaster, definite regret.

Slurping his coffee, he revelled in the aroma, the warmth of it in his belly, the comfort of a decent cup. Perhaps he'd spark the coffee machine up again, he thought as he stumped out his smoke and stood up, but then he saw the woman turn, a slight silhouette against the silvery sea.

He stepped back quickly into the shadows of the balcony even though she had not looked round, could not possibly have seen him. But there was something about her stance that warned him off. It was a private moment. He felt like an intruder. Yet he continued to watch, curiosity getting the better of him. And he squinted, as though that would somehow sharpen his focus, as all thought of coffee vanished.

He could tell she was not a local, not even Greek. The stupid coat, the awkward stance, the way her arms wrapped around her body tightly, all told him she was a stranger here and an anxious one at that. He stepped forward slightly to get a better view. It was early for tourist season. *Had she veered off track?* She turned suddenly, directly towards him, and for a second he feared he had been spotted, but she looked away easily, her face caught momentarily in the amber streetlight. Her lips were shut, her jaw clenched tight, her eyes barely visible below a hat of some sort. He watched as she bent down to collect her bag, long hair sliding across her chest and then flying back up with a flick as she straightened and turned away from town.

Nicholas's first reaction was to call out to her, to tell her she was going the wrong way, but something about her stride stopped him.

She no longer looked apprehensive. She was hurried, determined. Without doubt. It was clear she was heading towards Coso Point and, he assumed, the castle. He had better alert his mate. The tourists had come early this season.

As Nicholas returned inside, he had a niggling feeling the woman wasn't a tourist after all. There was something about those eyes, that jaw, the way she walked that told him she was no stranger to Sarisi.

He had seen them all before.

A tiny shiver trickled down his back.

EVE MAGAZINE

Tuesday stretched on. The phones kept ringing. Amelia never showed.

The deputy editor tried hard to mask her delight as she returned from her lunch break and noticed the editor's chair still vacant. She slipped behind her own desk, tapped her keyboard, then slid her eyes sideways and swivelled her chair around.

Why not? Alex thought. *Why not indeed!*

She stood up, pulled her shoulders back and made her way into Amelia's office.

It was absurdly oversized, really, with an enormous L-shaped wooden desk and a classic 1950s Eames high-back, leather office chair. One side of the room contained a small round conference table that sat four staffers, and behind that a metal bookshelf lined with every conceivable woman's title—from Italian *Vogue* and UK *Marie Claire* to *The Australian Women's Weekly* and US *Vanity Fair*. These were Amelia's personal copies, and in case you were thinking of sneaking in and pinching one, they were each plastered with a white sticker that read EDITOR'S COPY, HANDS OFF!

Alex stepped up to the shelf and began leafing through them, selecting the latest issues to take home and retain. Behind her, glass windows opened the office up to a sparkly Sydney harbour view, the kind of view that was wasted on a busy editor. The blinds had been let down halfway to avoid the glare, but she lifted them all the way up now, ignoring the sun that came smashing in. She wanted to drink in that view. She was almost giddy with delight.

"Alex?"

The deputy swung around to find the art director staring at her.

"Oh, Monty! Goodness, you gave me a fright. You're back from Hamilton Island."

"Just got in. What's going on?"

Monty Brennan glanced deliberately at the magazines in the deputy's hands. The look on her face spoke volumes, and Alex tried to regain her composure. The two women had never been friends. They were from different sides of the tracks. Alex was a middle-class suburban mum trying her hardest not to be, while Monty was the single career woman's pinup girl—painfully thin and smartly dressed in a shiny Stella McCartney suit and Pucci pumps. She was a very old friend of Amelia's and one of her "elite", part of the select posse who got to stay back each month and work on the illustrious cover. As though they were creating the next *Mona* bloody *Lisa*. And then, when it was finally complete—and God knows it could take days— they would celebrate at the latest swanky eatery, courtesy of Gerry, while the rest of them stayed back, eating soggy sandwiches or last night's leftovers like they'd been twiddling their thumbs all month. Like they were inconsequential.

Yet Alex was the deputy editor for goodness' sake! She once stayed back longer than anyone, neglecting her kids, ignoring her husband, pretending to fit in. But that was sometime ago…

She brushed her discounted Country Road suit down with one hand and tightened her grip around the precious magazines.

Monty frowned. "Where is Amelia?"

Your best friend's deserted you, Alex wanted to say. "She's vanished. Haven't you heard?"

"What do you mean vanished?"

"Nobody knows where she is."

"Don't be so melodramatic, Alex," Monty scoffed as she began to turn away. "She's probably in a meeting with Gerry or someone from advertising."

"No, Monty. I mean, we haven't seen Amelia in days."

She turned back. "Days?"

"Not since last Friday."

"*Friday?* Seriously?" She blew air through her lips. She did not believe Alex. "She must have called in."

Alex nudged her chin towards Brianna. The editor's assistant was watching them through the glass wall, and she shook her head no.

Monty frowned and reached for her mobile phone, stabbing at a few buttons, her tone still light when eventually she spoke. "Hey, lovely, it's me. I'm back. Just checking where you're at." Her eyes darted away from them both, her voice dropped. "Alex seems to have some crazy notion that you've vanished but, well, um… Just give us a bell. Okay?"

Clicking off, she began trawling through her messages. Nothing. Not so much as a bubble. Monty had been relieved by this earlier, now it made her feel nauseated.

"Why didn't anyone call me?"

"You were on holidays so—"

"I wasn't *on holidays*, Alex. I was on a fashion shoot. I was working."

Sure you were. Working on a tan more like. "Either way, she hasn't shown up all week; we've checked her house, it looks like she's cleared off. Gerry's in a flap, as you can imagine."

"She hasn't even called *Gerry*?"

"Nope. Pretty damn rude, if you ask me."

"Out of character is what it is!" She frowned. "Okay, leave it with me. I'll make a few calls. I'm sure her folks will know where she's at. She goes nowhere without them knowing."

Alex shrugged. Monty didn't get it. She really didn't care. Actually, that wasn't quite true. She *did* care. Just not about Amelia's whereabouts. She hoped the editor not only stayed away, she never came back. It's not that Alex hated Amelia, as such. She *despised* her, and that was a different kind of loathing. She glanced at the big chair behind the desk and thought about it for a moment, but nerves got the better of her, so she simply swept past Monty, out of the editor's office and back to her own desk, still clutching Amelia's magazines tight to her chest, like she was holding on to a life vest.

Monty, meanwhile, glared at her mobile phone like it was an emergency beacon that refused to work. She strode back to the designers' section of the office, greeting various staffers along the way, the phone still in one hand, silently begging it to vibrate.

When she got to her desk, she placed it beside the keyboard and kept darting glances at it, knowing she should be working— *God, she had so much to catch up on*—yet unable to focus.

Where, oh where was Amelia?

Monty knew she should call the parents immediately. Perhaps Beryl had the answer. But that was like tapping a sleeping grizzly on the shoulder and asking where her cub had got to. There had to be someone friendlier.

She scoffed to herself. *Who was she kidding?* She was Amelia's only friend or at least the only one she caught up with outside of publishing headquarters, and that was largely due to their history. They went back.

Back to when the infamous Amelia Malone was just plain Millie. Back when they were carefree travellers…

Monty's stomach tightened just thinking of it. Of the ferry. Of wanting to reach out, of wanting to grab Millie by her ponytail and keep her on board.

Why didn't she do that? Why did she let her get off with a stranger?

"You've got PTSD," someone told her a few years ago. A boyfriend who couldn't compete with the guilt he made love to every night.

"Don't be ridiculous," she had told him, but that was old news. She had already diagnosed herself.

She would never forget the anxious phone calls.

"What do you mean she got off the ferry with 'some Greek guy'?"

"What do you mean you continued on to Santorini?"

"Where on God's earth is my daughter?"

That was the mother. The father was much, much worse.

"Your best mate heads to some strange island you go there *with* her. What kind of friend are you?"

A bad one, she decided, a very bad one in fact. One with an ulterior motive.

She'd had a massive crush on Angus Tower, see, even though he only had eyes for Millie. Monty was certain she was a better match so was quietly elated by her friend's sudden desertion at Sarisi.

Now it was *her* chance to dazzle the better-looking one, to score the top prize.

It was as simple and as pathetic and as horrifying as that.

She wanted the hotter one to pick her for a change, and if both boys fought over her, all the better. Except they didn't, not really. They just used her up and spat her out, and when she returned to Sydney some time later, fully expecting Millie to be waiting in the wings, ready to giggle over her silly Greek love affair, she was nowhere to be found. Her parents hadn't heard from her. There was no gushing text or dull travel blog or reassuring call on Skype. This was before all of that.

There wasn't even a postcard.

"Must still be in the arms of her Greek god on Sarisi," she'd told everyone, still feeling envy then, still thinking *typical Millie!*

Oh how wrong she was.

When Millie finally returned, Monty's envy had morphed from worry to dread to remorse. She knew something terrible had happened, could tell from her friend's stiff mannerisms and vacant smile. Millie was back, but not really. The new Millie was different somehow, and it wasn't just the fact that she now insisted on using her full name, the name her teachers used to scold her with.

Amelia.

"I hate Millie now," she said, and Monty wasn't sure if she was referring to the name or to herself.

It took another year for the horror of what had happened to come out, and two more before Monty worked out what was missing. It was Amelia's heart. It had been snatched from her, along with her dignity, her ID and all her personal effects.

Monty groaned and reached for the phone. She could put it off no longer. It was time to wake the sleeping bear.

SHEPPERDIN VILLAGE

Tom groaned as he surveyed the open fridge, one callused hand holding the door wide. That's right, there was bugger all to eat. The final insult before Amy chose to bail. He'd managed to cobble some meals together for the past few days, but there was little he could do with some mangy veggies and slimy ham, and how was he supposed to do the shop? It was bad enough he had to steal away from work to get his kid to school and back—the school bus had been on the blink for weeks—he could hardly ask for time off to go to the supermarket. In this hick rural town it'd make him a laughingstock.

He slammed the door shut with so much ferocity he could hear his beer bottles clinking inside.

"Dad?"

That was Phil, eyes wide, a tiny crinkle cutting into his perfect little forehead. He'd had that expression for two days now, ever since Monday morning when he'd woken Tom with the news that his mum had vanished.

"Go back to sleep," Tom had told him, croakily, grumpily. "She's just up."

Well, she was usually up at that time, making Phil's school lunch. She always did it at the crack of dawn, didn't need to of course. Didn't need to be up for hours, but it was like she was bursting to get out of bed. *Away from him.* It made his heart wrench each and every time, her absence like a black hole in the bed.

An hour later, when he'd pulled himself from the covers and

shuffled into the kitchen, one hand scratching the stubble on his face, he had to concede his son was right. Amy was nowhere to be seen. Together they checked every nook and cranny in and around the house, the yard, the top shed.

"Shouldn't you call the cops?" his brother, Harry, had suggested later when they conferred over the back fence.

It wasn't so much a fence as a couple of scraggly bushes that Tom had planted some years earlier, a demarcation line of sorts. The property was Harry's, bequeathed to him by their father, and he'd chosen the better of the two houses as his own. Harry's was the newer, four-bedroom brick place, the one their parents had built back in the eighties, unable to stand the creaky, draughty old timber house they'd inherited from their own parents. That one was offered to Tom and Amy, who seemed genuinely delighted. She reckoned it had "stacks more character", but to Tom that was like admiring an ugly woman for her personality.

He wasn't buying it, but he couldn't afford anything else, so he'd graciously accepted and moved his then-pregnant wife in, even though it was where the bad memories were first forged, but what choice did he have? Beggars couldn't be choosers, and homeless couples had to take what they could get.

They moved in a week before Phil was born, and it was another three years before he erected the bushy barrier, as much to protect his own privacy as to keep Harry's brood out. And there were a lot of 'em to keep out.

His older brother and his wife of twenty years, Scarlett, had six children, all under the age of fourteen. They were a chaotic mob. A disaster zone if you asked Tom. Amy never envied their better house with its insulated brick walls and indoor toilet, but she did envy that snotty-nosed mob, and he could never fathom why.

"Amy's obviously taking some time out, mate; she hasn't been kidnapped," Tom explained to his brother over the fence that morning.

"And you know this how?"

"I just know it. That's all."

"Did you have a fight?"

"What? No, course not."

"Did you call her folks? She might've gone there."

He scowled, wasn't ready for that, but acknowledged the point.

She had run there before when things had been tougher.

Lately everything was good. At least he thought it was.

Harry added, "She's probably curled up in her mum's lap now, sobbing about her boring, miserable life."

"Shut up, mate."

But Harry wasn't being entirely unfair. It had been an open wound that seemed to fester between the couple with every passing year. Amy had had a career once, she liked to remind everyone, had worked as a feature writer for some flashy woman's magazine, but it always felt to him like she was admitting to some sleazy affair and left her looking grubby.

"I'm sure she'll be back in a day or so," he'd told his brother, and his brother had stared at him oddly, as though worried about *him*, not his missing wife.

"I'm starved," Phil said, breaking through Tom's thoughts. He looked around at the young boy with the old man's worry on his face.

"Come on then, matey, let's head to the Boot & Tucker."

SARISI ISLAND

A distant roar woke Millie from her sleep, and it took a few moments to work out where she was and why her body felt like it had morphed into a pretzel.

Ah, Greece. That's right.

She stretched her neck to one side and then to the other and tried to stand but found one leg had forgotten its purpose and refused to work. The other was crossed over it, clearly blocking the circulation, and she slowly straightened it out and looked around. It was still quite chilly, but a little sunlight was poking through a persistent cloud, and she was starting to sweat under the coat that was finally doing its job. She pulled it off as the roaring intensified.

There was a mechanical cough, a splutter and a whoosh as a motorbike came flying around the bend and up towards the woman at breakneck pace. That got her uncooperative leg working. She leapt up and out of the way as the rider came to a smoky halt, half a metre from her feet. The bikie wasn't wearing a helmet, and his oversized mirrored sunglasses could not mask the shock on his face.

"Sorry, sorry!" he was yelling. "I no see you!"

She dusted herself off and managed a smile. "Don't worry," she said stiffly. "I'm fine."

He pushed the sunnies up into his cropped, receding hairline and stared at her like she was a mirage, his scruffy eyebrows scrunched together incredulously. Leaning the bike to one side, he applied the stand and lumbered off. Well into his thirties, forty perhaps, the man had a chiselled goatee, a short, trunk-like body covered in lurid

24

orange jeans and a denim jacket, and an enormous, crooked nose that suggested one too many brawls. Or bad genes, perhaps.

"You come this morning?"

She nodded. "Flew into Santorini last night, got the early ferry across."

He looked awestruck. "The 1:25 a.m. Blue Star to Piraeus?" He chuckled. "Nobody get this ferry. Is too early! Only mad dogs and English man. You mad dog or English?"

"Australian."

He nodded as if that was basically the same thing. "You want bed?" The look of scepticism was still in place.

She frowned.

"Hostel no open, sorry." He was pulling a cluster of keys from his jacket and striding towards the front door as he spoke. "Season no start."

She grappled for her things and followed.

"But where's Sister Agnetha?"

He glanced back at her. "Your sister?"

"No, Sister *Agnetha*. The head nun."

He snorted. "No nuns! You see."

As he said it, he unlocked the heavy wooden door, then used both hands to shove it inwards and open. There was a loud creak followed by a burst of icy air that rushed out to greet them. He waved the woman through, and at first she hesitated, glancing into the cavernous room before stepping across the stone threshold.

And she did indeed see.

The place had changed considerably since she was there last. Oh not the bones, not the structure—arched corridors still led in various directions, stone slabs still occupied the floor, uneven and worn down—but everything else was missing. The enormous wooden crosses that once adorned the walls had vanished. So, too, the chipped statue of Mother Mary holding baby Jesus that once stood in the centre of the room, blocking the path of anyone who dared to whiz past. A most inconvenient position, she remembered, and as deliberate as a Stop sign. She could not recall how many times she nearly toppled it over in her youthful haste, a daily reminder of what was important, or so Agnetha said. The statue was gone, of course, and it was now an open thoroughfare adorned with a shaggy red carpet that looked straight out of an IKEA catalogue.

Priorities had certainly changed.

But worse than that, so much worse, the place had been whitewashed. Literally. Every wall had been plastered up and repainted a dazzling Santorini white where crumbling brown bricks once sat ticking off time. Her heart dropped further.

This was not how it was supposed to be.

The man was busy flicking on lights and opening shutters, oblivious to the disappointment that tasted like sour milk in the woman's mouth. He made his way across to a varnished wooden reception desk and then reached around behind a large desktop computer.

As it chimed its way to life, the woman cleared her throat. The hotelier glanced up as if surprised she was still there and then back at his screen. She stepped across.

"This used to be a convent, am I right?"

He looked up again. "Yes, *looong* time ago."

Thirteen years, she thought. Just a heartbeat.

"You come before, to Sarisi?" he asked.

She nodded, adding, "Also a long time ago."

He seemed happy to hear that and waved a pudgy hand about. "Is changed, yes?"

Yes, she thought. *Too much.* "So do you know where they went? The nuns?"

Kostas shrugged. He had no idea, and why would he? By Greek standards, he was a newcomer to the island, moved here four years ago, seeking work and an escape from his father's shoelace store in Athens. *Of all things,* he had thought, even as a young child, *shoelaces!* The shop was below street level, down a poky set of stairs into a darkened hovel of a space. And customers—mostly shoe shop owners needing to restock or local men wanting to gossip—would scuttle down at all hours to chat with his dad or barter for a better deal. It bored young Kostas senseless and embarrassed him too.

I mean, shoelaces! Really?

He swore when he was a man he'd get away, do something more important with his life. Yet it took him twenty years to work up the courage. But that was another story.

As for the nuns? Yes, there were nuns here once, but apart from the creepy paraphernalia they'd left behind—paraphernalia he had worked hard to exhume—it meant little to him. He'd never given them much thought until now.

Until she had shown up.

"Do they have a new convent here, or did they go back to Athens?" the woman pressed, sounding both desperate and demoralised.

"Sorry, Miss, I know nothing about nuns. They you friends, yes?"

"Yes."

"Okay, you speak to Effie."

The woman looked at him, stunned and silent.

"My friend Effie. She know."

He reached below the desk and returned with a printout of a map. He thumped it on the bench in front of her and stabbed a finger in the centre.

"We here, yes? You follow this road, back to town, to Casa Delfino. Down on—"

"I know the Delfy."

She even knew its nickname, and this surprised him too. "Okay, good!" He took the map back. "You talk to Effie. She give you good room. You stay with her. Tell her Kostas send you."

The woman's features had hardened, and she was looking about. "So this is a hostel, am I right?"

"*Yeeees.*" His tone said no.

"Then I'd like to stay here."

She wasn't asking, her tone steely, her eyebrows wedged together.

"Tonight?" She nodded. "We no open; you stay at Casa Delfino. Is good! Clean rooms. Hot water." Then he looked her over, taking in the silk shirt and pearl drop earrings, and added, "Is good for you, yes?"

"No, I'd like to stay here." Then, more gently, she added, "Please."

The manager was bewildered.

"Please," she said again. "I've come a very long way."

He sighed dramatically. "Okay, okay, is your lucky day!" It would be cash in his pocket. He would charge her double. "You want look?"

"No." She reached for her purse and produced a credit card and several red and green notes that Kostas vaguely recognised. "I only have Australian dollars. You can exchange some for me?"

He considered this. In six weeks' time the place would be swarming with boisterous Aussie backpackers—courtesy of their recent admission into *Lonely Planet's Guide to Greece*—so he knew he could off-load them eventually. He reached under the desk, located a fresh guestbook and opened it.

"Name and passport, please."

The woman rifled through her bag, retrieved a blue document and handed it across.

Opening it, he flipped a few pages then frowned. "You Am-eel-ea Mar-loney? You want me call you Amelia or Amy, maybe, for short?"

"Millie," she said quickly. "My name is Millie."

He nodded. *Yes, better.* "Okay, Millie, I take copy. I give back, okay?"

"Fine."

As he finished taking her details and exchanged some cash, the woman realised she must look a shambles and scraped thin fingers through her long, wavy hair. Eventually she gave up and pulled the whole lot into a knot on the top of her head, securing it with a black band she had around her wrist, then foraged through her bag again, this time looking for lip gloss. As she smothered it on, Kostas kept sneaking bemused glances her way.

She wasn't bad-looking, he thought. Bit bony for his tastes, but nothing a steady diet of moussaka couldn't fix. Pity about the crazed look in her eyes. Effie had the exact same look from time to time.

When he was done, he plucked some keys from a board behind him and led her through the reception to a narrow, stone staircase. He was feeling optimistic, suspected she would change her mind the second she saw the rooms, or at least he hoped she would. *He was still supposed to be on holidays, for goodness' sake!*

"Okay, my name Kostas. I do bed for forty Euro a night. Yes?" She nodded. "We have sheet, blanket, pillow. No towel." He turned back to the woman. "You got towel?"

"No."

"Don't worry, I get you towel." He shook his head. *Typical tourist. Lonely Planet must have left that bit out.* He stopped at the first-floor landing and was making his way towards a closed wooden door when the woman cleared her throat.

"I'd prefer upstairs, thanks."

He swung back. "Upstairs? Dormitory upstairs." He turned to

continue walking. "This single room is better."

"No," Millie said, stopping him again. "Please. I'd prefer the dormitory." She had an authoritative way of talking, but it was laced with anxiety as she added, "If you don't mind, Kostas."

He blinked at her like she was nuts, then shrugged, returned to the stairwell and continued up another flight to a sweeping dormitory with multiple bunk beds, small side tables between them, and a pile of variously coloured plastic beanbags in one corner. He walked to the far end of the room and swept a thick, red velvet curtain across, letting the sun pour in from two glass doors that led out to a small Juliet balcony.

"Any bed you want. Just one, please."

Millie was not listening to him; she was too busy pummelling through time. From the moment she had crossed the threshold to the second floor, she saw and tasted blood. Lots and lots of blood.

It was extraordinary, she thought, even now, how much blood one man could cause, one bad choice could create.

Her eyes went straight to the farthest wall, to another man, this one as bloodied as her but with none of the guilt and recriminations. He wasn't there anymore, the enormous crucifix had been removed, but she could still see him clearly, his arms out, his head dropped to one side, his eyes somehow more accusatory because they would not meet her own.

She reached for his eyes so many times; so many times he never looked her way.

Millie turned and glanced from bed to bed, but hers, too, was gone, replaced by a sturdy metal bunk with thick foam mattresses covered in plastic.

Fresh, clean, bloodless.

Kostas seemed oblivious to her time travel and sang out, "Okay, I bring clean sheets later. And what you call… blanket. Yes, I bring blanket too."

She dropped her bag and stepped across the room to where her bed once stood, the window above it now half-blocked by the top of a bunk. She placed her hand on the wall beside the window and remembered how often she had looked out that very window, how often she had thought and dreamed and imagined.

"Miss?" Kostas said and she turned, fabricating a smile.

God knows she'd had enough experience of that.

"Please," he said awkwardly. "Now I show you washroom and I show common room."

Millie followed him along a narrow corridor to the bathroom, also freshly renovated, the stench of new paint more powerful here than anywhere, and Kostas flipped the naked light bulb on. There was no toilet paper, he noticed, and a collection of dead beetles on the floor would need to be swept up.

"It's too early!" he hissed in Greek under his breath before striding down the corridor and throwing open another door. It led to a separate staircase, which he took, drawing her back to the main level. "Down here, common room and kitchen, but no food," he said as they walked. "You buy food in town, yes?"

She didn't appear to be listening, and again he hissed. "Is too early!" This time his English was loud and clear.

While Kostas strode off to fetch the linen, Millie took the opportunity to look around properly. The downstairs common room was unfamiliar, and she wondered if she had blanked it out or if it was the result of the makeover. New, brightly upholstered sofas sat sociably around the room, and one wall was lined with computers, four in all, and unheard of in her day. There was a giant-screen TV and a box of computer games. And every wall had been painted a particularly gaudy shade of something. Lime green. Candy pink. Baby blue. Thankfully there was no red, the only colour she associated with her past.

Kostas returned with a set of striped sheets, faded from one too many bleach jobs, and a towel, clean but ratty, and thrust them into her hands.

"And now I go," he said. "You have car? Bike?"

"No."

"You want lift to town, get food, wine?"

"Do you have Wi-Fi?"

"No, Miss. No connect, not yet. Casa Delfino has Wi-Fi. You talk to Effie."

Again, Millie appeared not to hear him. She was staring at a small arched doorway that was latched shut.

"This lead to cemetery. You no want. Come," he said, "I show you balcony. Is good, yes?"

Kostas strode across the common room and swept open two glass doors to the cobbled courtyard out the back, which offered a stunning view of the craggy coastline below.

"Gloomy today," he said, and he wasn't just referring to the weather.

~~~

At the end of the bridge, right before the road veered sharply left, the hostel manager slowed his motorbike for a final look back at the castle. And her. No amount of cajoling could dissuade the crazy tourist from staying. Not even the fact that Kostas would be gone for hours, that she would be there all alone. That usually scared the strays to their senses, but not this one. He had scribbled down the telephone number for the Delfy and hoped she'd soon use it.

"Any problem, you call Effie," he insisted, and the woman had stared at the number as if in a daze. And so Kostas had left, driven away earlier than intended. He cursed her aloud now. Had meant to finish going through the books, to start compiling a list of supplies for the upcoming season. But there was something about the newcomer that didn't invite company.

After another minute, he revved up his bike and turned towards town, feeling, for the first time in four years, that he was no longer the king of his old stone castle.

He had a niggling feeling he had just been overthrown. And his conqueror was a woman called Millie who had not just been here before, she had left her darkest secrets somewhere inside.
~~~

EVE MAGAZINE

Beryl Malone's voice was high-pitched, but there wasn't any panic. Not yet.

"No, Monty, of course my daughter's not here. Why would she be here? On a weekday? That's absurd."

Now that she'd said it, the idea did seem ludicrous.

Before Monty could respond, Beryl added, "You don't know where she is then?"

"Um, not at the moment, no. You see, I've been out of the office for a few days, so…"

She pictured Beryl in her neat little kitchen, her perfect doily tablecloth, a pot of tea stewing on the stove no doubt. She was like the proverbial '50s housewife, with her tidy aprons and home baking and scotch and dry ready for Ron when he returned from the office. Except it wasn't the 1950s and Ron was retired now, unless you counted worrying about Amelia as an occupation.

Amelia used to mock her mum for her dowdiness and lack of ambition, but Monty had been charmed by it. She first met Amelia's folks at their Year Ten speech night—Amelia was clutching a handful of books, lousy prizes for being top of English, History and Commerce (Monty was holding just one book for Art)—and found them delightfully old-fashioned. Even a little quaint, with their frumpy clothes and the way they clung to their daughter, pride oozing from their eyes. (Monty's own parents were so utterly un-parent-like. They dressed, drank and smoked like grad students and, when they weren't at each other's throats, were so entrenched in their careers—Monty's dad was in banking, her mum managed a clothing store in a swanky Sydney suburb—they barely had time to look up and certainly had no time to attend their children's awards night.)

When Monty's parents finally split at the end of her schooling, her two brothers just fifteen and twelve, the only thing left to squabble about was who was going to get lumped with the boys.

Monty had envied Amelia back then and wondered what it was like to grow up with sitcom-perfect parents, but then the *incident* happened, and she saw the downside of all that—the terror, the accusations, the overprotection, the guilt.

And she knew that if she didn't find Amelia in a hurry, it was about to rain down all over again.

"Didn't she have a meeting or something?" Beryl was saying, her voice still upbeat. "I'm sure she had a meeting, dear. Melbourne wasn't it?"

"That's next week. She usually goes down to the printers to check the cover. She's supposed to be *here* this week. In the office. We haven't even designed the cover yet. That's why I'm a little... Well, that's why I'm calling."

"Oh. Right."

Beryl's voice was still calm, which surprised Monty and buoyed her a little. If the mother's not panicking, she thought, but then she heard a distant voice and a fumble, and her heart sank.

"Hang on, dear. Ron would like a word."

Monty braced herself.

"What's this about my baby going missing?" Ron's voice was gruff but jovial.

He was waiting for the punch line, and she wished more than anything she could deliver one. For now she went into damage control.

"Oh, Ron, it's not that she's missing as such. She hasn't been in for a few days, and you know what Gerry's like. I'm pretty sure I know where she is." *Liar, liar.* "I thought I'd check with you first to see if you know—"

"Of course we don't know! How are we supposed to know?" *No more jovial tone then.* "You're the one who's supposed to know where she is, Monty. Why are you asking us this?"

"I just needed to check, that's all. We have a few more avenues. There's a spa she's been keen to try out. I bet she took herself there for a bit." Monty smacked a hand against her forehead as she said it.

"But surely she'd tell you! How could you not know?"

"She probably did and it slipped my mind. I've been away myself, see, and then my phone had no charge and I lost a bunch of messages." *Lies, more lies.* "I'm expecting to hear from her any minute."

"But I don't understand. Should... should we be calling the police? Should we—"

There was another fumble, and Beryl was back.

"For goodness' sake, he does carry on. Sorry about that, Monty. I'm sure everything's fine. Please don't get yourself into a lather. We've got the keys to Amelia's house. I'll get Ron to swing by there in the morning and see what's what. Maybe she's tucked up in bed, feeling out of sorts. In the meantime, you just focus on that magazine. I know she'd want you to get on with it."

"Thanks, Beryl." Thank God the mother wasn't overreacting. Yet.

Monty hung up and dropped her head onto the table. If only Amelia's parents were as crappy as hers.

As day turned to evening and the staff gradually slunk away— many earlier than normal because the cat, after all, hadn't been seen for days—Monty tried to return to her burgeoning workload but kept sneaking glances at her mobile phone, which mocked her with its silence.

Where the bloody hell was Amelia?

And what would possess her to be out of the office during this crucial period?

She shoved the phone under a stack of proofs and turned back to her computer screen, trying not to frown. She had earlier read that you could reverse the signs of aging by simply not exhibiting any expression. None at all. Like a character from a soap. At least that's what their beauty editor, Beatrice, had espoused, selecting an image to go with that priceless piece of advice—the unblemished face of a model who was sixteen if she was a day.

It wasn't lack of expression that ensured her unmarked features, thought Monty, grumpily, it was lack of life. *Just wait till you get to thirty-three, sweetie, that'll wipe the smug glint from your unlined eyes.*

"Monty?"

She snapped her head around, frowning despite the beauty editor's advice. Her senior designer was standing there, hands wedged into the pockets of his jeans. She dropped the frown and smiled back at him.

He was the only testosterone in the entire office, as good-looking as he was good-natured. Monty remembered when Amelia first hired Hank about two years back. He'd come straight from some music magazine but looked more suited to *Esquire* or *GQ*—clipped beard, black Ray-ban eyeglasses, Ralph Lauren jackets. Amelia had joked he'd be good eye candy for the girls—"give us all some relief"— and she was right. But he was also a sweetheart, and Monty had entertained the idea of asking him out several times before common sense prevailed. She was his boss; it would be inappropriate. Besides, who had time for dating? *How optimistic an idea was that?*

But Hank was more than a pretty face, he was a skilled designer. Too skilled for this job, Monty thought now. *He should be doing her job; she should be elsewhere.*

She shook the thought away. "What's up?"

"I've got a stack of layouts to be checked. Should I whip them past Alex first or…?"

Monty frowned harder. Amelia would die if she knew Alex was checking the designs. The deputy editor might be a whiz with words, but she wouldn't know a good layout if it smacked her between the eyes.

But what choice did they have? Deadline was fast approaching, and the hidden phone had offered no solace. She glanced at the darkening sky outside and said, "Just hold off until the morning. I'm *sure* Amelia will be back first thing."

He looked relieved as he turned away, but she hadn't convinced herself.

What if Amelia wasn't back? They didn't have any more time to waste. The issue was due at the printers next week, and they were already way behind.

Was Alex capable of getting them to the finish line?

Monty didn't think so. Amelia certainly never had.

She remembered the editor's hesitance before hiring Alex as her deputy. How unconvinced Amelia had been. She had spent hours trawling through job applications, reading and rereading, desperately trying to find a better match. Yet she kept coming back to Alex.

"She *is* a very good writer," she had told Monty. "Her CV's impeccable. I just don't know…"

"Don't know what?"

Amelia could never explain, but time had proven her instincts correct. There was just something *off* about Alex. She never quite fit in, never fully belonged. She was like a fish out of water who'd learned to breathe but still flapped about awkwardly making everyone awkward around her.

Monty's computer suddenly pinged. There was a fresh email, and she felt her heart leap. But it was a message from Alex, wondering where all the designs were.

"Don't forget, with Amelia AWOL, I need to approve everything first!"

The art director scowled so deeply she half expected Beatrice to appear with her blasted wrinkle cream.

How could Amelia do this to her? They were on to the final sections, the most crucial designs. And now Alex was to approve them? *Over her dead body.* She scooped up her desk phone and put a call through to Gerry.

She got as far as Gerry's assistant, a tiny woman with a towering reputation, almost as terrifying as her boss.

"You should know by now you have to book in, Monty," Lizzie Soda said. "Gerry's an extremely busy man."

Monty glared at the phone, then took a deep breath. "Yes, sorry, Lizzie, but this is really important."

"It always is, dear. Is this about Amelia? Has she finally shown up?"

"Yes, I mean, no, she's not back, but it is about the magazine. You see, with Amelia absent, Alex seems to think she's in charge, and quite frankly, I don't think she's up for it. She hasn't got a good grasp of the visual, and we need—"

"If you're not happy with Alex's work, you should take it up with Human Resources."

"Oh, it's not—"

"Gerry is far too busy for that sort of stuff."

"Yes, Lizzie, I understand that." She spoke through gritted teeth. "But we're trying to publish the very best issue we can possibly publish, and I know Gerry's never too busy for *that*."

She had her there and Lizzie knew it. The other woman sighed. "I'll call you if he gets a spare moment. In the meantime, let us know when Amelia returns. Gerry wants her up here pronto. I've managed to reschedule Revlon, but there's a meet and greet on Thursday that she simply must attend."

"Of course, Lizzie. I'm expecting her first thing in the morning."

But was she? Was she really?

SHEPPERDIN VILLAGE

They were just finishing their greasy T-bones and chips at the local pub when Polly What's-her-name came striding up, a boy with short hair at the back and sides, trailing behind.

"I saw you guys over here," she said, her voice high-pitched and chirpy. "How was your meal?"

"Good, thanks."

She tilted her head. "How are *things*?" The emphasis spoke volumes. He shrugged a reply, glancing towards his son.

Not in front of my boy, please.

She nodded, appearing to understand, and yet she continued on. "So, no news *at all*?"

The way she said it made him feel like sliding under the table. She must have sensed this because she quickly turned to Phil.

"Toby and I are heading off to get some ice cream. Are you interested in coming along, Phil?" Then she glanced back at Tom. "That is if you don't mind."

He wanted to tell her what she could do with that ice cream, he wanted to hold his son tight, but Phil's smile had suddenly appeared and it was like the sun appearing in a storm.

"You want?" he said to his son, and his son smiled wider.

Polly's eyes glinted victoriously. "Tell you what, why don't you come back to ours after that and we'll get you to school tomorrow?"

"But I haven't got my school bag and stuff," Phil said.

She flapped bejewelled fingers in the air. "Oh easy peasy, we can sort you out with a bag and some lunch and even get you in a fresh uniform, would you like that?"

Her eyes swept across the cruddy shirt Phil had been wearing for two days straight, and Tom felt a wave of shame. He hadn't had a chance to do a load of washing yet. She could reserve her judgement for Amy, thanks very much.

"Cool! Dad? Can I?"

He shook it off. "Sure, mate. Yeah, have fun and I'll get you after school tomorrow."

He watched as his son dashed off with Toby, and for a moment, just a moment, he felt a glimmer of appreciation for busybody Polly until he spotted the man hanging back, waiting his turn.

Geoffrey Pinter.

Tom's stomach clenched. The nod Geoff was now gifting Polly said it all, and he supposed he should have been grateful they'd removed Phil for this, but it didn't ease the tension in his belly.

He closed his eyes as Shepperdin's Local Area Commander approached.

"Tommo."

He opened his eyes. "Geoff."

"You all right?"

"Sure. You?"

He shrugged. "How about Amy?"

He closed his eyes again. *For God's sake.*

"She all right?"

"She's fine."

"So where's she at?"

He slapped his eyes at the town's chief of police. They had gone to school together. Best mates for six years until it all went south. He tried not to think about that.

"I'm not sure that's any of your business, mate."

The balding superintendent pulled a seat out and sat down next to him, leaning in closer. "I'm told she's been missing since Sunday. If you don't know where she is, mate, you have to report—"

"I know where she is."

His eyebrows lifted.

"She's on holidays. At her folks' place. She goes there regularly; it's no drama." Except she wasn't due there for another month, but Geoff didn't need to know that.

"Oh, great." He deliberately glanced around the pub. "It's just that a few of the ladies are worried."

"Gossiping more like."

"Just get her to call one of her gossips, get them up to speed so they can leave me alone, okay?" He smiled. "You know what they're like?"

"Yep. Right."

The policeman sat there for a few more minutes, offering Tom a sympathetic smile, then slowly got up and made his way out. Tom considered his options, then headed for the bar.

"The usual?" the publican asked, and Tom nodded.

"Thanks, Lennie."

"Oi, Tommo, over here!" someone called out from the pool table up the back.

He didn't bother to look round, simply waited for his beer, then produced his Visa card. Could've rattled off all sixteen numbers by heart if he'd wanted, but no one cared about numbers anymore, his party trick superfluous. Now you just waved the bloody thing in front of some gadget. Did all the work for you.

"Where's adorable Amy tonight?" Lennie asked, handing over the schooner of lager. He had the rose-coloured-glasses view of his wife. Most of them did.

"Just away for a few days. Having a break."

"Lucky bugger," he said, producing the aforementioned gadget.

Tom wondered if Lennie was referring to Amy or himself as he did the brainless wave then tucked his card away again.

Next he cleaned the froth off the top of the glass, wiped the back of his hand across his lips, then made his way to the poolroom where a thin man with a pregnant belly was leaning across the table, pool cue at the ready, about to strike the eight ball.

"You're killing yourself, Grant," Tom said.

"That's the idea," the other man replied, clicking the cue forward and slamming the eight ball into the corner pocket. "Bored with this shit. Let me grab a drink and we can pull up a pew."

He ordered his own schooner, then they made their way to the front bar where several tables were now occupied, a few older guys, a young couple, a family with three kids, all on their devices.

They sat down and drank their beers, then Grant couldn't help himself. "What the hell's going on? Steph reckons Amy's pissed off."

"Jesus Christ! What is it with this place? She's just having a few days off, mate. Why is that so hard for everyone to understand?"

"Without you? Without Phil?"

Tom shrugged. "Needed a break."

It had become a kind of mantra. What else could he say? *She's fallen out of love with me. She packed up and left.*

Grant scoffed. "The school run gettin' too stressful these days is it?"

Tom ignored that. It was okay for him to fire arrows, but Amy wasn't target practise for Grant. This was his wife he was talking about.

"She gonna come back?"

The look in Grant's eyes made Tom's blood simmer again. He should have shot off after his steak.

"Of course she's coming back. Jesus, man, what the hell?"

Grant's hands were in the air. "Okay, chill out. Just trying to help."

"*This* is helping?"

Grant said nothing for a while. Stood up. "'Nother one?"

Tom nodded. It was an apology of sorts, and it would do.

When Grant returned with the beers, the conversation moved on. Footy, the price of petrol these days, the big-breasted blonde who had recently perched herself at the bar. Grant was the one interested in that. Tom just pretended to be. He'd only ever been interested in one woman, and look where that had got him, batting away gossip in the local pub.

She had always been his downfall, Amy Malone; he knew that plain and simple. He'd stuck with her even after all that ugly business. Even when others warned him off, couldn't believe what he was doing. The *sacrifice* he was making. But he'd had a crush on her since day one, back when she was still Silly Millie and life was as fickle as her name. He'd been smitten since the first moment he'd clapped eyes on her, skipping down those Spanish Steps, weaving between other backpackers, her eyes locked on his mate Angus.

She was so radiant then, like she was lit up from within. Her hair was thick and glossy, her smile wide and wondrous, and the way she carried herself, a little hesitant, a little confident, a little too ready to take on the world, made his heart skip a beat. She might have picked Angus first, but his crush was patient. He knew then, even as he watched them flirt, that he could bide his time. He could wait it out.

Besides, he knew from their university days that Angus was a bad egg. More than that. A monster. And the monster would surface soon enough. Which it did.

And even after all the nasty business that came later, Tom was still smitten. His crush had not evaporated because she'd made one lousy decision. Eventually her eyes had turned to him, as he knew they would. Eventually she had seen him as her saviour, and that had cemented everything.

Or at least it had done, until last Sunday.

He took a large gulp of his beer and scowled. *Oh, hell, who was he kidding?* Amy had been crumbling away for years, their marriage on shaky foundation to start with. He wasn't stupid. He knew he'd always been the consolation prize. She'd never been happy, not really, never fully content. And it wasn't just the lack of career—there were no glossy magazines in this hellhole, only a country rag and a community newsletter she got involved with occasionally. There was something deeper behind her sadness, and there was nothing he could do about it, although God knows he'd tried. Nothing he could do now either. He just had to wait this one out.

It made his blood simmer again; it made him feel empty and worthless.

He turned his eyes towards the bar.

SARISI ISLAND

"**Y**assou!" Kostas called out to a tall Greek woman as he pulled up at the kerb in front of the Casa Delfino.

It was your typical Greek hotel, pretty as a postcard with glacial white walls, impossibly blue trim, and neat planter boxes made chaotic with bursts of pink bougainvillea. There was a small taverna at the front boasting FRESH SEA BASS & BBQ CALAMARI! and several tables and chairs straddled the footpath, their tablecloths billowing uneasily with each wind gust. Set on the other side of a pretty blue bay, there was nothing but a narrow, cobbled road and a bit of pebbled beach to separate the two, and today there was little passing traffic and certainly no bathers. It was not yet summer holiday season, and so only locals were going about their business, preparing for the onslaught.

The village of Sarisi had developed haphazardly over several centuries around the horseshoe-shaped bay with a fishing wharf at one end and the old stone convent-cum-hostel on a rocky cliff top at the other. Gleaming cubed houses were clustered across the escarpment and surrounding hills, like white Lego pieces scattered in various directions, walls colliding with rooftops colliding with sundrenched patios. And at various intervals, the steep, narrow road with its large, cemented pebbles and smudged donkey poo, winding its way down to the main town. At the bottom, the cobbled esplanade stretched from one end of town to the other, providing a border between the shops, cafés, and hotels and the main beach not yet decorated with summer's umbrellas and chairs. There were Lego pieces there too; houses and hotels perched right on the waterfront, some leaning out, defying gravity, one with an enormous squid dangling from a veranda, as though it was trying to escape.

There was another beach on the other side of the castle, its isolation and black volcanic sand luring fewer tourists, with only one hotel and café to accommodate them. It would be as quiet as a ghost town now.

"Hey, Effie," Kostas said again as he strode through the restaurant's courtyard, admiring the woman's long, tanned limbs and curly black hair. She wasn't bad for thirty, he thought. *Pity she was such a shrew.* "Nico inside?"

"*Nai,*" she replied using the Greek word for yes. "Where else?" she then snapped, and continued preparing the street-side tables, slapping forks atop serviettes as though they had misbehaved, while red-and-white-checked tablecloths slapped back at her, threatening to pick a fight.

Kostas stepped inside, past the small reception desk and staircase leading to the accommodation upstairs, and across the parquet floor, first glancing at the neon-lit bar, then to the kitchen at the back. He located Nicholas in the cold room, his nose hidden in a crate of tomatoes.

"Oi, Nico! Where's my morning coffee?" he demanded, one hand on hip, and Nicholas looked up and smiled.

"Where it always is, mate, help yourself."

"Come join me."

"Hey, you know my cousin. She's got me working like a dog, no time."

"Come on, man, I have some… how you say? Juicy gossip."

"You know I hate gossip, Kos. How many times I have to tell you that?"

"You like *this* gossip. I promise. Is about pretty lady. Strange lady. Just your type."

Nicholas plucked two tomatoes from the box and then closed the cold room door, groaning as if Kostas was holding his arm behind his back. "Fine."

He pushed past him and out into the restaurant where he took up position at the bar's espresso machine, measuring out the coffee, screwing the contraption into place, pushing two cups under the spout, and stabbing at a button. As the machine worked its magic, Kostas grabbed a discarded newspaper from a side table.

"Hey, Effie!" Kostas yelled outside in Greek. "Did your numbers come up last night?"

"As if!" she screeched back. "But they will!" And then in English, she added, "One day, Kostas, I escape. You see. I go to Melbourne with Nico."

Kostas shot his friend a wary glance. For some reason Nico hated all mention of his hometown; it was the only subject that turned him into his cousin, slapping him into a bad mood faster than a snakebite. Kostas had learned that the hard way, but the Greek Australian wasn't taking the bait today. Perhaps he was in too good a mood. Perhaps he was just distracted.

"So what's up?" Nicholas said when the milk had been frothed and heated and poured into one cup, which he now dumped in front of his friend.

"Huh?" Kos looked up from his paper. "Oh! Okay, so this lady, yes? She come to castle today. Is funny lady, little bit strange in her head."

"And?"

"Not just strange, she *Australian*." He let the last word linger in the air for effect, and Nicholas narrowed his eyes.

"Really?"

"Yes, really! Aussie. Like you, hey?"

Okay, he thought. He hadn't picked up on that, but then he'd only seen her from a distance. He'd been thinking Italian or Spanish perhaps. It wasn't so much the thick, dark hair as the light coat and flash of bare leg above her boots. Most Aussies who arrived this time of year wore everything they could find in their backpacks, always surprised that the Mediterranean could dip below boiling point.

Did none of them have a weather app?

"I didn't think you were open yet."

"Exactly!" Kostas pulled his cup towards him. "I tell her, why you want stay here? Go see Effie. Is better for you. She no care. Funny lady, but sexy."

"And?"

"And nothing. Is still there."

"On her own?"

"On her own! I tell you, crazy lady. Aussies are crazy people!" And he cackled, witchlike. "She say she looking for nuns, can you believe this?"

"What *nuns*?" Nico asked as a crash could be heard from the front of the hotel. He frowned and called out to Effie, "Hey! You all right out there?"

There was a moment of silence before she screeched back to him. "Bloody wind! I'm okay!"

She must have forgotten to staple the tablecloths down he thought as he shared a snigger with Kos. They were both fond of the hotelier, but she was renowned for her temper. Nico found it amusing once. Now, not so much. He turned back to Kostas. "You were saying something about nuns."

"Yes, from old convent. Before it become hostel."

He nodded. "Right, yeah, forgot about that. What did you tell her?"

"No nuns here. Don't you worry about nuns." He cackled again.

Nicholas gulped his espresso in one and glanced at his watch.

"Well, that was riveting." He sang out again, this time up a set of stairs: "Theo! Running late, mate. Let's move it or you'll miss the ferry!"

A few minutes later a teenage boy came crashing into the room like there was a zombie on the loose and he was next on the menu. He was wearing a blue-and-grey uniform and had a bulky backpack in one hand. Somehow he managed to pull up just short of Nicholas, offering him a grin and flicking his fringe from his eyes.

"D'ya bring my boots and shin pads?"

Nicholas frowned. "What do I look like? Your butler?"

"Just asking."

"Well don't *just ask*. You're old enough to worry about your own bloody soccer boots."

"*Football!* It's called football." Theo shared an eye roll with Kostas, and Nicholas pretended not to see. He couldn't seem to get anything right these days.

"We'll have to nip back and grab them on the way. Come on, your mum'll kill me if we miss the ferry again."

"Hang *on*!"

Theo bolted into the kitchen and as he went Nico couldn't help the lump that was forming in his throat. He loved that kid, would miss him acutely when Theo left for Athens, but he knew it was for the best. A classic oddball, a bit of a loner, Theo had few friends on Sarisi and, if it wasn't for his killer left kick, he'd have even fewer, Nico knew that. There was nothing like *football* to help build bridges. On the mainland he didn't have to do any building; there were more likeminded mates to choose from. He could be himself there.

Still it didn't mean Nicholas didn't miss him, didn't mean he didn't wish he was here each and every hour.

After a few minutes, Theo reappeared with an orange in one hand and what looked like a filo pastry hanging from his mouth. He called a garbled goodbye, first to Kostas, then once outside, to Effie, who pulled him into a bear hug.

"You know I love you," she said. "You know this, yeah?"

"*Yeahhhh.*" He wriggled out of his mum's arms with a groan but was grinning as he headed for Nico's dusty hatchback.

As they pulled out of the hotel driveway and onto the esplanade towards the wharf, neither of them noticed Effie still watching them, a grim look on her face, a piece of cracked crockery in each hand.

EVE MAGAZINE

Afresh Sydney morning, an empty editor's chair. Alex thought she would burst.

This time she didn't even bother sitting at her own desk, she simply scooped up her diary on the way past and headed straight for Amelia's office. Shoving her boss's things aside, she dumped her diary and sat down, adjusting the seating even though it was completely unnecessary. They were exactly the same height; it was about all they had in common.

"I'm in charge," she said quietly as she tapped at the computer, logging Amelia out and herself in. "I. Am. In. Charge," she said again, timing the words with each tap, then she took a moment to soak up the view through Amelia's office window—the dazzling white Opera House and the Sydney Harbour Bridge beyond.

Alex remembered the first time she had seen that view. It was the backdrop to her initial interview with the great Amelia Malone. Alex was quaking in her knock-off Jimmy Choos, but it was a good quake, like the buzz you get from a roller coaster you'd waited hours to ride. It was a genuine thrill to meet her mentor. The view paled in comparison. It was nowhere near as dazzling as Amelia.

Oh, she had heard all the horror stories of how hard Amelia worked her team, how demanding and unforgiving, but she didn't care. Alex was ambitious, she wanted to be in Amelia's shoes one day—hers were not fakes, hers were the real deal—and she would do whatever she needed to do to get there.

So when she sat down for that first job interview, she made sure she said and did everything necessary to get that result. And so she sold herself, her family and her soul in the process.

"There's no running out to pick up sick kids in this office," Amelia told her, leaning back in her plush leather chair, a silver pen at her lips.

"Of course not," Alex said, blocking the image of her daughter vomiting just the week before.

"Men don't need to do that, so why should we?"

Alex had nodded vehemently, not thinking to reply as she might now with the words "Because we want to?"

"I expect you to work yourself to the bone for me," Amelia continued. "I expect *Eve* to come first. Is that a problem for you, Alex? Will that be an issue?"

"Not at all," she had said, shaking her freshly styled locks. It had cost a small fortune to have the highlights added and the frizz ironed out, but it was an investment for the future and, let's face it, a key to getting the job. She'd just seen *The Devil Wears Prada*; she knew what was what.

"I couldn't think of anything else I'd rather do," she'd told Amelia that day, and she watched as the editor's eyes flashed back at her. Alex had thought it was admiration they were flashing. Now she wondered if it was victory, the knowing glint of a conqueror.

And it had been a glorious first year, very Hollywood movie-like: fashion shows, advertising lunches, flash bulbs on red carpets. She felt, for the first time, like she had escaped Castle Hill and her mother's boring clerical job, her father's constantly struggling small business. She now wore genuine designer fashion and drove a fashionably smart car. Even had her own car space with her name on it.

It took another year for Alex to realise that it didn't matter what she did to her hair or what clothes or car she bought, it would never quite be smart enough, and her name would never be Amelia Malone.

"Amelia's back!" someone cried out, and Alex's heart plummeted as she swivelled around to face the main office.

Monty was standing at the entrance and had mistaken Alex for the editor, that much was clear by her rapidly vanishing smile.

For her part, Monty felt her blood pressure spike—such relief and now such disappointment. She stared hard towards Alex.

The hide of the woman!

She watched as Alex started tapping at Amelia's desktop. *Unfuckingbelievable!*

She dumped her bag and stormed across. "What's going on?"

Alex waited a beat before she pulled her eyes from the computer. "Hey Monty. What's up?"

Monty waved a hand about. "What are you…?" *What the hell do you think you're doing in Amelia's chair?*

"She's not here is she? And this is a bigger screen, better to check the layouts on." Then Alex quickly added, "I'm trying to get the issue done, Monty. Somebody has to move it forward."

"But Amelia…"

"You and I both know Amelia would be here by now if she was coming in today. She's always in at the crack of dawn. So, hate to break it to you, honey, but it looks like *I'm* running the show." Her voice faltered a little. "Unless, of course, she shows up tomorrow, in which case we all go back to normal." She tried not to frown at the thought of that.

Monty blinked rapidly. "Is that what Gerry said?"

"He didn't have to! I *am* the deputy, Monty. That usually means second in charge, or at least it does in the rest of the publishing world." She lightened her tone. "I'm sure we can all survive without Amelia for a bit." Then she put on her best cheerleader voice. "Come on, Monty, we've got this! We can make this happen! Might even get the magazine to bed early for once."

Monty looked at Alex like she was deranged, so the deputy dropped the aural pom-poms and said, "I need all the layouts as fast as possible. For some reason Hank's ignoring my emails, so please tell him I need to see everything before it goes to the subs, yes? *Everything.* I'll edit Mel's self-defence story first thing, and meantime, you better get cracking on that swimsuit spread you just shot. I can see from the floor plan that it's supposed to make this issue, but you'll be cutting it fine."

I'll be cutting you fine, Monty thought as she stared at the deputy for a few more stunned seconds before turning around and heading back out and towards her corner of the office. *Corner of the ring, more like.* She felt like beating someone up, but it wasn't Alex she was thinking of now.

Call her optimistic, call her delusional, but Monty had fully expected to find Amelia back at her desk this morning, her eyes rolling as she reminded them all of whatever it was they had clearly forgotten.

"I was at that marketing conference, you eejits!" she would say, or *"I can't believe you'd forgotten about [whatever it is they'd all forgotten]!"*

Instead, it was like a horror show in here: Amelia still missing, Alex in the big chair and a magazine not even close to finished.

She glared at her mobile.

Come on, woman, ring!

"Call for you, Monty," came Brianna's monotone over the phone's intercom, and she felt her heart fly into her throat. But it wasn't the editor, it was the editor's mother, and for a moment there she felt a rush of relief. Beryl must have heard something! Her first words quickly put paid to that.

"No news yet, dear?"

Damn it. "No, Beryl."

"Never fear. I wanted to let you know we were just at her house this morning and everything's okay."

The spike of relief hit her again. "Really?"

"Yes, well, you had poor Ron in such a panic last night. First he wanted to call the police, then he wanted to rush right over. It was all I could do to stop him from getting in the car and driving straight there. He's got a dicky heart, see, and he really shouldn't get too excited. So I calmed him down, and we went over together this morning. And I'm so glad we did. Ron would have missed all the crucial signs. He's such a bloke, dear, he really is."

"Signs?" *What was she rabbiting on about?*

"Yes. Amelia's overnight bag was missing, you see. You know, the one she bought on that last trip to Singapore? The bulky one with the funny gold squiggles all over it."

"The Louis Vuitton keepall?"

"That's the one! Couldn't find it anywhere. Think some clothes might be missing, too. Ron would never've thought to check that."

"So what does this mean?"

"It means we're all a lot of worrywarts! Amelia wasn't lying there with a broken leg, dying of starvation or whatever my silly husband was thinking."

"But she wasn't there, right?"

"No! But she's clearly gone away of her own volition, taken her fancy bag with her. Probably on a well-earned break, I'd say."

"But… but why wouldn't she tell us?" Beryl was acting like it was all very obvious, but Monty still couldn't see it. "Why wouldn't she let Gerry know? And do you know *where* she went? Were there any— I don't know—brochures around the place? Any indication at all?"

"Not that I had noticed, but I'm sure the postcards will soon arrive in the mail and we'll all slap ourselves and want to slap her for not telling us."

"Oh there'll be slapping, on that we can agree," Monty said, trying to lighten her own tone, trying to make it all sound like the lark Beryl seemed to think it was. "Okay, thanks for letting me know."

But what she knew was still very sketchy, and it didn't explain anything.

What was Amelia up to? What was she playing at? You don't just pack your designer luggage and head off on holidays without any warning, without any word to your mother, let alone your boss. And you certainly don't do it if you're Amelia Malone and it's deadline week.

Why hadn't she scheduled annual leave like a normal person? Was her friend having an early midlife crisis? Had something *happened* to her?

Of course she didn't articulate these thoughts to the mother, simply thanked her again and promised to be in touch should the aforementioned postcard materialise. But she wouldn't be sending anyone down to the mailroom. Amelia would never just head off on holidays without telling anyone. It was laughable. The *Eve* editor, more than anyone, knew the dangers of doing that. And Monty wasn't thinking of the ferry trip now.

Holidays were a dangerous perk in this cutthroat industry. That was how Amelia scored her job in the first place, snatching the top position while the previous editor, Nancy Verew, snoozed on a banana lounge in Bali.

It had been an infamous coup.

Monty was the first of the two friends to join the magazine almost twelve years ago, starting as a lowly junior designer soon after returning from Greece via a brief stint in London that didn't bear thinking about. When Millie eventually returned—quiet, depressed, despondent—Monty didn't know how to help, so she suggested a job at *Eve*. They could work together! Wouldn't that be fun? And maybe it would assuage some guilt that was starting to gain momentum as her Greek tragedy slowly leaked out.

The only opening at *Eve*, however, was for the even lowlier editorial assistant, the job Brianna now had, which was several rungs below Amelia's skill set. She'd not only trained as a journalist at one of the country's finest colleges, she had already been a feature writer on a national magazine before that dreaded trip, so the obvious next step was features editor, not Nancy's lap-dog-cum-receptionist. But the idea seemed to embolden Amy, and Monty hoped it would come close to redeeming her, if not in her own eyes, at least in the eyes of Beryl and Ron.

It was Monty who organised the interview, who prepped her friend and polished her look, and who received the biggest lashing from Nancy when, after just nine months at *Eve*, Amelia ousted her from the top job.

"I went on a bloody holiday! My first in five years! And *this* is how I get repaid? Stabbed in the back by my *receptionist*!"

"I'm sorry, Nancy," Monty had said, but she wasn't sorry, not really. Amelia needed the job more than anyone knew. It had saved her life and saved Monty's bacon too. And besides, she was *so* much more than a receptionist.

Amelia had taken to that lowly editorial assistant job like her life depended upon it, and Monty half suspected it did. She poured everything into her work, was first in each morning and last out each night. She became indispensable, not only to Nancy but to everyone else in the office. Even though it wasn't in her job description, she started helping with little things and large. She studied how the bestsellers in the industry worked and began suggesting small but subtle ways they could improve an article or embellish a layout. She became the queen of snappy headlines and break-out box ideas, and when *Eve's* deputy editor, Penelope, an older woman with little passion and an inkling of what was to come, handed in her resignation six months after Amelia had started, Nancy didn't think twice about handing the job to Amelia, even though everybody knew it was a mammoth skip and jump, at least on paper.

The truth was, Nancy was stuck. She was due on holidays in a fortnight, and there was no time to advertise. The features editor was pregnant—*she was no use!*—and nobody else was putting their hand up.

"I'm giving you an extraordinary opportunity," she told Amelia at the time. "You're a very lucky woman; don't make me regret this."

Oh, how Nancy would regret it.

Not nearly as intuitive as her deserting deputy, Nancy didn't see the writing on the wall like the rest of the team. They had been bypassing both Nancy and Penelope for months, seeking out Amelia's advice. She had an uncanny eye for detail and an extraordinary knack for words, and they looked forward to Nancy's meetings with Gerry so they could head straight to Amelia's desk.

There was no getting around it. Amelia was a natural born editor who made Nancy look like a fraud. So when Nancy went on her infamous six-week break—one that would chain overworked editors to their desks for years to come—Amelia stepped it all up a notch.

This time she didn't just suggest ideas, she rewrote entire articles, gave them slicker headings, and had the entire magazine redesigned. She shifted sections around and dropped stock pages she'd never liked, and despite howls of protest from the art director and panic attacks from the production department whose job it was to keep a holidaying Nancy in the loop, the magazine had never looked so good.

It was as though it had been reborn.

Now more dynamic than anything else on the market, the advertisers lapped it up. Revenue doubled overnight, they had to go up a book size, and this was the only reason Nancy could not change it straight back when she returned, horrified, from her break.

When the new-look issue hit the stands two months later, it was the highest-selling issue in *Eve's* history, and Nancy's fate was sealed. Even if Gerry *had* wanted to keep the old editor, he had very little choice but to move her to "Special Projects"—which everybody knew was publishing speak for "out to pasture"—and hand the relative newcomer the job. It was the fastest rise to the top in Australian publishing history, seconded only by Amelia's immediate dismissal of *Eve's* disgruntled art director as she parachuted Monty into the coveted design spot.

For her part, Monty felt dreadful, but Amelia was unrepentant.

"Honey, the magazine was screaming for a makeover. Sales were plummeting, advertisers were jumping ship, and if I hadn't done what I'd done, we'd all be out of a job."

She had made it sound so reasonable, so *inevitable,* but Monty often wondered why Amelia couldn't work with Nancy to bring change, why she'd waited until Nancy was in Bali to make her move.

"It's a cutthroat world out there. It's kill or be killed," Amelia sometimes added, this attitude a by-product of that missing year in Greece.

"Besides," she'd predicted, "with us at the helm it'll be the top-selling woman's magazine in the country one day."

In fact, *Eve* quickly became the top-selling woman's magazine per capita in the world, eclipsing her more famous sisters *Cosmopolitan*, *Marie Claire* and *Elle*, and earning her a certain status with Gerry and his ilk that few other editors ever received. Even the formidable Lizzie seemed in thrall to her.

Yet despite it all, Amelia never seemed satisfied. She just got more intense as each year passed, more determined to increase circulation, to prove her worth over and over. But what else was there to prove? Hadn't she done enough? And was that why she'd suddenly upped and left? Monty wondered.

Perhaps she was exhausted. Perhaps she was hoping that one of them would do an Amelia and finally give her a break.

Monty scoffed. *That was as plausible as Beatrice's anti-aging advice.*

She put another call through to Gerry.

SHEPPERDIN VILLAGE

Tom didn't normally let his son sleep over at a friend's house on a school night, but then there was nothing normal about their life today. Still, he was glad Phil wasn't around to see how trashed he got last night, how quickly he trashed everything. Again, he had to thank Polly for that even though he hated being indebted to anyone.

As he waited for the kettle to boil, he slouched against the kitchen bench and wondered how his life had unravelled so fast.

A flash of something caught his eye through the side window, and he spotted his brother outside his own kitchen, waving him across. Tom ran a hand through his shaggy red hair, turned the kettle off and stepped out.

"You heading to work?" Harry indicated Tom's grubby overalls, the words *Shepperdin Building Supplies* embroidered across a front pocket.

"Someone's gotta pay the bills."

"Heard anything?"

"Nope."

"You call her parents?"

"Last night."

Just thinking about the call made his blood boil again. It had lasted less than two minutes. He asked if they knew where their daughter was. They sounded surprised then concerned, then as things started to heat up, he hung up. He already knew he was a disappointment, didn't need to hear it from them.

"*And?*" Harry was waiting.

Tom wished he had some good news. "They haven't heard from her. Not expecting her until next month."

"Shit! I was hoping she'd be there. Scarlett said everyone's tried her mobile phone and she's not picking up. You try her mobile?"

"I'm not a moron."

"Okay, chill out. It's just weird, right? I mean, sure, she might be cranky with you—"

"I didn't do—"

"I'm not saying you did! But you know what chicks are like. You probably left the toilet seat up again or something. I get why she might've walked out. We're not the most gallant of gentlemen, us Wilson brothers. But I don't get why she isn't talking to her friends. Why Scar and Polly haven't heard anything."

"You'll have to ask Amy that, mate."

"I would if I knew where she was."

The two brothers watched each other uncertainly for a moment, then Harry said, "How about you? Are you okay?"

"I'm fine. What about *you*?"

Harry held his gaze. "I'm not the one whose wife took off."

"Oh Jesus, man, like I need reminding. Good morning to you too." Tom turned to walk away.

"Hey, come on, Tommo, I'm on your side here."

"Then don't fuckin' rub it in."

Harry held both palms up. "Not rubbing anything in, just worried is all. She's been missing... what? Three days now? Four? That's... Well, it's a worry."

"Thanks, Harry. I do know what the situation is. I do have a bloody calendar."

He rubbed his bushy brown beard. "Geoff called again."

"What? Shit. Why?"

"He's a cop. It's his job. He's also worried."

"What's he worried about? I already told him she's okay."

"Yeah, but how do you know that, man? If she's not at her mum's, how do you—?"

"I just know!"

"Okay, easy. It's... Well, Amy wouldn't just up and leave Phil, would she? Why would she do that?"

"You'll have to find her and ask her."

"No, Tom, *you* have to find her. She's your wife last time I looked.

Make a bloody effort! And quick smart. The wagons are circling, and a few of them have had it in for you for a while."

He knew exactly to whom his brother was referring. While some old-timers liked him, there was a small posse, Amy's posse, who had grown increasingly cold. And this was *before* she'd vanished. He included Harry's wife Scarlett in that camp. Tom wasn't sure exactly what he'd done to earn their wrath, or what Amy had said. It wasn't his fault the single mums flirted, was it? Wasn't his fault there wasn't a job outside the local supermarket for his wife. Certainly wasn't his fault Amy was above that kind of yakka. Yet their antagonism had been growing, was clear in their haughty looks and flat smiles. They tolerated him, but they didn't think he was good enough for adorable Amy.

He scoffed to himself. *If only they knew the truth. If only they knew her past. How she made poor choices in Greece, and how he picked up the pieces afterwards.*

"I'm just saying, find Amy and fast. Get her to call home or Scarlett or someone. At least make a bloody attempt, Tommo. Just hanging around acting like nothing's happened makes you look suss."

"I'm not hanging around; I'm going to work."

"Even worse. Cross your t's, dot your i's, right?"

"Jesus. How come Amy gets to piss off on holidays and I get all the grief? Why isn't anyone worried about me?"

Harry looked at him sideways. "Should we be?"

He caught his eye. Sighed.

"I'm simply sayin', mate, I'm not the enemy here. You need to talk, you need to unwind, you know where I am."

"Yeah, can't miss you. Back there sniggering at my failed marriage." He went to go, then reeled back. "Bored with your own wife, hey? Not getting enough? Have to poke your nose into my life?"

"Hey, settle down. Now you're being a prick."

"And you're being a pain in the arse!"

Again Tom went to go, but Harry's next words caught him by surprise.

"Scarlett saw her, man."

He stopped, did not turn back.

"She saw her leave."

Tom's heart sank. He closed his eyes.

Harry was holding a palm up that he didn't see. "She hasn't said a word—it's your business, right? But get your shit together, Tom, for everyone's sake."

~~~

Standing in the hallway of his old wooden house, Tom couldn't get his brother's words out of his head.

"Get your shit together. Make a bloody effort."

Harry was right. He had to move past his own anger, his bitter disappointment, and make some progress. Do something to find his missing wife.

It was just after eight in the morning; he should be heading to work. Instead, he returned to his bedroom, *their* bedroom, although it hadn't felt like that in a long while. They hadn't had sex in a year. Maybe two. God, was it coming up to three?

He stared at her side of the bed and tried to find clues, answers, something. There were a few things he hadn't noticed before. *When had he stopped noticing?*

Amy's bedside table was cluttered with books and discarded jewellery and several glossy women's magazines—*Vogue, Eve, Grazia*. There were lotions too, and he saw a giant tub of something and picked it up. Anti-aging cream. It made his throat hurt. Amy was still as stunning as the day he had met her. *Why did she need that snake oil shit? Was she that insecure? Was that his fault too?*

He glanced at the magazines, his brow furrowing. They probably filled her beautiful head with that ugly nonsense. They were all about looking younger, being thinner, finding a better match, like every woman could be Gwyneth Paltry or whatever her bloody name was.

Amy had started in that inane industry, and while she spoke of it fondly, he was proud of himself for rescuing her from all that, giving her a proper sense of purpose. Again he had to wonder if he had done the wrong thing. Was she bored? Was that it? Was that why she wanted to take off?

Was she after some higher purpose?

He was just reaching for one of the magazines when the doorbell rang. He groaned and strode back to the front of the house, swung the door open, expecting it to be Harry, contrite, a loaf of Scarlett's
~~~

homemade bread in hand, perhaps. What he got was Belinda Mann. Another mum; one of the flirtatious ones.

"Hey honey, how are you holding up?"

"I'm okay thanks, Belinda. How are you?"

"Oh *I'm* fine!" She giggled at the question. "Listen"—she peered behind him—"I thought I'd grab Phil and get him to school for you, take one job off your plate."

He stretched his lips into a smile. "Already done."

"Oh? Already?"

Polly beat you to it, he wanted to say, but he knew it would set her off. He knew what these women were like. "Yes, but thanks," he said instead.

She smiled. "Okay, good, if there's anything I can do, anything at all..."

The way she said that, the way her words slithered out made him take a step back, as though her tongue might suddenly flick out along with it, and that's when he spotted Scarlett across the driveway, piling her kids into her station wagon, turning her head, looking up.

She raised a hand in what appeared to be a wave or perhaps it was a Stop sign. In any case, he quickly turned and shut the door on Belinda's startled face.

SARISI ISLAND

The nun's habit was crimson red, rendered brighter against the whitewashed walls. *Since when do nuns wear bright colours?* Millie wondered as she watched the old lady shuffle towards her, a smile on her lips.

"Morning. How are you feeling now?"

"Like shit."

"Language, dear," the older woman said, her voice stern, her eyes merry. "Just try to get some sleep."

Hadn't she slept enough? She closed her eyes and tried to drift away, but there was a low growl coming from somewhere, and she peeled them open again. The nun was still standing beside her bed, but there was something strange about her headwear.

Was it dripping?

"Are you okay?" Millie asked her.

"What is it, dear?"

"Your head… Did you…?" Then she saw it. *Him.* Just behind the nun. A man, hiding in the shadows. Lurking.

She scrunched her eyes shut and shook her head.

Go away, go away, go away.

Then forced her eyelids back up again.

The nun was still there, leaning down, just centimetres from her nose, but it wasn't Agnetha's face anymore, it was the face of the shadowy stranger, and he was grinning.

Millie woke with a gasp.

She was damp with sweat, her pulse racing, her breath heavy.

She looked around frantically. *Where was she? What was going on?* Then she remembered. Exhaled. Waited for her heartbeat to return to normal.

After a few more minutes, Millie untangled herself from the sheet and sat up, swinging her legs to the floor. Another calming breath before she stood up and reached for the mobile phone she'd placed on the bunk above her head, tapping the screen to check the time. It was almost 4:00 p.m., Greek time.

How had that happened? The early ferry had knocked her about.

Behind the clock she could see a screen bursting with text messages, lots of different numbers but mostly just one. She shuddered at the thought of calling him and dumped the phone before heading to the bathroom. There she washed her face with cold water, not meeting her eyes in the mirror, not willing to see the disappointment and disgust, then shuffled back and down the inner staircase, through the empty common room and out to the balcony beyond.

The temperature was cooling down again, and she wrapped her arms around herself, shivering a little. She'd forgotten how chilly it could get here at this time of year. But, oh, how gloriously blue! The sky above was cerulean, the sea below azure.

In her memory, in her dreams, Greece was always hot and always dripping red.

She approached the low stone edge and leaned down to watch the blue turn white and frothy as it smashed against the rocks. The sound, the smell, the energy that was rising towards her sent her pummelling through time again, and she held herself tighter, a ferocious regret smashing across her like the waves against those rocks.

Over the years, the regret had become manageable, something she could quash with a quick shake and a change of thought—with busyness and life—but not now. Not anymore. Lately regret had begun to overwhelm her, to distract her days and toss her through sleepless nights. It had become unmanageable, unfair to everyone around her, and she couldn't ignore it any longer.

He might be furious that she hadn't called, but she was doing him a favour. They were all better off without her.

A long, low whistle caught Millie's attention, and she swept her eyes back and forth across the rocks until she spotted the figure clambering along the south end, something in his hands.

Was it a spear?

She continued watching as the man—surely it was a man?—continued to whistle, the melody now jaunty until he reached what looked like a swimming hole, then bent down, stood up, and kept walking. He repeated this process several more times before reaching the edge of the point, then vanishing from sight, his whistle lingering a little longer while Millie stayed where she was, staring at the place he had been. She didn't think she knew the man, and yet there was something about the silhouette...

Her eyes narrowed as she returned inside. Her heart did a tiny somersault.

~~~

Heart in her mouth, Effie's dark eyes flickered constantly to the road outside the Casa Delfino, and back. Tried to calm her hammering heart. Tried to focus.

She had so much to do and there wasn't nearly enough time.

Pulling the cap down over her brow, she wiped the last of the lunch detritus from the red-and-white-checked tablecloths, then checked her watch for the umpteenth time.

Just a few more hours until the next boat to Athens. A few more hours and the Greek hotelier was off the hook.
~~~

EVE MAGAZINE

As the day continued, Alex tried hard to ignore the steady stream of raised eyebrows that heralded the arrival of each staff member, and she hunched over Amelia's computer, attempting to focus.

Yes, people, it was all very shocking—someone other than Queen Amelia was on the throne—but somebody had to get the magazine out.

She had finally finished editing the self-defence story and vastly improved on Melissa's morbid text and boring heading—Alex was the Queen of Alliteration—and was just emailing it to the design team now, adding the note:

Don't make it look too scary! We want this to feel empowering!

Then she swivelled towards the window, taking a few minutes to soak up the extraordinary city skyline again.

I could get used to this.

As Monty watched Alex daydream out the window, she wasn't sure she could be any angrier than she was right that moment with her old buddy Amelia.

How could she leave that incompetent fool in the Big Chair?

She glanced at her digital inbox. *Oops, spoke too soon.* There was another story from the deputy waiting to be laid out, and this one took the cake. Dubbed Seven Simple SOS Steps! it appeared to be about self-defence but was way too upbeat and perky. And Alex's accompanying note was beyond the pale.

Seriously? She expected the design team to make an article about sexual assault look like a *positive* thing for women? Monty wondered if she'd misunderstood the story completely and began wading through the text.

> *Feeling threatened? Facing a man with a knife? Here are seven simple steps to not only survive but to come away so much stronger!*
> ** SOS Step 1: Run, ladies, run for your lives!*

"No! Really?" Monty said, speaking aloud to the screen now. "I thought you'd hang around to see what pops up." She glanced at the byline and couldn't believe Mel was getting paid to write this drivel. Couldn't believe Alex had just signed off on it.

She kept reading.

> *Can't get away?*
> ** SOS Step 2: Scream, girls, scream like your lungs are on fire.*

I'll give you screaming, Monty thought, checking her mobile yet again in a vain hope that Amelia was sending an SOS of her own. The empty screen felt like an assault.

> *Nobody coming to save your soul?*
> ** SOS Step 3: Keep the bastard talking.*

This one got Monty thinking, and she glanced around to see if Brianna was at her desk. There was no one closer to the editor than the editor's assistant. And she wasn't referring to friendship. The young woman sat inches from Amelia's office. She had to know something.

Monty strode across the large room to find Brianna tapping furiously at her keyboard. She shook her head slowly, not even glancing up until she'd typed the last few words then clicked send.

"Sorry. Just updating Amelia's social media, pretending like everything's hunky-dory."

"It is hunky-dory! Or it will be." Monty hoped. "But that's a good point; has she added anything? Any posts on Facebook? Instagram?"

"Not even a like, but then I do most of it anyway, so she probably wouldn't. She hates this stuff."

Monty nodded. Yeah. They had both narrowly missed out on Digital Native status. Born a few years too early, yet it felt like they were generations apart from the likes of Brianna, who probably tweeted in her sleep.

"Listen, I was wondering about Amelia's last day," Monty began, perching on the edge of the desk. "I want to know everything that happened the day before Amelia took off."

"You mean Monday?"

"No, I mean Friday." *For heaven's sake, Brianna, keep up.* "Amelia was here last Friday when I got in at seven. She was already at her desk. I had to get some gear from the fashion cupboard for the trip. I said a quick hello and then I took off for the airport with Fleur. What happened after that?"

What did you all do to her?

"Nothing… really." There was something in Brianna's tone that sounded a little off.

"Was she here all Friday?"

"Yes, at least until I left at five thirty."

On the dot, Monty wanted to add on her behalf but bit her tongue.

Brianna was the office enigma, the puzzle none of them could solve. The twenty-year-old editorial assistant was famous for only ever giving *just enough*. In at nine, out at closing time. Never missed a lunch break, never sweated any blood or tears, and Amelia expected both bodily fluids from her team, especially during deadline week. She had little tolerance for those with other priorities, and it ensured a constant turnover of staff, but for some reason she held on to Brianna, even fought for her at one point, something Monty never understood.

It was like there was only room for one slacker in the office, and that was Brianna's job. She seemed untouchable, and Monty wondered about this now as the other woman stared at her dumbly.

"Okay, so you left at five thirty and she was still here then, right?"

"Right. Oh, hang on. That's right, sorry, I forgot, she needed me to stay back and check the ad placements, so I had to do that." Her tone was like an eye roll. "I didn't actually get away until just after six. I missed my usual train, late for dinner. Mum not happy."

Monty was blinking rapidly. "Hang on, advertisements? You don't normally check where they're placed until the end of the issue, right? I mean, layouts can change, ads can move about."

She shrugged. She hadn't thought about it, or maybe she just didn't care, but it suggested to Monty that Amelia might have preplanned her exit.

"Did anything else unusual happen? Come on, Brianna, think!"

"I honestly can't think of anything! I've really tried. Apart from the ads, it was business as usual. She was a bit cranky, busy with the latest issue, but then she's always busy." *Always cranky* she would have added if it were anyone but Monty asking. "She got a few phone calls—"

"From?"

"God I can't remember!"

"Think!"

"Okay, um, her mum, that's right, somebody from Chanel, some woman called Amanda Buggsly? I think she's from that domestic violence charity. A guy called Wilkins or Wilson or something. Oh and Lizzie called down about the meeting with Gerry, but apart from that—"

"Meeting with Gerry? What meeting?" As far as Monty knew, executive meetings were rarely if ever called close to deadline week. Amelia wouldn't allow it, even from the mighty publisher.

Brianna shrugged. "I don't know. Lizzie rang and said Gerry was ready for their two p.m. like it had been prearranged, and Amelia practically ran up there. Super keen. She was there for, oh, about half an hour or so."

"What was that about, do you know?"

"You'll have to ask Gerry. Or Lizzie might know."

Monty shuddered at the thought, not sure which of the two would be more terrifying.

"Okay, so who else was here after knock-off time, do you remember? Fleur was with me on the shoot, but where was everyone else?"

"Um, let me think… It was just Amelia and Alex by then. That's right, Mel took off for the train without me, *biatch*, and Hank and Beatrice were out doing the still-life shots. Never came in on Friday."

"And she never came in at all on Monday either? Amelia?"

"Not that I saw. As far as I know, no one has seen her since Friday."

"Okay, so if I've got this right, Alex was the last to see her on Friday arvo?"

She nodded but again there was a slight hesitation, a not-quite-meeting-of-the-eyes that piqued Monty's curiosity.

"What are you not telling me?"

"What? Nothing!"

Monty stared at her. Hard. "Did something happen between Amelia and Alex?"

There was a whiff of hesitation before Brianna said, "Well…"

"*Brianna.*"

The editorial assistant glanced around, then lowered her tone and said, "There might have been a little tiff. But you didn't hear it from me."

"Between Amelia and Alex? What about?"

She shrugged, then waved Monty closer. "All I know is they were having a quiet chat but then things started to escalate." She held up two palms. "I don't know what it was about but then…" She waved Monty even closer so their noses were almost touching and whispered, "I heard Alex say something about her husband and how he'd kill her, and then she stormed out."

"Hang on. Kill *who?* Who was Alex's husband going to kill?"

She shrugged and leaned back. "Amelia, I assume, but she obviously didn't mean it *literally*." She batted her eyelids. "Did she?"

Monty scowled. "Oh this is ridiculous."

She did a U-turn and headed straight for Alex, who now had her legs up on Amelia's desk, riding this self-promotion for all it was worth.

"Got a minute?" she asked, keeping her tone civil.

Alex dropped her legs to the floor. "Did Amelia call?"

"No, I just want to ask you a question."

It was shocking how quickly her legs returned to the desk.

"I'm trying to piece together what happened before Amelia vanished. Do a bit of sleuthing if you will. I heard you were the last to see her on Friday. Anything unusual happen?"

She didn't want to land Brianna in it; wanted to give Alex a chance to 'fess up.

Alex pushed her lips downwards. "Nah, not really. Why?"

"So you two didn't, I don't know, have a screaming match?"

Alex's lips straightened and a look of panic entered her eyes. *Or maybe Monty was just projecting.*

"I don't know what you're talking about," Alex said, and now Monty knew she was being evasive.

"You were overheard fighting. Threats were made. Something about your hubby and him not being happy about something."

Alex shot her eyes towards Brianna, who was already scuttling for the tearoom. She sighed. "It was nothing. You know what we're like?"

Monty crossed her arms and waited.

"Look, Amelia wanted me to come in over the weekend and finish the issue, that's all. I told her Tony would never forgive me, he'd have a meltdown, end of story."

"So did you? Come in and help out in the end?"

"What do you think?"

It was a stupid question. They both knew the answer to that.

A year ago Alex would have been tapping away at her screen right alongside Monty and Amelia, polishing things off. The three of them worked most weekends but especially during deadline. They were the three most crucial elements of the magazine—the axis of evil, Gerry once called them—and they took it seriously. It came with the pay packet; it came with the territory.

Then one day that all changed. Or at least Alex did.

The deputy editor was thinking about it now, too, about that day twelve months ago when she finally held up the white flag.

That Saturday had started typically enough. Alex pretended she would sleep in, her husband coiled around her like a koala in a gum tree, before gently edging her way out of his reach and into the shower. When she stepped back into the bedroom, hair in a towel, her body glistening naked, Tony had reached for her as he did each time and she had laughed him off. As she also did.

"Go back to sleep. I won't be there long."

"Come on, baby, for once, can you forget the job and stay home?"

"I'd love to, honey, you know that, but it's deadline week."

"You say that every week."

"I know, but this one truly is deadline week. We need to get the magazine—"

"—to bed, yeah yeah. What about putting yourself to bed right here." He tapped the sheets beside him, nudged his eyebrows suggestively.

And she laughed as she always did and said, "God, I wish. Sorry, honey."

This time things were different though. He didn't sigh and roll over and go back to sleep. He sat up, his jaw tense.

"I mean it, babe, come back to bed. Forget *Eve* and forget

Amelia fucking Malone."

She stared at him, shocked by the outburst. "You know I'd love to, Tony. Don't be like that. It's all just part of the job."

"Bollocks, Alex. You shouldn't need to work weekends if you're doing your job properly."

She blinked back tears. "I am! Besides, you work weekends too."

Tony was a plumber. Had his own small business. He looked offended by the comment. "I work very bloody rarely, you know that. I only ever work Saturdays when there's a genuine emergency, and even then I usually say no and tell them to find someone else. I put you and the kids first. You... you put *her* first!"

"Tones..."

"No, babe. It's true. You're missing your kids' childhood just to impress that bitch."

"We don't use that word, Tony, it's derogatory to women. She's not a bitch."

"No, she's a freakin' witch, and don't tell me that word's even worse. She *is* a witch! She's had you under some kind of psychotic spell since the first day you started there."

Alex sighed. "I promised her I wouldn't let her down, that the kids wouldn't make any difference—"

"No difference? They make all the difference in the world! They're little human beings; they need their *mother*."

She had scoffed at him then. "What about their father? You're being sexist."

"Oh leave your feminist bullshit at work, Al. We're not living on the pages of *Eve* magazine now. This is real life. The kids see enough of me for Christ's sake. It's their mother they want to see; it's you they want to hang out with. And all you want to do is hang out with her!"

"I don't want to, Tones, you know that! I don't have any choice."

"You have a choice, Alex, and you've made the same one every weekend since Hayley was six weeks old. For God's sake, when are you finally going to choose her?" He had paused then, his eyes flooding with tears she had rarely seen. He was normally so upbeat. "When are you going to choose *us*?"

And that's when she realised. It wasn't just her kids she was sacrificing, it was him. It was her marriage. And it hit her then like a bolt of lightning, that *this* was what Amelia had intended all along.

For everyone to be as pathetic and as lonely as she was.

And so that weekend she had simply not shown up. Instead of dragging on her jeans and moping into the cold *Eve* office, she had stayed in bed and clung to her husband like she was the koala, he was the gum, and a cyclone was fast approaching.

The following Monday, shoulders back, excuses at the ready, Alex had returned to work to find Amelia in a locked meeting with Monty. It was the beginning of many. It was the beginning of the end.

The axis of evil had turned into an arrow and it was aimed at her head.

"So?" Monty asked her now, perhaps for the second time. "Last Friday, Amelia must have known she was going away and wanted you to cover for her, did you ever think of that? You are the deputy, Alex. Maybe she wanted you in here on Saturday to tell you *where* she was going. But you didn't give her the chance."

Alex shrugged, like it didn't matter and said, "It's not my fault she took off."

But the way her eyes slithered away suggested otherwise.

SHEPPERDIN VILLAGE

Tom was racing to make the school bell but missed it by ten minutes. It might as well have been ten hours by the look the principal gave him.

"He went home with his cousins," she said.

You useless lump, came the silent echo. He nodded, thanked her and returned to his pick-up ute. By the time he got home, he had practised his excuse. *"Bloody boss made me drop off a load of gravel, son. Got lost trying to find the place. Sorry, mate."*

What else was he going to say? *I've been out at Grant's place, sinking beers, drowning my sorrows.*

Fortunately, Phil didn't demand any answers. Didn't even bother to look up as he bounced on his cousins' trampoline with three of Harry's kids, all pelting into each other, Scarlett watching on.

"I'm happy to bring him home from school, Tom," Scarlett said, her tone civil. "Besides, it's the least I can do—Pandanus and Jarrah are squatting in your sandpit as we speak. It's in much better shape than ours, that's for sure."

Tom had to hide his frown. He hated when her brood came over at the best of times, but what could he do? Demand they pack up their buckets and piss off? Besides, Phil hadn't used the sandpit all year. Practically lived there once, smashing his rusty Tonka trucks through the sand or climbing the old fig tree that hung over it like a pergola. Amy adored that fig, called it the *Avatar* tree, and she wasn't wrong. It was an enormous, sprawling beast.

"Anyway," Scarlett continued, watching the kids jump,

"Amy would want me to look out for Phil while she's…" She turned to catch his eye. "Where exactly *is* she, Tommo? Where did she go?"

He went to shrug, thought better of it and tried to swallow back a painful lump in his throat. "I… I don't know, Scar. I don't bloody know."

"Then why are you telling everyone she's at her mum's place or on some stupid bloody holiday?"

"What else should I say? She's left me? She's left Phil?"

"Yes, if that's the truth!"

"But I don't know… I don't…"

She followed his eyes to where Phil was now performing a precarious somersault. Amy would tell him to be careful. He just watched.

"You have no idea where she took off to, do you?"

He shook his head.

"Oh, Tommo! Something could have happened to her! Something really bad."

"Don't even say it, Scar, don't even think it."

"Somebody's got to! You can't ignore this." She reached out and touched his arm, then dropped her hand back quickly. "You have to call Geoff in. You have to make it official."

He looked at her, uncertainty in his eyes.

"She could be in trouble, Tommo. She could be somewhere out there, hurt." Then seeing his eyes fill with tears, she said more gently, "Just go and speak to Geoff. I'll look after Phil. Come on, he won't bite."

Tom nodded more certainly this time. He knew she was right, but it wasn't the top cop he was afraid of. It was the brutal truth. Of his marriage. Of Amy's despair. Of the quicksand that was their life.

~~~

Geoffrey Pinter might be the local chief of police, a superintendent no less, but Tom first knew him as Pimply Pinter then just Pinter then as his best mate, and he tried to remember that as he stepped into the police station late that afternoon to answer some "friendly questions".

Friendly fire more like.

"Thanks for coming in, mate," Geoff said, his tone also light,
~~~

like he, too, had history on his mind. "Just settling the horses, you know how it is?"

"You calling Scarlett a horse, Geoffrey? Or are you referring to Polly?"

The other man smiled, pretending that was a joke. "So. Amy."

"So. Amy," Tom repeated.

"Just for the record, can you tell me when you last saw your wife? Exactly?"

"Sunday night."

A deadpan look. "Can you give me a time, please?"

"Dunno." He rubbed at the orange bristle on his chin. "Let me think... She'd put Phil to bed—not that he needs putting to bed, mind, but she did anyway, always does. Kissed him like he was still five." Tom smiled now. He loved that about Amy, reminded him of his own mother. "So that was around nineish, give or take. Phil always complained, reckoned all his friends went to bed later, usual stuff. Um, I'd been watching telly but headed out the back to the shed—"

"Doing?"

"Bit of this, bit of that." Then as Geoff's stare hardened, he added, "I've been working on a birthday present for Amy, if you must know, a jewellery tree."

"A what?"

"It's stupid." He blushed. "Just a wooden thing, looks like a miniature tree, lots of branches coming out to hang your earrings and necklaces and shit. She wanted one." He smiled wanly. "She saw one in that overpriced excuse for a gift shop, you know, the one in the arcade? I told her I could make one bigger and better. And I did. Well, nearly. Not going to bother finishing it now." He wasn't smiling anymore.

"Why wouldn't you finish it?"

Tom frowned. "Would you give someone a present for walking out on you?"

Geoff leaned back in his seat. "Okay, we're getting off track here. I'm still a bit hazy. So she was putting Phil to bed, you went to your shed, what happened next?"

"No idea." Another stare. "Seriously. I'm as confused as you are. I came back in around eleven, eleven thirty. Amy wasn't on the couch. I assumed she was in bed, but she wasn't there either, so I assumed she was up in her writing cabin. Another thing I built for her." *More wasted energy.*

"That's a lot of assumptions. So does Amy normally go to her writing cabin that late?" Tom shrugged. "So what happened next?"

"Next thing I know Phil's waking me in the morning asking where his mum is."

"She never came to bed that night? Sunday night?"

He shrugged again, then thought better of it. He said, "It looked to me like her side of the bed had been slept in. The covers were down a bit, and her pillow was on the floor."

This had Geoff interested. "So what do you think happened?"

"I think she came in late, had a bad night's sleep—"

"Hang on, how did you *not* notice her come to bed?"

"I sleep like a tank, mate. Amy sleeps like a baby—you know, a newborn who wakes every hour."

He nodded. "Okay, so she came to bed and…?"

"I reckon she got up early, packed a bag and pissed off."

"There's a bag missing?"

"Think so. Can't find her baggy grey one anywhere."

"And she didn't leave you a note? Give you a reason?"

He shrugged again. "I'm sure she has her reasons; I just don't know what they are."

Geoff watched him for a few minutes. It was all very strange. He said, "I spoke to Mr and Mrs Malone this morning."

Tom said nothing.

"Why d'you lie to me, mate? Why d'you say she was there?"

"I didn't lie."

"You said your wife was at her folks' place."

"I said I *thought* she was there. Thought. Assumed."

"You're big on assumptions aren't you?"

"Hey, I don't know about you, Geoff, but when you're not expecting your wife to clear out, you don't automatically think the worst. You head straight for the simplest solution." The *kindest* solution he could have said. "She goes there every few months, I just joined the dots. So, what did they say? Her folks."

"They haven't heard anything. Not since you called and broke the news. They have a theory of their own, but I want to hear what you think now, what do you *assume?*"

"I told you before, I honestly don't know. But if I had to put a bet on it, I'd say Amy's booked herself into some quiet little bed and breaky somewhere and will be back by the weekend."

Geoff nodded, watching his old mate closely. Amy's parents thought the same. It had placated him somewhat. The mother, Beryl, insisted that Amy mentioned wanting a break, was planning a solo journey somewhere, but insisted she never really elaborated. "Wanted to find herself" the father had added, his tone denoting how frivolous he thought that idea. Neither parent suspected Tom of foul play, said he could be curt when he wanted to be but was genuinely loving, genuinely loyal. "Too loyal sometimes," Ron had thrown in, as though his daughter didn't deserve it.

Geoff sat forward in his chair and locked eyes on Tom. "Sadly for you, Tom, we can't work off assumptions, not when there're lives at stake."

"She's *fine*. I know she is!" *Or perhaps that was wishful thinking on his part.* Tom frowned. "Look, Amy said something… there was something I saw, something about a holiday…"

Geoff tried to mask his scepticism. "So *assuming* you're correct and she did go on some mystery holiday, any idea where? Is there a favourite place? Somewhere out of mobile phone range perhaps?"

"Nowhere I can think of."

"Does she normally up and leave? Just walk out on Phil like that?"

"Walked out on me too, mate!" Tom rubbed two hands across his face, clearly trying to calm down. "No, she doesn't. Like I said, she usually went to her folks in Sydney when she wanted some time out, so that's why I thought she was there. She liked it there, liked the luxury. Got a little tired of our old shack, the dunny out the back." He looked away but not before Geoff caught the shame in his eyes. "Who can blame her, really?"

You probably can. Geoff kept that to himself.

"Okay, so we know she didn't run back to her parents' luxurious indoor facilities, which begs the questions: Why did she leave this time, and where did she go?"

"I've been wracking my brain. I just don't know. She's coming up to another birthday, maybe that's been playing on her mind. Things have been busy at work for me, perhaps I wasn't giving her enough attention. You know how it is? You have a wife, right?"

Geoff stared at him hard again. Tom knew the answer to that

question better than anyone. Hadn't they fought over his wife, Jenny, once? Hadn't that marked the end of their friendship, mostly because Geoff had won the battle and Tom was a poor loser? Geoff tapped at his forehead as though erasing the thought, trying to remain professional. "I need to clarify, mate. Did you and Amy have a fight? Is everything okay with the marriage?"

Now it was Tom's turn to stare. "Taken up marriage counselling have ya, Geoff?"

"It's a simple question. Did you have a fight before she took off on this mystery holiday? Is that why you stormed off to your shed and she went up to the cabin? You can tell me, it's no big—"

"No!" He took a deep breath, rubbed his head again. "That's what's so bloody baffling about it all. We'd been *good* lately. I mean, I know she missed her old life, her career, her family, but I honestly thought she was settled."

"Did she take her handbag? Her mobile?"

He grimaced like he wished he'd thought of that. "I have tried calling her," he said, "but there's no answer." A frown. "Can you guys track down the phone? She's probably booked into a hotel somewhere to blow off some steam."

"We've checked all the hotels."

"In the whole damn country?"

He was snapping now, and Geoff was not in the mood for it. "Hey, I'm trying to locate your wife. Amy is now officially a missing person. She hasn't called you, she hasn't called her family, it's frankly worrying." He took a breath. "Did she have a passport?"

"She *had* one, but it'd be expired by now."

"We'll check that."

He scooped a pen from the table and scribbled something on a pad in front of him. He also wanted to check with the local stationmaster. Geoff already knew there was an express train to Sydney that departed Shepperdin around five each weekday morning and went every hour until eleven. She could easily have walked the thirty minutes it took to reach the station from her house and jumped aboard first thing Monday morning with very little fuss and nothing but dairy cows to witness it.

He threw the pen back on the table. "I have to say, Tom, none of this has filled me with any confidence, and I'm not waiting until the weekend. If Amy's not back by the morning, if no one's heard from her, I'm coming to the house. You are going to have to let me look around."

"Come! Look! But what would be the point? You think she's hiding in a cupboard or something?"

Geoff did not respond but it soon clicked.

"You think I *hurt* her? Is that what this is about? You think you're gonna find her chopped up into little pieces in the bathtub?"

"Of course I don't think that."

But plenty of others did, and Geoff wondered about that now. Despite their teenage friendship or maybe because of it, he wasn't Thomas Wilson's biggest fan, but he wasn't baying for blood either, not like some.

He recalled his conversation with Jenny over bacon and eggs that morning, how outraged she was by the accusations floating about. Mostly schoolyard gossip, of course, although she was taking it to heart.

"Prissy Miss Polly thinks Tom's batting above his weight, never deserved Amy," Jenny had said, and Geoff realised she had taken that as a criticism of her own dalliance with the bloke. "And Scarlett reckons he's been acting strange for days, but she won't elaborate." She tutted. "You can't just say stuff and then not back it up."

Geoff agreed with her and with them. While it was true the younger Wilson boy had married up, it didn't make him guilty of anything other than being a lucky bastard. And even though Tom could be secretive and grumpy and hold a grudge like no other, Geoff didn't honestly believe that he would hurt his wife.

Amy's parents didn't either. And that alone had filled him with hope.

For all his faults, Tom was a good husband, attentive and loving, like he knew he'd scored well and was trying hard to live up. Geoff didn't know what that jewellery tree was all about, but it didn't suggest a man who wanted to get rid of his wife.

"Just call me if you hear anything, okay? I'll get the gossips off your case."

"Thanks," Tom managed as he went to get up.

"And one other thing." Tom turned, eyes wide. "If there's no sign of her by midday tomorrow, I'm taking it all up a notch."

SARISI ISLAND

The seagulls had better keep their bloody distance, Nicholas thought as he flung his fishing line back out again. They'd been getting the better of him lately, but he had a new trick. He would outwit them this time. Sniggering, he wound the line back in a little and let it settle, repositioning his feet, checking the tide mark. He'd been washed off the rocks once before. Never again. He'd barely survived that first time, but then Kostas had appeared like an angel from heaven and wrenched him from the swirling sea, swearing and laughing as though he'd pulled him from a water slide, not certain death.

They became firm friends after that. "Friends for life!" Kostas liked to say, and Nico liked to retort that if he'd known that was the price, he would've let the sea take him. But he loved Kos like a brother now, the brother he never had. He was one more reason he'd hung around well past his use-by date.

Nico glanced casually back towards the shore, and that's when he spotted someone reaching down towards the rocks. The Aussie woman, had to be her, this time in dark sunglasses and more appropriate clothing.

"Oi!" he cried out. "What're you doin'?"

His voice must have carried elsewhere in the wind as she did not appear to hear, and he was about to yell out again when she recoiled with such speed, he also started. Even from this distance he could see her reach for her throat as she stumbled back, falling hard on her backside.

Curious, he began to reel his line back in, too hastily, knowing he was stuffing it up, sneaking glances back to watch as she struggled to her feet, crab walking backwards, still staring into the rock pool.

What had she seen? Was it really that horrific?

Clambering across the rocks with ease, Nicholas made his way towards her, his rod like a harpoon at his side. When he was almost upon her, he called out, "You okay?" and she was startled all over again.

Eyes wide, lips parted, she managed to straighten up and began to move away from the rock pool as though distancing herself from a crime. *Or was it from him?*

He kept his tone light as he called out, "Not pinching my dinner are ya?"

She stopped and shook her head furiously, clasping her arms around her chest. "I thought… I thought they were… stuck."

"Yeah they are stuck. It took me long enough to catch them. I don't want them going anywhere."

"Oh, right. Sorry." She glanced back towards the rock pool where several fish flapped in the shallows, blood billowing out from behind them, like distress flairs, clumps of seaweed nearby. She edged away again.

"You lost?" he asked, leaning down to cover his catch with the seaweed, then back up at her, his tangled fringe half obscuring his sleepy brown eyes.

The woman stared at him now as though she were staring at a ghost, her eyes widening, her skin paling a little.

"Seriously, you don't look so hot," he said, but she had already turned away.

"Hey!" he called out, but she was clambering back towards the beach.

This time she didn't miss a step as she made her escape.

~ ~ ~

An hour later and you would not have known the two Australians had ever met or that she had scuttled away at the sight of him on the rocks below the castle. The Aussie woman's stare was now blank, her tone perfectly neutral as she asked him, "Is Effie around?"

Nicholas had given up on his rock fishing after their strange encounter and returned to the hotel where he was scaling his catch in the kitchen sink when a voice sang out from inside the restaurant.

"Hello! Anyone here?"

He expected Effie to answer, so he ignored it for a bit, but when the voice called again, more persistent, he groaned and popped his head around the kitchen door.

"Can I help you?" he said before he realised who it was.

The woman, the Australian, stared at him again for a long, hard minute instead of paling and fleeing as she'd done last time, or apologising for that behaviour.

She seemed to relax a little and said, "Is Effie around?"

He blinked at her and then down at his scaling knife, which was still in his right hand. Now *this* she should be scared of, not some dead fish.

"Haven't seen her," he replied.

She seemed breathless, but he could already tell why. Her jumper was wrapped around her waist, her feet sandy, sneakers in her hands. She must have walked the scenic route from the castle, a good thirty-minute trek along the beach. Would've been faster to stick to the road like he had, but then you could never tell tourists that.

"We open for dinner in an hour," he said. "Can I help you with something?"

"No. No, it's okay."

She was already turning away, so he quickly called out, "Can I get your name at least?" And to her blossoming frown he added, "So I can tell Effie you're looking for her."

"Oh, of course." She hesitated as though trying to remember her name, then smiled and said, "Just tell her it's Millie."

And before he could say his own name, she was already striding away. He followed her to the door and watched as she walked back in the direction of the castle. When he turned around, he almost slammed into Effie.

"Bloody hell! You gave me a fright! And I'm the one holding the knife." He chuckled. "Where d'you disappear to?"

"I didn't disappear."

"There was a woman here asking for you. An Australian woman called Millie."

She pushed her lips south. "I don't know this Millie."

"Okay, well, she's obviously the one staying up with Kos. She's probably headed back there now. If you hurry you can catch——"

"I haven't got time for chasing tourists! You know I'm getting the sea jet to Athens in ten minutes, right?"

"Really? I thought it was next week."

She rounded on him. "You never listen!"

"Sorry!" He held fishy hands up protectively. "Bloody hell, Effie, chillax."

"Well, you boys, you only think with your lower bits! Use your brain, man! It is this week! I am picking up the orders. The pantry does not fill itself!"

"All right! So what do I tell this woman if she comes back?"

Effie stormed off to the kitchen and he followed, making a beeline for the sink.

"I don't care what you say," she said, then added more gently, "Just tell her I am not here. I am in Athens all week."

"So, hang on, how long *are* you gone for?"

"Arrgh, I have no time for your questions, Nicholas! Like always! A few days."

"Okay, so I'm stepping in for you from tonight?"

"Why? You can't?"

"No, it's fine. I'll do it. It's just that Kos and I were getting together to watch the soccer tonight."

"*Football.*" Kostas corrected him, appearing at the kitchen door as though he'd been waiting in the wings for this exact cue.

"Whatever you call it, you're on your own tonight. I'm working."

"No way! Is good match! Athens versus Piraeus!" he looked at Effie. "Why he work? Why you do this to me?"

Effie snarled and rattled off a series of expletives in Greek, then grabbed a notepad and started hunting around for a pencil.

The two men exchanged a look—they'd exchanged these looks many times before—then Nicholas returned to scaling the fish and Kostas loped out again, a stolen pita wrap in one hand, while Effie exhaled louder than she meant to and buried herself in the pantry.

EVE MAGAZINE

Wednesday morning drifted into afternoon at *Eve* magazine. Amelia never showed. And Monty's third call to Gerry's office was equally as disappointing.

Yes, Amelia and Gerry had a 2:00 p.m. meeting last Friday.

No, Lizzie would not be telling Monty all about it.

"But I can fit you in to see him at midday tomorrow, on the dot!"

Monty silently groaned, thanked her and hung up. She couldn't believe everyone's apathy towards the missing editor. Amelia's parents seemed to think she'd swanned off on some glamorous holiday. Her boss couldn't spare five minutes to discuss the matter. And Alex was acting like all her Christmases had come at once.

Monty stood up. It was time to take matters into her own hands again. Or Brianna's at least. She looked around, then followed the laughter trickling in from the tearoom and found Brianna by the urn, coffee mug in hand, chuckling at something Mel was saying. They both snapped to attention when she approached, almost as scared of Monty as they were of Amelia.

They were thick as thieves, those two, their dual ascendancy legendary.

"Got a minute?" Monty asked Brianna and before she could answer said, "I need you to swing by her house again."

"Whose? Amelia's?"

No. Lady Gaga's. Dimwit. She smiled patiently. "Yes."

Brianna looked annoyed by the request. Monty might scare her, but it was nothing compared to her fear of hard work.

Monty quickly added, "I want you to do a bit of sleuthing for me."

This piqued her interest, and she dumped her cup in the sink and followed her out. Only when they reached her desk did Monty speak again, aware of flapping ears and loose tongues.

"Amelia's parents were at her place this morning, and there's no sign of her," she explained, "but it looks like she may have packed her Vuitton and gone somewhere. So, that's good news; it'd just be helpful if we knew where."

"So where do I come in?"

"I'm thinking she must have mentioned something to someone, a friendly neighbour, the postman perhaps? There's a café down from her place. You know, the one on the corner? She often gets an early coffee there. Maybe she mentioned something to them. I mean, you don't just take off without telling *someone*."

Brianna was nodding. She liked this plan. Of course she did. Not only did it get her out of the office and away from those buzzing phones, she was probably already plotting a late-afternoon latté while she was interrogating the barista. Maybe he'd take pity on her and throw in a complimentary chocolate brownie.

~ ~ ~

Words not working? Think nobody cares?
**SOS Step 4: In case of emergency, just break glass!*

Monty leaned back in her chair, staring at her screen.

What the hell does that mean? She'd been working on the story for the past hour and was no closer to nailing it.

"Monty?"

She turned to find Hank standing behind her, a stunning redhead by his side. They both looked crestfallen.

"Is it true what everyone's saying?" he asked. "Amelia's not coming back."

Monty pushed away from her desk and faced them. "Don't be ridiculous, guys, of course she's coming back."

"So where is she?"

That was Fleur, the redhead, *Eve's* fashion editor, a failed model with the long legs and feline eyes. The catwalk's loss was *Eve's* gain. Fleur was as natural at fashion as Amelia was at editing, could pair an orange belt with a purple skirt and make it seem perfect. Hell, she'd start a fashion trend. In fact, since she'd accepted the job the year before, half the girls in the building were now donning cherry-red locks a la Fleur.

"Her parents say she went away on holidays," Monty said, trying to sound like that wasn't the craziest idea she'd ever heard, and they looked at her like she hadn't succeeded. "Don't worry! If *they're* not panicking, neither should we. I'm sure Amelia will be back before the issue gets put to bed."

That gave her until Monday. After that, all bets were off.

"I'm *baaaaaaaack.*"

Brianna was poking her head around the art department petition, looking pleased with herself, so Monty waved the others back to work, then turned to her expectantly.

"How'd you go? Tell me you found something."

"I think I might have."

Brianna dropped her handbag to the carpet and leaned against Monty's desk, feeling a little powerful again and liking it.

"So, I went straight to the café you suggested and spoke to a guy called Hilton." She grinned. He made a killer coffee. "He was sweet. Seemed to adore Amelia too." Her tone told Monty how inconceivable she thought that was. "Anyway, Hilton was even more worried than we are. Says he hasn't seen her in there *all week*, which is so not like her, and he nearly fell over when I said she hadn't shown up for work either. He says that's all she ever talks about. *Eve* this and *Eve* that. Like, duh! What else has she got in her life?"

"So they didn't have any idea where she might be? She told them nothing?"

"Not a thing. Hilton said she showed up for her usual macchiato last Friday morning, seemed perfectly fine, whatever that means, and he hasn't seen her since."

"Damn it. What about her neighbours?"

She waggled a hand in the air. "One side was deathly quiet, must be out, the other was an old biddy who's, frankly, not the sharpest tool in the shed. But she had something really interesting to report."

"Really?" Monty livened up.

"Again she thought Amelia was just lovely. Looks in on her from time to time, apparently, even stops for tea." Her top lip curled up again. More incredulity. "She also hasn't seen Amelia in ages, but she did say something a little curious."

"Yes?" Then, "For the love of God, Brianna, spit it out!"

Brianna smirked. "She said the last time she saw Amelia was… and this is where it gets a bit cloudy. *Might* have been last Friday, *might* have been Saturday. She doesn't have to work so I guess the days all blend together… Anyway, she said Amelia had a visitor. It was some, and I quote, 'handsome young chap in a white van and a high-viz vest'."

She stopped and looked at Monty like she'd just solved the riddle.

Monty blinked. "High-viz whatie?"

"You know, those fluorescent orange shirts all the tradesmen wear. My brother's a builder; he has one."

"Oh, I see." She felt her shoulders drop. "So someone came to repair a window or dig out the garden or something? Big whoop."

"That's what I said, right? But she seemed to think Amelia knew him. Said Amelia was coming out of her house when the guy called out her name, caught her by surprise and they had a few stern words—her words again—before Amelia shuffled him quickly inside the house like she was embarrassed or something."

"Okay, that's interesting…"

"I told you, right?"

"And this was last Friday or Saturday. Morning? Did she give a time?"

"She couldn't really remember so, like I said, not the brightest cookie. I'd take it all with a grain of soap."

"Salt."

"Sorry?"

"Never mind.

"What's this about?"

They both swung around to find Alex by the cubicle wall, hand on her hips, frown on her face. Monty quickly explained, telling her of Brianna's expedition. It did not erase the frown.

"Sorry, but aren't we losing a bit of focus here, Monty?" Alex said. "I mean, sure, it is concerning that Amelia's gone AWOL, but to tell you the truth, what I find even more concerning—and I'm frankly surprised that you don't—is that she's left us with twenty pages to finish, and the deadline, last time I looked, was in *two freaking days.* So, can we officially give up the case of the missing editor and focus on getting the magazine done? Maybe after that we can worry about a woman who clearly couldn't give a toss about any of us."

"That's a bit unfair, Alex," Monty began, but Alex was waving her index finger about.

"You know as well as I do, Monty, that if any one of us had dared not to show up *any* week, let alone *deadline* week and left Queen Amelia in the lurch, she wouldn't be out searching for us, she'd be writing us a termination letter. We'd be officially unemployed by the end of that first day. She's now been missing for *three days*. She hasn't phoned in. She's left no word, nothing, not even a half-written editor's letter we can use. So, sorry Monty, I know I sound like a cold cow but I'm actually being a lot kinder than she would be under the same circumstances. Amelia's gone and as far as I'm concerned, the who, what, where and why are irrelevant. We have a magazine to get out."

Monty sat back stunned while Brianna continued smirking.

"So, if it's all right with everybody, can we get back to work, please? Brianna, the phones are going berserk, and it's not Mel's job to answer the bloody things."

"Sorry!" she said, but the look she gave Alex as she swished past was one of renewed respect. *Who knew the deputy had balls?*

Alex turned her glare to Monty. "And I really need that SOS story back, ASAP. The production department is screaming for it."

"Fine, it's almost done."

"Good!"

"Good!"

Alex swept away, and Monty returned to stare at her screen, her fury at Alex's attitude fast dissolving as the truth of what she'd said hit home. The deputy was absolutely right. Not only would *their* absence be unforgivable to Amelia, she would dismiss it as quickly as she dismissed them and return to her first priority, *Eve*.

And so Monty must do the same.

She jiggled in her seat and clicked the SOS story open again. She had to focus; she knew that. But it didn't stop her wondering who the guy in the high-viz vest might be and what he was doing at Amelia's house around the time she vanished.

Did he have something to do with her departure? Were these seemingly inane SOS steps something Amelia might actually have benefited from? She shuddered just thinking about it.

~~~

Heart beating wildly, legs wobbling slightly, Alex returned to Amelia's office and closed the door carefully before heading straight to the desk. She sank into the chair and took a few calming breaths, closing her eyes and trying hard to think, then she opened them again and reached for her mobile phone.

It took a few seconds, but eventually the message service picked up. She silently cursed then waited for the beep.

"Don't come in, whatever you do, do *not* enter this building." Then, calmer, less wobbly: "I'll see you later. I'll explain it all then."

Then she dropped the phone to her desk and thought, *No wonder you can't look me in the eye, you silly, silly fool.*
~~~

SHEPPERDIN VILLAGE

Phil was not speaking to his dad. That much was obvious. Theirs was a relationship of few words anyway, but now Phil could barely look Tom in the eye and hadn't said so much as hello since he'd returned from next door two hours ago.

Scarlett had pumped the lad full of food (her words, not Phil's) and sent him home with a doggy bag for Tom, but he'd only dumped it on the kitchen bench and fled to his bedroom, slamming the door for good measure.

Who was Phil really angry with? Tom wondered, staring at the closed door. *Did he blame his dad for his mum's disappearance? Or her?*

Either way, Tom wasn't going to argue the point. He knew, more than anyone, that it was hard to disconnect the two in a kid's head, and so far he was coping pretty well. Tom had expected tears, fury, even a little hysteria, so silence wasn't unbearable, and he left him to his devices while he sat alone in the kitchen, picking at Scarlett's vegetarian lasagne.

When he'd had enough, he washed the plates and then made his way to the back shed, creaking open the door and stepping inside. He crossed to the workbench and looked at the handmade miniature tree, wondering why he'd bothered.

"How long does it take?" came a soft voice behind Tom, and he turned to find Phil standing at the shed door, half in, half out, as though the answer to this question would determine what happened next.

Except Tom wasn't sure what he was referring to. The jewellery tree he was making? Or his mother?

Before he could answer, Phil said, "It happened to you, didn't it? Your mum… Grandma… she took off too." Tom's eyebrows shot up. "Uncle Harry told me. Said you had to go through the same thing, around the same age."

Like it was a family tradition, a rite of passage. Was that why he was taking his mum's vanishing so well? Had he been expecting this somehow?

Then Phil repeated his earlier question. "So how long does it take? To get over it, I mean?"

Tom felt his heart break into a million useless pieces, and he wanted to reach out and grab the boy, but he knew he'd only turn and run. Theirs was also a relationship of few hugs.

"We'll find her, Phil," he began but could already see his son retreat, so he held a hand up to stall him. "You never get over it."

Phil stopped.

"That's the truth, son. It's horrendous and it hurts, and you cry for a long while, but then you just learn to live with it. That's all. You get on with living."

Phil thought about that for a moment, then stepped inside the shed.

For the next five minutes he wandered around, stroking the tools and glancing about, and Tom wondered why he didn't come to the shed more often, use the space a bit. Perhaps it was Tom's fault. Perhaps he should have lured him in with projects they could work on together. He looked back at the tree and realised it was a lost opportunity.

"For Mum?" Phil said, checking it over.

"Yep."

Phil walked around it and inspected every angle, and Tom was about to talk him through the woodwork, explain what he was intending, when Phil leaned closer to the object, his back to his dad.

"Why *did* she leave, do you think?"

Tom's throat felt like he'd drunk burnt coffee. He swallowed hard. "I don't know, mate." He wasn't talking about Amy now. "But Harry and I got through it, and you will too. We survived, and you know what? We came out better, stronger."

Phil turned around, his eyes glinting with anger. "How can Mum's leaving make me stronger or better? That's bullshit!"

The language caught Tom off guard, but he ignored it; it wasn't the time. Instead, he softened his tone and said, "It teaches you about love, matey, about what's right and wrong and"—he couldn't believe he was saying these words—"about fate and destiny. It teaches you that you can survive anything and maybe there's someone better out there anyway, someone you can trust."

"Someone better than *Mum*?" Again, Phil's eyes were fiery, and Tom noticed his hands were small fists by his side.

"I'm not trying to put shit on your mum, mate. I know she's your mother and you'll love her your whole life, just like I do."

"Hang on. So now you're saying I'm never going to see her again? My *whole life*?"

Tom sighed. *Jesus, he was botching this up.* "I'm not saying that either, mate. I hope she comes back." He sighed again. *Why give the kid false hope? It had never helped him.* "I'm just saying we love her, no matter what happens with your mum, whether she comes back tomorrow or she doesn't—and we don't know yet what's going to happen, right? What we do know—what I know for sure—is that one day you'll find another great love, like I did, and then you'll be able to move on. It'll all be okay."

"You met Mum."

Tom smiled. "Exactly."

Phil gave him a withering look. "And look how well that turned out."

Then he marched across the shed and slammed the door behind him.

Later that night after Tom had returned inside to find Phil fast asleep, his features now soft, like he wasn't thinking of his mum, he exhaled sadly and began to wander the house, trying to see it as a stranger might, as the police would tomorrow, but nothing stood out. Nothing gave any indication where Amy might be.

It seemed strange that Phil had already accepted her disappearance as a *fait accompli*, and he wondered what else Harry had told him and whether he thought he was helping. Tom knew it took them both many years to get over their own mother's desertion, and he wasn't lying to his son when he told him you never really got over it, but you somehow learned to live with it. Wasn't lying either when he said that meeting someone else—someone like Amy—was the key.

Amy had brought the light back into his life, the love, the way forward. But Phil was right. Now she was gone. Was the light gone too?

He glanced at the clock. He knew it was late, but he owed her parents another phone call, so he strode back to the bedroom, across to Amy's side, and reached for the old address book she kept in a drawer in the bedside table. He flipped until he found his way to *M* for Malone, then reached for his mobile phone and began tapping Amy's parents' number in, noticing a name from the past scribbled in at the bottom of the page that he hadn't noticed before.

Monty Brennan.

An old school friend of Amy's and as much her foe. He wondered about Monty for a moment as he waited for the line to pick up.

"Hello, this is the Malone residence, Beryl speaking."

His mother-in-law's tone was shrill, echoing the late hour.

"Beryl, hi, it's Tom."

There was a moment of hesitation—perhaps she had forgotten who Tom was (he rarely phoned her house) or perhaps she was delaying the inevitable—but then she asked about her daughter, and he explained that she was still missing, and it all turned to crap after that. Beryl's tone switched from high-pitched polite to deep thunder. She roared at him for many minutes, Ron following soon after, and he just held the phone to his ear and heard them out.

Back in the early days he'd been their favourite person, the one who'd saved their daughter's dignity after the horrendous business in Greece. After that arsehole had left her in a very bad way. But they seemed to have forgotten all that. Now they wanted to blame him for stuff they should be blaming Amy for. He guessed it was easier to turn the torch on someone you don't really love.

After twenty minutes he managed to settle them down, to assure them he would find her, to hang up. Then he sat on Amy's side of the bed for many minutes, trying to gather himself, to dam the tears that were starting to flow. He hated crying. Loathed it in fact. And he hated Amy in that moment for reducing him to this.

Eventually, slowly, the tears dried up and he looked around. Then he stood up and went in search of the laptop. He wasn't delusional about the holiday. He knew Amy was heading somewhere; he just couldn't work out where. There had to be an email about it, an e-ticket, a search history, something...

As Tom tapped and opened and clicked and swiped, he felt a

growing sense of frustration. Why didn't everybody understand he was the victim here, not Amy?

She wanted to leave this family; he knew that clear as day. *She* wanted to walk out on her husband and son and smash everything they had worked so hard to repair over the past thirteen years.

Tom knew it. Phil clearly knew it too. Now he just had to find the proof.

SARISI ISLAND

The taverna was busier than expected, buzzing with longtime locals enjoying a quiet dinner before the foreigners showed up and acted, as they always did, like they owned the place, and Nicholas barely had time to blink, let alone curse the missing manager who he was sure had got her Athens weeks mixed up.

He served the young couple who ran the paddleboat business and the old guy who hadn't yet opened his *pension* on the black beach for the season, and Joe-Joe the short fat Greek who owned the town's equivalent of a 7-Eleven, his voluptuous wife Catalina sitting across from him, watching Nico closely.

Luckily, the supplies weren't as low as Effie had said (more proof she had got her dates wrong!), and Nico didn't have to do any runs to Joe-Joe's on behalf of Pete, the Delfy's longtime chef. A cheerful sixty-something South African with a passion for food, and craters where the skin cancer had eaten his face, Pete once spent his summers in Greece and his winters in the Swiss Alps, but at some point, despite the skin cancer, the sun won out and he settled on Sarisi, taking up as Effie's head cook and occasional lover.

At least that's what the gossips said, but Nico didn't want to hear it, kept his ears closed. And he wondered now how much they all knew about him and Catalina and why she kept staring at him like he was on the menu.

Was she *trying* to get caught?

He shuddered at the thought. Not because he was worried about Joe-Joe so much. The guy was the size of a brick shithouse, would topple over at the first left hook, but his shop was like a lifeline on this island, and Nico did not want to have to avoid the place. Perhaps it was time to avoid Catalina instead. Perhaps he should have avoided her from the start. The affair was all his fault, he knew that. But the loneliness had caught up with him after Theo had left to start middle school on the mainland, and he was getting a little long in the tooth for stray backpackers these days.

His eyes slid to the esplanade where one such backpacker was walking, although the Aussie woman was as far from a backpacker as he was from what he'd call a decent bloke. Millie was holding what looked like souvlaki and picking at it with dainty fingers and a stern expression, a green bag hanging from the crook of one elbow, no doubt full of supplies from Joe-Joe's.

"You right for a bit?" he asked Pauly, the town's teenage postie who also waited tables at night.

Pauly swore something in Greek as he raced from the kitchen, hands laden with hot dishes, so he took that as a yes and stepped out onto the road.

"Hey!" he called out and had to call out again before she stopped and looked around.

"Oh, hi," Millie called back.

"Did you manage to catch Effie before she left?"

"She's *gone*?"

"Across to the mainland."

Millie seemed startled by that, then deflated.

"Sorry, I did tell her you were looking for her. She didn't seem to know you so…"

She smiled. It was a ghost of a smile. "No, I guess she doesn't." She stepped closer. "Do you have any idea when she'll be back?"

"She's usually over there for a few days, stocking up on supplies. I'm Nicholas, by the way. Everyone calls me Nico."

He held out his hand, and she switched the lamb stick to her left hand and wiped her right quickly before shaking his. "You sound Australian."

"Guilty as charged, but I have lots of family around these parts, all through the Cyclades and on Athens too."

"Lucky you," she said, and he smiled.

He'd never thought of himself as lucky.

"So, I hear you're trying to find some old convent." Nico didn't ask her why; he felt gossipy enough as it was.

"Oh, I found the convent. It's the nuns that have gone missing. I'm trying to find a woman called Sister Agnetha. You don't happen to know anything about her?"

He shook his head and saw her lips droop, watched as she leaned down to retrieve the bag she'd dropped at her feet, looking as though she were about to walk away.

"But I know someone who might."

She looked up.

"You should speak to Zoe, on Mikro. She knows everyone and everything. Nothing gets past Zoe."

"Mikro?"

"It's the tiny island just off the coast, on the other side of Coso Point. You can walk across in low tide but better to go by boat. I can ask some lads inside if you like. Maybe one of them can take you across in the morning. Doesn't take long."

She nodded, reaching for her things again. "That would be wonderful. Thank you." She stopped, turned back to him. "Why are you being so kind to me?"

He blinked. "Sorry. I wasn't aware I was."

And he wasn't at all sure why he was apologizing for it.

~~~

From the courtyard a man was watching their conversation and frowning. There was something familiar about the woman Nico was yakking with, something about her face that made him stop and look twice.

She had dark hair, long and wavy, but she didn't seem Greek. Definitely foreign yet oddly familiar…

That's when it hit him like a runaway ferry. He had a sudden flashback—to a dark night, a wet beach, a body bloody and battered. Then he remembered the screams and accusations, the pitchforks and police.

He grappled for his wallet, flung some Euro on the table, and slipped quietly out the back way.
~~~

EVE MAGAZINE

Monty had forgotten how diminutive Lizzie was. How petite and almost pretty. And she tried to keep that in mind as she loomed over Gerry's PA and begged to see the publisher.

For her part, Lizzie looked up at Monty like she was a flea on a rat. No, worse than that. What was the line? An amoeba on a flea on a rat.

"You're five minutes late. Gerry's completely booked out again. I told you yesterday that you needed to be here on time."

Monty grimaced. It was just after midday on Thursday, but she'd been ready for this meeting for hours. She'd arrived early, in fact—a quick glance at Amelia's office, another plunging heart—but then she got busy designing the final spreads and then sidetracked adjudicating a row between Alex and the fashion editor. Fleur was insisting that Amelia would *adore* the swimsuit shot she'd chosen for the style section's opening spread even though, as Alex pointed out, you could barely see a bikini thanks to the bright flash of light making everything look dark and hazy.

"That's the look Andres was going for," Fleur had replied.

"What? Crap and out of focus?"

"It's *art*, Monty! And Amelia loves that look. She also loves Andres and she'd want that as the opening shot."

"Do I look like Amelia to you?"

As Fleur's scowling eyes swept across the deputy's frizzy hair and down her ill-fitting suit, Monty had to jump in lest she said something she'd later regret and was now trying to explain all this to

Lizzie who wasn't scowling so much as looking completely disinterested.

"We'll reschedule," Lizzie announced. She turned to her desk diary and began gliding one finger downwards. "Now, let me see…"

She flipped the page over, then back again, and eventually stopped at an empty line towards the lower half of the page. She tapped it several times.

"I can pop you in this afternoon. Teeny window before Gerry has his conference call with London but *only* if you get here by 5:50. On the dot." She selected a pencil from a cup in front of her and looked up at Monty. "And I'm going to need a few more details. What exactly is this regarding?" She arched an eyebrow. "I'm guessing the prodigal editor has not returned?"

"No, and that's why I need to speak to Gerry. I think he might hold the key, and he may not realise it." She was still fixated on that 2:00 p.m. meeting they'd had, but she wasn't about to tell Lizzie that. "I promise, it'll be a quick chat."

"Dear." Lizzie tilted her face and eyeballed Monty above her spectacles. "Gerry doesn't have time for *chats*." She dropped the pencil back into the cup. "If he had any idea where Amelia was, he'd be shouting it from the rooftop. Her absence may have lost us the Revlon account, and if she doesn't front up to that Global Solutions soiree this evening, we can kiss another $50,000 account goodbye." Her phone began to ring. "Get in touch when you hear from Amelia," she said, reaching for it. "Gerry Henderson's office, Lizzie Soda speaking."

Then she offered Monty a stiff smile and glanced away.

Monty knew a defeat when she saw one and tried very hard not to curse aloud as she headed for the exit. Poor Amelia, she thought now, having to smash through that Berlin wall every time she wanted a quick *chat* with Gerry. If Alex thought Fleur was hard work, perhaps she should go a few rounds with Lizzie.

Out in the corridor, she headed for the elevators where she was quickly joined by the rake-thin editor of the country's leading design magazine, *House & Feather*.

"Monty darling, you look fabulous as always," Willow said, jabbing at the Down button even though it was alight. "Been in to see his royal highness have we?"

She nodded, feeling weary suddenly as Willow rattled on.

"I've been wrestling with the blasted advertising director who seems to think it's perfectly acceptable to mess with my cover. Honestly, that's a surefire way to lose sales!" As she spoke she pulled at the ends of her glossy black bob and patted her thick fringe down, and Monty realised she was checking out her reflection in the closed elevator doors. "Would *you* buy an interiors magazine with flat-pack furniture on the front?"

She pretended to shudder, then turned to face Monty. "Are you worried about your missing editor or the move across? If it's the latter, please don't be, sweetie. We're all very excited to have you aboard."

Monty looked back at her. "Sorry?"

"At *House*."

When Monty continued to stare at her blankly, Willow's meticulously sculpted eyebrows crinkled together. "Gerry did just tell you, didn't he?"

"Couldn't get past his itty-bitty bouncer."

"Oh, I see!" Willow bit her lower lip. "Oh blast it! I didn't just put my foot in it again did I? My team say I'm famous for it. Absolutely hopeless!"

"What's going on, Willow?"

She sighed. Lowered her voice. "Sorry darling, I assumed you knew. Hell, I assumed this is what you wanted."

Monty's eyes narrowed. "Still not making any sense."

Another dramatic sigh. "Darling, you're our new art director! I can't believe he didn't tell you. Or Amelia even more so! You're moving across. Next month."

"I am?"

"I hope so! I thought you must have asked for this. It's a massive promotion. Your wings are totally clipped at *Eve*; everybody knows that. We're getting you out of Amelia's shadow and helping you soar! Speaking of Amelia, where *is she*, darling? The whole place is abuzz with gossip! I'm thinking, some fabulous promotion overseas, but I'm afraid to say, most of my staff have their money on rehab."

"Rehab? What! No, look, sorry, can we back up a bit, Willow? I know nothing about any move to *House*."

"Oh dear, how very awkward."

The elevator pinged and the doors swept open. Seeing her escape, Willow all but leapt in.

"Go back and speak to Gerry, darling. I'm sure it'll all make perfect sense!"

And then she stabbed at the Close button and was swiftly swept away, her look of relief not lost on Monty, whose stunned expression was now being reflected back at her.

She swivelled and charged back to Gerry's office.

SHEPPERDIN VILLAGE

He knew they were coming, had expected their knock, but it still sounded like gunfire at dawn. Tom raced to the door before Phil could get to it, and let the officers in, his expression blank but his thoughts bitter, not helped by too many longnecks last night.

Geoff had rustled up some extra help from a neighbouring station, and there were six officers in all, each one going through her stuff. *Their stuff.* He wasn't sure what it was they expected to find, but he knew they'd find nothing, or at least nothing that would satiate their darkest thoughts. Because he knew what they were all thinking, the cops, his brother, that wife of his who was now watching openly from across the yard, a baby on one hip, another two kids at her feet.

"We're checking all avenues, you know that," Geoff told him, and he nodded. Yeah, he knew. "We might find something you missed. Some sign of what happened or where she headed off to."

He met the police chief's eyes and held them for a moment. He suspected Geoff didn't believe she'd gone anywhere, at least not of her own free will.

He swallowed the thought down, the lump catching in his throat, and he said a silent prayer to his wife.

Please help me get through this, baby. You know I don't deserve this. Please give them a sign, some proof, something.

"You all right, mate?"

Harry was standing beside him now as he waited in the driveway, Tom no longer welcome in his own home.

Scarlett had already fetched a worried-looking Phil, fed him breakfast and driven him to school, and she'd probably called Harry back from the paddocks while she was at it. That's where he usually spent his mornings, checking fence lines, tending the beasts.

Avoiding his busybody wife, Tom thought.

"Yeah, it's great fun having strangers crawl through your undies."

"They're just crossing their t's."

"Course they are." Then he turned to eyeball him. "Why d'you have to go and tell Phil about Mum? Why did you do that?"

Harry took a step back. "I can't believe you haven't. Why the secrecy? She left twenty years ago."

"So? That somehow makes it okay?"

Harry looked perplexed. He wasn't sure what Tom was on about. "Sorry if I overstepped, Tommo, but I assumed Phil knew what had gone on. I didn't give all the details. Just the basics How she also vanished when we were kids. Thought it might help."

"He's barely talking to me, so good work, mate."

"He barely talks to you anyway."

"What?"

"Nothing. I'm outta here." Harry stormed off, hands in his pockets just as Geoff approached.

"You two all right?" the police chief asked.

"Never better," Tom said, and Geoff glanced back towards the retreating brother and wondered now about their relationship.

The Wilson boys had always been close—you picked on one at school, you picked on both—which was why the news that their dad had left the entire property to Harry had seemed such a cruel blow, almost as though he was intending to break them up. In any case it hadn't worked. Harry had done the brotherly thing and offered a slice of the property to Tom, righting a wrong and keeping the relationship close. Geoff wondered now what else Harry would do for his brother.

Would he lie for him, for instance?

He turned back to Tom and tapped his watch. "I'm not waiting any longer, mate. I've arranged the press briefing for three o'clock so we can get it on the news tonight. I know you've got work, but I've already cleared it with Jimbo. He said to take the rest of the day off."

"What?"

"Now don't get angry. I figured he'd be more likely to say yes if I was the one doing the asking."

That wasn't what Tom was angry about. In fact, he wasn't angry at all, he was surprised. "So that's it. You're done?"

"Here, yeah, sure." He shook his head. "I didn't really expect to find a smoking gun. I just had to tick that one off."

Tom felt a surge of disappointment. Of course there was no smoking gun, but he had assumed they'd find some evidence of the holiday she was clearly planning. If six trained police officers couldn't find it, what hope did he have?

"We'll need you in there by about two thirty, okay? No later. Come to the front desk and ask for Ommie. She's the media manager."

"You guys have a media manager?"

He smiled. "It's a slick operation we run, mate."

SARISI ISLAND

The fishing boat was made of fibreglass-reinforced wood, the hull painted a cheerful Greek blue with a tiny cockpit for the skipper, a ragged Greek flag at the stern and very little else to ingratiate itself. Millie had initially been assisted to a wooden bench seat behind the cockpit that had been furnished with a mouldy plastic cushion, but it left her choking up diesel fumes, and she was soon standing next to the skipper, making small talk. Eventually she groped her way down the starboard side, almost to the stern where Nicholas was sitting, legs dangling over the edge, holding what looked like a rusty tin can.

Despite the movement of the boat, the water below them was almost serene, yet Millie had been on so few boats she was yet to find her sea legs and thanked the heavens for the handrail as she made her way to him, finally dropping down clumsily by his side.

Nicholas looked up from the can—a makeshift fishing rod with line twined around it, one end reaching down into the water. He didn't usually fish off a moving vessel, but they were going so slowly he thought he'd try his luck.

"Sorry!" he yelled, his voice rising with the sound of the motor and the wind. "She's the flashiest vessel I could find at late notice."

"Oh it's fine," she yelled back. "I'm just so appreciative he could take me." She glanced forward. "This skipper fellow, I get the feeling he doesn't speak much English."

"Giannis? Not a word!" Nico laughed. "How long did it take you to work that out?" He laughed again. "Nah, half the islanders don't speak any English. It's the only reason they tolerate me around here. I help to translate."

"You speak Greek?"

He waggled his free hand. "I understand a bit. Come from a big Greek family, so some of it sunk in."

"You're from Melbourne?"

He glanced back at her. "I knew you were smart."

But it was an easy guess. One of the largest Greek populations outside Athens could be found in that Australian city.

"Don't you miss your family?" she asked, watching as he fished, and he shrugged and focused on his line.

He'd gone quiet, and she wondered whether he preferred to fish alone when he said, "We'll be on Mikro in about ten. It's close, but this old tug is slow, which is why I jumped on. Ideal for fishing." Then he glanced across at her. "Hope you don't mind my tagging along. I can get some decent bream out here. Saves me having to go out on the rocks this arvo."

"Not at all. Thanks so much for organising this. I'm sure Giannis had better plans for the day. Besides, maybe you can translate for me, with Zoe."

That brought the smile back to his face.

"What?" she asked.

"It's not translation you'll need help with, not when it comes to Zoe."

He chuckled and she was about to enquire further when he said, "Whoah! We have a live one!" Nicholas began to wind the line in, his hands working overtime when he suddenly growled and relaxed it again. "False alarm."

She watched as he continued to wind it in to check the bait and, realising it had been pilfered, reached into his shirt pocket to scoop out a small plastic bag with something mushy inside. It looked like squid, and he pulled a slippery morsel out and pushed it through the hook, then released some line before flinging it outwards again.

After watching him for a while longer, Millie said, "You must love your fish."

He laughed again. "Can't stand the scaly critters!"

"Really?"

"Yeah. Just do it for Pete—the chef at Delfys. I sell him my catch. And because it's therapeutic, fishing. You should try it."

He had a hunch it would help.

Nico hadn't yet worked out why the woman was searching for nuns, but it smacked of something deep and heavy. *I mean, you don't look up old nuns to go partying with, right?* He felt the line tug again, tugged it back to check, but it was nothing. Just the tide playing tricks.

"So what do you do for a living?" she asked, pulling her flyaway hair into a ponytail. "Apart from sell fish you don't like and wait tables for Effie. Or is that it?"

"Is that not enough?" He smiled and gave it some thought. "I do whatever comes along. Never really settled on one job to be honest. I get bored easily. Need to stretch myself, try new things."

"Wow," she said. "I wish I was that brave."

"What about you then? What do you do, apart from nun-hunting that is?"

But before she could answer Nico found himself laughing again.

"What's so funny?" she demanded.

"Sorry, it's just... *nuns*? Really?"

"What's wrong with nuns?"

"They give me the creeps, that's all. Bit too smarmy. And what's with their getup? It's a little too KKK to me."

"Oh stop it!" She smacked him on the arm. "Most of the nuns I've met are lovely and very few wear a uniform anymore."

"Still," he persisted. "Nuns aren't what most people come asking about. They usually want to know where the beach is or how soon they can get the first ferry to Santorini."

"Well, I'm not most people."

"Yep," he said, peering into her dark glasses, "I've already worked that one out."

She met his stare for a moment, and her lips turned skyward in a smile. He felt his breath catch—what a smile! He wanted to see her smile again, but she was looking away and saying, "I think you got a bite."

Nico swivelled back to see his line flying away from him, and he grabbed it and began to haul it in while she watched and laughed. She had a lovely laugh too, strong, confident, like a galloping horse, but she was already pulling in the reins, bringing it to a canter, and he felt a flash of disappointment. He had a sudden desire to hear that gallop again, but she was already pulling herself up by the railing.

"I'll stop distracting you," she said. "Besides, we're nearly there."

They both stared out towards the rocky islet that was fast closing in and towards a large woman with long white hair who was standing on a wooden jetty, waving one arm like a windsock at them.

"Zoe," Nicholas said, as if it needed explaining.

And in some ways it did.

Zoe was not at all what Millie had been expecting. No wizened Greek widow with chin whiskers and black garb, she was surprisingly glamorous. If Millie knew her designers—and she hadn't read all those magazines for nothing—that was a $1,000 *Camilla* kaftan she was sporting over paint-splattered jeans. And, of all things, she was British. No wonder Nico had been laughing at her suggestion he translate.

But still, there was something a little kooky about the woman, starting with the fact that she didn't seem to care why the boat had suddenly shown up and a stranger was now asking for a chat.

She simply said, rather cryptically, "Of course, my darling! I knew you would come!" Then she waved the men off like they were a distraction.

Nico looked uncertain for a moment, but Millie assured him she'd be fine.

"We'll putter about for a bit and do some more fishing," he said. "Just give us a holler when you're ready. Do you have a mobile?"

She shook her head. She'd left it at the castle. The constant stream of messages was beginning to tug at her heart, and she wasn't ready to call. Not yet.

"Then just wave your hands like a maniac, and we'll keep an eye out."

"She'll be fine!" Zoe announced, all but pushing the men back onto the boat.

No sooner had they launched, the older woman launched herself at Millie grabbing her chin and moving her face from left to right as if inspecting a race horse or a cover model.

"Look at you!" she gushed. "So beautiful. And just as I imagined."

Millie balked at that and pulled away. "Sorry, do I know you? Have we met?"

Zoe cackled. "No, darling girl, not yet, but come, let's change that."

Then she took Millie's hand like she was a small child and led her along the creaky jetty and across the rocky bay to her house. It was actually a series of houses, more like yurts, some simple, some ramshackle, some looking new or newly renovated at least.

"I run an artists' colony out here," she explained, "although we're low on numbers at the moment. But don't be deceived; the sun always brings them back." She stopped to offer her effusive wave to a middle-aged man and woman who were exiting one of the yurts, and they smiled widely and waved back. "That's my Canadian couple," Zoe explained. "They're sorting out their marital issues through ceramics." Before Millie had a chance to digest that, she added, "Come, the rosehip will be ready."

They continued on, past the couple and towards the oldest and most ramshackle of the yurts where Millie spotted two goats nibbling on what looked like a vegetable patch.

Zoe spotted them too and let out an almighty shriek, then raced off to scare them away, surprisingly nimble for her age—which Millie assumed was well into her seventies—arms flailing about until the goats had trotted off and into a fenced area around the back. She followed them across and secured the gate.

When she returned to Millie's side, she said, "Nigel and Nora are particularly fond of getting amorous around my spinach!"

For the life of her, Millie wasn't sure if she was referring to the goats or the Canadians. She let it drop and followed the woman through the front door of her yurt.

The interior room, if that's what you could call it, for it was really a series of circular rooms each one opening out from the other, was cluttered and cosy with a motley collection of furnishings and a myriad of knickknacks. There were elaborate vases with flowers (fresh, dried and synthetic), several rusty birdcages (empty as far as Millie could see), glass cupboards jammed with bright pottery, and old paint pallets and easels at every glance.

But it was the walls that caught her eye.

Everywhere you looked, enormous canvasses were hanging, leaning or piled up, each with oversized faces dripping out of them, some laughing, some crying, one screaming (that one looked suspiciously like the face of the Canadian man she'd just seen), another staring, bemused, her expression now matching Millie's.

Zoe cackled again. "Don't you love them!"

"They're amazing. Did you paint them?"

"Of course. And I'd love to paint you one day, if you will let me."

"Oh, well, I'm not going to be here for long, so…"

Zoe tsked. "Of course you are. We'll schedule you in another time."

Then before Millie could object, she was striding into the kitchen and towards a white ceramic teapot that was decorated in hand-painted yellow and black flowers.

"Meg's creation," she said, nudging her head back towards the front door. "It was one of the few she didn't lob at her husband's head."

She cackled again as she reached for mismatched cups and a strainer. After pouring for them both, not asking about milk or sugar, she thrust a cup in Millie's hand and then padded into the centre of the room and settled on the rug, her legs folded meditation-style beneath her.

Millie hadn't sat cross-legged on the floor since childhood, so she glanced around, spotting the only armchair without books piled up on it, and said, "May I?"

"Of course!"

Zoe watched and waited until Millie had sat down and taken a few sips of her tea, then she said very matter-of-factly, "So you're looking for Aggie."

Then she cackled again at the younger woman's surprise. "Oh I am psychic, but not quite *that* psychic. News travels fast even out here." Then she crossed herself and said, "Poor Aggie, may she rest in peace."

Millie's heart nosedived. *No, no, no.*

"Oh my darling, I can see this news did not quite travel fast enough. Or should I say far enough. You have come from Australia?"

"Yes. A few days ago."

"But you cannot be surprised? Agnetha was older even than me."

"I guess not… I never thought…" She stopped, took another fortifying sip. "She seemed ageless, invincible."

"It's hard to tell with nuns. They're very clever; they hide their grey hairs beneath a white habit. She was a good friend to you."

It wasn't a question, but Millie nodded anyway. "For a while, yes."

"She was formidable."

"That too."

"Then you know how much we all miss her around here. And not just here, all the surrounding islands. She saved a lot of lives."

"I know," she said, thinking, *She saved me.* "She should have been a doctor," Millie said. "She was so talented."

"She should have *trained* as a doctor, that is true. Maybe then she wouldn't have got in quite so much trouble." Then to Millie's blank expression she said, "Ah you never heard that either."

"Heard what?"

Zoe took a good gulp of her own tea, then placed it on the floor before her. "Dear Aggie. She lost someone, about six years ago, administering her usual medicine, her usual magic—at least that's what the imbecilic policeman called it, and it wasn't a compliment, I can tell you that. In any case, it was an utter nightmare. The poor darling bled out, a helicopter was called, mad dash to Athens, but it was too late. The officials came down hard on Aggie after that. Oh don't worry, she didn't get charged, there were too many skeletons for that, but there would be no more needy souls through the convent doors." She stopped, stared at a spot behind Millie's head. "Aggie was never quite the same after that, never quite as formidable. Neither was the convent for that matter."

"What happened to it all? I know the convent's now a hostel, but what happened to all the other nuns who were there?"

And why couldn't she remember any of their names and faces?

"Eventually..." Zoe stopped, shook her head. "No, *quickly* when you think about it, the sisters began to leave, took posts elsewhere, and who could blame them? Aggie had lost her spark, her *raison d'être.* I think you all gave her something to live for but after that... well..."

"That's so tragic," Millie said, tears welling in her eyes.

"And not just for Aggie. For all of Sarisi. She was the only one with any medical nous. Now all we've got is a vet, and he's only good if you've got four feet and not even very good then. If anything goes wrong, we have to scoot off to the mainland. It's a dreadful six-hour ferry ride away. But that you do know about, yes?"

Yes. She took a long drink from her cup. "How did she...?"

"Peacefully as it turns out. About four years ago. They found her in bed. Rosary beads in her hands. Mozart playing."

Millie's heart swelled. She had forgotten all about the classical music that tinkled through the convent from various transistor radios set up by Aggie. It had become a soundtrack to her time in Greece, and so Millie avoided anything remotely like it when she returned home, flicking past Classic FM whenever she tuned her radio.

She suddenly had a yearning for Mozart or her then-favourite Chopin. Instead, all she could hear was the lapping of the waves nearby and what sounded like laughter. Again, she couldn't work out if it was the couple or the goats.

Zoe's face had darkened. "I can't help wondering," she said, "if I could have done more. Perhaps I should have whisked her out of that old castle and dragged her here."

"She seemed invincible," Millie said again, and it was her way of redeeming them all.

The older woman nodded. "We thought she was. Thousands came for the funeral, and not only patients, not only Greeks. They poured in off the boats and the airplanes. Young and old, men and women, lots of children. Every nationality. So many souls, saved by one little lady."

"I wish I'd known," said Millie, "about the funeral that is." But would she have flown out from Australia? *Probably not.* She was still caught up in her own lies back then. She was only working out how to shed them now.

Millie sensed a mood change and noticed that Zoe was now watching her carefully. Her eyes were not unlike Agnetha's. They seemed to be having a conversation of their own, and Millie wasn't sure she liked where it was heading.

She placed her cup on the table in front of her and said, "I've probably taken enough of your time. Thanks for letting me know about Aggie and what happened."

Then, cutting off Zoe even though she hadn't actually spoken, she quickly said, "I really just wanted to see her again, that's all. I wanted to say thank you. Wanted to say goodbye."

But they both knew that was a lie. She wanted a lot more from Aggie than that, and now it was too late.

On the windy walk back to the jetty, Millie let Zoe do all the talking—about her artwork and her students—and she let her mind stray. Not to ugly thoughts, she couldn't go there yet. Instead she remembered the first time she met Sister Agnetha or at least the first time she remembered clapping eyes on the elderly Greek.

Zoe was only half right. It wasn't just the white habit that hid Aggie's age, her energy and optimism also camouflaged her wrinkles and frail bones.

"You want to hang around this time?" were the first words Agnetha uttered or at least the first Millie could remember. There was no judgement, just inquiry.

She managed to nod.

"Good! We've been waiting for you. Welcome back."

And the smile she offered Millie was like an elixir.

Thinking about it now, she knew that it was Aggy who got her through that coma and kept her alive. Not through any medicine or even silly magic—although God knows what she'd tried while Millie was unconscious those first three weeks—but through gentle hands and nonjudgemental care.

Millie felt a sob catch in her throat. Those were the very things she needed now, and she suddenly ached for a woman she barely knew, let's face it, and had not seen or spoken to in over a decade.

"Millie?" That was Zoe and she must have asked a question, her eyebrows high.

"Sorry, Zoe. I'm a bit distracted."

"You have reason to be, my darling. It has been a shock."

She nodded as they reached the jetty and noticed that Giannis's boat was already closing in. Zoe must have signalled for them.

As they watched it approach, Zoe grabbed Millie's hand and pulled her close.

"I'm sorry I cannot give you all the answers you need, my darling girl, but it is not my place. I hope you can understand that."

Again Millie was bemused, but she saw that the older woman was looking more worried, her tone growing in urgency.

"But you must keep going," Zoe said. "Do not turn back now."

"What do you mean—?"

"I know you have given so much already, Millie, but sometimes you have to give it all—every last bit of it, no matter how painful, how heart-wrenching—in order to be truly free. It might be time to face the beautiful, brutal truth."

Then she pulled her into a hug, waved at the approaching vessel, and swiftly turned away, leaving Millie feeling like she'd been slapped with answers to questions she had never asked and couldn't begin to comprehend.

EVE MAGAZINE

"**E**xcuse me, Monty. Monty? Monty Brennan! You cannot go in there… Monty!"

Ignoring the increasingly shrill tones of the publisher's bouncer, Monty strode straight towards Gerry's closed door, turned the brass knob and pushed it open.

Barging in like this was probably a sackable offence, Monty realised as she proceeded. It was certainly sure to put her on Lizzie's black list for the rest of her career, yet she suddenly didn't care. She was furious. Her anger so intense it shimmered from every pore.

No wonder Amelia had walked out! No wonder Amelia couldn't face her when she returned from the shoot. Her dear friend, her boss, must have heard about the move from Gerry or Willow and felt deeply, desperately betrayed.

Yet it wasn't true! Monty hadn't requested a move to the design magazine or anywhere for that matter. She would never do that to her friend. It was a pact she had made not so much to Amelia as to herself many years ago. No matter how many times she was headhunted, she always said no. She was there for Amelia; she had her back. She had been missing in action once, had let her down with almost fatal consequences. She would never make that mistake again.

The publisher was at his desk, feet up, phone at one ear, eyes fixed on Monty. He seemed curious at this stage, probably the result of hearing his normally phlegmatic PA screeching, but he wasn't angry, at least not yet. The surprise was holding that at bay.

"I'll call you back, Ted," he said before clunking the phone onto its hook and dropping his feet to the floor. "Monty Brennan, what can I do for you?" And then, "Did you find her?"

For just a moment Monty had no idea what Gerry was talking about, and she stopped mid-march. "What? Oh, no, Amelia's still... well, no."

"I'm so terribly sorry, Gerry," came Lizzie's breathless voice behind her, but Gerry already had a hand up and was waving her back out.

Monty heard the door click behind her and exhaled.

"There better be a bloody good reason for you—" he began, but she couldn't wait for a dressing down.

"What's this I hear about *House*?"

"*House*?"

"I just ran into Willow. You're moving me to *House & Feather*?"

"Ah."

"Ah indeed, Gerry. When were you going to tell me?" She took a deep breath, remembering he was her boss and quickly added, "Sir."

"So you *don't* want to work on *House*?"

"No, it's not that. It's just..."

"Just nothing. Finish the latest issue of *Eve*, and we'll get you across." He reached for his mobile phone as if the conversation was over, but Monty wasn't finished yet.

"But we've discussed this before, Gerry." Many times in fact. He tried moving her to *House* three years ago and then last year to the new men's title he had in the works, but she always put him off. No amount of money would change her mind.

"You know I can't leave *Eve*," she said now. "You know very well that I would never desert Amelia."

He looked up from his phone. "And yet she's left you, has she not?"

"No! I mean, well, I don't know. I have no idea what's going on, but she wouldn't leave me either, and she'd be furious if she learned you had moved me across."

"Don't see why. She was the one who suggested it."

"Sorry?"

He sighed. Annoyance had edged out his curiosity. "Take a seat, Monty, you're giving me the shits."

She dropped into a plush chair in front of his enormous glass-topped desk just as the door swept open and Lizzie reappeared, her face an icy mask. "Can I get you anything?"

Monty assumed she was talking to Gerry but he was now stabbing away at the phone, oblivious to her presence so she waved a hand to her breast. The woman stared at her. There was something disturbing about that stare.

"Oh, um, no, thank you, Lizzie. I'm fine."

Lizzie pushed her lips into a smile as foreboding as the stare and then turned and closed the door again.

Eventually, after several more stabs at his phone, Gerry flung it back on his desk and sighed.

"I don't know what the hell's been going on down there at *Eve*. It's chaos by the sound of it, but I figured Amelia would do the honours and let you know about the job before she pissed off. But, like I say, chaos!"

"But I don't understand. Why would Amelia want me to move to *House*?"

"Beats me. She swept in here last Friday and demanded you be moved off *Eve*. When I asked what the problem was she said, 'I want her gone.' That's a direct quote."

Monty crumbled at that, her chest caving in. "But…?"

But why? What could she possibly have done to make Amelia push her away like that?

Gerry was still talking. "Willow's been after you for years, and she's dead right. You're wasted on *Eve*. I mean, it suits our girl Amelia, she lives and breathes that commercial crap, but it's not your style. *House & Feather* is your style. And now that Willow's head designer is up the duff, well, it a win-win." He stopped. "You're not bloody pregnant are you?"

She shook her head although she felt like vomiting.

"I figured you girls must have had yourselves a catfight, but I wasn't gonna lose sleep over it. So you want the bloody job or not?"

Monty shook the nausea away. *Yes! No.* She didn't know.

"Work it out, Monty."

He grabbed his phone again and she stood up, her legs shaky. As she reached the door he called out to her.

"You ever storm in here again uninvited, it'll be the last time you come in. I don't care how good you are. Got it?"

Her legs shook again as she left the office.

By the time Monty found herself back at *Eve*, Lizzie had already enacted her revenge. During the long elevator ride down—it was lunchtime and stopped at every *damn* floor—Monty's mind was racing and she was trying to make sense of it.

Why would Amelia secretly oust her from the magazine and so unceremoniously? She was a bloody good art director, she knew that. It was the reason Willow was so thrilled to have her on board. So what happened to make Amelia turn against her?

What had she done?

She trawled her memory, trying to think of something she had said or done, but kept coming up blank. The last time she saw Amelia, the woman was putting her in a cab and hugging her goodbye. No anger, no animosity. Then, later that same day, she was plotting her removal. It was absurd.

"This one's got your name on it, honey."

Monty looked up as she approached her desk to find Alex hovering, a gilded invitation in one hand.

"Well, it's really for Amelia, but there's no way I can manage it," said Alex. "A meet and greet tonight, would you believe? Six p.m.! How can I possibly make that? I've got groceries to buy, children to feed. It's ridiculous, *and* it's for some digital technology company. I'm not even sure *why* she was invited to this."

Monty exhaled loudly. "It's the life of an editor, Alex." *The life I thought you wanted*, she would have added if she had an ounce of Amelia's gumption.

Alex was already dumping the glossy invitation onto her desk. "Well, I'm not going, and it doesn't matter anyway because Lizzie said to give it to you. Said it'd be your reward, whatever that means."

Monty winced. "I bet she did."

She glanced at it and then away. Then back again.

"Tower Global Solutions?"

"Yeah, that's the bonus I suppose. You get to meet the dishy top dog. I hear he's hot. Might snag yourself a hubby if you're not careful."

Alex sniggered as she walked away, but Monty's mind was off and racing again, this time in a very different direction, backwards, towards some Spanish Steps.

She madly tapped at her keyboard, starting a Google search, and sat back, stunned, when the results came in.

It was just as she thought.

This wasn't any old public relations event. It was a corporate meet and greet with Tower Global Solutions CEO, and the last time she looked there was one man who ran that company—a university student she first met on some crowded steps in Rome and got to know a whole lot better on a boat to Santorini.

She tapped the invitation against her lips.

Well isn't that interesting…

SHEPPERDIN VILLAGE

Though he woman with the dusting brush was closing in, and he gave her the evil eye.

"It takes the shine off," she said, but he held a palm up.

"This isn't a fashion shoot, love." He knew all about fashion shoots. Amy used to do them in a past life.

The woman smiled, dropped the brush. "Fair enough. Can I just...?" She indicated his hair and he scraped some fingers through it. She gave him two thumbs-up and backed away.

"You ready?" This was Geoff, seated at the trestle table beside him, his official uniform on, hat in front. He had opted for the powder and looked like a clown.

"As I'll ever be," Tom said, regretting this instantly.

Oh, who was he fooling? He'd regretted it ever since he'd agreed to the publicity stunt. He knew how these things worked. Parade the poor husband across the telly and hope to God somebody, preferably the wayward wife, would see the heart-shattering story and return home promptly. Or perhaps someone would ring in and reveal her whereabouts. Might have seen her wandering the corridors of their local supermarket. He wondered if it ever succeeded, and glancing about now, he also wondered how far the coverage would get them.

There was only one camera crew for the regional TV news and a young guy with bad acne holding what he assumed was a tape-recorder for the local paper.

"Radio's late," said the makeup woman who now had a clipboard and a mobile phone in her hand. She was also the police media manager. That is, when she wasn't at the front desk answering phones.

"We'll give Claude another five thanks, Ommie, and then we'll start without him," Geoff said, turning back to Tom. "He's always bloody late."

"So how does this work?" Tom asked.

"I'll start us off, throw some questions at you and— Oh there you are Claude, great."

A thin man with a wispy ponytail rushed in with his microphone and straight to the desk where he set it up at the midway point between both men. Then he held a hand up and reached for something in his bag. It was the SunshineFM logo, and he clipped it to the microphone, for the benefit of the camera no doubt.

Tom saw the cameraman roll his eyes and then wondered whether there was a TV reporter, when a blonde strolled up. She was thin and pretty but not quite thin and pretty enough for the metropolitan stations. Had ample confidence, though, and was offering them all a wide, smug smile as she dragged a chair noisily to the side of the camera and sat down.

"Nice you could make it, Nene," Geoff said.

She winked. "It's not every day we get a missing spouse."

Tom saw her flash him a quick look then, but it wasn't one of sympathy. It was more like curiosity, followed by something else. Excitement maybe? Delight? He guessed this kind of story was leaving all the local media salivating.

"Okay, people, let's make this happen!"

That was Ommie, and Geoff cleared his throat and gave a quick nod as the camera light flashed on and left everyone looking startled.

"Thanks for being here, folks," Geoff began. "We have a matter of great urgency that we'd like the public's assistance with. I will read a short statement, and then we can throw to some questions."

Nene's eyes glinted wickedly, like she'd just been offered a line of coke.

~~~

The shoot had run over, and once again, he was racing to meet the three-o'clock school bell, only just making it. Scarlett had offered to collect Phil for him, but he saw that as a statement on his parenting
~~~

and was determined to step up.

"Hey Tom," came a high, melodic voice he instantly recognised. He felt that slithering feeling in his stomach again.

"Hi, Belinda," he said as they reached the school gate at the same time. "How are you today?"

"I'm good, honey, how are *you*? We're all so worried."

"Don't be. I'm fine." He knew Belinda and he knew it wasn't his wife she was worried about. She already had a hand on his bicep and was squeezing it, as if sizing him up.

"Need anything?" she was asking, her hand rubbing the bicep now. "Anything at all?"

He stared at her. It wasn't a casserole she was offering, and he knew it.

Belinda had been a shameless flirt since they'd met at the local swimming pool nine years earlier when he first dropped his son off for swim class. She'd idled up in a bikini two sizes too small, oblivious to the leering looks from Phil's teenage swimming instructor and offered him a look of her own. He had laughed her off at the time, laughed her off for years, but now he wondered whether he should have taken it all a little more seriously. Perhaps he should have let her lead him into the changerooms or the back of her Mazda or wherever the hell it was her mind was wandering.

But he didn't do that. Of course he didn't do that. He was the good husband. He was the devoted one. Faithful. Yet now it stood for nothing. Now he wondered why he'd bothered. His devotion to his wife felt about as useful as that bloody jewellery tree. He turned to Belinda and smiled.

From a distance Polly was watching, lips squished to one side. She reached for her mobile phone and stabbed at some buttons. When it picked up, she covered the mouthpiece with her spare hand.

"Hey, I'm at the school gates," she said. "Yep, can see him now. Hm-mm, usual stuff. ... What? Oh, I guess he's collecting Phil, but... Yeah, yeah, you should see Belinda having a crack." A chuckle then deadpan: "No, I don't think so. I mean, he wouldn't, *would he*?" She listened for some time, nodding like a yoyo as if the person on the receiving end could possibly see her. "I will. I promise. You take care and be safe, yeah? And don't worry. I've got a plan. You'll see."

Then she ended the call and strode swiftly towards a group of women who were chatting merrily at the pickup zone.

"Hello, ladies," she said. "Want to do a little detective work?"

SARISI ISLAND

As the boat approached Mikro to tie up for the second time that day, Nicholas could tell that Zoe had done a job on Millie. She had seemed so happy, so hopeful when they'd dropped her off, now she looked like one of Zoe's monstrous portraits. Her cheeks were pale, her eyebrows wedged together, her arms wrapped tightly around her torso, her thick hair flying loosely about her face.

"Everything okay?" he asked as he secured the boat at the jetty and helped her jump across.

"Yep. Fine," she mumbled, then edged her way to the mouldy seat just behind the skipper. There she turned her whole body away from the islet to face the sea.

Whatever had happened on the island, whatever was said, it was not what Millie wanted to hear, that much was obvious, and Nicholas felt like leaping back onto the jetty and chasing the old witch down. Demanding she take it all back!

But the truth was he blamed himself. He should have warned Millie about Zoe. Probably shouldn't have mentioned the crazy coot in the first place. *Why did he bring her here?* He'd heard so many stories about the so-called witch of Mikro as Kostas jokingly dubbed her. But he didn't believe in that nonsense. Until now.

The Aussie woman looked like she was under some kind of nasty spell, and it was clear that whatever she had heard about her friend Agnetha, it wasn't good either. She looked miserable and he gave her some space, first helping Giannis get the boat away, then settling at the port side this time, legs dangling over the edge. He didn't bother to fish now, simply watched the wake below his feet, now dark and frothy.

The weather had turned and the journey back was even slower and rockier, the wind now howling, making conversation virtually impossible. It wasn't until they'd cleared Coso Point that the wind dropped back and he decided it was now or never. He clambered to his feet and shuffled up the deck towards Millie, who gave him a reassuring smile as he approached.

He took it as a welcome sign and said, "Didn't go so well, huh?"

Her smile deflated, and for a moment he thought he'd overstepped, but then she said softly, the wind nearly swallowing the words away, "Agnetha's dead. I should've come earlier. My bad."

She gave him a chin-up grin, but he wasn't buying it. Millie looked crushed. This Agnetha must have been a very important person once, a very dear friend.

"I'm sorry I didn't warn you about Zoe," he said. "You can't take anything she says seriously. She's put noses out of joint all over Sarisi. That's why she hides out here. Even *she* knows we can only handle her in small doses."

"Oh Zoe's fine." She tried to smile. "Let's talk about something else!" She tried again, this one more convincing. "So, how long have you been here then? On Sarisi?"

"Two years, give or take."

"If you don't like fish, and you've got such a big family back in Melbourne, why do you live so far away?"

"Well, there's Theo."

"Theo?"

His eyes lit up. "One very mischievous teenage boy." He chuckled. "Bit of an oddball, but that's what I like about him. He dances to his own beat, that one, could care less about 'fitting in'. Whip smart, too, and can pop a soccer ball into a net from midhalf without even trying."

Millie knew nothing about soccer, but his tone told her everything. "He sounds terrific."

"Ooh he can be a nightmare, too, when he sets his mind to it. But yeah, he's a good kid."

"And his mum? Is she…" Her voice was swallowed up by the wind, and he misunderstood the question.

"Effie? I wouldn't call *her* good. Cranky's more apt."

"Effie?" She was clearly doing some mental backtracking.

"Yeah, Theo's mum."

"Oh, I didn't realise you were together. Oh, right."

Millie stopped and blushed deeply, and he watched her confused for a moment, then burst out laughing.

"No! Effie and me, we're not—" He laughed some more. "She's my *cousin*. Jesus don't wish her upon me!" Then he quickly added, "Theo's not my son if that's what you thought."

Millie's shoulders dropped as the penny dropped along with it. "Sorry, it's just the way you spoke about him, I thought…"

"Well, we're close. Real close in fact. His old man has never really been on the scene, and now that Theo's getting older, Effie wanted a male role model about. So she dragged me out from Melbourne to help."

Like it took any convincing. He couldn't get on the plane fast enough. Had first met Theo as a toddler on a brief holiday to Sarisi and been smitten from the start.

"And have you?" she asked. "Helped?"

His eyes lost a little of their sparkle. "Theo's currently at school on the mainland, stays with his *yaya* in Athens most of the time, so what does that tell you?" He forced himself to smile.

"Sounds like a cool kid," she said.

He didn't know it, but her mind was actually on another cool kid, a teenager with a wild mop of black curls and a mischievous wink, a young woman whose very nature had helped her heal.

"What about you? Any…" Nico hesitated. "Anyone special back at home?" Wasn't sure why he was asking. Wasn't sure he wanted to know specifics, and she shrugged, clearly not wanting to give any.

"I want to hear more about Theo. How often do you get to see him now?"

"He's back weekends. Effie grants me that at least."

"So if Theo is now away at school, will you still hang around? Or will you go back to Australia?"

He shrugged and turned his eyes out to sea. His mum wanted him back desperately. So did his five sisters, imploring him through regular phone calls, Facebook messages and WhatsApp, which were becoming increasingly urgent, increasingly annoying.

His duty was with *them*, they told him. He was supposed to be *their* male role model, but he'd never felt that. For starters, they were all married; there were plenty of males about. And it wasn't a role model they were after, if they were being honest. They wanted their beloved Bubba back. Used to dress him up in dolls' clothes when he was little, fight over who was going to sing him to sleep. They loved him deeply and he loved them just as much, but it was not enough and too much all at the same time. Both suffocating and unsatisfying.

When Bubba hit forty, it came to a head. He felt like a fraud, like he was still playing the role of the baby brother and not living his own life, an *adult* life. The problem was he hadn't worked out what his own life should be. He was all over the place, floating on the wind, could stick at nothing and no one.

Until Sarisi. Until Theo.

"You're really fond of him aren't you?"

She was reading his mind, and he nodded but knew it was much worse than that.

He loved him like his own.

"You know how it is?" he said flippantly, and she frowned and turned away.

Millie thought about his question and wondered, Do I? Do I really know *how it is*? What it is to be a family? To love someone so completely, you'd give up your whole life for them? And happily? Because she hadn't been happy, that was certain. She had spent the past decade pretending she was and fooling nobody. Her mind flittered to home. Her heart ached. She damped it down as she always had. Zoe was right. She was nowhere near ready to face the truth.

By the time they returned to Sarisi, Millie was exhausted. She thanked the two men and headed straight back to the castle. She needed a rest. A "nanna nap" as her mother would say.

Kostas was at his post at the front desk and looked up surprised when she entered, like she had been a mirage, a figment of his imagination. She pointed upwards and he nodded.

Once upstairs she made her way straight to bed, slipping off her shoes and settling under the covers. She wanted to sleep, to forget what Zoe had said, but the brutal reality was hitting her now and she tossed and turned and could not doze off.

Agnetha was dead. The other sisters had dispersed.

How was she going to find him now? How would she ever get the answers she so desperately needed?

She thought of Nico then and felt her heart lighten. He reminded her of the past, of another man on another boat but this one a very different man, a very different journey. Then she remembered what he'd said about nuns and she burst out laughing. The sound echoed across the walls and down the stone staircase towards Kostas, who looked up from his account-keeping with a start.

"KKK indeed!" she said, twisting under the sheets. "What a cheeky bugger!"

Agnetha would be horrified to be compared to that lynch mob, was the antithesis in fact, but still, it made Millie chuckle. The truth was she *had* been a little terrified of the nuns in those early days.

"Up, up!" Agnetha had snapped one day, her patience waning with every fading bruise. "We can cry and we can wallow, but that will get us precisely nowhere except wet and friendless."

She spoke perfect English for a local, as did all her flock, another seven sisters who must have all had names and personalities of their own, but for the life of her, Millie couldn't remember any of them. They all seemed like one universe orbiting around Sister Agnetha.

But young Millie was feeling morose that day. She was scared of the old lady, she remembered that clearly, but she was also still hurting, still bitter and angry, and those were the stronger emotions. She *wanted* to wallow, couldn't care less about making friends. Friends had got her exactly nowhere to this point. Agnetha was persistent.

"Come on, Miss Australia, you have to earn your keep like the rest of us." She shoved a bristly scrubbing brush in Millie's hands. "You can start at the top of the stairwell and work your way down."

Millie stared at her, scowling. Surely she was too battered, too traumatised for idle housework? Then she noticed the girl from the next bed, the one with the magnificent curls and the mischievous smile. She was at the end of the dormitory, straw broom in hand, sweeping away.

She had been in an even worse state when she came in, sobbing into her pillow day and night, but was now working like a Trojan.

The girl caught Millie's eye and gave her a wink.

"Come on, Effie," Agnetha said. "Let's get this lazy bones up!"

The girl giggled and dropped the broom, then skipped across the room and grabbed one of Millie's long, bony arms while Agnetha took hold of the other, and together they pulled her up.

And through that one simple gesture, the healing had begun.

EVE MAGAZINE

As she raced up the marble stairs of the ornate art gallery in stilettos, leaving flat-heeled women struggling in her wake, Monty thanked the Lord for Fleur and her bottomless fashion cupboard. After a momentary panic attack—goodness she looked a mess!—the fashion editor stepped in and helped her select just the right outfit for the last-minute event, a black, body-hugging dress with a high neckline and a plunging back, high-ankle pumps, and a strappy silver handbag. It was sexy yet classy, the two things she remembered most about Angus Tower.

Fleur had also helped her repair her face and swished her unwashed hair into a knot at the top of her head that looked cool but carefree—more Angus traits—and the exact opposite of how she felt as she teetered her way towards the front desk where a beaming PR girl and a set of name tags beckoned.

"Welcome to Tower Global Solutions! Name and title?"

"Monty Brennan, *Eve* magazine."

The woman searched the tags, frowning, so Monty added, "I'm the art director, standing in for the editor, Amelia Malone."

"Oh. Right. Great." The woman's chipper tone barely masked her disappointment.

Monty knew how these things worked. It was always better to get the top dog along to your publicity events, not a lowly staffer, even if you were the top dog's BFF. But no PR girl worth her weight in gift bags would ever let on. She reached for a blank tag and scribbled Monty's name down, then handed it across.

"There're drinks and nibbles inside, Monty. Speeches in twenty."

Monty thanked her and made her way in. She recognised lots of faces, mostly from their editor's letters or other shindigs she'd accompanied Amelia to, some she knew well enough to stop and air-kiss, but she didn't stop for long.

She was on a mission.

It wasn't until Monty had wrestled her way to the front of the makeshift bar and was waiting for the harried barmen to notice her that she spotted him in the middle of the crowd. Monty's breath caught in her throat. Her stomach clenched, she felt a blush creep up her neck and wished now that she wasn't revealing so much flesh.

Angus Tower. The Sydney business student they had met in Rome.

The one who had fallen for Amelia.

The one she had secretly adored.

He was standing in a gaggle of girls, women really, but the way they hung on to his every word, eyelids batting, glossy lips parted, reminded her of herself many moons ago. He still looked amazing, debonair now with his slicked-back hair and exquisitely tailored suit. Sure, the good life had caught up with him a little and he was carrying a few extra kilos, but that potent aura still hung around him, helped considerably by the giggling girls.

Angus glanced up and towards her then, and before Monty could look away he had caught her eye and frowned for a second, as if trying to place her, then turned back to the women around him and continued talking.

She didn't know whether to be relieved he hadn't recognised her or offended.

"What can I get you?" a barman asked, returning her attention to the bar.

"A wine thanks."

He looked at her deadpan. "Shiraz? Semillon? Sparkling wine? Prosecco—"

"Prosecco, thanks." As he reached for a champagne glass, Monty wondered whether it would be a little lush-like to ask for two.

She needed a few drinks tonight and not just to face her past. It was the future she was struggling to get her head around, one where she was no longer working beside the indomitable Amelia Malone. If she was honest, there was a sliver of relief in the thought, but her sense of outrage was blocking it out. All she felt was an intense anger at Amelia, a deep sense of betrayal. And a feeling, too, that she had somehow brought it upon herself, if only she could work out what the hell she'd done wrong.

None of it made an ounce of sense, not really, she thought as she was handed her glass. Not Amelia's disappearance, not Monty's posting to another magazine, not the simple, strange fact that it had all happened without a hint. Not so much as a whisper to her boss or parents or, most cutting of all, her best friend. Because wasn't that what they were? If you stripped away everything else—the job, the past—they were each other's rock. And now Amelia had dislodged herself, handed Monty to the highest bidder and then skipped away like a pebble across the bay. Just like that infamous ferry ride. Except Monty had been given no warning this time. No chance to try to snatch the pebble back.

"Monty Brennan, well, well, well."

The art director took a deep breath when she heard the familiar voice, the one that could still make her stomach flutter, and slowly turned to face him.

"Hello Angus," she managed.

He leaned in and kissed her on both cheeks. He smelled of something subtle and expensive, still had that certain something she could never quite articulate. Just being in his radius was electrifying, even now, after all these years, even with the heavier jowl and the slightly thinning hair.

"God, how long has it been?" He had stepped back and was running his eyes over her, his smile widening.

She smiled back. *Thirteen long and lonely years.* "Ages!" she replied.

He stared at her then, smiling, clearly flirting, and she rushed to fill the silence, rushed to distract him from the blush that was creeping along her cheeks and ruining her makeup.

"So," she said, glancing around, "you made your millions then."

His smile turned into a look of bemusement.

"You always said you'd make your first million by the age of twenty-five."

"I did?" He stared at her for a moment longer, then belly laughed. "Christ I was a bit of an arrogant tosser, wasn't I?"

She laughed too, enjoying the release. "I think we were all a bit cocky back then."

"No, no." He was shaking a finger now. "Not you, Monty Brennan. You were always a little shy, a little behind Millie's enormous shadow."

He laughed again, oblivious to the dagger he'd just stuck in her heart. She didn't remember it that way.

"So where is she?" he said, looking about.

"Amelia? Oh, she's, well, she's having some time off. On holidays."

Lizzie had sent her a simple text as she rode the cab to the event: *Not a word about A. She is just on "holidays".* And for a moment Monty had felt a rush of relief. Amelia must have called and explained her absence to Gerry. Then she slumped as she noticed the inverted commas. She might not be an editor but she knew what they meant. It was a PR exercise for them, a cover-up.

"Holiday? That doesn't sound like Amelia—from what I've heard."

"Well…"

He tilted his head to one side. "Come on, 'fess up."

Her eyes narrowed. *Oh shit, the news was out.*

"It was something I said, wasn't it? Was I too frank last time?"

She stopped, smiled, stammered, "Sorry?"

"I *knew* I'd offended her. Please tell Millie I'm sorry, that wasn't my intention. We'll blame it on that last martini, which she talked me into, by the way."

"Oh." Monty's smile was waning. "I didn't realise you guys were still in touch."

"I wouldn't go that far, although I was hoping we could rekindle something, that's the reason for the invite." He paused, sensing her confusion. "She didn't tell you? That's how this all came about. We ran into each other at the new iPhone launch about ten days ago. I don't usually attend that crap, but they're too big to ignore."

Monty tried to think back. She recalled the invitation, Amelia's pleas for her to accompany her and how she had put her off. They'd been working around the clock lately; she needed some time out.

They dubbed these events "Free beer and chicken nights" even though they both knew it would be more champagne and sushi and there was nothing free about them. If you wanted Apple's advertising revenue, some regular double-page spreads showing off their latest gleaming device, you fronted up whether you were tired or not.

"I didn't realise she went to that," Monty said. In fact, she was pretty sure Amelia had told her she hadn't. *So why the lies?*

"She was there all right. Turned out to be quite a night, lots of glitz and glamour. And to run into Millie, well that was the highlight. At least it was for me. We had a good yarn. I thought... well, I thought everything was fine. She'd convinced me to place an ad, even though we all know Global Solutions is as suited to *Eve* as I am to—" He stopped, laughed. "Well, you, I suppose!"

He laughed some more as Monty's heart continued to shred itself.

Luckily, she had a moment to recover while Angus stopped to shake hands with two passing suits. He told them he'd catch up with them, then turned back to her.

"So where is Silly Millie? What's she really doing? Simmering at her desk? Throwing darts at a board with my face on it? Or is it you she's angry at?"

"Why would she be angry at me?" Monty said as a sliver of ice began trickling down her back.

He hadn't told her about them? Surely.

"Nah, you're right. She seemed fine with it." He looked around, then back at her. "Although I'm surprised you never mentioned it to her before. Aren't you two like the Topsy Twins?"

As he glanced around the room again, Monty's insides also turned to ice, and she tried to keep her tone calm as she said, "You didn't mention *us*, did you? How we... you know?"

She'd been swallowing the words down for almost thirteen years and couldn't bring herself to finally spit them out.

"...hooked up?" he said, finishing the sentence and having another belly laugh.

Of course he told her. He was a bloke, wasn't he?

"I can't believe you never mentioned it yourself," he was saying, oblivious to her turmoil. "I mean, all those late nights working on that magazine together, can't believe it never came up."

Monty realised then that he was only thinking of himself. How could one of his conquests *not* want to shout it from the rooftop? But that was a fleeting thought. Her mind was now settling on Amelia; things were starting to make more sense.

"Don't sweat it, Monty, she thought it was a great joke." Then, finally sensing that she was indeed sweating, he added, "Hey, we were all kids, right? Young and foolish. Honestly, Amelia didn't care! How could she? She was the one who jumped ship first, remember. She got her just deserts."

Monty stared at him then, searching his face. *What did he mean by that?*

Then another fleeting thought—*he holds it against her!* He can't believe she chose a Greek stranger over him. He can't believe he was left back on deck with sloppy seconds.

Angus reached for her hand, his tone now conciliatory. "Sorry if I put my foot in it, but she was such a fatalist, remember? The one who believed everything happened for a reason. If she holds it against you, just tell her to reread that stupid book; that'll set her straight."

"Book?"

"You know? The one she dragged everywhere? Kept banging on about? The *Prophecy* or something."

"*The Celestine Prophecy.*"

"That's the one. I couldn't make sense of it, but she loved it."

Pity she lost it, Monty thought, absentmindedly. Except that wasn't quite true. Amelia hadn't lost her copy, it had been snatched from her on a soggy Greek beach, along with her purse and her ID, her dignity and her sense of self. It was the reason no one knew who she was for so long, why no one could get her help until she'd come out of the coma and uttered her first words in that surprising Australian accent.

But he didn't need to hear all that, and she had heard enough. Monty downed the rest of the drink and forced herself to change the subject.

"So, how's your old buddy Thomas? Seen him lately?"

A frown appeared and he didn't look quite so handsome with a deep scratch between his eyes.

"Ahh, Tom Wilson, what can I say? We catch up every now and then, sink a few beers, reminisce."

"How's he doing? What's he up to?"

"Not much these days. He's had some trying times, that's for sure. Never quite got his shit together, you know? Floundering a bit." As he spoke, Angus waved yet again and Monty finally turned to see who was stealing his attention. She spotted the PR woman standing near the stage at the back, looking flustered despite the glacial smile.

"Bloody speeches. I better stop putting it off."

He leaned in again, but this time he embraced her, bringing her to the warmth of his warm, wide chest.

"Give my love to Millie, yeah? And tell her not to be a stranger." He tapped his top pocket and produced a business card. "You too. Stay in touch."

He handed it to her, then swept away, shaking hands with more ogling guests as he strode towards the lectern.

Watching him go, Monty felt chilled to the bone and wished she'd agreed to bring a wrap as Fleur had suggested. At least it was all making more sense now. This had to be the reason Amelia had booted her from *Eve*, shoved her onto *House* and then done a runner. Because, just ten days earlier, Amelia had learned what she should have learned more than ten years earlier, what a good friend would have mentioned at the first opportunity—that Monty and Angus had ended up together, at least for a little while. Not because it mattered—he was right, they were kids, Amelia had already chosen someone else—but because by *not* saying it, by acting like it meant nothing, she had made it mean everything.

Amelia was not the traitor. It had been Monty all along.

She slipped his card into her silver handbag, downed the rest of her Prosecco, then turned back to the bar and ordered two more.

SHEPPERDIN VILLAGE

Tom watched the seven-o'clock news bulletin and recoiled at his own oily orange face. His expression was pinched, his voice jittery, his eyes darting about like a homicidal maniac. He wished he'd opted for the powder, and his heart sank as he remembered the real reason they paraded haggard husbands across the evening news—to see how guilty they looked under the spotlight.

But then who wouldn't look shifty under all that startling light? Tom thought sullenly. Even the Dalai Lama would come away looking dodgy.

He snapped the TV off and flung the remote control at the couch, wondering if Phil had seen it, grateful yet again that he had plenty of mates to keep him distracted. He was with Belinda's boy tonight and couldn't get into her Mazda fast enough. Tom couldn't blame him. His poor boy was going through his agony all alone.

At least Tom and Harry had had each other.

Of course, if it were up to Tom, Phil would have had another brother to turn to for solace. Or a sister, he wasn't fussed. But Amy was never interested. Despite envying Scarlett's brood, she didn't want more of her own. She was an only child; it had worked well for her, she had said. Why mess with the template?

"For company?" he had suggested initially, but the truth was Phil was never short of that. It wasn't simply that his son made friends easily, he also had six cousins just a backyard and a few bushes away, each of them vying to be his favourite.

He wondered now if he should have pushed her on the baby

thing. Perhaps she might have been more fulfilled. Perhaps she might have stayed...

The doorbell rang, cutting through Tom's thoughts, and he growled like a caged animal. *Now who wants their pound of flesh?*

He swung it open to find Polly at the door, two women standing just behind her, two familiar faces whose names he could not remember. He wasn't sure he'd ever said a word to either of them.

"Hey there," Polly sang, glancing through to the room behind him. "Do you mind if we come in. Just for a minute?"

No, he wanted to tell them. *Leave me alone.* But he opened the door wider.

They seemed surprised by the move and exchanged glances with each other, then stepped inside and began looking around as though for lost treasure. He wondered if they'd ever been inside the house before. Had Amy ever invited anyone over?

"We heard you were on the news tonight," Polly said, adding quickly, "We just held a special P&C meeting so we didn't get to see it. But we've taped it. Will watch it later."

Please don't, he wanted to tell them as another voice said, "Has it helped, do you know? Any word yet?"

This was the shorter, fatter of the women. The butcher's wife if he recalled correctly. He shook his head. He said, "Not that I know of."

All three nodded as though expecting this, and Polly cleared her throat.

"I hope you don't think we're interfering..."

"But?"

She stopped and swapped another cryptic glance with her friends before continuing. "But the P&C have met and we'd like to help, if we can."

"How do you mean?"

"We were thinking fliers? Door knocking? We could start a Facebook campaign? You know, 'Have you seen our friend?,' that kind of thing?"

He nodded. What could he say? *No, piss off, I've got this.*

"Maybe even a Go Fund Me page?" the butcher's wife added, her eyes darting around the room, zeroing in on the old blue lounge. Amy had liked that lounge, insisted it was comfy. Now he saw it for what it was—tip fodder.

"No," he said at last. "I mean, thank you but not the fund-raising thingy. I don't need charity."

"Of course not," Polly said, "it's just to help—"

"No."

"No worries! But we'll get the fliers out and put that Facebook page up, okay?"

"Thank you."

"And we'll send you a friend request?" said the third woman, scrawny with a voice to match. She sounded nervous.

"I'm not on that shit."

"Oh! Right. I see."

What, woman? What do you see? He plastered a smile to his lips. "If that's all ladies, it's… well, it's been a big day."

"Of course!" said Polly. "Come on, girls, let's leave the poor man alone." She bustled them through the hallway, back to the front door, then stopped and turned around. "We're desperate to help, Tom. We all loved Millie so much."

Loved? They were using the past tense already?

"I appreciate that," was all he could manage.

SARISI ISLAND

When Millie strolled into the Casa Delfino that evening and asked for a table out the front, Nico felt a range of emotions but mostly surprise. He knew what she had learned, that Sister Agnetha was six feet under, and he expected she would take off on the first ferry out. Had watched one chug away less than an hour ago and assumed she was on it, had felt a stab of disappointment that she hadn't said goodbye.

Yet here she was ordering grilled sea bream, a traditional Greek salad, and a half carafe of the house white. She didn't look like she was going anywhere in a hurry, and now he felt a surge of joy.

It was quickly tempered by the busy night, and Nico was so run off his feet he didn't get a chance to stop and speak to Millie properly, only managing a few smiles as he swept past, then scowls as he watched Kostas join her at the courtyard table.

Kostas rarely sat out there. He usually perched himself at the bar inside, close enough to the kitchen to swipe whatever free food was going. Yet here he was, ordering his own meal and flirting outrageously with the Aussie.

Nico felt his heart sink. *She wouldn't go for someone like Kostas, would she?*

It's not that he expected anything to happen between himself and Millie—she was so far out of his league, he'd decided—he simply enjoyed her company, found her intriguing, mesmerising...

"Oi!" someone yelled. "Plates up!" It was Pete the chef, and he was looking uncharacteristically cranky.

Nico nodded and returned to the kitchen. Over the following hour he had to settle for brief glimpses of Millie between order taking and food delivery and cleaning up the night's rubble. When Kostas finally appeared at the cash register to settle both his bill and Millie's—a minor miracle in itself—he grabbed the opportunity to get some answers.

"What's the story? How long's she staying?"

"Who?"

"*Kos*," he growled, a note of warning.

"Millie?" Kostas looked delighted, nudged his eyebrows up and down. "You don't like gossip! Why you want gossip now?"

"Just spit it out, mate."

"She stay longer. She say she wait for Effie to come back."

"Effie? I thought they didn't know each other."

Why would she wait around for a stranger or at least one who didn't seem to remember her?

He glanced at the galley. There were no dishes to be brought out, and there was no one lined up to pay, so he slammed Kostas's change into his hands and made his way out to the front. Millie had an empty carafe and plate before her and was just reaching for a handbag that was hanging from her chair.

"Can I get you another wine?" Nico said. "Some dessert perhaps? We do a great *Galaktobureko*."

"That sounds exotic but no thanks, I'm done." She tapped her belly. "That was delicious. Especially the grilled fish. Was it one you caught today?"

He nodded. "Good to see someone eat the scaly critters."

She smiled and scooped the bag up.

"So, you're heading back to the castle now, hey?"

Before she could answer, his name was being shouted out from inside the restaurant again, but he ignored it. "Listen, I hear you're staying a bit longer, to see Effie."

"That's right," she said. Not elaborating.

He blushed. God he hated gossip, but he needed to know more, so he swallowed his pride and said, "So how do you know her again? Sorry to be nosy, but she is my cousin. And she didn't seem to know you so…"

Millie pulled the bag over her shoulder and then retrieved some hair that had got swept under.

"It's okay," she said casually. "Effie probably didn't recognise my name after all this time We knew each other quite some years ago when I was first here. I wasn't well. I was staying at the convent."

She hesitated, searching his eyes.

"And that's when you met Effie? Was she running the Delfy back then?"

"Um, no." She hesitated again. "It's really not my place... You need to ask Effie about that."

"About what?" *Exactly.*

Millie sighed then, but it came out wistful. "All I can say is it was a different time, a different place back then, Nico. The convent was like a haven for Effie and me. Sister Agnetha, she was like, well, she took us lost souls in, helped us out."

"Effie was in the convent?" He had to swallow back a smile. "*Effie* was a lost soul? Can't picture that." Didn't believe it for a second.

She smiled, she shrugged, she repeated the line "Not my place, Nico", then she looked startled by those words and seemed suddenly lost in thought.

Nicholas couldn't inquire further. Pauly was now hollering for him while a customer screeched profanities from inside. He groaned, wished her a good night's sleep, then raced back in to handle the dispute at the cash register.

By the time he returned to the courtyard, Millie was long gone, so he reached for her empty wineglass and began cleaning up.

"This one, she play hard to get, hey Nicholas?"

He looked around to find Catalina, still perched in the chair where she'd sat across from her husband. He'd shuffled off an hour ago.

"What's that?"

She nudged her head towards Coso Point. "This Aussie. She no look interested to me." Catalina's voice was singsong, almost melodic, but it left him cold. He heard her snigger. "I interested. You know that. I no play games."

He shook his head and continued cleaning up.

"Joe-Joe leave for Athens tomorrow," she whispered, a smile creeping across her face. "I come over? Yes?"

Not turning around this time, he said, "No thanks, Cat."

Her smile flickered out and she sat back in her chair. "So, you do not know then. You have not worked it out?"

He glanced at her and back to the table. "What are you on about?"

She went to say something and then seemed to reconsider. Her smile reignited as she tapped her eyebrows up and down. "Come, Nicholas, why you be so cranky? You know I give you what you want."

This time he had lost his patience. He turned to face her, his eyes flashing with annoyance. "But I don't want it, Catalina." He lowered his voice. "Not anymore, okay?" *I never really did*, he wanted to tell her. *I was lonely, I was stupid.* He took some deep breaths. "Now please, Cat, we're packing up, dinner's over."

Catalina remained in her seat, her smile twitching again. "You think this girl give you what you want? This Australian woman?" She shook her head. "She too posh for you."

Nicholas stared at her for a moment, then shook his head. "You don't know anything about her."

He gathered the last of the plates and began to walk away.

"I know she so posh she won't sleep with Greek man."

He stopped.

"I know she so posh Greek man has to take it from her."

He turned back. "What did you say?"

Catalina was finally getting to her feet, gathering her things. She stopped and met him head-on. "You be very careful, my love." She hissed. "She seem sweet, yes, but she is dangerous that one." She swept the hair back from her face and added, "Is no good for you. Is only here to hurt you."

Nicholas strode across the courtyard until he was inches from her face, then he leaned in, barely containing his fury as he spat out the words, "Go home, Catalina. Go home to your *husband.*"

Then he walked swiftly inside, his heart thumping, his pride too strong to ask her what the hell she was on about.

EVE MAGAZINE

**SOS Rule 5: Call, call, call for help! If you have a mobile handy, use it!*

No shit, Sherlock, Monty thought as she attempted to squeeze the extralong subtitle into the given space in the layout on her screen. *I thought you handed your phone over and asked him to film it.*

She was in a bad mood, and this inane article wasn't helping. It was now Friday morning, and Monty's head was punishing her for too much Prosecco, too little sleep, and a decade of guilt.

Why hadn't she told Amelia about her fling with Angus all those years ago? In the scheme of things, what did it even matter? Why should anyone care? Yet it did matter, Monty knew that. She knew she had stuffed up.

It mattered not because of the action—first just a clumsy fumble on a dark Santorini night. She hadn't even enjoyed it, if truth be told, and he had seemed distracted. She wondered now if he was thinking of Millie and tried to shake the thought away. It mattered because of everything that had come later, how she had not done as she should have done and backtracked to Sarisi to look for her friend. How she let Angus talk her into travelling on to London, where their relationship quickly soured, Angus hooking up with an English girl faster than she could say "Cad!" How she had been so crestfallen she'd ditched the whole idea of staying longer and working in a pub—a dream she had once shared with Millie—and simply caught the first plane home without so much as a glance towards the

Mediterranean. And then taken the very first job that came along. The job at *Eve*.

Yet none of this was ever broached. Long after Millie finally returned, the conversation never came up. Even as Millie morphed from a broken bird into Queen Amelia, Monty had had her opportunity; she'd had her chance.

Hadn't they watched Angus's star rise together? Hadn't they sniggered and giggled and flirted with the idea of getting back in touch? Her stomach clenched, remembering how often she had put Amelia off, how time and again she had urged her not to phone him.

"You're so much better than him," Monty had said, her message couched in concern. "He's a player, babe. He'll break your heart."

Like he broke mine, she should have added, could easily have said.

And yet she never did.

Monty forced herself to think back to that fateful ferry ride now. The moment of no return.

She remembered their startled expressions as Amelia—Silly Millie back then—grabbed her backpack and ran for the gangway, stopping for just a moment to look back, a sliver of something on her face— was it excitement? Exhilaration? Terror?—before she vanished, off the boat and into the darkest chapter of her life, while they all just watched her go.

They *let* her dash towards her fate.

"What the fuck?" Angus had said, staring hard at Thomas then.

"She'll be back," Thomas assured him. But how could he know that? They'd only known each other a week.

Monty had said nothing at first. Speechless. Gobsmacked. Eventually she found her feet and raced for the railing to watch as her friend skipped down the gangway and towards the guy she had spotted her flirting with earlier.

What the hell, Millie? What are you doing? Was her first thought, but there was another thought too. She knew it even then. *Good. Keep going.*

There was still a chance, just a few frozen minutes, when she could have called out or, better yet, grabbed her own pack and raced to catch her friend, but she didn't do that. She just watched as Amelia strode along the deck towards a complete stranger and then away. She kept watching as a whistle pierced the air, and the ferrymen began flinging ropes and the ship began churning, and the island began moving swiftly out of focus.

When she finally returned to where they had been sitting, Sarisi simply a blot on the hot horizon again, she gave the guys a shrug and sat back down. But this time she didn't place her head in Thomas's lap where it had been the entire journey. She sat between them and pointed her feet towards his best friend.

A soft *ding* brought Monty back to the present, and she glanced at the top of her screen. A message from Alex: *How's SOS coming along? You've been at it for days!!!* She grimaced and glanced back at the layout.

Maybe it was the subject matter, maybe it was the timing, or perhaps it was the flippant way in which it was being discussed, but Monty couldn't make the self-defence story work. She stared at the accompanying image. The model looked a little determined, a little annoyed, like overcoming her attacker was just one of many things on her to-do list. Perhaps Monty should ditch the picture and find a bright mobile phone shot instead.

If only they'd had mobile phones back then, she thought, her mind wandering again to Greece. This was before mobiles were commonplace, back before international roaming and text messages.

She sat back, her head racing. Phone... messages... Wilkins... Wilson...

She pulled herself up and headed for the editorial assistant.

"Brianna, you said something the other day about Amelia's phone calls. You mentioned someone called Wilson."

"Hey? What?"

Brianna was tapping away at her keyboard, adding what looked like yet another Facebook post. *How much social media did they need to do?* Monty wondered, before clicking her fingers impatiently. It was something Amelia would do. She stopped, thrust her hands into her pockets.

"Last Friday. You said Amelia got a bunch of calls, right? From her mum and that Amanda woman, and some guy, you said his name was Wilkins or Wilson."

"Yeah, so?"

"So, which one was it? Wilkins or Wilson?"

"I can't remember, sorry. I think it might have been Wilson."

Brianna reached for a spike with a stack of yellow stickies and white note pages attached and began flicking through them.

"Did he at least leave a first name?"

She continued wading. "Not sure, give me a minute!" Then, sensing the urgency, she stopped and looked up at her. "Why? Is it the guy in the high-viz vest?"

Monty ignored the question and waved her on. "You must remember why he was calling; he must have left a message."

"I honestly don't know."

"How do you not know? Aren't you her assistant? Why didn't you ask?"

Brianna bristled at that. "He was returning *her* call!"

That stopped Monty in her tracks. "Really?"

Why in God's name would Amelia have called Thomas Wilson?

"Really. Aha! Here it is!" She pulled a message slip from the spike and waved it at the designer as if it were the proverbial Golden Ticket.

Monty snatched it from her and read the details. *Tom Wilson, returning call 10:33 a.m. Friday.* There was a number scribbled at the bottom.

Montana tapped the note against her lips. Why would Amelia call Thomas after all these years? What did she want with him? Unless it was a different Tom Wilson? She shook her head. It had to be the same guy. It was too much of a coincidence.

First Angus from the ferry, now Thomas.

What the hell was going on?

SHEPPERDIN VILLAGE

Tom hadn't enjoyed a day at work more in a long while. It was Friday morning. His wife had been missing five days now, but his boss, Jimbo, simply issued orders like he normally did, then returned to the converted shipping container that doubled as the headquarters of Shepperdin Building Supplies. As if he didn't care. As if everything was hunky-dory.

It was such a blessed relief, not being treated like a criminal or, worse, a bad husband, and Tom enjoyed the physical toil, the shearing of timber, the oiling of giant slabs, the shifting of rocks and gravel. It helped to feel normal again, to feel physically weary, to forget if only briefly that his life had just fallen apart.

The only indication that things were different now was Jimbo's casual nod when Tom tapped on his door that afternoon and asked to knock off early.

"Gotta get my kid at two today," he explained. "He's got a thing—"

"No worries."

Jimbo didn't want to hear it, and this left Tom frowning. A week ago the older man would've snorted at Tom and told him he was whipped. Today he added, "Take all the time you need," ruining Tom's buzz.

Two hours later, his buzz now back, Tom pulled up outside his home and sat in his truck for a moment, not willing to get out, not willing to face his empty house.

"Thomas Bloody Wilson," came a voice through the open window, and he jumped, nearly hitting his head on the roof of the vehicle.

"Jesus!" he said, holding on to his chest, then he looked out and up towards the familiar figure that was leaning in. "Jesus," he said again and flung the door open. "Angus Bloody Tower, what the hell are you doing out here in the sticks?"

"Good to see you too, mate," Angus said, holding out a hand and pulling him in for a hug. "Been to the beach?"

"What?"

Angus pointed to a smattering of leaves and other debris caught in Tom's red curls, then looked past him and back into his truck.

"Where's young Phillip then?"

Tom shook his fringe out and said, "Went home with a mate. Kid's got a better social life than the Kardashians. Nothing like a missing mum to bring out the leeches."

Tom hoped Angus knew he was referring to him. Didn't show it.

"I heard about Millie. Are you okay?"

"I'm fine, it's *Amy* we're worried about."

"Of course. Amy... yeah, Amy." Angus said her name slowly, still trying to get used to the name change. "And how's Phillip, is he..."

"My son is fine." His jaw tensed. "We're both fine in fact. Seriously, you needn't have come. Haven't you got your millions to count? Heard business is booming, you're a bigwig these days, quite the celebrity."

"Yeah, well, I gave myself a hall pass." Angus offered an apologetic smile. "Besides, it's your face I'm seeing all over the news. You and Mil...I mean *Amy*."

Tom shoved his hands into his pockets and looked away.

"I'm here to help, Thomas. Last night's news gave me quite a fright. Is it true? She's vanished into thin air?"

Tom nodded, felt the shame of it suddenly, slumping back against his ute while Angus reached out and squeezed his shoulder.

"I'm so sorry, man. You want to go inside? Talk about it?" He waved towards the house, but Tom was shaking his head.

"Let's head to the pub, hey?" Tom said. "Like old times?"

"Sure. Whatever works. How about I drive?"

Angus clicked a set of keys, and Tom saw a silver sports car come to life, just on the edge of Harry's driveway, parked there as if he'd mistaken the house. The vehicle looked fancy, like a Maserati perhaps, but then what would Tom know. He'd never got past the used-car lot.

He frowned momentarily, then shook his head again. "I need to clean up first. I'll meet you there. You know the one? The pub on the corner, near the bank."

Angus nodded, went to laugh remembering a few too many beers there one very long night, but must've decided against it. They both knew this wasn't the time for laughter.

"This isn't a courtesy visit is it?" Tom said half an hour later as he plonked two schooner glasses on the table in front of his old friend, who had the remains of a glass of red wine in front of him.

Angus shrugged and reached for the beer. "Told you, I'm worried about you. You and Phillip."

"That's the third time you've mentioned him, Angus." Tom's tone had a very slight chill at the edges. "What's going on?"

Angus held a palm up. "Just asking."

"Phil's fine. Great, in fact. Never better."

"Really? Even though his mum's gone missing?"

Tom ignored this.

"I'm just looking in on him, seeing if there's anything I can do to help. He's a good kid. Got a good head on his shoulders that one."

"And how would you—?" He stopped. "Oh stupid, stupid me." He felt like a complete fool. "So when did you meet him?"

"She didn't tell you any of this?"

"Nah, she likes her secrets, my wife. Big on secrets. So come on, spill."

"Just a few times, when she came to Sydney."

"Sydney?"

"You *knew* she came to Sydney?"

Tom felt a prickle of heat, tried to douse it down. *Yes, of course he knew his wife went to Sydney.* But he thought it was to see her folks not buddy up with a lecher like him. Another one of Amy's secrets.

"She wanted us to get to know each other, that's all, mate. She said I had a right—"

"A *right?*"

A slight blush crept up Angus's neck. "Mate, we're all adults now, can we just talk about this?"

"Nothing to talk about."

"He could be—"

"He's not."

"But she said—"

"She's yanking your chain."

Angus smacked his lips together, took a big gulp of his beer. "Listen, I'm not here to cause trouble. I know you've been a good husband and father."

"Bloody good."

"Yes, she said that. But I need you to know I can help now that... well, if she doesn't come back."

"She's coming back."

"Of course, right." He shook his head, pushed his beer away. "Listen, this is all coming out wrong. I know she wanted me to have some input."

"What input?"

"What? No, um, I'm just saying, I know she wanted me to have some involvement—"

"How could you possibly have *some involvement*? You live two hours away! What are you going to do? Come up and take him out for cosy play dates? This late in the game?" He took deep, calming breaths. "Why should you anyway? What right do you have?"

"I'm talking financially, that's all. I can help Phillip out. And, you know, if he ever wants to come to Sydney, maybe for his education or something..."

"His *education*? What are you talking about? Why would he want to do that? There's schools here; his mates are here. Jesus, Angus."

"Okay, sorry, just trying to—"

"We don't need your help. You weren't there for Amy when you left her broken on the beach that night—"

"Fuck's sake, mate. Keep your voice *down*." Angus glanced around and back. "It wasn't like that. You know it wasn't like that."

"I know you treated Amy like garbage. You used her then you moved on to her mate. Monty. I was there when Amy found out, when she tried to get that creepy nun to make it all go away. But it wasn't going anywhere, and that was thanks to *me*. I was the one who saved Phil from the scrapheap. He might hate my guts, so might she, they might both treat me like a piece of crap, but I rescued them both. Not you. So you don't get to ride in on your fancy fucking charger and try to steal the glory now, right?"

Angus seemed stunned by the outburst, which had caused a few patrons to look up, but he was also embarrassed. Tom knew why. Angus was indeed a bigwig these days. Had a reputation to uphold, a certain image to maintain, and he didn't need strangers thinking he was a monster, deep down.

Angus leaned towards Tom and lowered his voice. "Let's leave the past in the past, shall we, mate? We all behaved badly. I'm only here to offer some help and do the right thing. That's all this is."

"You're thirteen years too late. *Mate*."

Then Tom stood up, pushed his beer so hard half of it slopped across the table, and he walked out.

The man in the corner had seen it all. It was just good luck that Geoff was at the pub so early that Friday. Just good luck that he'd taken the afternoon off and headed straight home where he promptly had a fight with the missus. She reckoned he'd never quite got over her "little fling" with Tom, as she dubbed it this arvo, and told him to stop holding that against the poor bloke, to be more objective. She clearly still believed in the man's innocence, but Geoff was beginning to wonder about that, was beginning to buy into what she called "salacious, small-town gossip". It seemed like half the town adored the guy and the other half wanted to string him up. And Geoff didn't know what to think. As a friend, there was no one more loyal than Tom. As an enemy he could be, frankly, terrifying.

They'd bickered about it while Jenny started making dinner. Went frosty well before she'd finished, so he'd cleared out to give her a chance to warm back up. The roast lamb she was preparing smelled delicious, and he didn't want to risk going hungry tonight.

Spotting Tom deep in conversation with a stranger had been a lucky coincidence, and he was even luckier that the normally hyperalert local hadn't spotted him slink in and steal a seat on the other side of the bar. From there he couldn't see Tom's face, but he could see his drinking buddy clear as day. The guy looked vaguely familiar and completely out of place. Like Cary Grant had stumbled onto the set of a *Wild West* film and needed to return to wardrobe pronto. His suit was too fancy, his hair too coiffed, and he looked increasingly uncomfortable as the conversation progressed.

Geoff couldn't hear what they were saying, but the body language spoke volumes, and he thought they would come to blows at one point, had considered intervening. But then Tom spilt his beer and stormed out, so Geoff waited a few beats, then pushed his own beer aside and made his way across.

"Geoff Pinter, Local Area Commander," he said, indicating a chair. "Mind if I?"

The other man looked surprised for a moment, then nodded. Geoff could smell expensive aftershave, and too much of it.

"You're a friend of Tom's?"

The man held out his hand to shake, showing off a gleaming gold watch. "Angus Tower. I was. A friend, that is. I'm not sure he's too fond of me right about now."

"Mind telling me what's going on?"

The other man hesitated. "Is this an interrogation?"

"Just asking that's all. Nothing official. I went to school with Tom. I know his wife."

"Got any idea yet where she is?"

He shook his head. "We're concerned though. You knew Amy?"

The man's expression softened. "Long time ago. Back when we called her Millie. Silly Millie. Seems so trivial now." He sighed. "Met her while backpacking in Europe, same time Thomas did."

Thomas? He hadn't heard the guy referred to like that in a while. "But Tommo got the girl, hey?"

Angus's face hardened. He didn't answer.

"What brings you round these parts?"

"I heard the news, of course. It's all over the internet. I thought… Well, I just wanted to offer him and the young lad some help, that's all."

"And it wasn't welcome."

"How do you know that?"

"Stormed out, didn't he?"

Angus nodded and slid his eyes away.

"When did you last see Amy?" the detective asked, and his eyes slid back.

"Ages ago."

"Can you be more specific?"

"Um, five, six months ago, I suppose."

"With Tom?"

"With Phillip actually. In Sydney." And to the man's raised

eyebrows he quickly explained, "She was visiting her folks, wanted to catch up, reminisce about our days in Greece."

"With her son in tow?"

He shrugged. "What else was she going to do with him?"

"Leave him with his grandparents."

"Yes, well, she didn't. She brought him along, we had a nice catch-up. It was as simple as that."

"And what did you talk about?"

He shrugged. "The state of the country, the drought, her dreams of living in Sydney one day."

"She said that?"

He looked like a rabbit caught in headlights suddenly. "She missed the place, that's all. She used to work there once. I think she missed her folks, her career and wanted more for the lad, that's all. Look, perhaps you should talk to her parents; they'd know more about all this. Can't remember their names but they live in—"

"We've spoken to Amy's parents. They know nothing."

"Oh right," he said, then glanced at his watch. "Look, I wish I could be more help, really I do, but it was just a friendly catch-up with an old *amoureux*, and I haven't seen her since." He looked at his watch more pointedly this time. "I honestly do need to get going. I've got a long drive ahead of me."

"Can I have your details, please?" Geoff asked, causing Angus to frown. "In case we have any more questions."

He slapped his jacket pocket then reached in and pulled out a thin leather wallet, selecting a glossy business card from inside and handing it over.

Geoff read the words TOWER GLOBAL SOLUTIONS and realised now where he'd seen him before. If it wasn't the financial pages of the national paper it was probably in one of his wife's trash mags. If he remembered correctly, the guy was one of the country's most eligible bachelors. A George Clooney type.

"My assistant's name is Wanda," Angus was saying. "She'll set something up."

Like Geoff was discussing a business deal, not the disappearance of... *What had he called her in French? An old lover?*

As though reading his mind, Angus quickly added, "Look, I'm really just an old friend trying to do my bit. I want to help find Amy. I'm as worried as the rest of you, but I'm not sure there's much

I can do, to be honest."

He buttoned up his jacket, then nodded his head at the card still in Geoff's hands. "But, please, do call me if you hear anything."

Then he patted his jacket down and strode swiftly out of the bar.

As he went, Geoff watched and wondered what that was all about. Word of Amy's disappearance had only hit the news last night. Yet here he was, less than twenty-four hours later, pretending to care yet offering nothing of any substance.

Angus Tower was a busy man, by all accounts. Ran some top-notch tech company. Yet had time to make the four-hour return drive to Shepperdin, and for what? To offer his help and then assure him he was no use anyway.

Why was Angus Tower really here? What was that about? And why had Thomas looked like he wanted to knock his block off before he stormed out?

There was history there, sure, but there was something else. Secrets. This "old friend" was clearly hiding something. The whole thing reeked of bullshit to Geoff, and no amount of expensive aftershave could hide that fact.

SARISI ISLAND

Seagulls swooped low, like feathered signposts, but she didn't need them to find her way to Nicholas. He was fishing in the same spot he'd been fishing every morning since she'd arrived on the island, and most afternoons, down on the rocky outcrop beyond the castle.

It gave her some comfort to see him there, like a sentinel on guard below the tower, and she'd pulled on her sneakers, grabbed her jumper, then made her way out to join him. As she clambered down the rock face and skipped across the bloody pools where yet more fish were snagged, she felt lighter, stronger, less anxious than she had when she'd first arrived.

He glanced up as she approached but didn't quite smile. Just edged his lips northward and called out, "Hey!" before turning his attention back to his rod.

Perhaps she'd misinterpreted last night, she thought, noticing the mood change. Or perhaps he wasn't a morning person.

"Any bites yet?" she asked, keeping her tone light.

"Not yet. Playing hard to get today."

For a moment she wondered if he was talking about himself, but she brushed it aside and held a hand above her eyes as she peered out at the shockingly bright Aegean.

She said, "I think I had the best sleep of my life last night. I was out for the count. Must be all the good food and fresh air."

He nodded without speaking.

"So." She tried again. "I was wondering..." He didn't look around. "If you have any idea when Effie's returning."

Her tone was casual but Nicholas could sense an undercurrent. Or maybe that was just him brooding over what Catalina had said last night. He was glad Millie got some sleep because he hadn't slept a wink. Cat's words kept circling through his brain until they were in knots and made even less sense than before.

What did she mean about Millie being dangerous? And what was that comment about being too posh for Greek guys? That Greeks had to take it from her? What kind of creepy comment was that?

He shook the words away and tried to lighten up.

Cat was simply jealous. That's all this was. A rejected lover lashing out.

"I think she's due back this evening," he said of Effie, trying to shake off his moodiness. "She better be. I'm supposed to be having the night off. Why?"

"Oh, just wondering that's all." Then, a little less casually, "If you happen to speak to her again, could you do me a big favour and tell her I'm staying for a bit?"

"Sure."

He recalled how happy that news had made him feel last night. Now all he felt was trepidation.

Bloody Catalina, she was ruining everything.

But Millie wasn't finished. "Maybe let Effie know, if you don't mind, that I'm not going anywhere. Not leaving the island until she gets back. Tell her I'm *determined* to see her."

Nicholas nodded again, too preoccupied with his own thoughts to hear the threat in Millie's tone. If he had, he might have acted very differently after that. Instead, he watched her smile suddenly appear as a fish leapt from the water, then heard her laugh—*oh God, the laugh!*—as he grappled with his rod and tried desperately to reel the whopper in.

Her laughter was intoxicating, exploding out of her like a wild animal, and before the fish was even in the bucket he had forgotten Catalina's warning and was falling for her all over again.

But this time he knew there was no going back.

EVE MAGAZINE

The inner-city street was pumping with the midmorning coffee set, every café—and there were lots of them—packed with espresso-sipping sorts. Mostly hipsters by the look of it, Monty thought as she stood on the sidewalk, watching the bleached blondes and bearded types who seemed to have nothing better to do than sit about looking beautiful. Others, including yummy mummies with tank-size strollers and middle-aged women impersonating Sporty Spice in their yoga pants and ponytails, walked hurriedly between vintage clothing stores and record shops, retro music pelting out from some of them.

Five years ago Monty would have thought this location cool with its mixed bag of restaurants, clubs, shops and residences, mostly dusty terrace houses, flanked with metal bars. Now it made her feel old and cynical. She wondered how Thomas could stand living amongst the crime and drugs and booming bars. If she recalled correctly, he was from a small country town somewhere. Quite the opposite of all this.

She glanced at the paper in her hand, at the words she'd scribbled down hastily—*263A Darlo Street*—then continued to walk.

Number 263 was wedged between a tobacconist and a shoe shop boasting shiny Doc Martens, and she smiled at a past memory of buying the exact same pair in a shop in London. She had adored those shoes once, now they just looked stiff and uncomfortable. And if she was being honest, trekking the world in them had not made them any more relaxed. *Bit like Amelia,* she thought. *Bit like herself.*

Monty glanced at the paper in her hand again. Number 263A. That didn't make sense. She stared at the door to 263. Was the *A* missing? Did she have the wrong address? Stepping back, she peered up at the shuttered veranda, the freshly painted veneer, then she looked around and towards a narrow laneway on the other side of the shoe shop. She waited for a cyclist to pass and then made her way down.

There was just one shop wedged in here, a tiny jewellers with its door closed, and she noticed the back of some restaurant, Italian by the look of the debris overflowing from various garbage bins— pizza boxes, pasta packets, the pungent smell of garlic.

There was a deeper stench though, and she realised it was urine, so she breathed through her mouth as she hurried along to a faded red door with the numbers 263A scratched into it.

Monty wasn't sure what to expect when Thomas swung the front door open, but he was older than she'd imagined, certainly hadn't aged as well as Angus, despite being thinner with all his thick, red locks. There was something about him that looked *tired*, and she quickly ran a hand through her own hair in case he was thinking the same.

"Monty Brennan!" He was smiling broadly. "Come here, girl."

As he pulled her into a hug, she exhaled and hugged him back. When she called him an hour earlier, she had prepared herself for the cold shoulder, even some animosity, but he seemed delighted to hear from her and insisted she come straight over, which she did lest she lose her nerve.

"Wow, look at you in your fancy suit, hey!" he said, pushing her back to look her over.

She laughed. "Hi, Thomas, how are you?"

"Ah, just call me Tommo. I'm great, yeah, never better. So tell me what's going on."

"Can we talk?"

"Well, I assume you're not here for my killer coffee."

He still had her hand and was pulling her through the doorway and up a steep set of stairs to the first-floor landing. There he led her into a dark living space, flicking on a lamp to reveal sparse furnishings and smudged walls in dire need of a paint. A radio was blaring from a distant room, a shock-jock by the sound of it, and she smelled a mixture of tobacco, tomato sauce and mould. He clearly hadn't done as well from his business studies as his best mate, but he seemed happy enough as he led her to a sofa and then stepped towards a doorway that opened into the kitchen.

"Or maybe we should go straight for the beer?"

She laughed. "It's not even noon!"

"So? We used to put 'em away earlier than that on Santorini remember?"

"See any Greeks around here?"

He laughed like he'd never heard anything funnier, then clapped his hands together and said, "Killer coffee it is."

As he vanished around the corner, Monty stood back up and strolled the room, looking about. He had a few photos on display, most of the countryside—cow paddocks, an old timber house, and a bright red tractor with a man standing in front of it who looked a little like Thomas. She vaguely recalled another brother and wondered if he still lived out there somewhere and why Tommo hadn't returned to join him. There was a bookshelf too, mostly jammed with CDs, but she did spot a few self-help books, including that ridiculous *Celestine Prophecy*, the one Amelia had liked, as well as a handful of what you could only call airport reads by Wilbur Smith, James Patterson, Candice Fox.

"You like a good thriller?" she called out, and he reappeared at the doorway, a beer in one hand, a mug in the other.

"Who doesn't?"

Me, she thought but let it drop as she took the mug from him. They had always been chalk and cheese, she and Thomas. It seemed silly now, how they had turned to each other soon after they all met. Like they had no other choice but to get together once Angus had chosen Millie.

Why didn't we just stay friends? Monty wondered, swishing her lips to one side. *What was the point of all that?*

"So." He was sitting on the sofa now and patting the cushion beside him. "Come, tell me why I'm everybody's favourite person all of a sudden. I don't hear from anyone for over a decade, and suddenly you're all breaking down my door. What's going on?"

Was there a slight edge to his voice? Was he feeling offended?

"I'm sorry we lost touch," she began, rushing to sit down. "I didn't think you'd want to hear from me, to be honest."

"Why not?" His eyes were steady and she wondered if he was joking.

She glanced at her lap, swept some invisible dust away. "I don't know. Just, you know, the way things ended up."

When she glanced back up, Tom looked genuinely confused.

"How did things end up? What are you talking about?" Then the penny must have dropped because his face creased into a smile again. "You mean you and me?"

"Well, you know, we did break up…"

"Jesus, Monty, we were barely together! I haven't been crying myself to sleep over it if that's what you think."

He was almost sniggering, and she could feel her cheeks burning. "No! Of course not." She grappled for her coffee again. *Subject change,* she thought. *Now!* "Anyway, it's good to see you. What have you been up to?"

"Bit of this, bit of that."

She nodded, trying not to glance around, not to focus on the general shabbiness of the place. "How's all the family? You were from somewhere out west was it?"

"Shepperdin, just a few hours away." He glanced at the picture on the tabletop. "Dad died a few years back."

"Sorry."

"What for? He was a prick. Left the property to my brother, wrote me out of the whole lot. Two hundred acres of dairy farm, all gifted to Harry."

"Oh." No wonder he hadn't returned. No wonder Angus said he was floundering.

"It seems I was never to be forgiven for getting above my station." He noticed her puzzled look and explained: "Dad loathed my business degree. Expected me to be a good little boy and stay on the land like Harry." Then he offered her a cheerless smile. "Harry got his reward, and so did I."

"Oh, Tom, I'm so sorry."

"Nah, don't be. Harry did the right thing, offered me a bit of land but I couldn't go back. Besides, his wife's a total ball-buster. Couldn't stand the thought of living so close." He scratched at his chin stubble, seemed lost in a bubble for a moment before glancing back at her. "But I don't think you've come all this way to hear my sob story."

He smiled. He sat back. He waited.

Offering her own apologetic smile, Monty said, "No, you're right. I'm here about Amelia."

"Amelia?"

"Millie."

"Right, Millie. Yeah, she dropped in last week. She was looking good. Said you two were still close. Work together, am I right? On some chick mag? The big one? *Eve* is it?" She nodded. "Wow, that's quite a bond."

"She's my bestie. Has been since school, remember?"

His lips dipped downwards, and he looked like he was about to object to that but thought better of it and shrugged. "So, what about Millie?"

"She's gone missing." Truth was probably the best option, she decided; they'd beaten about the bush long enough.

"Missing?" He sat forward.

"Yes. She hasn't been seen since last Friday."

He sat back and rubbed his chin again. "Wow, she's vanished again, hey?" Then he smiled. "You check for Greek blokes?"

When Monty didn't smile along, he said, "I'm sure she'll turn up again; she's the boomerang kid that one."

"I'm sure she will too, but I'd rather not wait so long this time. I know she came to see you the day before she vanished."

"And you think I had something to do with it?"

His tone definitely had an edge now, and she held a hand up.

"God no! I'm not saying that at all. I-I'm just wondering if she told you anything, gave you any indication where she might be heading, that's all."

"Nope. But then she wouldn't, would she? I mean if she didn't tell you—her *bestie*—why would she tell me?"

He took a good, long gulp of his beer and then leaned back as though that was the end of it. He wasn't going to make it easy, she realised.

Taking another deep breath, Monty tried again. "Do you mind telling me what you two talked about? When she came to visit? Maybe it'll shed some light on where she went."

He looked at her surprised, the beer at his lips again, and she held one palm out.

"Look, I know I'm being nosy, but something's obviously

happened. She wouldn't just take off."

"She did once."

Monty let that one go to the keeper. "I saw Angus last night."

He seemed surprised to hear that but said nothing.

"He told Amelia about how he and I had, well, you know…?" Again she didn't have the courage to articulate it.

"And what? You think she was so crushed she ran out and killed herself or something?"

"No, of course not!" *What a ridiculous notion!* Although now that he'd said it, she wondered if that was what she had been thinking. She shook the horrendous thought away. "It's just that I'd never told her before about Angus and me, and, well, I wondered whether she brought that up with you last Friday? Whether she was hurt by the revelation, maybe she came here to commiserate or something?"

"Oh, Monty, Monty, Monty." Tom was looking at her like she was a small child and a dim one at that. "Stop making this such a big deal, babe. Amelia's taken off again. It's what she does, right? And I'm sorry to say I have no idea where she is this time. I'm as clueless as you are. I get this bloody strange call last Thursday, a cryptic message from a ghost from my past, begging to see me. I call her the next day, text her the address, she comes over and is here for, oh, about three minutes when she turns and runs out. I mean, I know I haven't aged well, but yikes." He half smiled, his eyes dropping.

He looked disappointed.

"And you have no idea what she wanted? She never asked you about Angus and me?"

He shook his head. "We'd barely got past pleasantries. I mean, I was curious, right? Kind of looking forward to catching up, hearing her news, and then—pfft! Vanishes down the lane. I started to wonder if I'd hallucinated the whole thing." He chuckled. "Wouldn't be the first time." Chuckled again.

But Monty wasn't chuckling. "Right, well, she's vanished for good. She hasn't been at work, hasn't been in touch with her parents. None of us have seen her since that Friday. There was one potential sighting on Saturday but… well, you're one of the last people to see her so—"

He thumped his beer on the table. "You really do think I had something to do with this."

"No, of course not! That's not what I'm saying. Look, sorry. I…

well, I'm not explaining myself very well."

He stood up. "I know exactly what you're saying. She's taken off again and you're trying to blame somebody other than her. This is textbook Millie. She pisses off without thinking about anybody else but herself. I know she's your 'bestie' and all that crap, but she was always a selfish, entitled bitch and it sounds like that hasn't changed."

Monty was shocked by the language, by the very sentiment, but he didn't seem angry so much as bored by the whole subject. And she couldn't blame him for that. As far as she knew, Tom had no idea what happened to Millie the last time she vanished, and she wasn't about to tell him now. As far as he knew, Millie had skipped off into the sunset with a Greek stranger, letting down his best mate.

So she pushed her cup aside and followed him across the room and down the staircase.

At the bottom, he swung the front door wide and turned back.

"Maybe it's time to stop looking at everyone else and start putting the blame where it belongs—with Millie. Or, I don't know, here's an even better idea. Maybe it's time to forget precious Millie and get on with your own life. Maybe it's time to stop cleaning up after that chick, hey?"

Monty stepped out onto the road. He was right. Of course he was right. *God, why was she doing this all over again?*

"I'm sorry, Tom, if you thought…"

He grabbed her hand, squeezed it for a second, then let it drop. It reminded her of something, of before, and she offered him a sad smile.

"Let's try to catch up, properly next time," she said, and he nodded blankly at her as he closed the door.

She knew he wouldn't be holding his breath.

SHEPPERDIN VILLAGE

Tom stepped heavily as he made his way through the overgrown grass to the secluded cabin on the top part of his block, smacking the stick against the earth, warning the brown snakes and pythons he was entering their territory.

Her territory, actually, but the undisturbed grass testified to just how often she bothered to visit. It also proved that Geoff wasn't as smart as he thought he was. His team clearly hadn't thought to look up here. Tom had built the place for her. Years ago. Her haven, he called it. A place for her to hide away, write, paint, or whatever she needed to do to get happy.

Wasted energy as it turns out. Like the jewellery tree. Like the boy.

She feigned delight when he first led her here, eyes closed, hand tiny in his.

"So this is what you guys have been working on all this time!" she'd said. "Another shed!"

"It's not a bloody shed, Millie. It's an art space. *Your* art space."

"Mine? Really?" She threw herself into his arms. "Oh my God, you're amazing!"

But he'd seen the slight crinkle of her brow, the twitch of her lips before she'd hidden her face in his chest. She didn't like it, that was obvious.

"I love it, my God, but honey, you shouldn't have! Don't you want it?"

"I've already got a shed. I want you to have your own space."

"Oh, okay, wow, thanks."

It took another two weeks before she returned, books and paints in hand.

Two months later she stopped pretending and continued pottering about in the sunroom at the back of the house, doing the odd painting, scribbling the odd short story.

"I like to be near the action," she said when he pressed her on it. "You know I have loads of washing to do, and I need to be near the phone in case Mum calls or the school. But I do love it and I'll use it, don't worry."

Creaking the door open now, thick spiderwebs pulling apart as he did so, he could see she never did. At least not recently. He swung the door wide and waited a beat, allowing any critters to find a home before he stepped inside.

He was kicking himself for not doing this earlier. *Why hadn't he thought of this?* Perhaps he was as dumb as Geoff.

There was a desk against one wall, a wooden chair in front of it, large, distressed wooden windows above it, looking out at the towering ghost gums that were one big storm away from destroying it all anyway. On the other side was a small table, a fan, a bookshelf and a single bed now covered in dead insects and rat shit. He'd hung vintage paintings on the walls and retro light fixtures he'd taken care to find at a Trash or Treasure shop an hour's drive away. And all for nothing. He should've rented it out on Airbnb.

He noticed Amy had found time to add some books to the shelf and he stepped across. *The Seven Spiritual Laws of Success, The Road Less Traveled,* and at least five books by some dude called Dyer, including *You'll See It When You Believe It.* He snorted at that one.

Yeah right. That's all it takes. A bit of conviction and your life is rosy.

He surveyed the bookshelf again but couldn't see what he was looking for.

It had to be here, there had to be something. Angus's words kept circling through his head. His words about Phillip.

"She wanted me to have input. She wanted me to be involved."

It sent molten lava through his spine, and he looked around again. There had to be some proof, something... Glancing back at the desk he spotted the drawer and pulled it open. Ants scuttled across the dust and over a few unlit tea candles, but it was otherwise empty. He glanced around again, then he saw it. The tiny drawer in the table by the bed. It was easy to miss, but he wasn't stupid.

He strode across, just two steps, and pulled at it. It didn't budge. He yanked, and this time it creaked and then flew out, spilling contents as it went, and he leapt upon them, darting his eyes back to the door, his heart hammering in his chest.

He didn't know why he was feeling nervous, there was nobody else around, yet it felt like he was invading someone's privacy. *Her* privacy in fact, and guilt tugged at his heart. Ignoring it, he picked the contents up and placed them carefully on the bed. There were old crayon drawings and more recent report cards, all belonging to Phil, as well as copies of his birth certificate and immunisation record. But beneath it all he saw it, a thick white envelope with a fancy blue logo on the front. A logo he recognised.

His heart stopped. His head felt light. He glanced back at the door, then he reached for it.

SARISI ISLAND

It was Thursday morning on Sarisi. The 11:00 a.m. ferry from Piraeus had come and gone, and Millie tried to hide her disappointment as she left the wharf and returned to the road again. She was just passing the Casa Delfino when Nicholas appeared in the courtyard, an apron around his waist, a smile on his lips, his earlier mood now forgotten.

"She wasn't on it?" he called out, and she shook her head.

He threw his arms in the air. "Sorry, what can I say? I think Effie's avoiding us!"

Millie had a pretty good idea who Effie was avoiding, but she kept that to herself.

"She hasn't called?" she asked.

"Nope. Hasn't returned my call either. But then she wouldn't. Not unless I've rung to tell her the Delfy's on fire." He chuckled. Had considered lighting the place up himself a few times this week. It really had been manic without her. "Don't worry. She's gotta be back by the weekend; that's when Theo returns. She won't want to miss that. Plus there is the minor matter of a hotel to run. Speaking of which…" He swallowed his reservations and asked, "Got plans for lunch? Wanna grab a table and I'll see if I can rustle up that fish I caught this morning?"

"No thank you," she replied.

His heart deflated. "Oh, okay."

"But if you can spare some time, I've got a much better idea."

He held his breath.

"I was wondering," she said, smiling bashfully, "if you'd teach me how to catch my own lunch."

"What? Go fishing?" She nodded, her eyes twinkling. "Sure! No worries!" Then, about to turn away he quickly added, "Don't move an inch, I'll be straight back!"

Nicholas raced inside, whipping his apron off and grabbing one of the rods he kept at the door outside the kitchen. Then he ducked into the pantry to retrieve a small bag of frozen octopus and told the frowning chef, "I'll be less than an hour! Back before the rush, I promise."

"Sure you will!" Pete scoffed, but he wasn't angry. He recognised a smitten man when he saw one.

As he returned to the road, Millie's eyes twinkled again. "I wondered if you'd let me use one of your fancy rods."

"Oh you're not getting the fancy one. I've got a rusty tin can and some old wire for you, my dear."

And she laughed like she'd never heard anything funnier.

Millie was still laughing twenty minutes later when she'd caught her first fish, and as she sat on the rocks giggling while he released it from the hook, he said, "Who knew fishing could be so funny?"

"Sorry," she said, throwing a hand to her mouth. "Truth is, I was remembering this inane article I once wrote for a magazine, many moons ago."

"You work in magazines?"

"Many moons ago," she repeated. *It felt like a lifetime now.* "We called the story Fishing for Mr Right." She almost snorted. "It was all about how women shouldn't worry, there were plenty of fish in the sea."

"And is there?"

"God no! That's just what we tell single women to make them feel better so they'll buy the magazine." She laughed again, but it was less convincing. "Anyway, the point is we took the theme so seriously. Had a break-out box with little fish logos and this kind of Adonis guy with a naked torso and a hook in his mouth."

"Eww."

"I know! Woeful stuff. But the point is, we were so full of crap. I don't think any of us had ever been fishing. Couldn't imagine us in our kitten heels ever stepping onto rocks let alone throwing a line out. The closest we came to fish was grilled snapper at the gourmet Thai restaurant down from the office." She smiled wistfully now. "We thought we were so clever, but we were ridiculous."

"Ah, but not anymore. Now you've tried fishing. You can go back and speak with some authority."

Her smile faded and she looked away. She didn't think she wanted to go back. All those years she thought that's the life she wanted, the one that would save her, and now she couldn't think of anything she wanted less.

"So tell me about this magazine of yours," he said, sensing her slip away.

She thought about the question as she watched him rebait the hook.

"It was just a stupid women's mag, like any women's mag."

"Yeah, except I'm not a woman, right? You did get that?"

She smiled. "Right. Well, let's see. It was jammed with all the stuff we 'experts' deemed essential for a woman's life, like fashion and beauty and relationship 'advice'."

She used her fingers to denote the quotation marks, and the sarcasm in her voice showed him what she thought of that. He frowned.

"You sound like an old cynic."

"You did just hear my story about fishing, right?"

He smiled. "So why are you still there?"

"Yeah, except I'm not there, right. You did get that?" She turned back with a gotcha smile and he laughed.

"Fair enough."

She gave the question some thought, though, as she watched him secure the bait, then said, "I think I believed all our lies at the beginning, I really did. I thought we were doing good work and I found it so easy to justify. We're empowering women! It's *for* women *by* women! But it just holds women up to a standard they can't possibly reach and worse, it pits women against each other."

"How so?"

She stared at him. "Again, that story about fishing! And there were plenty more where that came from. Stories like, Drop a Dress Size by Saturday."

"That was a story? Seriously?"

"Seriously." She sighed. "It wasn't all rubbish. We did some good stuff; there was always at least one 'worthy' story."

"Worthy story?"

"Yeah, you know, highlighting women's issues and inequality—what it's like being a woman under Taliban rule or how women still retire with almost 40 percent less savings than men and what we can all do about it."

"That does sound worthy."

She glanced back at him quickly, and he held a hand up.

"I'm being serious. They sound like good stories."

"And they were, but they weren't the real reason women bought the mag even though it made them feel better and gave them an excuse for buying it."

He laughed again. "Bit like *Playboy* then. You realise men only ever buy it for the articles, right?"

"Exactly."

"So is that what this is about then?"

"Sorry?"

"You finally clicked that it was crap and handed in your notice."

A wistful look came over her face again. "The truth is, I worked out it was crap a long time ago. I'm only just admitting it to myself now. I thought it was what I wanted, what I dreamed of doing my whole life, the thing that would make me truly happy." She shook her head. "I'm only just realising it's not where I want to be, not really. I got it all wrong. Everything."

Nicholas looked at her confused. *So had she left her job recently or was it years ago?* The woman talked in riddles, and they were way beyond his pea brain. He lightened the tone and thrust the rod back to her saying, "So just your classic midlife crisis then?"

"Hey, who are you calling middle-aged!" She slapped him lightly across the shoulder, then took the rod.

"Sorry, no offence. I'm simply wondering, is this a chance to catch your breath, start afresh maybe?"

Or are you just here fishing? He wanted to say. But he wasn't brave enough.

She stood up and said, "Something like that."

Then she made her way back to the water's edge.

An hour later Nicholas had forgotten all about his promise to Pete and was still squatting on the rocks below the castle watching the

Sydney woman as she continued fishing. She'd taken to it like a duck to water, and it surprised the hell out of both of them. He had to choke back his own laughter every time she snagged a fish and let out an enormous scream. Like she was shocked that it had actually worked! Like it was a revelation!

As she threw out another line, he wondered why she was still here, in Sarisi that is. And he knew it had nothing to do with fishing, and he didn't really think it was an early midlife crisis, or at least he hoped it wasn't. No, he had a horrible hunch it had everything to do with Effie. She seemed a little too interested in his cousin.

But for the moment, at least, he didn't care. He was interested in her. Intrigued. Millie was like no one he had ever met before. The backpackers around these parts were usually pretty vacant, just out for a laugh, void of substance. And the local Greek women were generally a variation on Catalina and Effie—loud, bossy, slightly unhinged. Either that or they were like his loving sisters—loud, bossy and wanting to mother him. And hadn't he come all this way to escape that?

But this woman was different. There was an energy in her, an intelligence and yet there was also something slightly broken. He could sense it beneath her radiant smile and in her strange way of talking. They might speak the same language, but she spoke in riddles, evaded questions, was definitely hiding something. Perhaps Catalina was right. Perhaps he should be careful. But he couldn't help himself. He wanted to unravel the riddle, to find out who exactly this mysterious stranger was, with the galloping laugh and the sudden interest in fishing.

And he hoped to God Effie would stay away a little longer because he had a feeling it would all come crashing down the moment his cousin returned.

Those two had history. He was no fool, and they were fooling nobody.

He had a hunch Millie was on a fishing expedition, but it had nothing to do with fish or, sadly for him, hooking herself a Greek Adonis.

EVE MAGAZINE

If magazines were motion pictures, thought Monty as she placed the overladen tray on the wet tabletop and watched the team snatch their respective drinks, this one would be that Kevin Costner dud *Waterworld*. They'd pulled it off, but it was a pretty pathetic effort, and at what cost?

Alex was clearly thinking more along the lines of *Citizen Kane* and made them all toast themselves as soon as they had drinks in hand. The issue wasn't strictly finished, someone had to rustle up an editor's letter—they all knew who was gagging to do that—and there were still proofs to check and several layouts to tweak, not to mention the cover. Monty couldn't even get her head around designing the cover with Alex, but the bulk of the magazine was finished, and it was a minor miracle, even by publishing standards.

They may all bitch and gripe, but Amelia sure was a smooth operator. It had been extremely hard work without her.

It was just after six on Friday night, and they were having drinks at a noisy wine bar just down from the office. This was rare for the *Eve* team. Most of them scattered at the end of each week, as happy to get away from the magazine as each other, but Amelia's disappearance had united them somehow. Even Alex had tagged along, and she never tagged along. Not lately, anyway.

"To getting through the week from hell!" sang Mel, reading Monty's thoughts not Alex's.

The deputy editor bristled. "Hey, we did good, guys. We did it! No thanks to you know who."

Several sets of eyes darted across to Monty, but she ignored them as she stared into her wineglass. She'd need a few more of these to deal with what came next. The Malones had insisted she drop over later, and she didn't have a good feeling about it.

"Any word yet?" asked Mel, still playing mind reader.

"Nope."

Monty gulped back half her wine and tried to focus on some silly story that Beatrice was telling, something about a misadventure with fake tan, but all she could think of was Amelia and how she had let her down.

"You okay?" This was Alex now.

"I'm worried about Amelia, of course."

"Why? She left us in the lurch, honey. You should be *cranky* with her." A slight hesitation and then, "Why are you so loyal to her?"

"Sorry?"

"Amelia? You'd give her your left tit if she asked."

"And she has, several times," Monty said, trying to lighten the mood, to change the subject, but Alex didn't laugh.

"Has she got something on you?"

"What?"

"I heard about the promotion. *House & Feather*. How you didn't take it for years."

"It's a sideways step."

"It's a giant step up! Much more stylish than our popular rag. Why didn't you? You can't seriously be that smitten with *Eve*, or Amelia for that matter."

Monty brought her glass to her lips. "You don't know everything, Alex." She took a small sip. "It's not as black and white as you think. Amelia's had it tougher than most people realise, and we've known each other a long time, have always had each other's backs." *Well, not always.* "I wouldn't desert her. Not now."

Alex cocked her head to one side and raised her own glass. "That's very gallant, Monty, but if I'm not mistaken, the one who's been deserted here is you."

It was the second time that week that she had heard the sentiment, and it infuriated her now. Why did everyone assume *she* was the one being deserted? Why did they all insist *she* take it personally? She might have been the trigger—perhaps Amelia couldn't get past Monty's deceit—but she wasn't the only one Amelia had turned her back on. There was the entire *Eve* staff, the publisher, Gerry, and worst of all her parents.

She sighed just thinking about them, swallowed the rest of her wine and stood up. It was time to face the music.

~~~

Amelia's parents lived in a safe, middle-class suburb of Sydney, a mostly elderly enclave with more hip replacements than hipsters, and a direct train ride straight from the city. Monty didn't have a car, had never needed one, so she took the twenty-minute journey and then walked the last ten-minute leg to their quarter-acre block.

It was a familiar trail. She and Amelia had loped along this road many times after school together, then later, staggered and giggled their way back from whatever party or club they'd been to, but today it felt like enemy territory. She stiffened her shoulders and rehearsed her battle cry.

It's not my fault! She's a grown up; it's not my fault!

But Ron didn't want to hear a word of it.

"You lost my little girl? Again?"

Monty folded her arms across her chest. She was standing at the doorway to the Malone home, not as oversized and showy as the neighbours but big enough to know they weren't stressing over power prices.

"She's not lost, Ron." Monty said, wanting to add *and she's not your little girl anymore either. She's a thirty-three-year-old career woman for goodness' sake.*

"Then where is she? Why hasn't she called?"

"I don't— Look, she'll show up."

Ron's expression was sceptical. He had heard that once before and yes, sure, she had shown up eventually, but they all knew at what cost. His craggy features contorted from fear and despair to disbelief and fury, all in a matter of seconds. "How could this happen? How could you let her vanish again?"

"I was away, Ron. She sent me away."

"You didn't smell a rat? I thought you were supposed to be the smart one."

"Don't know where you got that idea."

Ron glared at her then exhaled loudly, despair winning out again
~~~

as he waved her in. For a moment there Monty didn't think she was getting through the door, was almost relieved at the possibility of being shut out, but of course there was more of this to come.

Amelia's mother hadn't yet had her turn, and while she had sounded calm enough on the phone earlier, Monty knew the panic would have settled in by now. Beryl had already told her there was still no postcard, so she braced herself for the worst and, once again, was pleasantly surprised.

As she dragged herself up from her creamy-coloured lounge, Beryl did not look distressed. Grim, sure, and a little worried, but it was Monty she seemed most worried about.

"How are *you*, my dear?" she said, pulling Monty into a warm embrace. "Are you okay?"

Her eyes narrowed. "I'm fine, I guess. How are you guys holding up?"

"We're holding up just fine, aren't we, Ron?" She didn't wait for a response. "Please come in, come sit with me."

Monty dared a glance Ron's way as she took her seat, but he was heading for the liquor cabinet on the other side of the room.

"Drink?" he barked when he got there, his back still turned.

"Thank you," she called out. "I'll have whatever's going."

He grunted something and reached for a glass tumbler.

"So," Beryl began. "No word yet from our girl?"

Monty's shoulders slumped. "No, Beryl. I'm so sorry. She hasn't called, she hasn't left messages—"

"She's fine. Don't panic."

"You honestly think so?"

"Of course, dear." The mother pulled Monty's hands into her own. "She's not a baby anymore. She can make her own choices. Despite what Ron thinks, nothing's happened to her."

"But how can you be so sure?"

She looked blank for a moment. "The bag!" she said suddenly. "Her clothes! She obviously packed a bag and has gone somewhere for some valuable time out. She will come back. She came back last time. She will come back again."

"You think?"

"Yes!"

There was a loud clunk of glass at the other side of the room, and Monty glanced around to find Ron holding on to the edge of the bar, his back still turned. He didn't say a word. He didn't need to. That clunk said it all.

Beryl's eyes never left Monty. "Ignore him, he still thinks Amelia's twenty. No, *twelve*. Me, I think it's about time she got herself a life."

Monty was shocked. In all the years she'd known Beryl, through all their conversations—and God knows there had been many of those—she had only ever played the worried mum. Now she sounded like a liberated friend.

"She *has* a life," Ron growled, striding across the room and thrusting a gin and tonic towards Monty.

Beryl was unrepentant. "So, shoot me," she said, releasing Monty's hand so she could take her drink. "I want grandkids. Best-selling magazines aren't going to give me that, are they?"

"Neither is a missing daughter."

"She is not missing, Ron!" Beryl spat each word out slowly, her relaxed mood fast diminishing.

"We haven't heard from her!" he countered. "She hasn't turned up to work. She's not at her house. That's the definition of missing." He drew his eyes to Monty. "If I don't hear from my baby girl by Sunday, I'm calling in the police!"

"Oh, for goodness' sake, Ron. You're being very dramatic."

"And you're not being dramatic enough!"

"But how do you know for sure?" asked Monty, dragging the conversation back to neutral territory. "Beryl, I can't believe you're not more worried."

"Of course I'm *worried*, dear. Please don't take this as proof that I don't care. But I saw her bag was missing. I think she's gone somewhere for a bit of a break and she'll be back before we know it."

"Back from where? Do you know—?"

"I have no idea where she is!" Her voice was rising again. "But she will be back. Call it a mother's intuition, call it what you like, but I just know she'll be back."

"You know nothing," Ron growled, but before Beryl could respond, Monty had dropped her glass on the coffee table and grabbed the woman's hands again.

She wanted relaxed Beryl back. "So if you really believe that, Beryl, and I'm loving your positivity by the way, why did you want to chat?"

Why did you drag me halfway across Sydney when I'd rather be drowning my sorrows with my colleagues? she might have added, but she was too polite and adored the woman too much.

"I want you to tell that boss of hers she won't be back."

She dropped Beryl's hands like they were on fire. "What?"

"Just tell that dreadful man, Amelia's free and she's done with the place. Hand in her resignation for her. Please."

"But…" Monty glanced from Beryl to Ron, who was now perched on the edge of the sofa, looking as though he might slip off it, and staring into his glass. He didn't seem surprised by this, but he also didn't look like he agreed.

"Shouldn't we wait to hear from Amelia?" Monty said. "I mean, you're probably right and she'll be back tomorrow, and if she is she'll be furious at us for even considering it."

"Hope not," Beryl said emphatically, and this time Ron groaned. "I don't want her to go back. I hope she's got as far as she can from that horrendous magazine and its ridiculous long hours as possible."

"But… but I thought you liked *Eve!*"

"It's not about *Eve*, dear. It never was. It's about *Amelia*, her life, her choices. Sure, *Eve* helped at a very… *difficult* time, we all know that." Another groan from Ron. "But enough's enough. She's given everything to that blasted magazine. It's time to give back to herself."

"To herself or to you?" That was Ron, now meeting his wife's eyes.

"*Ron,*" she replied, her voice low and growly, like a Rottweiler. She knew where he was headed with this. They had clearly had this conversation many times in the past few days, perhaps the past few years judging by the woman's conviction.

"You don't even want to try to track her down," he said. A statement of fact. "What if something horrendous has happened? What if she's lying in a hospital somewhere?"

Beryl shook her head. "She's a big girl, Ron. I'm sure she's okay. But you…" Beryl turned back to Monty again. "I need you to be okay too. You do what's right for you now, leave us to find our daughter. And tell that Gerald Henderson that Millie is done with publishing and that's the final word on the subject."

"But…"

"No buts, my dear. Not anymore." Beryl was already dragging Monty to her feet, leading her back towards the front door. "Enough's enough. Now you go out and enjoy the rest of your evening and just worry about yourself."

She *was* worried about herself and was pretty sure Gerry would skin her alive if she dared to suggest his top editor was now stepping aside. And she had a hunch his top editor wouldn't clap her on the back for it either. So she made no promises as she bid the parents good night and left them to their inevitable row, returning to the trail more baffled than ever.

That had not gone at all as she'd expected. As for what was right *for her?* She'd forgotten what that was or even how to go about finding it.

SHEPPERDIN VILLAGE

Tom sat on the dusty bed in Amy's cabin and stared at the envelope unable to believe his eyes. It was her greatest betrayal yet, worse even than her desertion. He pulled out the dossier and scowled even harder. It was for a private school in Sydney, an exclusive boys' boarding school with a fancy logo and an even fancier name.

He would have preferred love letters, the lease on a Sydney apartment, a sex tape!

He stormed out of the cabin and down to the backyard, stomping hard across the sandpit and below her beloved *Avatar* tree and towards the rusty incinerator, collecting twigs along the way. He dumped in the kindling, followed by the package, then reached for his lighter and lit the whole thing up, flames leaping skyward within seconds. But the warmth of the fire only left him cold.

How could she tear his son away from him? Did she really want a bunch of strangers to bring up their boy? How could she even contemplate the idea? And how had he not suspected a thing?

If it wasn't for Angus and his clumsy arrival, Tom never would have guessed. Could not believe she'd been in touch with him all this time. Another deceit! All those weekends, dragging Phil to Sydney to 'bond' with his grandparents, it turns out he was bonding with Angus instead!

And why? So the tech mogul could deign to take him out from boarding school occasionally? Even thinking that made Tom bristle. Angus had done nothing more than defile Amy, then run for the nearest ferry, her best friend under his arm. As if the egomaniac had time for the young lad, as if he had the heart!

What kind of *role model* did she think Angus was? Why would Amy *want* him to have any involvement in their son's life, after the monstrous things he'd done? Was it purely financial? Was it vengeance? Was she using the rich prick to pay for Phil's schooling, or was it more about getting Phil far away from Tom? Was she using Angus so *she'd* have a place to run?

He blinked, staring hard into the fire as the revelation hit him like a branch from the fig. This was about *him*, not Phil, or even Angus. This was Amy's way of leaving him.

But why? When and how had *Tom* become the monster in all this?

Suddenly Tom was running, back through the yard and into the house, his blood boiling. He felt bitter, furious, betrayed. And grateful, oh so grateful again, that Phil was at Zac's place tonight.

There was no controlling his rage this time.

He headed straight for Amy's side of the bed, scooped up her stupid wrinkle cream and threw it against the wall, watching as it bounced off, not even smashing. It only enflamed him further. He reached a hand and swiped at her stuff, watching as her precious beads went flying across the room, no lovingly made jewellery tree to contain them now. He picked up her address book and tore it in half, then swiped at her precious magazines, sending them fluttering towards the carpet. Then he dropped onto the bed, grabbed her pillow and smashed it, smashed it, smashed it before stopping, dropping and sobbing into the soft case.

He inhaled deeply, didn't want to release her smell.

Oh Amy, Amy, Amy. His beautiful, beautiful girl.

Tom lay down slowly and hugged her pillow to his chest, wrapping his legs beneath him and coiling into the foetal position. As he blinked back tears, he glanced towards the carpet and that's when he saw it, a face he hadn't seen in more than a decade.

He sat up with a jolt.

A magazine was spread open on the floor where it had landed, a brassy redhead smiling out at him below a painfully blue sky, a dark-haired man behind her. And behind him, an eerily familiar castle.

He leapt off the bed and reached for it, the latest issue of *House & Feather*. He read for just a minute before he dropped it back to the carpet as if it too was on fire.

SARISI ISLAND

Effie pulled her cap low across her face, inhaled deeply, and stepped off the gangplank.

The ferry ride from Athens had been calm, but that made little difference. Her stomach was aflutter. It was late afternoon and few passengers were disembarking at Sarisi. Even fewer were hanging back, waiting their turn to board. She quickly scanned the faces, then released a long, slow breath.

Good. Perhaps she'd already left.

"Looking for someone?"

Effie swung around, her heart fluttering again, to find Zoe treading towards her, bag of apples in hand, her crazy white hair flapping about behind her.

"Oh, Zoe, *yassou!*" she called out, calming her breathing down. "How have you been?"

She smiled. "Always good, you know me. I see you've been stocking up."

Effie nodded, then turned to the group who were piling down the plank behind her.

"Get that stuff straight to the Delfy, *nai?* Cold stuff will be off before we know it."

They continued walking; they knew their job, had done it faithfully many times.

Zoe watched them for a moment, then turned back to Effie. "I had a very interesting visitor yesterday," she said. Effie held her breath. "An Australian lady. Pretty as a picture. Not an unfamiliar picture in fact." She let those words linger for a little, then said, "She was asking about Agnetha."

Effie feigned a scoff. "That's ancient history."

"Not to her it's not. She was most disappointed to hear Aggie was gone. Wanted to speak to her, seemed terribly desperate actually."

Effie reached for her sunglasses and thrust them on.

"Even more disappointed to hear you weren't around," Zoe added.

"Well, I can't hang around to chat to every sentimental tourist, can I? Hurry up, Aris! Be careful with that last crate!" Effie wedged a smile to her lips. "I have to get this stuff in. Good to see you, Zoe. Come for dinner one night, yes?"

The English woman smiled. "You can't avoid the past forever."

Effie stopped, heartbeat rising again.

"And you certainly can't hide the truth," Zoe continued. "But then I think you already know that, my darling, don't you?" Then she took a large bite of one apple, smiled again and turned away, unable to see Effie's terror through the dark sunglasses but sensing it anyway.

~~~

As the witch of Mikro walked away, a man was watching from the esplanade. He had been waiting to talk to Effie for days. But now he hesitated.

Did he really want to bring it all up again? All the recriminations and turmoil?

He remembered that awful, bleak day, how the police had arrived by the boatload, how they'd swept the island and fingerprinted all the men. They were hunting for a rapist, a single man, yet somehow everyone was left feeling violated.

Gossip began to surface, suspicion began to grow, and at least two lives were ruined, probably more. Eventually, slowly, things settled down again and Sarisi returned to some semblance of normality. But he knew that the police had it all wrong from the start, and he wasn't surprised they never found their man. They were looking for evil, but they were hunting in all the wrong places.

He, alone, had seen the face of evil that night, and it was not an unfamiliar one.
~~~

EVE MAGAZINE

It was ten o'clock Saturday morning on a bustling Sydney street. Most people were heading to the shopping centres or cinemas or the neighbouring parks, but not Monty. It was later than normal and she was wearing jeans, but otherwise it was another work day. There was so much still to be done. As she approached her office building, she glanced up and spotted a light in the eighth-floor window. *Eve's* window.

Monty's heart skipped a beat. She felt a surge of emotion— part joy, part relief, part something else entirely.

It couldn't be, could it? Was Amelia back?

She raced to the front entrance and rapped loudly on the sliding doors, then tapped her feet impatiently as the overweight security guard shuffled across and slowly unlocked it, drew her to the front desk, insisted she sign in as she'd signed in almost every Saturday since their infamous coup. Like she might have turned into a terrorist overnight.

Eventually he waved her through, and she raced for the elevator, jabbing at the Up button over and over until the damn doors opened and closed and it began to ascend.

By floor four, her head went *ping!*

It had to be Hank. Hadn't he mentioned something about popping in to help her get the final pages out?

Hank rarely worked Saturdays. Monty would not let him; they didn't pay him enough for that. But she was glad of the offer and hadn't tried to dissuade him this time. She needed the help, and she didn't want to work alone.

By floor six she was sure it was the cleaners.

They usually came through at night. Perhaps someone had simply left the lights on?

When she finally arrived at the eighth floor and rushed through *Eve's* open doors, she couldn't have been more surprised.

"Cripes, Monty, you don't need to look quite so shocked," Alex called out to her from the editor's office at the back. "The editor's letter's not going to write itself."

Then she swivelled back to her screen while Monty stared at her a moment longer, as if expecting her to vanish into thin air, just as Amelia had done. She couldn't remember the last time she'd seen the deputy editor work weekends. Remembered that long, dark day she first refused to come in, the darkness all Amelia's as she ranted and railed about the "traitorous lowlife" and how she suspected the woman would let her down eventually and how she could bloody well kiss any future payrise goodbye.

Monty had nodded along, as she always did, and agreed it was slack, because it was, a little. They were always under the pump that final week; the more hands on deck, the better. But it was also incredibly brave, and she secretly envied Alex's sleep-in, quietly admired the guts it must have taken for her to stay under the covers, knowing the consequences and snoozing anyway.

Of course Monty hadn't said any of that to Amelia. She rarely crossed swords with her best friend, and she wondered about this now as she made her way to her desk and brought her own computer to life.

We were supposed to be friends, she thought, keying in her password and accessing the cover template, but it was an uneven friendship, everyone knew that, a one-way street heading straight to Amelia's door. They might have started out as equals, but they had soon morphed into something else entirely.

Something very off-balance.

As she pulled up last month's cover and began discarding the old image, rearranging the parts, searching for the model shot she had put aside for this month, it occurred to Monty what she was really feeling when she spotted that office light from the street below. Sure, there was some joy and relief, but there was something darker too. She had felt the bitter sting of disappointment. Not at the thought of Amelia returning (for all her faults she loved her friend, was genuinely worried about her), but at the thought of everything returning to the way it was, of the scales tipping back in Amelia's favour. Of thinking, *I'll say I'm sorry for lying about Angus and I'll refuse the House job and everything will go back to normal.*

But she didn't want to go back. Not now. Not ever.

"You finally finished the SOS story," Alex said, appearing at her desk. "You did a good job. It looks a little dark, but it also looks so empowering."

Monty nodded. "You didn't make it easy."

The other woman laughed. "I learned from the master! You can blame Amelia for that." Her smile dropped. "I honestly thought we might see her here today. I don't know why."

"Me too."

"Do you have any idea where she is? Has there been any news at all? Any clues?"

Monty dropped her head to one side. "I thought you only wanted to focus on the magazine, Alex." She knew she was being unfair, but it was the first real sign that the woman even cared.

"I'm curious, that's all," she replied defensively. "And I'm not completely heartless either."

"Sorry," Monty said. "I'm beginning to feel very stressed. She still hasn't called her parents, and she always calls her parents. Always. I'm wondering when we should start panicking."

Alex brought a hand to her lips. It looked a little like it was trembling. "You're seriously worried, aren't you Monty? Do they think… Is there any chance something *bad* might have happened?"

"Oh God, I hope not." Oh God, she couldn't handle that, not again. "Her dad says he's calling in the police if she hasn't contacted anyone by tomorrow."

Alex's hand definitely shook now and she dropped it back down. But Monty had seen it, and wondered now why Alex was suddenly acting so… *strange.*

"Anyway, the fact still remains, you were right about one thing," Monty said. "Worrying about Amelia won't get this magazine done. It's just you and me now, Alex. You think you're up for it?"

The deputy quickly nodded. "Good idea," she said. "Let's return our focus to that."

"Oh, and Hank's coming in, too, a bit later. To help out."

"Great," Alex called as she walked back to her desk. "He better be bringing coffee and chocolate."

Hank brought nothing but his knack for hard work and innate design talent, and as they pulled together to tweak the last designs, create a cover in record time, and help Alex pull off her first-ever Acting Editor's letter, Monty promised herself she'd brave Lizzie again and demand Gerry hire Hank as her replacement. He was so much more than eye candy. He deserved the senior role at *Eve*.

And *she* deserved *House & Feather*!

Monty was still no closer to understanding why Amelia had upped sticks and vanished, but she would do as Beryl insisted and start looking out for herself again.

It was her turn to jump ship.

~~~

As the last of the afternoon light filtered through the office, the three colleagues stood in the centre of the room, coffee cups in hand, and stared at the large internal wall. The entire issue, including the cover and advertisements, had been copied onto small, A6-sized pieces of paper and pasted up in order of how it would appear in the magazine. Monty did this every issue to see how the designs worked, if any sections jarred, and to get a feel for the overall flow.

"Not too shabby," Hank said, and Monty flashed him a smile.

Yeah, they'd done okay, considering.

"When will you go down to the printers?" Alex asked Monty. "First thing Monday?"

Monty surprised them both by shaking her head. "Amelia usually checks the cover, so *you* can fly to Melbourne this time, Alex."

Hank looked as stunned as Alex at the suggestion, but it was Alex who had to hide her face in her mug lest they see the tears that were welling in her eyes.

Later, after Hank had waved them farewell and raced to meet friends for the night, the two women remained in the belly of the darkening office, something holding them there, something pulling them together.

"Why do you hate her so much?" Monty asked, watching as Alex
~~~

sipped from the mug again, this time swallowing something much stronger.

Monty had a secret stash of vodka in her desk's bottom drawer and ignored Alex's raised eyebrows as she produced the bottle and proceeded to pour them both a shot.

"What are you talking about?" Alex said.

"You've never liked Amelia. Why?"

"It's not that I don't *like* her," she replied, a blush creeping into her cheeks. Then, to Monty's own arched eyebrows, a quick, "No seriously, it's not that. It's just…"

"Fear and loathing?"

She raised a shoulder, stared out at the encroaching darkness. "Something like that." She thought about it more seriously. "She's so rigid and demanding. So obsessed! Slightly psycho, perhaps."

She smiled but Monty could tell she wasn't joking.

Alex said, "I get that you need to be tough to be a good editor, but I don't believe you need to play favourites or demand that your team give up their own lives, their own *loves*, to make a magazine successful. Like you." She waved her cup at Monty. "You've given up everything for this magazine, don't you sometimes wonder if it's all worth it?"

Monty laughed, surprising them both. "If you're referring to my 'spinsterhood', you can take your mind out of the 1950s, Alex."

"No, it's not just that. We've all wondered why you stayed; we know you've been headhunted time and again." She took another sip and winced, not used to hard liquor. "No offence, but *Eve* would survive perfectly fine without you, and so would Amelia for that matter."

"It's more complicated than that."

"You keep saying that."

"Because it's true. There's a backstory, yeah? There's stuff you don't know."

Alex rolled her eyes. "I'm sick of hearing that! It's utter bullshit!" Her voice was rising, the blush replaced by splotches of anger. "I don't care what your background, nobody should act like a God, wielding power over their minions, forcing us to work ridiculous hours and make choices between family and work. Family and *her*, is what it really is. Every single day was a test, and every single day I failed."

Now Monty tried not to roll her eyes. "Oh, diddums! You're still here aren't you? You've got an amazing job. She gave you an amazing opportunity."

"Yes, and she never let me forget it." She sighed. "Sorry, but you get it good from her. You're one of Amelia's favourites, you and Brianna—and God knows why she likes Brianna so much—so you'll never fully understand, but she treats the rest of us like we're inconsequential, dispensable. Without talent."

"She doesn't believe that. She admires you all. Says you're the best writer in the building."

Alex looked shocked by that, not quite believing the sentiment. "So why not show it?"

"She has her reasons."

Alex was now beyond eye rolling. She slammed the cup onto the table and stood up. "I'm going home to my family."

Monty watched her pack her things and suddenly felt the urge to explain. Perhaps it was time. Perhaps it was long overdue.

"Amelia was badly hurt by a man once—" she began, but Alex was already moving towards the exit.

"We've all had bad breakups, Monty," she sang back as she walked. "She's not the first person to be dumped, and she won't be the last."

"She wasn't *dumped*, Alex. She was brutally assaulted."

Alex stopped.

"She nearly died, was in a coma for weeks. Took her years to get over it. I'm not sure she ever has."

The deputy had turned around, and Monty was surprised to see the horror in her eyes. What she didn't know was that it was herself she was horrified by. All her loathing, all her venom now felt misplaced.

"When… when did it happen?"

"Oh, well before your time. Thirteen years ago when she was a young thing, travelling overseas. It was extremely brutal and… I wasn't there to help." She shuddered. Didn't want to go into that. "So, you know, she kind've shut down after that; it was the only way she could move forward, survive. She put everything into her career, never trusted anyone again. I know it's wrong, I know what she demands of us all is wrong, but well, there is a reason. She's not psycho." She smiled. "Or perhaps she is, a little bit, but there's a reason for it. And it's the reason she's married to the job and expecting everyone else to be too. Because *Eve* is the only thing that keeps the wolves at bay. It's the only thing that keeps her sane."

Alex blinked quickly, trying to process it all. She sat back down, her bag in her lap and exhaled loudly. "Wow, okay, wow."

"Sorry to throw that at you, and I'm sure she'd be furious with me for even mentioning it, but—"

"No, thank you! My God, I wish I'd known!" They might have had a better relationship if she had.

"Please don't tell anyone," Monty said, gathering her own things now. "I don't know where Amelia is or if she'll ever return, but if she does I don't think she'll want your sympathy. She never handled sympathy very well."

Alex nodded, pretended to zip her lips, then stood back up and followed the art director out, shutting off lights as they made their way to the elevator.

"Try not to give it another thought," Monty said as they rode the lift down. "No matter what, no matter the reasons, Amelia is a bloody good editor and that's never changed. You mustn't treat her differently."

Alex nodded but she disagreed. How could she not? Everything was different now. So much of Amelia's ferocity and determination made sense.

And now what Alex's husband did was so much worse.

SHEPPERDIN VILLAGE

As the motley search party gathered outside the police station—pulling on hats, slathering on sunscreen—the police commander watched them through the bay window and wondered if this would all come back to bite him.

It was Sunday morning in Shepperdin, and half the town could not believe he had not called in the hounds earlier. The other half, the half Geoff's wife was in, scoffed at the mere suggestion that Amy was officially missing and had come to some dark and devious end. They believed Tom's theory that she'd taken off, had always known the woman was not a happy camper. "Too good for the likes of us" was how Lennie the publican put it. "Too bloody up herself" was Lennie's girlfriend's take on it.

But what could he do? Amy had been missing for six days now and still no word to anyone, including her parents and her beloved son. As far as Geoff was concerned, that was "officially missing" no matter where you pitched your tent.

So he watched as the locals from that first camp assembled, frowns on some faces, excitable grins on others—because there was nothing like searching for a body to bring out the ghoul in all of us—and waited while his deputy walked between them, handing out smudged photocopies of the search rules and protocols—*who knew searching for a corpse could be so fraught?*—and wondered again about Tom and why he wasn't here, helping.

"On his way to Sydney, mate," Harry told him when he rocked up that morning, not to search for Amy—he was firmly in the second camp—but to bring in some of Amy's clothes so they could dress up a look-alike mannequin and erect it outside the train station in case it twigged anyone's memory. The stationmaster hadn't been much use. Didn't recall seeing Amy that Monday but said she often took the train to Sydney, so he'd probably stopped noticing.

Tom would be on the outskirts of Sydney now, driving Phil to his grandparents' place so he could remove him from the small-town gossip that had finally infiltrated the schoolyard and caused friction between his friends.

"Poor kid is shattered by all this," Harry told Geoff, "and so is Tom."

Geoff thought that was a good plan and didn't blame either of them. The problem was the rest of the town might. It looked like Tom was running away when he should have been stepping up and leading the search.

Because to believe one thing was fine, to be confident and hopeful was all very well, but until there was proof, you had to keep your options open, and one option was very bleak indeed, whether you wanted to face it or not. He wished his old mate could understand how bad it made him look. How disinterested. How guilty.

Geoff was just pulling on his hat and glancing around for his own water bottle when a familiar face caught his eye. There was a woman walking determinedly through the crowd, but instead of hiking boots and a sheet of instructions, she wore glittery sandals and a sheepish expression. He recognised that expression, had seen it many times before.

"Can we have a quiet word?" she said when she reached the station door, and he nodded, ushering her past the other officers and inside.

Then he told the team to head off without him and dumped his hat back on his desk. He wouldn't be going anywhere for a bit. He had a pretty good idea what this woman was here to tell him, and if he was right, it was about to blow the case wide open.

SARISI ISLAND

Millie spotted Nicholas striding through the courtyard of the Casa Delfino, apron around his waist, and felt a stab of disappointment. If Nico was back at his post, waiting tables tonight, that meant Effie must still be in Athens.

She tried to find her smile as she approached. She liked Nico more than she cared to admit, but she had bigger fish to fry. Fortunately, Nico was in a world of his own and didn't notice her close in or the way her eyes widened as he yanked the apron off, dumped it in a flower bed, and swept out of the courtyard and away.

"Nico!" she called out, but he had his head down and didn't hear, so she strapped her bag tight across her chest and chased after him.

It wasn't until he had reached the far end of the esplanade, the southern end of the beach where the fishing boats bobbed about, that she was able to catch up.

"Hey, Nico! Wait up!" she yelled this time, almost out of breath.

He swung around and stopped, looking surprised to see her. Hesitated for a moment, then started back towards her.

"Hey, Millie," he called out.

"What's going on? Are you okay?"

"Yeah. No. Not really."

She smiled. "So is that a yes or a no?"

Nicholas did not smile back. "Bloody Effie!" he said and she nodded.

"Still in Athens?"

"What? No, she's back."

"She's *back*?"

"Yes, but she hasn't brought Theo with her. I could kill her!"

Millie could tell he wasn't joking, was barely holding his anger in check.

"She's left him in bloody Athens for the weekend, can you believe it?"

"He usually returns on weekends?"

"Yes! But *she's* just been over there, says she's already caught up with him so what's the point of dragging him home? Like what am I? Chopped liver?"

"Um…"

"Don't I deserve to see Theo? Didn't I give up my whole life for that kid? She was so worried about him. Said he had few friends, no father figure, so I moved from the other side of the world, but she's forgotten all that now! Why else does she think I'm here? For the fishing? To work like a galley slave in her stupid bloody restaurant?"

"No, I'm sure, she—"

"She is a selfish cow is what she is. She doesn't need me anymore. Theo's happy at school, so my needs… pft!"

"He's a teenager, Nico. Maybe he wants to hang in the city for the weekend?" Millie said trying to draw him down to a nearby bench seat, but he wasn't having it, was striding backwards and forwards now, gesticulating with his hands, his temper growing. "Maybe he had some plans over there?"

"*We* had plans, Theo and me! We were going to watch a game this weekend, with Kos, it was all booked in, a boys' weekend. She's just jealous because she wasn't invited! She's jealous because he loves me and she can't handle sharing him!"

"That can't be true," Millie said. "She asked you to come here, didn't she? She obviously wanted you to have some input."

"Then why leave him in Athens? I'm furious."

Millie could see that. "Listen, why don't you come back with me and we'll get something to eat, grab a bottle of wine, maybe drink it on the beach?"

"Nope, sorry. I-I need to get home. I'm too bloody angry."

"Fair enough. If you change your mind or you just need to talk, you know where to find me."

"Yeah, sure," he muttered, turning away.

As she watched him go, Millie felt a strong urge to follow,

to somehow ease this man's pain, but she had to shake the urge away and focus on her mission, the reason she was on the island in the first place.

She swivelled and turned back towards the Delfy.

~~~

The Greek woman had barely changed. Sure, she was a good deal heavier, but her legs were still impossibly long, her hair still thick and unwieldy, although shorter now, like a curly black helmet on the top of her head, and as she barked instructions to someone at the door to the kitchen, Millie could see she still had the fire in her belly, the bossiness in her manner.

She waited a beat, then said, "G'day, Effie."

Effie's back stiffened for a moment, and Millie thought she must have imagined it as the Greek turned to face her with a wide, warm smile.

"Oh my God! Miss Australia!" she said, striding the two paces to draw her into an embrace. "I thought I had missed you! I was so worried!"

Millie smiled and hugged her back. She wanted to believe that, she really did.

There were no words for a few minutes, just a long, trembling cuddle, then Effie said, "Come, sit! Just... just give me one minute," and she strode back to the kitchen.

Millie wondered whether she was going to run away again but scoffed at herself and selected a seat by the window. Surely she was just being paranoid.

After what seemed like ages, Millie's paranoia now setting in, Effie did return, this time with a bottle of ouzo, two shot glasses and a bowl of olives and *dolmades*. She dumped them on the table, then scraped a chair back and sat across from the Australian.

"You look good," she said, pouring them both a shot.

"So do you."

"Nah, I'm fat girl now! Stealing too much food from the kitchen."

Millie smiled. "Well, it suits you."

Effie held her glass up and said, "*Yamas!*" then waited until they had both drunk before pouring them another.

She laughed. "Remember when Aggy caught us in the chapel?
~~~

With Father Karpathakis's wine?"

Millie laughed too. "God, she was so angry! At the time I thought she was a party pooper, but bloody hell, Effie, in our condition? No wonder she was cranky! We shouldn't have been drinking!"

Effie's smile deflated and she stared at her glass. "I didn't think you were ever coming back. You said you would never return."

"And I wasn't going to. But something happened. I needed to come." Millie shook the dark memory away. "Anyway, how have you been?"

"Me? Good! Never better."

"And your boy?"

Effie shrugged. "He is at school. In Athens."

"So I hear. Getting a good education, that's great."

She shrugged again, helped herself to an olive.

"I remember when I first met you Effie, you were pregnant with him. You were so defiant, so proud. So…" She smiled sadly. "Well, so different to me. Did you ever go back? To Paros? To Theo's dad?"

"No." She reached for her glass and poured them another shot, her lips wedged downwards as she did so. "He was no good. Bad man. I stayed here, worked with Aggy for a bit, then I took over the Delfy."

"I know," Millie said as she glanced around the room. "You've done so well. The place looks amazing. I remember it used to be a bit of a dive."

"Thank you." She held her glass up and said, "*Yamas!*"

They drank again and then Millie said, "Don't you miss him?"

Effie wiped her mouth. "Who?"

"Your son, Theo. Athens seems so far away."

"It's only a ferry ride." She dropped her glass on the table and got up. "I must get back. Dinner rush starts soon."

Millie took a deep breath.

It was time. Hell, it was long overdue.

She called out: "I need to see him, Effie."

The woman was midway to the kitchen and stopped in her tracks. She did not look back. "See who?"

Millie smiled. "You know who I'm talking about. I need to know where he is. You need to tell me."

Effie swung around, but this time there was no smile. "Why? Why you need to do this?"

"I just… I just need it, Effie."

"It is bullshit!" She strode back and leaned down towards Millie's startled face. "You think seeing him will help? How it help? It can't stop what happened. It can't make it all good for you."

"No, but it might help me get some closure; it might help me move on."

Effie stared at her for a long while, then straightened up, her voice lighter, almost a whisper. "Don't do this, Millie. It will only break your heart."

"My heart's already broken, Effie, you know that."

She nudged her lips downward and collected the glassware from the table. "Anyway," she said, almost flippantly, "I don't know where he is."

"But…"

"Only Aggie knows, and she is dead now, so you waste your time. You need to go home."

"I'm not going anywhere until—"

Effie slammed the ouzo bottle back down. "Even if I did know, I would not tell you! It will not help!" Millie looked at her aghast. "It is for your own good, Millie. You don't understand this now, but it is good for everybody. Just leave it alone!" Her voice softened again. "*Please*. Everything has settled now. You will only hurt him. You will only hurt yourself. You have to stop thinking about him. Just let him go!"

Then she left the bottle and fled into the kitchen, leaving Millie gasping in her wake. That had not gone at all as she had expected. She couldn't understand Effie's aggression, her reticence.

She was once so brave and strong. Now she was acting like a jittery child, and it didn't make an ounce of sense.

~~~

Nicholas stood on the other side of the restaurant door, perplexed.

What the hell was that about?

Having circled back soon after running into Millie, wanting to apologise and take her up on her drink offer, he found her deep in conversation with his cousin, and it all sounded very obscure.
~~~

Wasn't she here to find some nuns? If so, who was this bloke she was suddenly asking about, and what if anything did he have to do with Effie?

More tellingly, why did Effie sound so terrified?

He heard a chair scrape across the floor, so he ducked back through the courtyard and down the side of the taverna to the kitchen.

Perhaps it was time to confront his cousin.

EVE MAGAZINE

Alex was left floating in the wind. Unanchored.

As the deputy editor made her way home from the *Eve* office that Saturday, she couldn't help hearing Monty's words like a grand denouement at the end of a long and exhausting mystery.

"Brutally assaulted."

"Nearly died."

"In a coma for weeks."

It wasn't the explanation she was expecting. It wasn't the answer she wanted. Now everything was out of balance. She didn't know how to steady the ship or where to go from here. Her loathing of the editor had sustained Alex for so long, had driven her on, despite herself, despite what her husband said. Now... Well, how could she continue to loathe a woman who had been treated so badly? A woman she was now supposed to *sympathise* with? And how could she forgive herself for all she had thought and said about the editor?

How could she forgive her husband?

When she reached her house, Tony's white van was back in its usual spot. She gave it a wide berth, like it was a loaded weapon, then strode to the front door, took a few steadying breaths, and let herself in.

"Hey babe!" Tony called out, the TV blaring from the living room. "Kids are asleep, there's leftovers in the oven."

She stepped across to him and tried to smile, tried to thank him but the only words she could think to say were, "How could you?"

He glanced from the TV screen to her, eyes wide. "What?"

"It was you, wasn't it? At Amelia's place last Saturday morning. I wondered what took you so long."

She had avoided this conversation for days, but the way his eyes didn't quite meet hers, the way his jaw began to tense, told her everything.

"What were you trying to achieve?" she said. "What were you going to do? Bully my boss into being nice to me?"

Tony reached for the remote control and switched off the television, then turned in his chair to meet her head-on. "I paid her a quick visit after that emergency call-out, that's all. I just wanted a chat, a face-to-face."

"Why would you do that? What did you *say*?"

"I wanted to appeal to her as a human being, babe! I wanted to show her pictures of our kids, to show—"

"*Pictures of our kids?* Are you crazy?"

He had grabbed Alex's hands and was dragging her to the ground in front of him now, his eyes imploring, his tone desperate. "I wanted her to understand where you were coming from, that's all. Why you don't work weekends anymore. That you aren't being slack or lazy or whatever she thinks. That you have other commitments. That you have a *life*."

"Oh Tones…"

"It's just that you seem so sad and angry all the time, and it's all my fault. Don't look at me like that! It's true. I know you want to do the right thing by her, that you *want* to go in and do your bit, but it's because of me that you don't. I wanted her to see that, to understand, to stop blaming you."

"Tony, you're not the reason—"

"I'm the one who moans every time you get home from work late, and I'm the one who bullied you into staying back on weekends. I'm as bad as Amelia!"

She was shaking her head. "But you were right, Tony. I shouldn't have to work weekends to get the work done."

"You went in today."

"Because we're down one person, one very crucial person I might add, and extremely behind. But if I *ever* ended up editing a magazine—and I'm not even sure I want to anymore—but if I ever did I would make sure I had enough staff, that we worked hard enough during the hours we have to get the magazine done. I would incentivise my team, not intimidate and bully them into doing overtime."

"See! Listen to you! You're amazing." Tony looked at his wife with awe. It was the kind of look she had never received from Amelia. "That's what I wanted to tell her. I wanted Amelia to understand that."

"I'm not amazing, Tony, I just differ to her, that's all. We have different ways of working." Different motivations she learned today. "That's why we clash. That's all it is."

She pulled herself up and into his lap, and they hugged for several minutes, then she released him and nudged her eyebrows together. "What did she say? When you said all of that. How did she react? She must have gone ballistic!"

"No, that's the weird thing. She said, 'You're right. She's a good mum.'"

"Really?"

"Yes. She was actually quite nice, damn her. I was expecting a monster."

Alex smiled. *Bloody Amelia. Trust her to charm the husband.*

"I'm sorry," he said. "I know I was out of line. But she was cool with it. We spoke for about ten minutes, and then she said you'd get your chance and I should stop worrying."

"Hang on, what? *My chance?*"

"Yeah! I wanted to tell you, but then I'd have to admit I'd gone to see her. But yeah, she said, 'Alex will be an editor before she knows it' or something like that. And I didn't... well, I didn't know that she was going to piss off like that, leave you in the top job..."

"She didn't just piss off, Tony, she's vanished. Everyone's extremely worried."

He sat back and could barely meet her eyes again.

"She hasn't been seen since last Friday. You saw her on Saturday. Did she say anything? Give any indication that she was going away?"

"No, nothing."

"And what was she like when you left her?"

"I didn't *do* anything to her! I promise. Nothing happened!"

She stared at him aghast. "Of course nothing happened! Jesus, Tony." Did he honestly think she believed otherwise?

He looked panicked. "It's just... shit, Alex. I could have been the last person to see her alive. Maybe they'll try to pin it on me."

"We don't even know if anything's happened to her yet, Tony."

Do we?

He was watching her and he sensed some doubt. "What if she doesn't show up, or worse, she turns up dead? I could be in big trouble! I know some old woman saw me at her house, some neighbour. They could think I had something to do with it!"

"They? Who is this 'they'?"

He faltered. He whispered, "You."

She pulled him towards her and kept him at her breast as she patted his hair down and made soothing sounds. "Oh, Tones." She sighed. "No wonder you've been weird lately. How can you possibly believe I could ever suspect you of hurting anyone? Even my boss? Stop being so silly and get that out of your head."

As she continued stroking his hair and felt his body melt into hers, Alex wondered about what Tony had said and tried very hard to stop the doubts that were indeed creeping up.

Like: What really happened when Tony met up with her boss? And did Amelia simply smile and agree that Alex deserved to be the editor? If that was true, then Amelia had had a personality transplant.

Alex held her husband tighter and tried to shake those doubts away.

Of course Tony had nothing to do with it.

He wouldn't hurt a fly.

Would he?

SHEPPERDIN VILLAGE

Tom would not have recognised her if they had passed in the street. Oh, she still had that pointy nose and the flyaway hair, but now it was dyed an extreme cherry-red colour and she had a stack of makeup on. Her clothes were grander, too, her heels ridiculously high, and she was clearly someone important because she had a posse of younger things at those heels, racing out of the elevator and towards the foyer with her. No, *behind* her, following as if she was the Messiah.

"Monty!" he called out and she stopped and looked up, like she'd heard a ghost.

She swung around, causing her apostles to almost stumble at her feet.

He was standing just on the other side of the security desk. Had waited three hours for her to appear, and he wasn't going to let her vanish again.

He called again, louder this time, "Where is my wife?"

The young things looked across at him with concern, so he quickly added, "What have you done with Amy?"

Monty's expression morphed from curiosity to surprise to what looked a little like fear, and her mouth opened and closed, opened and closed, while the minions stared from Monty to this new invader and back again. *Who was this madman who had caused such a stir in their otherwise unflappable leader?*

She collected herself quickly, the consummate professional, and turned back to the bemused group. "I'll meet you in the conference room later."

One or two hesitated and she shot them a frown. "Do I have to repeat myself?"

They scuttled off, several glancing back, worried, while she wedged a smile to her face and took a step towards Tom.

"Thomas," she said, her tone flat.

"Monty," he replied.

"It's Montana now."

"Of course it is."

She frowned, recognising an insult when she heard one, then said, "Shall we get a coffee?"

Montana was pointing to the automatic glass doors that spilled out to the bustling street beyond, but he shook his head firmly.

"This isn't a courtesy call. I want to know where my wife is. And I want to know now."

"I don't—" She stopped and glanced around, noticing all the eyes upon her, the security guards, bored visitors, several colleagues who were passing. "Can we at least move this to my office, please?"

He shrugged and let her lead him back to the elevator and up. They did not speak as they ascended even though they had the elevator to themselves, and he wondered whether she was gathering her nerves or fabricating her lies.

The doors swept open at the tenth floor to reveal a glossy marble interior with a large gold sign that read *House & Feather*. He heard the general buzzing of phones and idle conversation but kept his eyes fixed to Montana's back as she waved the ogling receptionist off, then swept past her and into the main office. There were more ogling glances in there, the staffers now silent as she marched on and towards a separate, glassed office in the farthest corner. Montana stopped outside at a desk where a young man was seated. He was dressed in black from top to toe and had a Sanskrit tattoo up his neck.

"Hold all my calls, Pascal. Oh and fetch us some coffees would you?"

"Of course, Montana," he said, barely glancing at the interloper.

She held the door to her office open and waved Tom through, then shut the door behind her, staring out for just a moment longer as though plotting her escape. Eventually, slowly, she turned around to face him.

"What exactly is this about?" she said, shoulders back, still standing by the exit.

He smiled widely, surprising her. "It's good to see you too, *Montana.*" Then he added, "We were fond of each other once."

"We were also young and stupid." She swept past him to take her seat behind the large wooden desk and waved him into the chair in front. "What do you want? I haven't got much time."

He glanced around as he sat down. "You've done all right for yourself. Pretty fancy office. And what a title! Creative director, that's very impressive."

Her eyebrows crinkled together.

"I had some time to kill in the foyer, waiting for you to appear."

She smiled grimly. "Do I need to ask a third time?"

"Amy's missing."

"Amy?"

"Millie. Amelia. Whatever you want to call her. She's gone." He spread his fingers wide like he was releasing a dove.

Montana frowned and leaned forward. "When?"

"Like you don't know."

"*When,* Thomas?"

"A week now. How do you *not* know that? Aren't you in the media? It's all over the news! Oh, that's right." He glanced around again. "This isn't news, it's fluff."

She ignored that comment, her expression now stony. (In fact, Montana had heard something about a missing woman, somewhere in the country, but it hadn't clicked until now. Amy Wilson was her old friend Millie Malone.) "When you say missing, do you mean—"

"I mean she's vanished. Left me and our boy. Just pissed off."

She leaned back. "Did she say where…?"

"Just slunk off at the crack of dawn. No goodbye, not even a note. Just took off like we meant nothing."

"But it's only been a week, Thomas, how do you know she won't be back?"

"She's gone, Monty, and you know that as well as I do, so you can cut the crap and tell me where the hell my wife is."

"But…" She held her palms out. "Why do you think I would know?"

"Because you two were best buds once."

"Yes, *once.* A long time ago. The prehistoric age."

"And yet she had your phone number. I saw it in her address book the other day."

"So? We were school friends, remember? Of course she had my number."

"It was a *mobile* phone number." He smiled. "No mobiles in the prehistoric age."

Montana blanched as he knew she would. *He had her!* He had her exactly where he wanted her, and as the door clicked open behind him, he said, "I want to know exactly where my wife is and I want to know now!"

The well-dressed assistant approached with two eco-mugs in hand and didn't say a word as he placed one in front of Tom and then handed one to Montana. She gave him a very subtle shake of her head, but Tom saw it. He knew what that meant.

"Shall I ask young Pascal here then? Shall I? Perhaps he knows something?"

Tom stared at Pascal, who met his eyes with a vacant stare. He looked like a model strutting down a catwalk, bored, disinterested.

"Did you see my wife in here, Pascal?" Tom persisted. "Maybe you're the one who booked the ticket for her, hey? Maybe you helped her escape."

Pascal's expression did not change as he glanced across to Montana again, then left the office, and Tom rolled his eyes as he turned back.

"Wow you've got them well trained, I'll give you that. But I'm sure a copper could beat it out of him in no time. That tattoo's fooling nobody."

Montana watched the scene with growing annoyance. "What the hell do you want, Thomas?" she said at last. "Why do you think I have any answers for you? Or Pascal for that matter. Why are you even here now? Not at home searching for Millie?"

"Because she's not at home, Monty. You know that as well as I do. And it's Amy now! *Amy!*"

"Okay, sorry, but I don't know anything!"

"Yes you do. She called you! I know she called you!"

Montana reached for her mug and held it to her breast while she considered how best to play this. Eventually she placed the mug back down and said, "Okay, sure, you're right." She held a manicured finger up. "But only about one thing. Mil... *Amy* did call me. A few months ago. Asking about those days, reminiscing I guess."

"And?"

"And nothing! I told her they were best left in the past and we'd all moved on and to let it go."

"Let what go?"

She dipped her head to one side. "You know what I'm talking about, Thomas."

"It's Tom now. I don't go in for fancy names anymore. And neither did Amy until, oh, *a few months ago*. Suddenly she's all restless, suddenly I'm not good enough for her anymore. I knew something was up." He paused. "She met with you didn't she? You got her thinking."

Again the palms were out, but they were shaking now. She was nervous. "We just... Look, we had a quick coffee, Thomas. Tom. That's all it was. Just two friends meeting for a catch-up."

"You talked about *him*, didn't you? You told her to go back."

She stared at him. "I don't know what you mean."

He shook his head as he reached into his jacket, then pulled out a folded piece of paper and flung it towards her, missing the desk so she had to reach down and pick it up from the floor where it had landed.

Montana knew what it was even before she had unfolded it and spread it out in front of her. Of course she knew. Had read every word, overseen the design.

It was creased but glossy, had been ripped from a magazine— *her magazine*—and showed a series of shots, of two models on a beach, of a photographer, lens poised, of a thirty-something woman with cherry-red locks and an index finger up. She is directing the shoot while one of the models, a dark, handsome man, looks on, and behind him, an old castle swallows up half the skyline. You didn't need to read the column of text down the side to know where these photos were taken.

"That's you, *Montana*. That's you on Sarisi Island."

She straightened the page out, caressing the glossy paper, her hands trembling ever so slightly. Then she reached for her coffee and took a gulp.

"So," she said, exhaling with the word. "I went to Greece for a shoot. So what?"

"My wife saw that in your stupid magazine. It got her wondering. It got her questioning. It made her restless." She said nothing. "Did you see him on the island?"

"What? Who?"

"That Greek sleazebag! I keep forgetting about the guy on the ferry. I'm such an *idiot*. When she took off for Sarisi all those years ago, I thought it was for the convent. I'd heard what they do. But... Jesus, I had it all wrong. She was looking for him, wasn't she? All that time."

"Convent? Him? What are you talking about? You're making no sense!"

"Like you have no idea. Did you run into him and then tell my wife? Did you make her want to desert her beloved boy, her *loving husband* for some... some wog she met for five seconds on a fucking ferry thirteen years ago?"

Montana looked shocked by his words and placed the cup back on the table, then scrunched her eyes shut as if trying to think. When she opened them again she seemed calmer, almost relieved and it made him frown.

She said, "You think Millie flew back to Sarisi. You think she's in Greece. Looking for that... that guy from the ferry? The one she spoke to while she was getting a coffee?"

He hesitated, his own eyes squinting. "Of course. Where else would she be?"

She sat back in her seat. "Okay, now it makes sense."

He leaned forward. "What? What makes sense? What are you saying?"

Montana pushed her chair away from her desk and stood up. She walked past him and across the room, then swung the glass door wide.

"I'm done here," she said. "I've got a conference to run."

Tom stared at her without moving. "That's it? That's all you're going to tell me?"

She waved a hand out the door, and for just a moment it looked like he wasn't going to budge, then he reached for the clipping on her desk, folding it and shoving it back into his pocket as he got to his feet.

"Sure, keep your secrets, what do I care?" he said, walking

towards her now. "Doesn't change the fact that it's not my fault anymore, it's all on you." He stopped inches from her face. "You need to speak to the police; this is all your doing. Amy was happy. *We* were happy. And then she spoke to you and booked a flight to Greece."

He stepped through the door and towards Pascal, flashing him a scowl as he began to move away, but then he heard the word "Good," and he spun around like he'd just been shot.

"What did you say?"

Montana was closing her door, and for a split second she looked panicked, but then she pushed her shoulders back and held his stare.

"I'm sorry, Tom, but I hope she went back. I honestly do. I hope she got the hell away from you and that bloody awful farm and her boring bloody life, and I hope she found what she was looking for. I hope she found what she needed."

He couldn't believe what he was hearing. His face turned a deep shade of red, and Pascal looked up alarmed now, half standing from his chair. But Montana gave him another subtle head shake and stood her ground, turning steely eyes back to Tom.

"Just go home, Tom," she said calmly. "Go home to your boy."

Then she turned, closed the glass door and left him staring through it.

Montana inhaled deeply as she walked slowly back to her desk. Kept breathing in as she tapped her screen to life, waiting five more seconds before she dared to glance up and out. Tom had vanished, but Pascal was staring in at her with a look that said "What the fuck?"

Only then did she allow herself a long, loud exhale. Only then did she let her shoulders drop and a hand reach for her mouth.

"Oh God, Millie," she said, muffling the sound with her palm. "Oh you silly, silly girl, what have you done?"

SARISI ISLAND

Nicholas didn't get a chance to question Effie until Delfy's dinner rush was done, but he was a patient man and so he sat at the edge of the pier, smoking hand-rolled cigarettes and waiting until the last of the diners stumbled out and eventually Pete and then Pauly. It was only as the lights inside the Delfy began to dim that he made his approach, half-chilled from sitting outside for so long, half-warmed from his sense of outrage and anger.

He had no idea what the conversation between the two women had been about, but he was determined to get some straight answers for a change. Millie wasn't here looking for some nun, she was searching for a man, that much was obvious. But who? An old lover? And if so why didn't she tell him? Why lead him on?

Catalina's words kept circling through his brain—"She will hurt you, she is dangerous"—but they didn't make any sense and he needed them to make some sense. So he stubbed out his cigarette and strode swiftly across.

When she saw him, Effie did not look alarmed, just weary to the core. "I'm sorry about Theo," she said, "but he'll be back next weekend, so can we just drop it?"

"I'm not here about Theo."

"Oh?"

"What's going on? Who is this woman, really? Millie? Why is she here? I know she didn't come here to chew the fat with an old nun, and she's certainly not here for the sun. There's something going on."

Effie stopped, frowned. "You know her?"

"Yes, I know her! I've been keeping her company while you've been hiding out in Athens. You want to tell me why you've been hiding and what's really going on? What were you two talking about earlier?"

"You heard us?"

"Some of it. Who is this guy she wants to find? A past lover? Is that it?"

"You sound jealous."

"It's not that… It's… well, we've been getting to know each other. I like her. She's—"

"She is not for you," Effie said as if that was the final word on the subject, and it kindled his temper again.

"Piss off, Effie. It's none of your business who I—"

"I'm telling you!" she yelled. "This woman she is not some stupid backpacker you can sleep with and then throw away."

"I know that! I'm not an idiot! Bloody hell, Effie, I like Millie. A lot."

Effie took a step back looking horrified.

"Are you going to tell me what's going on, or do I have to go and drag it out of her?" he persisted.

"Just leave her alone!" Effie's voice was a roar now and it surprised him. But before he could react, she was shaking her head and softening her voice. "Please," she said, "I'm begging you, Nico, for everyone's sake, let it go."

"But…"

"You need to trust me on this, cousin. Please, just forget you ever met this woman; she is no good, she is dangerous!"

Catalina's words suddenly circled back to meet him, and he said, "I don't understand why you're all saying that." Millie seemed so sweet, so harmless, so benign. "Maybe if you tell me what's going on, I can—"

"Just stop!" Effie had a hand up, her voice more irritable now than angry. "Just go back to Melbourne, Nico. Just get a fucking life!"

He recoiled. "Fuck you too, Effie!"

Then he pushed a chair over on his way back out while Effie closed her eyes and hoped to God he'd keep walking.

It was probably just as well her eyes were closed because she did not see her cousin veer off the main road and head in the direction of

Joe-Joe's corner shop. And she did not see him glance around furtively before he snuck down the laneway and towards Catalina's door.

EVE MAGAZINE

When Monty strode into *Eve* on Monday morning, she realised it was Alex she expected to see seated at the editor's desk, not Amelia. Like she had given up on her friend completely. As it turns out, neither woman was there. Brianna informed her that Alex had caught an early flight to Melbourne to check the printing of the cover, and Amelia was still AWOL.

Still missing after more than a week. She remembered what Ron had said, how he'd call the police in if they hadn't heard by Sunday, and she turned back to Brianna and said, "Any visitors or phone calls for me?"

"No, except Alex. She called from the airport, said she needs to talk to you urgently about her husband or something."

"Tony?"

She shrugged.

"Okay, thanks. And no call from Amelia's folks? No word at all?"

She shrugged again, and Monty wandered across the office to her section, wondering why the parents weren't panicking yet. Ron said he'd call the police, so where were they? Why wasn't the office crawling with detectives? Why weren't they going through her things? Interrogating them all?

She stopped. Had a sudden thought. Slapped a palm to her head.

Oh God, she'd been such a fool!

She swept around and made a beeline for the elevator, yelling, "Brianna hold all my calls. I'll be back later."

Then she stabbed the button angrily.

~~~

Beryl Malone was far too relaxed.

Monty couldn't believe she hadn't noticed it before. Her relief at being let off the hook this time had clouded her judgement entirely.

"You know where she is, don't you?" she said the moment the older woman swung open her front door.

Beryl blinked rapidly as a blush crept into her cheeks, giving Monty all the answer she required. She pushed past Beryl and into the house where she found Ron on the couch this time, staring glumly at the TV. He could not meet Monty's eyes, and she realised he knew, too, but only recently by the look of him.

"Where is she?" Monty demanded, first of Ron, then back to Beryl.

"Can I get you something to drink, dear? Juice? Tea?"

"Beryl!" Monty said while Ron sighed and switched the TV on mute.

"She's okay, Monty. She's safe."

"You don't know that!" Ron retorted and Beryl rolled her eyes and revised her statement.

"I'm *sure* she's safe."

"So you *do* know where she is?" Monty was gripping the back of a dining room chair.

She went to nod and then stopped. "Not exactly. But I have a vague idea."

"Vague's the word for it!" growled Ron. "I've had enough."

He pulled himself up as though dragging a great weight from the lounge and shuffled towards the hallway like he was a hundred years old. He couldn't be more than sixty-five, Monty thought, watching him go. She remembered how he had changed when Amelia had first vanished, how she'd watched him age as the year dragged on. This time he looked like he'd added another decade overnight.

She turned back to Beryl, who was now standing by the window.

"So tell me! Where is she?"

"She went back. To Greece. To Sarisi."

Monty pulled the chair out from beneath the table and slumped into it.

She hadn't expected that.
~~~

Eventually she found her voice. "But… but she wouldn't… would she?"

"I would," Beryl snapped. "And about time too. What happened there, that day… it's haunted her for the past decade. Enough's enough. I'm glad she's finally trying to exorcise the ghosts."

"Exorcise?" Ron growled, shuffling back into the room. "She could get hurt! Or worse. Is that what you want?"

"I want her to *feel* something, Ron! *Anything!*" Beryl was growling too now. They were like two cats circling each other, knowing each other's moves, as though they had circled each other for years and were exhausted by the effort.

Beryl tapped a hand to her chest as if trying to still her heart. "Our baby used to be so happy and confident and carefree." She half smiled as she glanced back at Monty. "What did you all call her? Silly Millie?" Her smile deflated. "When she first came back, she was so cold. Just blank and cold, do you remember? She wasn't Silly Millie anymore; she wasn't my baby girl." Her eyes reached for Ron's. "You want her to stay cold, is that it? Stay boxed in and angry? To sleepwalk the rest of her life? Because of what some monster did to her? You think bubble-wrapping her away has made her happier? Do you? You tell him, Monty! You tell him just how happy our little girl is!"

Monty groaned. She was right. Amelia wasn't happy. Hadn't been happy for over a decade, and immersing herself in a busy career had not helped. Hadn't helped either of them in fact. She looked at Ron, but he wasn't ready to hear any of it.

"I want my baby girl back. I don't care what she's like. I just want…" He choked on the final words and Beryl stepped towards him, but he waved her off and shuffled out.

Monty met Beryl's eyes and saw that her bark had gone. She simply looked sad.

"I think we all got it terribly wrong, Monty. I think trying to forget the assault only made it all worse. And I'm sorry, not just for my baby, but for you."

"You *really* think she flew to Sarisi?" She was still trying to get her head around the concept. Never in a million years would she have guessed that.

She remembered the last time the conversation had come up. Fleur had mentioned a swimsuit shoot in the Greek islands, including

Santorini and Sarisi. The Greek Tourist Board was splashing money about, offering free trips to almost every magazine in the country in exchange for publicity. She remembered how Amelia had nixed the idea before it got up, saying something like, "That place still gives me the creeps."

That's how she and Fleur had ended up on Queensland's Hamilton Island, a glamorous enough location to shoot swimsuits, but nothing like Sarisi. Monty wondered about that now but shook the thought away, trying to focus on what Beryl was saying.

"Amelia said she was flying out last Saturday, that's what she told me. She said she was heading straight for Athens, then getting a direct flight to Santorini. Then…" She gulped. "Then she was going to try to make her way back to that island, she wasn't sure how. But she said it was important to go back, that she needed the time and space to get there."

"But why didn't you tell me? You know I've been worried sick!"

"I'm so sorry dear. But she begged me not to tell anybody, and she swore me to secrecy. She knew that Ron would not allow it, would try to stop her and persuade her to return. She knew you would too, all of you at *Eve*. She made me promise I wouldn't tell a soul."

"But why?"

"She needed the time and space to find him."

This sent a shiver racing down Monty's back. She gulped. "Him?"

Beryl nodded, dislodging a tear. "She said it was time. Long overdue, she said. She promised me she'd call as soon as she found him."

"Okay and has she? Called you I mean?"

Beryl's eyes flooded with tears, and her hand reached for her heart again. "No." She sniffed. "Not yet." Then, more confidently, "But she will! I just know it! Very soon."

Monty tried to digest this news, couldn't get her head around it. "I have to go over there. I don't care what she says. I have to find her, help her out."

Beryl shook her head firmly. "No, dear. I told you before. Amelia was adamant about this. She didn't want anyone following her."

"But…"

"We *all* need to let her grow up, Monty, let her face her own demons, and you, my dear…" She walked across the room and reached for Monty's hands, folded them into her own. "You need to get on with your own life. I never did quite understand why you stayed, why you helped so much."

"She's my best friend." Now Monty's voice was cracking.

Beryl nodded, squeezing her hands tighter. "But she's not your whole life. You need to get on with your own life."

Didn't she already know that? Hadn't she been telling herself that for twelve years?

The first year or two were easy. They patched each other up. But then it became habit, one she couldn't quite work out how to break. Was that what Amelia was doing, she wondered as she squeezed Beryl's hand back.

Was she helping me break the habit?

SHEPPERDIN VILLAGE

The Shepperdin police station was abuzz with activity when Tom burst in late Monday afternoon, having driven straight from the city, not even stopping to fill the car with petrol or his stomach with much-needed nourishment. The fuel gauge was as red as his mood. He needed to get this out. He needed to get this done. And he was thankful, yet again, that Phil was in safe hands, ensconced with Amy's family in their snobby Sydney suburb.

The Malones were cold and distant when he dropped Phil off, Ron barely able to look at him, and he understood their fears and hoped that the news he was about to give Geoffrey would clear his name and change all that.

"Hey!" he called out as the screen door behind him slammed with a thud and the uniformed officer on the front desk looked up with momentary panic. "You bastards need to talk to Monty Brennan! Now!"

The admitting sergeant relaxed a little when he realised it was Tom, but he knew the situation, everybody knew the situation now, and he was about to ask him to stand back when the superintendent appeared.

"*Tommo*," Geoff said, a warning sound in his tone. "We've been looking for you."

"Yeah, well, I went to Sydney, doing your job for you! Call your dogs off, Geoff! That bitch has sent her back to Greece! That's where she is!" There was spittle flying from Tom's lips. "She's sleeping her way around the Greek islands while I'm stuck here being branded a killer!"

Geoff stepped in front of the officer and released the latch to let Tom through. "Nobody's branded you anything." *Yet.* "Just take a deep breath and settle down, okay?"

"You settle down!" Tom yelled, glancing around to see that the buzz had stopped and several officers were now moving towards him, hands at their holsters.

Geoff held a palm out to his lackeys, just as Montana had done.

"Let's get to my office, mate, and you can tell me all about it."

As they walked across the room, Tom started up again.

"I've been dealing with your suspicions and accusations for days now, but I'm the victim here! My wife is exactly where I knew she'd be. She's on fucking holidays! And I've got two witnesses to prove it."

Geoff nodded as they walked, then bypassed his office and headed towards an interview room, nodding at his sergeant as he went.

It was only when they were seated that Tom took a breath and looked around. There was a uniformed officer standing guard at the door and another seated beside Geoff who had a folder in his hands. He placed it on the table as Tom frowned.

"What's going on?"

"I'm glad you're here. We have a few questions for you. Just some discrepancies we need to clear up."

"Hang on, *what*? You're still questioning *me*? You should be halfway to Sydney by now! Hauling Monty Brennan back here! She's the one with answers."

Geoff was writing something down in the folder. "Monty Brennan?"

"Amy's old school friend, *Montana*. She knows exactly where my wife is." He had the clipping out again. "She works at this magazine. See, this chick." He was stabbing a finger at Montana's creased face. "She went to this island, this place called Sarisi. She told Amy about some guy there. That's where Amy's gone. To see this fella. I promise you! Just talk to Montana. She'll set you straight."

Geoff took the page from him, glanced across it and then placed it in the folder.

"We'll get onto that later. For now, I want to talk to *you*."

He looked past him to the officer by the door. "How about a bottle of water, hey, Constable Dobson? Or would you prefer a cuppa?"

Tom scowled. "I'd prefer that you listen to me. I'm trying to tell you what happened to Amy. There's a guy there, see? On that island in the picture. Someone she fell for years ago. She's obviously gone back to find him. To Greece. She's—"

"We've already checked customs, Tom. She does have a new passport as it turns out, but she hasn't left the country."

That caught him by surprise. He blinked. "What?"

"They have no trace of her."

"Then she's using a false passport."

Geoff cocked his head to one side. "This isn't a spy novel, mate."

Tom let out a loud sigh. "Well, then, she must be holed up somewhere, maybe waiting for her flight. She might not have left yet, but you mark my words. She's on her way there. She's having an affair."

"See, here's my problem, Tom. As far as I can see, *you're* the one having the affair." His voice was perfectly calm, but it caused the other man to start.

"What?"

"Belinda Mann came in yesterday. She told us all about it."

His mouth gaped. Geoff waited a moment, giving his old friend a chance to speak up, but when he did, his words just made Geoff feel sad.

"Told you about what?"

He waited some more.

"Seriously, Geoff? Belinda and me? Oh give me a little credit!"

And finally, as Geoff's expression morphed from sadness to disappointment, Tom said, "Come on, Geoffrey. Everyone knows she's the town bike, has been trying her luck for years. But I never took her up on it. Just ask anyone."

Geoff nodded. "She told us all that herself, Tom. Said it was always a game to her, she flirted, you flirted back, but you never took up the offer." Tom's shoulders relaxed considerably, so he quickly added, "Until last Friday." The shoulders jumped sky-high again. "At the school gates, when the game suddenly changed."

Tom's cheeks began to mottle.

"She said you couldn't palm Phil off fast enough, dumped him on his friend Zac and followed her home. Said she was taken aback and

not just by your sudden interest. Said it was, and I quote…"
He glanced at a sheet of paper in front of him. "'Kind of weird'."
He looked up at Tom. "You like it *alfresco*, hey, Tommo? Out in the
open for all to see?"

Tom now blushed a deep beetroot red and his eyes were boring
into his lap.

"And we know she's not the first."

Now the eyes were scrunched shut.

"We know about the blonde. Scarlett saw her leave your place.
Last Wednesday morning. Crack of dawn."

Tom seemed to sink into himself then, his shoulders so hunched
forward he looked like he might tip onto the desk. A water bottle
appeared before him, but he ignored it, shaking his head over and
over while Geoff sat back and watched, waited, wondered if this was
anything more than a sad, pathetic sleazebag. Hoped that's all it was.

Eventually Tom looked up, wiping something from his nose.
"Stupid." He sniffed.

"What was that, Tom?"

"It was stupid, okay? I know that. Bloody stupid! But I was lonely.
She was there. That's all it was."

"To whom are we referring, Tom? The blonde or Belinda?
Or were there others?"

"No! Of course not!"

"But how do we know that? Looks like a pattern to us."

"It was only them. Just the two. I've never done anything like that
before. You know I only had eyes for Amy, you know that! Cassie…
the blonde, she came into the Boot & Tucker. I was… drunk.
I was… angry."

"Yeah. We know, with Amy. Your wife. Do you get angry with
Amy often?"

"What? No! Never. Until she left me. She's the one who's left *me*
for some other man, can we remember that before we start pointing
the finger!"

"But you don't know that for a fact, do you, Tom? You only
assume that, like you assume everything."

"You talk to Monty Brennan. She'll tell you. Her secretary guy will
back me up. She'll explain about the Greek bloke, about Sarisi."
Tears were streaming down Tom's face. "Please, man, you gotta
believe me. I know I'm a bastard, I know it was wrong. Belinda…"

He shuddered thinking about her. "I shouldn't have gone there. She's poison. I always knew that about her. And the other chick, that was just the grog, the desperation. I needed somebody that night."

Geoff was looking at him with a disgust he could not disguise.

"It makes you look guilty, don't you see that, Tom? You tell us you're the grieving husband, but all I'm seeing is a man out and about having a good time."

"A good time? Have you ever *been* with Belinda?" He almost smiled. "Come *on,* man, you *know* me. Jenny knows me—"

"You leave my wife out of this." Geoff's voice was a low, deep rumble that made both officers look towards him.

"I'm just saying, she'll vouch for me. She knows I'm a good guy. I'm the one who rescued Amy, remember? You know the story. You know the truth. When she got knocked up, I'm the one who looked after her, took her in. Not Angus. Me!"

"Angus Tower? Your Sydney mate? Are you telling me *he's* Phil's dad?"

Geoff had long known Tom was not the biological father, most of the town had worked that out—Phil looked nothing like his so-called dad, and why else would someone like Amy be with someone like Tom? But Geoff had never been told who got Amy pregnant and had never felt the need to ask. Now he felt like kicking himself.

"Why didn't you tell me that?" Geoff said. "Why didn't Angus?"

"You spoke to Angus?" Tom rolled his eyes. "'Course you did. You've been following me around like a criminal since this started. Well here's something else Angus wouldn't tell you. He *laughed.* That's right! Laughed his bloody head off when he learned Amy was pregnant. Like it was trivial! It's his fault she ended up at that convent, trying to discard Phil like a piece of chewing gum."

"Hang on, what convent?"

"Doesn't matter now. Point is, I saved him, and her. I got them out of there. I got them home. And I've never cheated on her, not once while…"

"While she was alive?"

"She *is* alive! You ask Monty. You fucking do your job!" Then he pushed the chair back and stood up. "You do your job."

As he walked out, smacking away his tears and swallowing back the snot, Geoff let him go, wondering if he had ever really known the guy or if he was reading him all wrong.

Then he handed the crumpled magazine clipping to the officer beside him and said, "See if you can track down this Monty Brennan, Dave. See if we can get her in here pronto. And while you're at it, let's get Angus Tower back. It's time to get some straight answers. I've had enough of all the bullshit."

SARISI ISLAND

The moon was full, almost absurdly so, and Nicholas appreciated the light as he strode up the hill towards the castle. It was a long trek, and he also appreciated the chance to calm himself down and clear his head.

He had no idea why Effie had turned so vile so fast, but he'd just got up to speed on a little ancient history that he knew was far from buried. For all of them, it would seem.

When he finally got to the hostel, he was surprised to see Kostas, feet up, snoozing in front of a blaring television, like he was on guard or waiting for something. The manager usually slept in a small bedsit in town preseason, but his one guest must have changed all that.

"Kos, mate," Nicholas said, and he woke with a start, nearly toppling off his chair.

"Oh, shit man! You scare me!"

"Sorry about that. Is she here?"

"Who?"

He gave Kos one of his looks.

"Is upstairs packing. She get red-eye to Athens soon."

Nicholas felt like he'd been slapped. He checked his watch and then charged up, first checking the single rooms, then taking another flight of stairs to the dormitory. There was a large leather carry bag sitting on the bunk, some clothes spilling out of it, but otherwise the room was empty, and he was about to head back downstairs when he noticed the rippling velvet curtain.

He took a few breaths, then stepped out onto the Juliet balcony.

Millie was standing at the edge, jacket and beanie on, looking up at the ridiculous moon.

"So it's true?" he said and she turned around, eyes wide.

"Oh, Nico, hi."

"Is it true?" he asked again. "You're just going to slink away?"

"I'm heading home; there's nothing for me here now."

"Really? Nothing? Nothing at all."

She looked away and back at the moon, and he felt his heart crack but let that one pass.

"So that's it? You're going to take Effie's word for it and not chase down this animal?"

Millie glanced back at him, her eyes now hardening. "What?"

"You're going to let that bastard get away with it?"

"You don't know what you're talking about, Nico."

"I know that there was a man on a ferry. I just spoke to Catalina. A longtime local. She told me."

Millie looked away, reaching for the edge of the balcony.

"I know you got off with him and he…" He took a deep breath, still trying to digest the shocking news himself. "I know he hurt you, Millie, and I'm so, so sorry about that."

She was now swaying, and he stepped towards her, but she held a hand up. That hand said back away. So he did but he couldn't seem to stop the words that were flowing from his mouth even though he knew they must be painful to hear, even after all these years.

"I know that bastard left you for dead on the beach near here. I know it happened a long time ago but—"

"Exactly!" she said, turning back to him. "It happened a long time ago. I'm over it."

"No, you're not."

Her jaw dropped, she shook her head. "How do you know that?"

"Because I'm looking at you, and you have so much pain."

"You have no idea what I'm feeling or who the hell you're looking at."

"Let me help you find him—"

"He's not here! The monster has gone. That's the end of it."

"It doesn't have to be!"

"It does! For me to survive it does!" She had palms up in the air as if pushing him away. "I can't be here anymore, I'm sorry… I just can't…" She went to walk past him, but he held his ground.

"Why didn't you tell me about what happened to you? I thought we had a connection—"

"A connection?"

"Yes, you and me, on the boat to Zoe's."

"That was a *conversation*," she said as he took a step back. "That's all it was, Nico, just a conversation."

"That's how you see it? That's how you see the past few days?"

"That's how I've learned to see life." She dropped her head to the side. "You're such a dreamer, Nicholas."

"And what are you then?"

Her head straightened. "Oh I shed my dreams a long time ago."

"Really? Then what are you doing here in Sarisi?"

She looked away.

"You're full of shit, Millie. There *was* something there, between us. I felt it, you felt it—"

"No, you just *wished* there was something there, it's not the same thing."

Millie saw him flinch. She knew she was hurting him. Yet she couldn't seem to stop. "I'm sorry, Nico, I know it sounds cruel, but life is cruel. Surely you're old enough to have worked that one out by now. Don't read so much into everything."

"I didn't read anything into it. I thought you and I... I thought it was..." He stopped, looking for the words, and now she almost laughed.

"*Fate?*" she said, loading the word with sarcasm. "*Destiny?* Not everything happens for a reason, Nicholas, have you not learned that by now? Did you seriously think it was our *destiny* to meet on Sarisi?"

He slumped, whispered, "Maybe."

She shook her head sadly and brushed past him to go inside.

When she reached the doorway, she turned back and said, "Sorry to burst your bubble, Nico, but we're just two people who went on a boat and had a conversation."

Nicholas stood out on the balcony for many minutes, feeling once again like he'd been slapped. No, worse than that, pummelled. Beaten to a pulp. What an idiot he'd been. What a classic fool. He swallowed painfully and brushed his hair back, then took many deep breaths before he ventured inside.

Millie was still there, now seated on the bed, her bag zipped up, the beanie in her hands. He stepped towards her, reaching into his pocket.

"There was a guy," he said softly as he pulled something out. It was a scrap of paper with words scribbled across it. He dropped it to the bed, adding, "There was a witness."

And he left it at that.

EVE MAGAZINE

By the time she returned to the publishing house on Monday afternoon, Monty's mood had gone from bleak relief to breathless rage. At first she was happy to know her friend was okay, but now she was feeling both bitter and betrayed.

How dare Amelia do this to her again! How *could* she? After everything they'd been through? How could she simply take off for Greece without a word, not offer her so much as an explanation, then expect her to sit around and pick up the pieces? They were supposed to be friends, they were supposed to be equals, so why couldn't Amelia trust her with the truth? Why all the stupid secrecy?

"You need to focus on *Eve* now," Beryl had said, "and she needs to find herself."

Fuck her and fuck *Eve*, she thought as she rode the elevator up.

Once more it was all about Amelia, no thought for anybody else and what they were going through. What had Thomas said last week? Something about her cleaning up after Millie again.

Not anymore, she thought. *Never again.*

As soon as she reached the office, she headed straight for the interior wall and began pulling at the photocopied issue, ripping the pages and grunting loudly as she did it.

"You okay, Monty?" This was Hank, standing behind her, eyebrows wedged together.

"I'm so sick of this bloody magazine," she spat back. "I don't want to see it anymore!"

He thought she was just referring to that particular issue. "I don't blame you. That was the monster month from hell. Want me to help?"

She stopped. "No, why don't you take the rest of the day off, Hank, you've earned it." Then she turned and pulled him into a hug. "Thank you for everything. You've been such a loyal friend."

He drew back and looked at her like she'd gone a little nuts, then smiled sheepishly and said, "Okay, well, thanks, I guess." Then he hesitated before asking, "Do you maybe want to go get some lunch or a drink or something?"

Monty didn't notice the catch in his voice and swept back to the wall saying, "No, thanks, honey. You go have fun!" as she kept pulling and ripping and throwing scraps of paper in a nearby recycling bin.

She also didn't catch the look of dejection as he loped away.

It was only when Monty got to a glossy, double-page advertisement that she stopped and focused. It was the ad Angus had taken out for his digital technology company and he was right, it wasn't *Eve's* usual run of designer fashion and obscenely priced accessories. But he'd paid top dollar for that front-of-book space, and she wondered now why he would do that. It didn't make good business sense.

Good Lord, she thought as the penny dropped. He's still got a crush on her! Angus Tower is trying to win Amelia back!

Well, fuck her! Monty abandoned the wall and pulled out her mobile phone. *She's not here is she, so now he's fair game.*

What else had both Beryl and Thomas said? Something about moving on and living her own life?

"I'll move on all right," she said aloud now, causing several colleagues to swap worried glances. She charged back to her desk and rifled through the silver handbag she'd dumped there days ago until she found Angus's business card. She tapped the number into her phone before her nerves caught up with her.

"Angus Tower, who is this?"

Her breath caught. She had not expected him to pick up. "Hey, Angus, it's Monty." Then, because he didn't say anything, she quickly added, "Monty Brennan." And scrunched her eyes shut, hoping she didn't have to add more.

"Oh, Monty! What a surprise. Nice to hear from you. How did you wash up the other night?"

"Bit seedy, actually." She giggled. "One too many Proseccos." Then remembering his heady aftershave and his smooth demeanour and, most of all, Alex's insinuation that she was a washed-up spinster, she said, "Speaking of drinks, do you—"

"And how's Silly Millie going?" he said, cutting in.

"Sorry, what?"

"She finally back in the hot seat?" Before she could answer, he said, "I hope so because she owes me a dinner at least. We've put a big ad spend on your title this month."

"Yes, I saw that." She slunk into her chair, wishing she hadn't made this call, feeling like a fool. "Um, no, she's not back yet, but she will be, so…"

"Really? Because Wilson didn't sound so convinced."

"Wilson?"

"Yeah, Thomas. He called yesterday, said you'd been to see him. Said something strange about Millie vanishing again. What's that about?"

"Oh, no, she's just away. On holidays." *Chasing down Greek guys* she wanted to say but couldn't find her mean streak.

"That's a relief. I thought he was being melodramatic, but then you know how freaked out he got last time."

"What do you mean?"

"You know he never really settled down after that trip, not like the rest of us anyway." She rolled her eyes at that. *If only he knew.* "To be honest, I don't think he ever got over having his heart ripped to shreds."

She felt herself flush. "I didn't mean to hurt Thomas, honestly I didn't."

There was another pause, an embarrassed laugh. "No, Monty, I'm not talking about you. I'm talking about Millie."

"Millie?"

"You didn't notice?"

Something heavy seemed to settle in the bottom of her stomach. "Millie?"

"He had a major crush on her. It was pretty obvious." He chuckled. "Look, don't take this the wrong way, but we both had a thing for Millie at the start, when we met in Rome. You must have seen that. But then she chose me and he was a bit pissed off at first, but he's a mate, right, so he let it go."

And he reached out to me, Monty thought, suddenly feeling queasy.

"Anyway, I got my comeuppance in the end. She ran off the ferry with that Greek bloke and I was left all alone."

No you weren't, you bastard! She wanted to scream. *You were left with me!*

They hadn't just had a fling. They returned to London together and went out for six weeks before his eyes strayed elsewhere and she was tossed on the scrap heap. It was exactly as Thomas had predicted that very first night they all met up.

"Chicks always fall for Angus," he'd told the two girls. *"But he's a flake, quickly moves on to the next one."*

She'd called Thomas jealous then, but she hadn't meant it, not really.

"So Thomas had a crush on Millie, hey?" For some reason she was not surprised.

"More than a crush, he was like a man obsessed. So furious when she jumped ship, like it was him who'd been rejected." He snorted. "Reckons he's over it now, but I've got my doubts. He still has her book, so it makes you wonder…"

"Book?"

"Yeah that loopy *Prophecy* one, you know the one she lived by back then. At least he had it last time I dropped over."

Monty reached a hand to her throat as he added, almost flippantly, "I told Millie all of this. At that Apple launch. She'd seemed a bit shocked to hear about you and me, so I told her she should get that book back off Thomas and read it again—remind herself about fate and destiny and how everything happens for a reason. You know, all that crap she used to believe in."

"Except she doesn't believe it anymore," Monty said, her voice barely audible.

"Sorry?" he said, then she heard a mumble in the background. "Look, I've got to go. Been nice catching up. Tell that runaway editor that I want to hear from her when she gets back."

With that, the line went dead, and Monty was left staring at the receiver, frozen with thought, her stomach in knots, her mind racing.

A book.

A crush.

A brutal rape.

"All good?"

She looked up and saw Fleur, her hands overloaded with last month's fashion bagged and ready to return. She had some handbags, too, as well as a piece of luggage. A bulky piece, one with "funny gold squiggles".

"Where'd you get that Louis Vuitton keepall?" Monty asked, ice trickling through her veins.

Fleur glanced down at it. "I don't know. I guess they sent it to us to use in a shoot."

Did they? She wondered. Or is that Amelia's missing luggage?

"Oh shit!" Monty leapt to her feet, flung her phone into her handbag and then glanced around for her jacket.

Stupid, stupid Beryl! Believing her daughter had packed a bag and was safe in Greece. But how did she know that? Really? No one had seen her since Saturday. Had she ever even left the country?

Monty pulled her jacket on and headed for the exit.

"You off again?" Fleur looked surprised.

"Yes! Hold my calls. Except for Millie!"

"Millie?"

She shook her head. "I mean Amelia! If she calls—*God, I hope she calls*—tell her to call my mobile immediately."

Then she bolted for the elevator.

SHEPPERDIN VILLAGE

Scarlett knew Tom would be on the warpath. Felt guilty that she'd dobbed him in to the Shepperdin police.

"But he was cheating on her, Harry," she told her husband as they sat at the table that night, the remains of dinner scattered around them. "I saw that blond girl slink out of his house. It made my blood run cold."

The children had all been excused, most of them now tumbling about in the family room, the TV blaring some cartoon or another, a stereo popping from somewhere deep within the house, the older ones in their bedrooms, hooked to screens no doubt.

"Still, Scar," Harry said, picking up the bottle of Shiraz to replenish their glasses. "You promised me you wouldn't say anything. You'd let me get to the bottom of it first."

"And I wasn't going to, you know that! But then Polly told me about Belinda and the creepy way he was with her and I—"

"Jesus, Scar."

"Sorry, but apparently he made Belinda do it out in the backyard, where the kids play for goodness' sake! Among her boy's plastic buckets. I mean, that's weird, honey. That's just wrong."

"What's wrong is Geoff telling his wife any of this. That was a confidential police interview. Jenny should not be gossiping about it with the school mums."

"Jenny doesn't normally gossip, honey, but she was upset. She's the only one who's ever stood up for that bastard, so she felt betrayed. I think she needed to vent, and Polly was there."

"Doesn't matter. Geoff shouldn't have said anything to her; she shouldn't have said anything to Polly. Jesus what a pack of gossips! Besides, he probably only did it outside so he wouldn't desecrate Belinda's bed or something."

She raised an eyebrow at him, then whipped a hand out to grab a young boy who was toddling through the kitchen, naked and laughing. She gave him a hug, patted his little bottom and sent him on his way. "It's just sick."

"That's my brother you're talking about, babe. He's family. I can't believe you said anything."

"And so is Amy! So is Phil. They're your family too. I can't believe you said nothing." Then she snapped her head around and screamed, "Bethy! That television's too loud!"

The sound instantly dropped, and she turned back to her husband.

"How do we know he hasn't cheated before? How do we know it's not all because of him?"

Harry knew what she was talking about, but he kept shaking his head. "You would know, love. You've been watching him like a hawk for years. Waiting for exactly that."

"That's not fair."

"True though, yeah?" He kicked her foot under the table, trying to give her a small smile, but Scarlett was still feeling tense. She was worried and not just for herself.

Harry said, "I know you've never warmed to him."

"Not only me! The kids all think he's weird. Your own father wrote him out of the will for goodness' sake."

"That had nothing to do with him being *weird*. He was a traitor."

"I know, because he left for Sydney University, got too high and mighty." It had become the family mantra.

"It went further than that."

"I don't care. He *is* an oddball. There's something not quite right about your brother, and Amy knew it. She never said it to me, she was too damn loyal, but I could tell. I really hope she did leave him, and I hope she's far, far away."

He frowned, realising he hoped that, too, but for very different reasons. He glanced out the kitchen window, towards Tom's house, which sat dark and foreboding just beyond the bushes. He sighed. His hope turned to a feeling of desperation.

"Let's keep our distance for a bit, hey?" he said. "Let's keep the kids in our yard from now on. Just don't give him any more reason to be grumpy with us."

"They don't like going over there anyway. You know that. Apart from his pristine sandpit, there's nothing there for them now. Phil's in Sydney, and I hope he stays there for a bit, safe and sound with his nana." She reached for the dirty dishes and began to gather them up. "I feel for that poor kid. He loved his mum so, so much. That's what's got me worried. If she did take off, why didn't she take Phil?" She stood up and stared at the plates. "What if she doesn't come back, Harry? What will happen to him?"

He frowned. "My brother will look after Phil, of course. Jesus, Scarlett. He might be a weirdo and a lousy husband, but he's a good father. Jesus."

She nodded, taking the plates across to the sink. But she did not believe him.

For his part, Harry didn't notice her insincere nod. He was lost in his own thoughts.

There was something Scarlett had said, something that sounded so out of character for his brother…

He tried to shake off a growing sense of unease.

~~~

Tom saw the lights twinkling in Harry's house. Heard the TV blaring, a base sound beating from a back bedroom, a kid calling out to another kid, a woman screaming for them all to shut up.

A happy family, he supposed. He was no expert at that.

His own father had disowned him many years ago, long before he went to Sydney to get that wasted business degree. It had nothing to do with him getting above his station and everything to do with his mother. The moment his mum shot off, his dad turned on him, like it was all his fault.

And perhaps he was right.

Of both sons, Tom was the mummy's boy, Linda's favourite, although not mummy's boy enough to keep mummy at home. He'd let them all down. His dad was right. And now he'd let Phil down too.

Couldn't keep a mother. Couldn't keep a wife.

Tom sighed and turned away from the happy household.
~~~

Sat down at the dark kitchen table and reached for his beer. His fourth for the night. *Or was it his fifth?* He remembered his mother's last evening, although he hadn't known it at the time. It was like any other night. They ate dinner in silence, at this very table in fact, his dad shooting off soon after for "a quick one with the lads", Harry and Tom disappearing to their respective bedrooms where they spent most evenings now. Hiding from the unhappiness.

She came to tuck him in, his mother, but later than she normally did. He was ten, too old for hugs, but she hugged him anyway, tighter than she normally hugged him, and she was a tight hugger as it was. She said stuff he didn't understand then, words like *destiny* and *fate*, words that meant nothing until he met Amy.

Millie Malone. The woman on the Spanish Steps. The one who reminded him so much of his mother. It wasn't just her luscious brown hair and sparkling green eyes. It was the way she spoke, the things she believed in. The words she used. So like Linda.

The two sets of friends had followed each other to a small bar in the Piazza Navona, and with each glass of vino, Millie began to open up.

"We were *meant* to meet here," she philosophised to the boys. "You might think it's all chance, but it's not!"

"Millie doesn't believe in coincidences anymore," said Monty, the plainer one, the one with the wispy hair and the crazy dress sense. "Not since she read that stupid *Celestine Prophecy.*"

"Shut up! It is true! Just look at us. Thousands of miles from Sydney and here we are, together. How did that happen?"

"We're all tourists and we met at Rome's most popular tourist spot?" Angus suggested with a smile, but she was shaking her head.

"Nope. Millions of people go to the Spanish Steps every year. How come *we* met, us four, this evening? Huh? I'm telling you, everything happens for a reason! It's *destiny.*"

And while Angus muted his mockery and pretended to agree— he'd agree to anything to get his leg over—Tom nodded fervently. She sounded just like his mother! And suddenly, in the middle of a foreign land, he felt like he was home.

He lapped her words up back then, had lived by them ever since. And even when she chose Angus that first night instead of him, he was fine with it.

It was destiny.

When she nearly got off that ferry that day en route to Santorini, those agonising few minutes when he thought she was lost forever, he was willing to accept that too. It was fate, wasn't it? He would somehow find her again.

But then she didn't get off! It was like a miracle!

She simply laughed at her own folly, dropped her backpack down, and fell into Angus's arms. And Tom was fine with that too.

Fine, fine, fine.

Because he knew then exactly what would happen and it turns out he was right. Millie fell pregnant to a monster who left her to fend for herself, and Thomas stepped up as he knew he would because that was *his* true destiny.

She was his fate. Amy. It had only ever been Amy. And finally, one balmy Greek night, everything made perfect sense. *This* was why his mother left. To give him the gift of Amy.

Without Linda's departure he would never have left for Sydney and then for Europe, searching the world for his mother and finding, instead, a young backpacker called Millie Malone.

God, she really was like his mother, young Millie! So bright and sparkly; so full of love and laughter and hugs so tight.

And even after it happened, after she lost her sparkle and turned to that ugly old witch on Sarisi, like she was some kind of Messiah, it was *Tom* who got her back while Angus made a beeline for Monty.

It was *Tom* who rescued Amy. He was the destiny she always spoke of. She just hadn't realised it until then.

Tom now recalled their first night together. How soft he was. How careful. And how, as she softly snored in his arms afterward, he hugged her as tight as he could without waking her.

And whispered thank you to his mother.

SARISI ISLAND

The witness was an elderly, windswept man named Artemis. He ran a beachside *pension* on the other side of the castle, called Sofi's. Sofi had fled years ago, not long after he first found Millie lying battered on the sand nearby. Sofi didn't like how fixated it made him, how crazed and haunted, and had soon found a younger man with no dark thoughts and very little else going on upstairs, or at least that's how Artemis put it. They were now happily living on Mykonos.

He told all this to Millie as she sat on a plastic chair beside him, hands wedged in her lap, teary eyes looking out at the beach she never thought she'd be brave enough to set foot on again.

"Everybody think I mad," he said. "Everybody say, 'Artemis, he crazy!' but I know what I see. I tell them about this man but nobody believe me. I tell Effie, yesterday, but she no believe."

"Tell me," she said quietly. "I'll believe."

He nodded. "But first we have breakfast." Like they both needed the strength, and he was probably right.

It was 6:30 a.m., and Millie had not yet eaten, hadn't meant to come so early, but she hadn't slept a wink since Nicholas dropped his bombshell and couldn't wait a moment longer, grateful to find Kostas up and smoking his first cigarette when she appeared in the lobby at sunrise.

The hostel manager had been happy to hear she wasn't leaving and given her directions to Sofi's, which was located on the quieter side of Coso Point, the one with volcanic sand and budget tourists.

He didn't know why she was asking, but he had a pretty good idea. Unlike Nico, he had his ear to the ground and already knew the story, or at least scraps of it because it wasn't exactly a favourite topic around these parts.

Millie's attack had left a dark smudge on the island's soul and pitted police against locals, and neighbours against neighbours. Because of this, some of them were anxious that Millie was back while others hoped things would be different this time, that they could somehow redeem themselves and their beloved island.

Of course Kostas told Millie none of that, but she had already worked it out from the wary expressions she received from old-timers and the way they scuttled in a different direction, as though just crossing paths with her would bring another decade of bad luck.

Not Nicholas though. He ran towards Millie, embraced her, and it was clear even before last night that he had no idea about the past. And that's what she liked about him. He was a clean slate. She had enjoyed their time together, if only because it made her feel like none of it had happened.

He made her feel clean and sparkly.

But of course it had happened, and this elderly witness was about to make it very real, so she appreciated the murky Greek coffee he produced and the breakfast platter of cheese and yogurt with honey and a sesame bagel he called *koulouri*, trying to swallow as much of it as she could before her appetite was chipped away with every passing sentence.

"I tell police," he said now, rolling a cigarette. "I tell everybody but nobody listen. I know who do this to you. I know this man."

She felt her heart charge and said, "You saw him attack me?"

"No, no! I no see!" He was offended by the suggestion. "If I see, I stop, yes? But I see him go to beach where I find you. I see him that night. Next morning, he take early ferry. He leave quick. Quick mean guilty. He only here one night, then he go. Why he go? I know guilty man when I see guilty man. This man guilty."

She nodded. It wasn't exactly a smoking gun.

"This guilty man..." He hesitated. "This man he *Australian*."

Artemis waited for that to settle in, for the shock of it to subside, but she didn't seem shocked at all, was still nodding at him, staring out at the sea.

"He come on evening ferry from Santorini, yes? He book room, here! He stay one night, he go. I tell police, I tell Sister Agnetha, but next day he gone! Nobody believe me. They all think Greek boy do it. Like they want Greek boy do it. But I know. I see this man. I see evil in his eye."

Millie shivered now and wrapped her cardigan tighter. She hadn't seen the evil, he had crept up from behind, but she had felt it and would feel it for the rest of her life.

"What did he look like?" She needed confirmation.

There was hesitation, an embarrassed glance. "Is like Aussie tourist. You all look same to me."

"So how do you know…?" She stopped. "I'm not saying he wasn't Australian, but how do you know for sure? Was it his accent?"

"This man, he wear Aussie hat. You know, from *Crocodile Dundee*."

She sighed. Every second Aussie tourist wore those hats back then. "Did you see the colour of his hair? His eyes?"

"Hair under hat, he wear hat all the time, even inside! This strange, yes? This make me think he bad man."

She almost laughed then with the idiocy of it. He was certainly guilty of having bad manners, but was this man her attacker?

"But his eyes different to crocodile man," Artemis continued. "Crocodile man is kind, this man, he evil. He has evil eyes."

She nodded yet again, but it wasn't really why she was here. She had a question to ask, a difficult, terrifying question. She swallowed and said, "What happened to Aki?"

Akakios. The Greek stranger on the ferry; the one she'd flirted with. The innocent man as it turns out.

Artemis's eyes looked hooded, and he dragged on his rollie for a long time, then blew the smoke out and shrugged. "He go away. He no come back."

"He didn't get in trouble?"

He half shrugged. He didn't have the words, didn't have the heart, but later she would learn that Aki left under a dark cloud. He'd been seen with Millie that evening and was hauled in for questioning when the police arrived. He insisted he was innocent, insisted she was British, too, which set police on the wrong path entirely. Some locals thought he'd done that deliberately, but he'd misunderstood her accent, and while he was eventually cleared, his reputation never recovered.

Mud sticks, after all.

"He never come back," Artemis repeated.

She nodded sadly and drained her cup. If only she could see Aki again and tell him how deeply sorry she was. How she, too, had blamed him all those years. How she could never equate the sweet man on the ferry with the monster that attacked her that night.

If only she could turn back that boat, not flirt with him over cheap coffee or follow him off the boat like a foolish schoolgirl. But of course she couldn't do any of that, and she wondered now as she had wondered all week, why she was putting herself through this.

What was the point?

She pushed her plate aside and stood up. "Thank you, Artemis," she said. "I'm sorry nobody believed him, and I'm so sorry nobody believed you. I certainly do, but I'm not sure there's enough proof. I think it might be too late."

He looked sad but not surprised and dragged on his rollie again, then, as she reached for her purse, he held that hand out.

"No, no, no!" he began, but she shook him off.

"I will pay for this meal, Artemis. It's important to me that I pay, okay? You don't owe me anything." *You've paid enough.*

As Millie rifled through her purse, she began to frown. "Damn it, I gave Kostas all my cash last night." She plucked a credit card out. "Do you take Visa? Is that okay?"

Artemis waved her indoors towards the cash register. "You Aussies," he said as he took the card from her and swiped it across his machine. "You like your credit cards. You know your number too?"

"Sorry?"

"This man, this evil man I see, he know his card number, he say it to me without looking. He think he so clever."

Millie felt suddenly faint. She already knew that, didn't she? Yet it was the last compelling piece of the puzzle. Her worst fears had been realised, and now it made everything real.

Worse than that, it made everything she did afterwards utterly unforgivable.

EVE MAGAZINE

It was early evening when Monty reached Darlinghurst and already getting dark down that stinking, narrow laneway, and she breathed in through her mouth and wrapped her jacket tighter as she headed to number 263A.

"Monty Brennan!" Thomas said, his eyes lighting up as he opened the door. "My, my, two visits in a week. Somebody got a little crush?"

"Hey Tom, can I come in?"

He smiled. "Sure." He held the door wide but didn't move so she was forced to step in and under his armpit. Again she tried not to inhale as she made her way up.

When she got to the living room, she stopped and said, "I'll have that beer now, if it's still on offer."

"Really?" He looked surprised. "That's more like my old Monty. Great, just give me a sec."

He vanished into the kitchen and she watched him go, then turned and dashed to the bookshelf, running her fingers along the dusty covers.

Where is it, where is it, where is it...

"You looking for this?"

She swung around to find Tom holding a battered copy of *The Celestine Prophecy.* Her stomach clenched.

"It's hers, isn't it?" she said, knowing she was steering into dangerous territory. When he just blinked at her, she clarified. "The book, it's Amelia's, right?"

"Millie. Her name is Millie. Why do you keep calling her Amelia?

It doesn't suit that stupid slut."

He said the words so casually, but she felt like she'd been punched.

"Yeah, you're right," she managed. "Sorry… So… how about that beer?"

His eyes narrowed and for a moment she thought he was going to refuse, but then he slapped the book on the coffee table and returned to the kitchen. This time she heard him open the fridge door. She heard the clink of glass bottles and she slipped onto the sofa and grabbed the book, flicking open the front page to see what she already knew had been scribbled there in smudged blue ink many years earlier:

Millie Jane Malone 1998 xo

When he stepped behind her, she tried not to jump. She steadied her breathing as she flung the book back.

"What a load of nonsense, hey?"

There was deathly silence, then Tom handed her the open beer, dropping it over her shoulder so it hovered, dripping near her breast, and she grabbed it quickly, thanked him and took a long, steadying gulp.

He sat down on the stained armchair opposite her now and drank from his own bottle, watching her.

"Why are you here, Monty?"

She leant back, trying to look relaxed. "I don't know, maybe I just wanted to be around an old friend. Forget about life for a while."

His eyes narrowed further. "Silly Millie still missing then?"

She told him yes but had a terrifying feeling he already knew that. She said, "I'm sick of the whole subject to be honest. I'm sick of it always being about Millie. Maybe I want to be around someone who saw through it all, just like I did."

He kept staring at her, so she ploughed on.

"I gave her the best years of my life, you know, and for what? She was the boss, not me. She got the big pay cheque, all the glory, I did all the work. You're right about that. I was a fool."

He smiled. "You wouldn't be the first."

"I know! She didn't deserve me. Didn't deserve either of us."

"Us? There was no *us*. She never even looked sideways at me."

"I know, right? What a bitch. You're such a catch." She wondered if she was overdoing it Sank her mouth around her bottle.

But he was warming to the topic now. "She ruined my life too, you know."

"Oh?"

"Yeah, we did do it, just the once. Did you know that?"

So that's what he was calling it. She felt her stomach turn.

"She was a cold bitch. Don't know why I bothered." His eyes began to flutter down Monty's neck and towards her décolletage. "Pity you and I never stuck."

She tried to smile, was sure she hadn't quite delivered.

"You got a boyfriend? A husband? Somebody?"

"Yes," she lied. "Going out with a guy from work. Hank."

He swept his eyes back up. "Then why are you here with me?"

She laughed nervously and dropped her beer on the table, struggled to her feet. "You're right. I should get back."

He sat forward. "That's a pity. I thought we were just getting warmed up."

"Oh, ha, ha, I wish! No, I… um, I have to return. Deadline."

"Thought you didn't give a shit about that anymore."

"No, I don't but, well, it's the last issue. I'm putting the magazine to bed and then I'm out."

"How about I put you to bed?"

She laughed again, but this time it definitely came out strangled and she had to do everything in her power not to run for the front door, expecting him to grab her at any point, but he didn't. He simply followed her across the room and stood at the top of the staircase, watching her go.

When she reached the bottom, she swung the door open and then called back, "I'll be in touch, yeah?"

He did not reply.

SHEPPERDIN VILLAGE

Montana shook her cherry-red curls and gasped at the classic Queenslander in front of her. For a police station it would make a really lovely family home. Of course you'd have to replace the parochial white timber with a more in-trend shade of grey and open up that wondrous wraparound veranda, which some *short-sighted delinquent* had thought to enclose. Built on stilts with steps sweeping up to it, the timber structure looked almost cheerful with its clump of rosebushes out the front, and if it wasn't for the signage, you'd swear you were given a bum steer.

"It's not so charming inside," came a gravelly voice beside her.

Montana looked around to find Angus Tower standing there, hands deep in his pockets, giving her a flirtatious grin. She hadn't seen him in years and was momentarily spellbound—he was still so handsome, more so now that he'd swapped his casual jeans and Polo shirts for a slick Hugo Boss suit—but soon found herself in his embrace, soaking up the heady aftershave and the memories. They held each other for a few seconds before turning to stare at the station again.

"Tom and I spent a night in here once, did we ever tell you that?" He chuckled. "I was visiting on uni holidays, and we'd gotten so filthy drunk some old copper confiscated our car keys, dumped us in the lockup, and didn't let us out until we'd sobered up. Even made us bacon and eggs the next morning." He shook his head. "Gotta love the country."

"No you don't," she snapped back, shuddering as she glanced

around at the quarter-acre block with its overgrown grass and what looked like a lone sheep just behind one of the patrol cars. "The country gives me the creeps. Too much space, not enough privacy."

"You look amazing. Really, quite stunning."

She laughed at the subject change as much as his comment and eye-rolled him. "You know that shit doesn't work on me anymore, Angus. I am now officially immune to flattery."

"Pity. It worked a treat back then."

"Hey!"

She slapped him lightly across the arm, but it was a subject that cut deep. She had been so smitten with Angus and had been treated so shabbily. And for some reason it had become like a festering sore between her and Millie, even though neither woman had ended up with him.

"Sorry," he said, smirking a little. "I forgot our mantra: what happens on holidays stays on holidays."

"Yes, except I have a feeling that policy's not going to wash today." She looked at the station, then at his dissolving smirk. "Why else do you think they've dragged us in here?"

"You don't seriously think they care about our backpacking days, do you?"

She shrugged. "He came to see me."

"Tom?"

"Yesterday, scared the *bejesus* out of me and half my team. He's angry, really angry. Blames me for everything. Says I put the idea in her head to go back to Greece."

"He thinks *that's* where she is?"

"Yes, and he thinks it's my fault. He saw a fashion spread we did in the Greek islands, says she saw it too and that's why she ran. Do you think that's why they've dragged us here? They're going to pin this on me?"

He smiled. "I don't think they can arrest you for sending someone on a Greek holiday, Montana." Then he stopped smiling. "If indeed that's where she is." He swung an arm around her shoulder. "Come on, let's see if they're still offering bacon and eggs."

Superintendent Geoff Pinter had no idea what designer outfit the woman sitting before him was wearing—it looked like frayed wool in a particularly nauseating shade of salmon—but he had a hunch it was pricey. It was exactly like the kind of stuff Jenny pored over in those glossy magazines she scored off Amy at the end of every month. Lots of fancy buttons and flashy trims and price tags to make you laugh out loud. Or worse, no price at all.

"'Price on application'!" his wife read aloud once. "Yikes, it must be a million bucks!"

"For those ugly leather slacks?" he replied, and she'd howled with laughter.

"We don't call them *slacks* anymore, Geoffy! Oh dear, what an old fossil I married."

He felt positively stone-age today in his steel-rimmed glasses and boring blue police suit. Angus was in even fancier threads than the woman, fancier than the gear he had on last week. He did look a million bucks, although a recent Google search showed the guy was worth so much more than that. Had made *Forbes'* list of Australia's Richest 100 last year, and it wasn't his first time.

He studied them as they took their chairs in front of his desk. Could picture Amy and Montana being friends, the former never quite able to hide her posh self, but Tom seemed a very unlikely match for Mr Moneybags here.

"Thank you for coming all the way in," he said. "Can I offer you something to drink?"

This wasn't an official interrogation, but he suspected these two knew something, and he needed them to feel comfortable enough to spit it out.

"I'll have bottled water," Montana said to no one in particular. "Cold, please. And a glass."

"Just a black coffee for me," added Angus.

Geoff smiled. They were used to being waited on, these two, and he passed the order on to Constable Dobson, then placed his hands on the desk in front of him and waited another beat. Neither of them said a word. Just stared back at him, expressionless, prepared for anything. Pros, it seemed. Neither had records of any kind—he'd looked that up too—but they knew a deliberate pause when they heard one and knew not to rush in.

"So," he began, "as you know Amy Wilson née Malone has been missing since last Sunday evening, and we are beginning to hold grave fears for her safety."

They nodded, not looking surprised but not looking panicked either, and he wondered about that.

"I believe you two are old friends of the missing woman?"

Montana said, "Millie and I go back to year ten high school, but we've kind of lost touch lately. We both met Angus—and Thomas for that matter—in the late nineties, in Italy. We were all backpacking at the time."

"The awesome foursome," Angus said, his tone droll.

"I know I've asked you this before, Mr Tower, but I need to ask again. Over the past ten days have either of you seen or heard from… let's call her Amy, shall we? That's how we know her around these parts."

Now they were both shaking their heads.

"When *did* you last see or hear from her? Ms Brennan?"

Montana frowned. "I'm surprised Thomas's not in here telling you all about it. He came to my office yesterday, completely manic."

"I'd like to hear it from you."

"Sure. As I said, Amy and I had lost touch. We were Facebook friends, of course, liked each other's posts occasionally, but she rarely had much to say, just posted pix of her kid really, and she never came to Sydney, so there wasn't much chance to catch up."

Angus shifted in his seat but said nothing. Geoff noticed it but waved Montana on.

"But she did come to town about two, three months ago. Wanted to catch up. I told Thomas all of this."

"What did you and Amy talk about?"

"Nothing much. She'd seen some of my Facebook posts on my trip to Greece. I'd just come back from Santorini and a smaller island called Sarisi—"

"You went *there*? To *Sarisi*?" This was Angus and he sounded gobsmacked.

"Yes, like I told you. For one of our fashion-meets-food shoots. The Greek Tourist Board paid for us to fly a team out. I did the styling. We flew a model in from Milan, another from Athens, a chef from Melbourne. It's in the last issue of *House*. Anyway, Tom definitely saw that and came charging into my office yesterday like a man possessed, accusing me of convincing his wife to leave him and run back to Sarisi. He had some ludicrous notion that I'd met up with that bloke…" She turned back to Angus. "You know? That guy on the ferry that she got a crush on? Remember, we all thought she was about to jump ship with him? Gave us all a heart attack."

Angus frowned and said, "And did you?"

"Meet the guy? Don't be absurd! I wouldn't recognise him in a lineup. I doubt she would either." She turned her eyes to Geoff, who had been watching this exchange curiously. "It was thirteen years ago. She had a bit of a flirt with this Greek guy on the way to Santorini. Thought he was hot. They had 'chemistry'." She wiggled her fingers in the air. Sighed. "She kind of regretted not jumping ship with him, kept saying how she might have missed the love of her life, her 'soul mate'. But he could've been a serial killer for all she knew."

"Hang on." This was Angus. "Did she say that recently or are you talking about back then?" *Back when they were hooking up.*

"Both, but I honestly didn't think she was going to desert Tom and fly back to Sarisi!" She turned to Geoff. "You seriously think she's there?"

He didn't answer. Had turned his eyes to Angus. "What do you think?"

"I don't know anything about this bloke and whether she ran off to find him, but she'd have to have lost her marbles if she did."

"Why? Because he's not you?" said Montana.

He scoffed. "Because he's not Tom! And I know Tom adored Amy. He lived for her, in fact. It would gut him if she ran away."

"But if she didn't go to Sarisi, where is she?" Montana asked, and they frowned at each other.

"Okay, so, Mr Tower, you last saw Amy..." Geoff glanced at his papers. "Five or six months ago I think you said."

He shifted in his seat again. "Actually, it was more like three weeks."

Now Geoff was frowning. "So why lie to me?"

"Apologies for that. It's like I said, Tom adored Amy and I know this place is gossip central. If word had got back to Tom, well..." He offered an apologetic smile. "Look, he'd *really* fly off the handle if he knew all this, but Amy started to contact me about two years ago; we met regularly after that. Every couple of months or so. Turns out Tom knew nothing about it."

Montana clearly didn't either because she had turned to stare directly at him, eyes wide. He noticed and directed the next sentence to her.

"She liked to talk about the old days, the backpacking days, when things were good."

"And things *weren't* good now?" This was Geoff.

He shrugged. "You'd have to ask Tom that."

"Except I'm asking you."

He shrugged again. "She never quite came out and said it. I just…"

He stopped as the coffee was handed to him, didn't bother to thank the officer, simply placed it on his crossed knee.

Geoff hoped he didn't spill it all over his fancy *slacks*.

"I got the impression she wasn't happy," Angus continued. "I mean, you wouldn't be sentimental for the past if you were enjoying the present, would you?"

"And where would you two *meet*?" That last word was loaded, and Angus scowled.

"Usually at a café near my office. It wasn't an affair, if that's what you're insinuating. Not at all. It wasn't like that."

"What was it like then?" This was Montana, her tone cold.

"It was just two friends reminiscing."

Montana looked sceptical, and Geoff wasn't buying it either. The man ran a multimillion-dollar business—regular travel, staff of hundreds. No time for breezy chats with old buddies as far as he could tell.

"Does this have anything to do with Phil?" Geoff asked.

Angus was bringing the cup to his lips and stopped, looked up sharply at the superintendent while Montana did a double take.

"*Phil?*" she said. "Amy's son, Phil?" Her eyes were darting between the two men.

"Angus's son, too, if I'm not mistaken."

Angus brought the cup back to his lips and took a good gulp before answering, now ignoring the look of shock on Montana's face.

"So Amy said. We never did the DNA test, and she did hook up with Tom very quickly after me, but, well, he probably is my son. He looks a lot like me." He smiled cheekily. "He's a pretty handsome devil."

Montana did not smile back. She had turned completely in her chair now and was staring at him open-mouthed. "You two were together for about five seconds! How could Phil be yours?"

"Only takes one second to get pregnant, Montana."

Montana scowled as the penny slowly began to drop. She remembered that night Millie had dragged Angus off to the beach for "a chat". How he'd soon come looking for her at the hostel bar. He didn't mention any pregnancy. Just said they'd split up. After six weeks of island hopping, things were "now boring". His exact words; hideous in retrospect. He said Millie was taking off to some other island; didn't want anyone to follow. It didn't make any sense, of course, but he acted so casual, so cavalier about it. And she so desperately wanted her chance with Angus, so she bought it, hook, line and sinker.

Montana only learned about Millie's "condition" many months later, after they'd all returned home. Had always assumed the child was Thomas's because Angus was right, those two had hooked up so quickly. It was Thomas who'd tracked her down. It was Thomas she'd made her life with.

She felt herself blush and stared down at her lap. *No wonder their friendship went sour.* If only Millie had told her the truth after that "chat" on the beach with Angus, then she never would have jumped into bed with him so quickly. Never!

She was a bad friend. But she wasn't a *monster.*

Geoff watched her blush deepen, sensing she and Angus also had some history, but he wasn't sure how relevant that was so he ploughed on. He had another bone to pick.

"Why didn't you inform me of this the other night, Mr Tower?"

"I told you—small town, loose lips. Besides, I didn't think it was important. I can't see how it would be."

"I get to decide what is and isn't important." Geoff shook his head irritably. "So let's back up a bit. When Amy met with you on these visits to Sydney, did you discuss Phil?"

"Of course, that's why she wanted to meet."

"And *now* we're getting somewhere." Geoff sounded almost relieved. "What did you talk about? Exactly?"

"Just how the kid was going. Occasionally he'd be there but usually it was just her, wanting to discuss Phillip's future. She wanted to make sure he was okay. Had booked him into a very good boarding school which she couldn't afford. Asked if I'd pay the fees."

"And would you?" This was Monty, an eyebrow raised high.

"Of course! I said I would, but then she seemed to give up on the idea. I never heard another word about it. She must've changed her mind."

"Or maybe Tom changed it for her," said Geoff.

Angus shook his head. "I don't believe Tom knew. At least he didn't mention it the other night at the pub, and I think he would have. He seemed surprised I'd even met Phillip."

Geoff sighed and sat back. It was all so convoluted. He wasn't sure what any of this had to do with Amy's disappearance, but it had to be connected.

As if reading his mind, Montana said, "You know Tom could be half right. I don't know if Sarisi was on the itinerary, but perhaps Amy did leave him. That's why she wanted to put her boy in boarding school, so she could be free. She clearly wasn't happy. I got the same sense as Angus, but she never came out and said as much. It was just a vibe. And I mean, seriously? If you're rendezvousing with an old boyfriend every few months behind your hubby's back—"

"Nothing happened!"

"*Still*, it's not a ringing endorsement for your marriage is it? Tom might've loved her, but she was clearly miserable. I know she told me she had regrets about giving up magazines for marriage and small-town life." She glanced at Geoff. "She could have taken off. She's done it before." Then she flashed a sour look back at Angus.

Geoff watched and let it drop. She was right. Everything pointed to that, but he hadn't been lying to Tom. So far, there was no record of Amy Wilson leaving the country. She had applied for a new passport almost three months ago, but it had not yet been used. Maybe it would be soon though. Maybe Tom was right and she was holed up somewhere biding her time.

But why leave a man who adores you? Why leave a son you adore even more? And why not speak up once your face hits the news?

It didn't add up. None of it added up.

Geoff's mind kept returning to Tom and wondering how much he did and didn't know and how he'd cope if he did uncover the truth. Because the only truth they all agreed on was that Tom adored Amy.

Did he adore her too much to let her go?

SARISI ISLAND

Millie stared up at the old castle and wished she hadn't burned all her photographs when she left Sarisi. Wished there'd been mobile phone cameras back then. Then she could've flashed a picture in front of Artemis and cracked the case wide open. Instead, she had to go with her instincts and her instincts were hyperventilating.

There was only one man she had ever known who could quote his sixteen-digit credit card number by heart. It couldn't be him, could it? But she already knew it could. She had worked it out ten days ago; she just hadn't come to terms with it yet.

The elderly Greek was watching her, eyes narrowing. "You know this man."

She nodded. *Yes she did.*

"This man, he no good."

She stopped nodding. She had never suspected that of him. At least not until recently. This news would take some getting used to. She had been so sure, she had been so certain.

"You find this man," Artemis said. "You call police! You tell world, not Greek man hurt you. This man! This *Australian.*"

She was nodding but what would be the point? It had been so many years and the evidence had long washed away. Suspecting someone of evil did not make him evil, and surely he wasn't the only man in the world who wore an Akubra and could recite his Visa number. There was her signed copy of *The Celestine Prophecy*, of course, the book that was stolen after the rape, but she suspected that would soon go missing. Holding onto it would be suicide for him.

"Thank you, Artemis," she said softly. "I do believe you, and I am so sorry that nobody else did." Then she reached in and kissed him on the cheek. "I'm sorry. About everything."

"No, no, no! No be sorry! Is not your fault, yes?"

She nodded, almost believing him.

~~~

Nicholas opened his front door to find Millie standing there, a sheepish expression on her face, a plastic Joe-Joe's bag in one hand.

"A thank-you present," she said, thrusting it towards him. "For helping."

He glanced into the bag and saw a fresh three-hundred-yard roll of fishing line, a small plastic container of assorted fish hooks, and some brightly coloured artificial baits.

"Very cool," he said and decided he'd also take it as a makeup gift and a peace offering. "So are you okay? How'd it go?"

"Good," she replied although that wasn't the right word, not even close.

"Did you... did you find the answer you were looking for?"

"Yes." But it wasn't really the right question either, and she smiled at him sadly. Nicholas didn't understand.

"Can I come in?"

"Of course!"

He waved her through, wishing he'd thought to clean up. He hadn't yet made his bed, and there were clothes and wet towels strewn about the place. As she took a seat on the small armchair by the window, he hoped she didn't find one of Catalina's bras lost down the side or notice the smudged lipstick on one of the wineglasses, forgotten beside a cluster of photo frames on the side table by her chair. The truth was he hadn't slept with Catalina since he'd first clapped eyes on Millie, but still he cringed at the thought of her knowing.

"How did you find my place?"

She smiled. "Kostas told me. Not that I asked, mind you. He insisted on giving me directions when I got up this morning."

"God I love that guy." He chuckled. "So, can I make you a coffee or get you a drink of—"

"No, thank you." She waved at the seat next to her and said,
~~~

"Can we talk? I need to explain—"

"You don't have to explain anything."

"Oh, I think I do." She waited as he sat down, then chose her words carefully, starting with, "You already know what happened to me, about how I was attacked."

"Yes and now you know who did it, maybe now you can get some justice."

"I had already worked it out, Nico." He frowned. "It was a guy I was travelling with back then, an Australian. I didn't realise it at the time."

He looked surprised. "So it wasn't a local?"

"No. It was not."

"Okay, but that's a good thing, right? You know his name. Now you can track him down in Australia and—"

"I already know exactly where he lives."

He stopped, stunned. "Really?" *So why was she here? Why was she asking Effie about him?* "Did you call the police? Did you confront him?"

"No." She gave him the ghost of a smile. "I had to get out of there. I got on the first flight to Greece."

"What?" *Now she'd really lost him.*

Millie sighed and tucked her feet up under herself; tried to explain.

"I never saw my attacked. Had no idea, until last week, when I stumbled across the truth. It's a long story and I don't have the energy right now…" She sighed again. "Anyway, I finally realised who it was, and I had to get back here as fast as possible. I booked the first flight out. Didn't tell anyone. Well, just one person, but they'll keep it to themselves. I hope. I just   took off."

She was still surprised by what she had done, still baffled that she'd had the courage, but he was looking at her like she was insane, and there was something else in his expression—was it worry? Disappointment?

"So you came back to the scene of your… *attack?* Why would you do that? What for?"

"That's not why I'm here. Not really."

He was still looking worried. Bemused. She realised it was time to stop talking in riddles. Time to explain herself.

She swallowed hard. "What I'm trying to tell you, Nico, what I should have told you days ago…"

She got to her feet and stepped across to him. Knelt down at his legs and placed her hands on his knees. "It's the reason I stayed at the convent for so long."

"You were hurt. You were depressed. You were—"

"I was pregnant."

He stopped, his breath catching. Yes, Catalina had tried to tell him this. He had refused to listen. "I heard something…," he began. "I know there were rumours, but I don't listen to rumours."

"Well you should." She offered him a grim smile and stood up. "He… my attacker, he left me pregnant. By the time I came out of the coma and found the will to live, it was too late to do anything about it and I didn't want to anyway. I felt…" She swallowed again. "I felt like it was just punishment—"

"No, you can't—"

"Nico, please, let me finish." He nodded. "I wanted to stay hidden away on Sarisi. I wanted to have the baby and then I never wanted to see any of it again. And so I did, I stayed in the convent and Agnetha cared for me, and then, one day, one very painful, bloody day, I had my baby. A beautiful, beautiful boy."

Her eyes flooded with tears, and she caught one as it trickled down her face.

"I had him for two weeks, Nico, two glorious, unforgettable weeks, and then I let him go."

She returned to her chair and looked out at the bay beyond as though that was the end of the conversation and he couldn't help the frown that was forming on his forehead.

"But how? How could you…?" His frown deepened. It was unfathomable to Nico.

She glanced back at him. "I loved my baby, Nico."

"Then *why*?"

"Because I was terrified I'd grow to hate him!"

He gasped at that and she seemed winded, too. She hadn't ever said it out loud, had never fully articulated this fear. He went to get up but she held a hand out to stop him.

She needed to say it, if only for herself. "I wasn't lying about him being beautiful. So cherubic, you could have put him on the cover of a baby magazine. But I knew that would change. I knew that one day

I would look at him and I wouldn't see *him* anymore, I'd see someone else."

"Who? What are you talking about?"

"That man, the man who hurt me." Her voice choked, she swiped at more tears. "I knew that every time I looked at my boy I would not just be looking at my son, I'd be looking for signs of that monster. And then one horrifying day it would happen! I would see. And then how could I unsee that? It terrified me!"

"But Millie—"

"No! You don't understand! It's not how a mother should look at her child! It wouldn't be fair to him. I couldn't bear to hate him. And I couldn't bear for him to see that hate. I thought it was better... better for him to grow up with only love in his mother's eyes. He needed a new mother. And so I gave him away."

She hugged her torso and let the tears stream freely now. He nodded, he understood that, but he didn't know what to say to her, he didn't know how to stop her tears, and he feared that if he went to her she'd suddenly crack.

He reached for a box of tissues and held them out.

She sniffed and took one. "Sister Agnetha said she'd find a good home for my boy, a loving home, a loving mother." She stopped to blow her nose. "That's why I'm here, Nico, not to find my rapist but to find my son."

Okay, it was finally starting to make more sense. "So last night, when you were talking to Effie, you weren't asking about your attacker, you were asking about your boy? You wanted to find your son. I thought..."

"I know that's what you thought." She sniffed again and tried to smile. "I thank you for trying to help me, for sending me to Artemis. But I already knew, deep down, who did it to me, and that's what makes it all so unforgivable."

He blinked back at her. Now he was lost again.

"Don't you see? What I did to that poor little baby? I left him here, floating in the wind. He's not Greek, Nico! He's *Australian*—both his parents are Australian—and I abandoned him to strangers! There's a boy somewhere on one of these islands and he's missing a mum and he's missing a dad—"

"He's better off without that monster!"

"I know that, but it doesn't change the facts. He's not Greek, he never was. He must feel so out of place… He must feel so, so different."

Nicholas stared at her, his spine tingling, thinking, *I know someone just like that. Someone who has never fitted in.* He jumped up like he'd been bitten. "I think it's time to get that drink."

He strode into the kitchen, Effie's last words circling his brain, echoing Catalina's: *"Just forget you ever met this woman. She's no good. She is dangerous!"*

He opened the fridge and stared inside. *What did they mean by that? Why was she so…*

He heard the door slam and looked up.

"Millie?" he called out.

Nothing.

He returned to the living room to find it empty, and he glanced around. *What just happened? Where did she go?* He stared at her armchair. *Had she found Catalina's bra after all? Is that it?* Then he spotted one of the picture frames sitting facedown on the table next to the chair and frowned. Had Millie turned to look at it while he was fetching drinks? He strode across and picked it up. He turned it around. It showed a young boy with sparkling green eyes and a hint of red in his dark brown hair, smiling and laughing and squinting into the sun as he held a fish up for the photographer to capture.

It was his favourite photo of Theo.

EVE MAGAZINE

The wave of relief that rushed through Monty when she left Thomas's place was her first mistake. Her steady pace, the fact that she didn't bolt for her life, was her second.

She had only just stepped out into the inner-city laneway when she heard a click behind her. Her heart constricted but she was too slow to react. Thomas had one hand around her throat, the other pulling her back. She tried to scream, but she could barely breathe, and he was panting so loudly now. He pulled her inwards, but she kicked him from behind and managed to escape, but only briefly. She was barely a quarter of the way down the lane when he caught up, grabbing her again, this time slamming her against a brick wall with no means of escape.

"Thomas!" she cried, but he slapped her hard across the face, causing her to fly sideways and land in a huddle beside a cluster of rubbish bins. It was the back of the Italian restaurant, but the door was bolted shut.

"You and that stupid bitch," he said, looming over her. "Why didn't you both leave me the hell alone? You think you're so damn hot. But you, you never even came close to her, so how dare you even try to reject me."

"I… I'm not… rejecting you, Thomas, I'm…"

"Shut the fuck up!"

She recoiled, sinking back towards the bins.

"You don't get to reject me! I reject you, right?"

She nodded, breathing quickly, trying to look around, hoping to

God someone was close, but all she could see was an empty laneway and just one dark shop front. Whatever they were selling, they clearly weren't selling it now. Then she remembered; it was a jewellery store! Her heart sank lower. Jewellery stores didn't open at night.

"You were always sloppy seconds," Tom continued, stepping closer, kicking a small metal bin out of his way, the lid rolling towards Monty, "so don't act like you're better than me."

"I'm not…," she managed and then found herself saying, "But she was."

She couldn't believe she'd said it and neither could he. He stopped, fists clenched.

"What the fuck did you say?"

Monty recoiled again, waiting for a kick of his boot, wondering if this was how Amelia felt on that dark lonely beach thirteen years ago. And instead of terrifying her, she felt emboldened by the thought.

Millie had survived then and she would survive now. Somehow she had to survive.

The kick came hard and heavy, straight towards her chest, but Monty managed to get her knees up in time so they took the bulk of the blow. She felt a pain shoot through her right leg and wondered if he'd fractured something, wondered how she could possibly flee with a broken knee.

That's when she remembered the article. Mel's stupid SOS story.

It was too late for step number one: *Run, ladies, run for your lives*, and she knew the second step—something about screaming—would cop her a boot in the throat, so she moved to step three: *Keep the bastard talking.*

She took a ragged breath. "You were angry with her for jumping off the ferry, Tom. I don't blame you."

He was leaning down then and stopped, frowned at her.

"You were angry with me for hooking up with Angus. I get that."

It was the wrong thing to say, his foot lifted again and this time it hit its target, smashing into her jaw and sending her flying again, back to the brick wall, writhing in agony.

"You dumb bitch," he said, stepping back and wiping his forehead. "I didn't give a shit about you! You honestly thought I was sobbing on a Santorini beach. Over *you?*"

She shook her head madly. *No, of course not. He only had eyes for Millie.*

She croaked: "So *that's* when you went back? When Angus and I were together?"

He didn't say anything.

"You caught the ferry back to Sarisi. You found Millie… You… you… raped her."

"It wasn't rape!" He pulled Monty up by the shoulders and spat his words out. "She owed me. She led us boys on a merry dance, and then she ditched us both like we didn't matter! Jumped ship for some wog she met for five fucking seconds! She was more like my mother than I realised. Both stupid sluts, both not worthy!"

Monty wasn't sure what he was on about now but she had to regain control of the conversation. She said, "Did Angus know? Did he—"

"He didn't want to know! Didn't want to do anything about it, but I sure did. You don't get to bat your eyes at us for a week and then just waltz away."

Monty held her nerve, staring him in the face as she said, "She had to pay."

He smiled suddenly, his teeth gleaming white. "You know what they say, Monty? Someone's got to pay the ferryman."

The words were almost as painful as the boot and she recoiled, feeling sick to the stomach, but she couldn't avoid his sneer. He had his face close to her now and was pushing her back up against the brick wall, wedging his body against hers. It was so tight she couldn't lift her legs to kick him where it hurt, and she wondered idly why Mel hadn't thought to include that step. Why Alex hadn't edited it in.

Probably for this very reason; probably because it so rarely worked.

"And you were the ferryman?" she managed to say.

He snickered as his eyes began to run down her body, and she ignored the bile that was rising in her throat. *Keep talking,* she told herself. *Just keep talking.*

"How did you find her?" she croaked again, trying to see behind him as his eyes kept roving downwards. There was still no sign of life. *Where were all the residents now? Where were the fucking hipsters and their fucking lattés?*

"Wasn't hard," he said, his eyes flickering back. "She was with that wog on the black beach. But then he just took off. Didn't even want her after all that! Can you believe it? She betrayed us and all for nothing. I saw my chance. I took what was mine."

He had one hand at Monty's neck again, his face was centimetres from hers. "And now I'll take some more."

Then he pushed her back towards the bins, lodging her body between a green recycling bin and the old metal one, as Monty tried desperately to remember step number four.

What was SOS step four?

Think, Monty, think!

Then it came to her in a whoosh, and she grappled behind her, reaching out for something, anything. When she produced the metal bin lid he didn't flinch, just looked amused as she held it up.

"Who do you think you are? Wonder Woman? You think that's gonna save you?"

She nodded and gasped. "SOS step four. In case of emergency… just break glass."

"What?"

"Don't bother screaming," she added, slowly twisting her wrist, "nobody cares."

This surprised him and he stepped back a bit, laughing. "Fuckin' right they don't. Nobody gives a shit about you or your friend."

"No… but they do care about… their stuff."

Then she took another enormous breath, twisted her wrist and flung the metal lid like a frisbee towards the jewellery shop window opposite them, and they both watched with awe as the lid hit the glass and then bounced off without shattering it. And for another horrifying moment Monty realised the game was up, there would be no more steps for her tonight.

And then a scream suddenly pierced the night air. The shop's burglar alarm had been activated.

If Tom had hung around a second longer, he would have seen the faces appear at the windows above, the people running down the laneway, the siren that came soon after. But he had already scuttled off and she was left slumped against the bins again, gasping for breath and sobbing like a child.

By the time the police reached her and the paramedics after that, Tom had long gone, probably via the fire exit at the back of his building.

"Don't worry, ma'am," a soothing policewoman told her. "We know where he lives. We'll find him."

She nodded, wiping her wet eyes and holding the icepack to her jaw. But it wasn't Thomas she wanted to find. Amelia was still missing. Amelia was her priority. And now she had to wonder what she didn't want to contemplate.

Had that monster found her first? And had he finished her off properly this time?

SHEPPERDIN VILLAGE

Harry Wilson sat in his dusty station wagon and waited. He'd been here for hours, not looking forward to uncovering the truth but needing to anyway.

He had spent an entire life covering for his brother Tom, but there would be no more cover-ups. He had seen that backyard. He knew what was what. Tom was the laziest bastard this side of Sydney. It was one of the many reasons their father had left the land to Harry.

He couldn't remember the last time Tom had mowed his own bloody lawn let alone cleaned up about the place, and he certainly wouldn't bother replenishing any of Phil's old play spaces.

The only reason Tom ever got that writing cabin built for Amy was because Scarlett had insisted on it—she thought it would cheer Amy up, give her some much-needed purpose, a place to hide out, not that she'd mentioned that last part to Tom. But Harry had done most of the work. Tom just stood around, sinking beers and telling him which bits he wasn't getting straight.

And what would Tom know? Couldn't even pull off a stupid jewellery tree. Had been working on the bloody contraption for months.

Harry shook his head, felt a lump in his stomach. Wished life had turned out differently. Wished he'd never offered his brother a house. Maybe then…

But he couldn't think of that. Not yet. He needed proof, and there was one man who could provide it.

When Jimbo's shiny four-wheel drive finally swept into the car park of Shepperdin Building Supplies, Harry waited a few minutes, giving the guy a chance to gather his gear and unlock the place. Then he pulled his shoulders back and stepped out of his vehicle.

There were some difficult questions to ask, but somebody had to ask them.

SARISI ISLAND

"Oh darling girl! I did not hear you arrive. Did you come alone? Did you steal a boat?" Zoe was seated on a wicker chair at the back of her yurt, legs up, a book in her lap, the sun bearing down upon her face.

"It's low tide," Millie said. "I walked across."

Ran, really, like she'd been running for the past decade, but this time she was running towards the truth, this time she was ready to face it, her legs almost buckling under her as she made her way to Mikro.

"Why didn't you tell me?" Millie demanded, breathless but still calm at this point.

Zoe looked at her sharply and dropped her legs to the floor. "I'll get us some tea."

"I'm not here for your blasted tea, Zoe. I want the truth. I came here the other day for the truth."

"No, darling, you were not ready then."

"Well, I'm ready now!"

"I can see that, yes. This week has been good for you. Nicholas, he has helped?"

"What?" *What was she going on about?* "I didn't come for a bloody holiday, Zoe."

"And yet that is exactly what you needed."

"You have no idea what I need. What do you even know about me?"

"I know that you wear your fancy clothes and speak your haughty

263

way, but I see you, Millie. I see you."

The hide of the woman, in her designer kaftans and plum accent. "You are such a hypocrite."

"No, I live by my truth. Do you?" Then she sighed wearily and struggled to her feet. "And now I will get us that tea."

As the elderly lady prepared the pot, boiling the water on the gas stove top, scooping in the loose leaves, Millie watched her, angry at first, then irritable and finally feeling foolish.

What was she even doing here? This had nothing to do with Zoe. Yet it felt like the right place, the *only* place where she might get some honest answers.

Millie waited until the tea was done steeping and they both had mugs in hand, then followed Zoe back to the sunny spot where they sat down on wicker chairs. She had no idea what the woman put in her tea, but it calmed her almost instantly, and she felt stronger with every sip.

"You knew, didn't you?" Millie said eventually. "You knew it the second you saw me."

Zoe smiled. "As clear as your green eyes, my darling. I'm surprised Nicholas did not see it, but then he's a man. They see what they want to see. They see what is convenient."

"So I'm like an inconvenience that's just arrived on the scene?"

"What did you expect? A ticker tape parade?"

No, Zoe was right. She hadn't thought this through. Had not considered the consequences of her actions, had *reacted*, something she never did, at least not since that fateful day on the ferry.

"I always knew Effie's story was not right," Zoe was saying. "I knew she came out from Paros about the same time as you. I didn't know the details, but I knew her baby was lost and then suddenly her baby was found." She sipped from her cup, smiled. "Everything else you must hear from Effie."

"I tried. She lied to me."

"She's a mother; you cannot blame her for that."

Millie shook her head. "Please...," she said, needing to hear it confirmed, but Zoe was staring into the distance now.

"It is not my place, my darling. And you know that. You have waited this long, you need to hear it properly. Go back to Effie. Find her. Ask her. Face the truth."

The beautiful, brutal truth.

EVE MAGAZINE

Monty was still shaking when she got to the Malone residence. She was battered and bruised, looked like she'd gone a few rounds with Mike Tyson, but luckily nothing was broken and Beryl, bless her heart, managed to conceal her horror as she helped her gently inside and got her straight onto the couch.

Ron had a glass of something stiff and strong in her hands before she could stop him, and she said, "I think it might be time for me to cut back on these."

He snorted. "You're still in shock, Monty. You can start AA tomorrow."

She smiled and clung onto the glass.

"I am so, so sorry," Beryl was saying, a tumbler of whisky also in her hands. "If I had known this was going to happen, I would never—"

"Please, Beryl. I'll survive. I did survive, in fact, all thanks to *Eve*." She shook her head and ignored Beryl's confused look as she thought of that silly little SOS story and how it may have saved her life.

"What a nasty piece of work," Beryl was saying. "I can't believe he was a friend of yours."

I can't believe I once slept with him. Monty remembered that first night near the Spanish Steps. How Angus had chosen Millie or, as she'd just learned, how Millie had chosen Angus, leaving one man smug and another resentful. She couldn't believe she hadn't sensed it, had continued sleeping with Thomas for that week in Rome then discarded him so breezily for Angus after Millie jumped ship.

She shuddered thinking how lucky she was that Thomas hadn't held that against *her*, wasn't as fixated with her as he had been with Millie. She might also have found herself brutalised on a beach somewhere. Because didn't that book now prove everything? Tom had Amelia's copy of *The Celestine Prophecy*, the one that had been stolen from her the night she was attacked. If it was in Thomas's possession, then he had to be her attacker, there could be no other conclusion.

"Oh you're still shivering, dear. Ron, get the poor girl a blanket!"

"I'm okay," she said, but Beryl wouldn't hear of it and fussed around her for many minutes, tucking a cashmere throw carefully around her aching limbs and fetching the soup she'd been warming up.

"This'll comfort you," she said as she handed the bowl over.

But how could Monty ever feel comfortable again? How could she possibly rest until she knew that Amelia was okay? That she'd made it out of the country and was safely in Greece?

Earlier she had told the policewoman the whole story and been urged to make a statement at her local station the next day.

"We can get in touch with Interpol," the officer told her. "We can try to track your friend down. That is, if she's even over there."

She told Ron and Beryl all of this as she slurped the chicken soup, but Ron was having none of it. He had dallied long enough. He strode out of the room, and when he returned a few minutes later he had his wife's mobile phone in his hands.

"I just did my first text message," he told the two women, Beryl gulping as Monty smiled. "I told Amelia that if she didn't reply to me in the next hour, I'd be getting on the first flight to Greece."

"But what time is it over there, Ron? She might be asleep for all you know!"

"It'd be daytime now," Monty said, giving Ron the thumbs-up.

He nodded, his face grim. "If that doesn't get her calling, *then* we can be worried."

SHEPPERDIN VILLAGE

Tom knew there was no hope the second he spotted the flashing blue and red lights, was glad he'd downed a few beers at the pub with Grant earlier, it would help buffer him from the brutality of what was to come.

There were several squad cars blocking the road and two vans parked up his driveway, a woman in a plastic bodysuit pulling something from a trunk. But worst of all was the sight of the small digger perched in his backyard.

Constable Dobson pulled Tom's car up well before the driveway and demanded he get out. Then frogmarched him the final fifty metres towards his house.

He spotted Scarlett standing in her yard again, no kids at her feet this time, scowl on her face, and he went to wave but thought better of it and looked away. That's when he saw his brother, standing to the right of Geoff Pinter, under the shade of Amy's beast of a tree.

Harry wouldn't meet his eyes.

"We found her," Geoff said as soon as Tom reached him. Then he nodded his head towards the sandpit, which had been partially dug out, and to what looked like a baggy grey suitcase on the other side.

It was Amy, of course, now lying in a body bag, and Tom felt his throat constrict and his eyes well with tears.

"How could you?" This was Harry, now glowering at him, but Geoff had a hand up.

"Mate, I told you, if you're gonna get emotional you need to move back."

"You'd still be looking for her if it wasn't for me!" he retorted.

"*You?*" Tom gasped at his brother and Harry glared at him again.

"Jimbo told me about the stolen sand. How it went missing on Sunday night. Same time as your poor wife!"

Tom looked away, hung his head. He thought he had been so clever, the sandpit such a perfect burial place, her body rotting in a deep hole beneath her special spot, the very place she once pottered with their son, the child she then plotted to rip from him. He had driven to work very late that night, pinched a few bags of sand to cover her over, didn't think anyone would notice.

He watched as a forensics examiner squatted at the edge of the sandpit, shifting through it as if looking for gold nuggets.

He probably would have got away with it if Harry hadn't said something. People always suspect freshly turned soil, but sandpits were frequently turned over, the sand frequently freshened up. Who would think to look below the surface of a child's beloved playground? Only Harry would have known that Tom hated that sandpit almost as much as he hated the blasted fig and hadn't replaced the sand since Phil was four. He'd loathed the way the two of them would spend hours out there, digging and laughing and *avoiding him.*

Then he snickered at the memory of Harry's snotty-nosed kids recently playing just above Amy's rotting flesh.

Geoff watched as Tom stared at the sandpit, his face void of emotion. Couldn't believe what his old mate had turned into.

"Why did you do this?" he asked. "Because she was leaving you?"

"Not just *leaving* me, Geoff. Taking my kid. Hiding him away in some posh boarding school so she could head to Greece and hook up with some wog she met for five seconds on some ferry a million years ago. Who did she think she was?"

"But how did you know she was heading for Greece?"

Scarlett told Geoff that Amy was good at keeping secrets, that there was no way she would have told him if she was planning to run, but Tom was shaking his head incredulously now.

"I didn't, not until I saw Monty's magazine. Amy must have seen that story, too. It must have put the idea in her head."

"It also put ideas into your head, didn't it?" Geoff said. "You saw it as your get-out-of-gaol-free card. So you went zooming down to

Monty's Sydney office, made a big song and dance. Made sure everyone saw you there, accusing her of sending your wife to Greece, wanted us all to be distracted by that, not realising that in fact your wife never went anywhere. She was lying in your own backyard."

"But… but if you didn't know… then *why*?" This was Harry, also grappling to understand, barely able to contain his rage.

"Because she was leaving me!" Tom bellowed suddenly, like that was reason enough. "Told me calm as day, like it was all very normal behaviour thanks very much."

Geoff sighed, his heart twisting for Amy. Wishing she wasn't quite so loyal, quite so honest. That was one secret she should have kept to herself.

"She'd just put Phil to bed," Tom said, his voice barely a whisper. "She came to my shed, looking so damn pleased with herself. Said very calmly, 'I have to leave you Tom. I need to go away.' I thought she meant to her mum's for a bit, but then she showed me her new passport. Like she was so proud of it! Said she needed to go overseas, to find herself again." He sniggered, the sound making his brother flinch. "I thought she meant Paris or something. I didn't even twig she meant Sarisi! She said she needed a few weeks, then she'd come back for Phil. Like, yeah no worries, babe, you go spend all my hard-earned money on some fabulous holiday, then return and take my son away. Good fuckin' plan that one!"

"You tried to stop her?"

"I didn't have to stop her. I was never going to allow it."

"So you killed her."

Tom glanced at the policeman sharply. "It didn't happen like that. It was an accident. I… I was so angry and she was so surprised, like, 'Oh, I thought you'd be cool with this.' My God what rock was she living under? 'Course I wasn't *cool* with it."

"She wanted to be honest with you, Tom. Should she have lied? Should she have run off without telling you?"

He thought about that and shrugged. "I would've tracked her down anyway. She was never going anywhere."

And that's when it hit Geoff, the inevitability of it all. Poor Amy never stood a chance. Scarlett was wrong, she would have died either way. Perhaps she wanted to face life—death as it happens—with honesty, not sneak off like a rat in the dead of night. He had a hunch the forensics team would find her shiny new passport on or near her body. Her mobile phone smashed beside it.

As if reading his mind, Tom said, "If she'd just stayed where she bloody belonged. If she'd just been the good wife and mother, well, none of this had to happen, see? She asked for this. It was her own damn fault. I gave her a good life. I saved her and her unborn baby. I cleaned up after that monster!"

"What monster?" said Harry. "You talking about Angus? He was just a young fool who got a girl pregnant. That's all he did."

"It was *enough*. He defiled her. It left her broken. She was going to get some nun to help her get rid of it. Or... or maybe she thought that Greek arsehole was going to save her. I don't know anymore."

He looked frantic. His eyes darting about. "I... I just know I'm the one who got her back. I'm the one who saved her and Phil. *I'm* the one who made her happy!"

Harry scoffed and so did Geoff. He wasn't sure what Tom was now rambling about. Nun? What nun? But he did know there was nothing happy about Amy. She was already dead inside, living in a loveless marriage, where he probably reminded her every day what she "owed" him. How he "saved" her.

It would destroy her eventually anyway. Tom's innate evil streak was beginning to surface. His aggression had been escalating as their marriage deteriorated. Geoff had seen it in so many marriages so many times before. It started with "love", then with control, then escalated into violence. Maybe it hadn't yet, but it was coming.

Amy's only mistake was not to try to cut and run. Now they would never know if she ever stood a chance. Maybe, just maybe, she might have got away. Maybe she might have made it back to Sarisi to rekindle things with some Greek stranger they all seemed to know about. Or maybe she wasn't fleeing to find true love, or even herself.

Maybe she was fleeing to stay alive.

In any case they would never know. Now Phil would be left without a mother because she had proven too honest, too loyal, too dutiful to the real monster—the only monster—in this entire saga.

"So how did it happen?" Geoff asked, trying to keep his tone casual.

He knew he should be doing all this properly, at the station, but he needed to hear the truth and suspected a good lawyer would shut Tom up. That it might never come out otherwise.

"It was an accident," Tom said again. "She came into the shed to tell me about her plans. I'd just pulled the jewellery tree apart, fucking thing wasn't working, so I turned and… and…"

And finally he broke down, falling to his knees and sobbing, and it was a relief to see, at least for Harry who had listened to this exchange with shock and horror, no longer recognising his own flesh and blood.

They would later learn from the autopsy that Tom had smashed his wife across the back of the skull with the heavy wooden trunk of the miniature tree. She must have been walking towards the shed door at that point, perhaps her last thoughts were of freedom. In any case, he then washed the blood off and reconstructed the tree. Had let his own son look at it, touch it, inspect the very thing that had snuffed his mother's life out.

They didn't know any of this yet. For now, Tom was just sobbing, choking back tears and snot and his anger, but Geoff was not quite finished yet.

"So you drove straight to your workplace late that Sunday night, yeah? You pinched a few bags of fresh sand and you used it to hide your wife's body under the sandpit."

He shrugged, dropping down onto his bottom. "She always did like the beach." Then he wiped his face and shook his tears away. Half sniggered. "I wanted to do Belinda on the sandpit, but bloody Scarlett and Polly and all those bitches were always watching! Had to make do with Belinda's sandpit instead."

"You disgusting, disloyal bastard!" This was Harry now, and he was about to launch himself at his brother, so Geoff grabbed one of his arms to hold him in place.

Tom seemed more outraged by Harry's comment than anything else and turned to him with fury. "Don't you get it, man? I was the loyal one! Not Amy! We were meant to be together. It was our fucking destiny. How could she leave me? If she left me it didn't just make a mockery of my marriage, it made a mockery of our mother."

"*What?*" Harry's face was contorted with confusion and disgust. "What are you saying about Mum?"

"That's why she left, don't you see? Mum left so I could be free to leave, too, to travel and find Amy. By leaving, Mum enabled me to meet Amy and—"

"She left because she met another bloke, you moron."

"What? No! Dad wasn't good enough for her. She sacrificed herself for me."

"It had nothing to do with you!" Harry was barely containing his rage, his body shaking under Geoff's tight grip. "God, now I see why Scarlett calls you a narcissist, why Dad left you nothing! Because after everything, all Mum's affairs, you still took her side, you refused to see. Her pissing off had nothing to do with you, and it certainly had nothing to do with a woman you met ten years later. Mum left because she loved some other bloke more than all of us combined, and that's the end of that sad, pathetic tale."

"No!" Tom scrambled to his feet and reached for Harry, his fists clenched, but Dobson had a hold of him and Geoff had one palm out.

"Enough!" he said. "That's enough for today."

Then he gave Dobson the nod and the officer yanked Tom away, another officer helping to secure his hands behind his back. They were all eager to lock the bastard up. They'd seen the poor woman's body, wrapped in a paint-splattered drop-sheet beneath the sand and plastic toys, and it had ripped their hearts out, the creepiness and obscenity of her burial place. Most of them had kids of their own, some would be sitting in their own sandpits now, shovelling dirty sand into their Tonka trucks.

As Dobson dragged Tom to a paddy wagon, Geoff released his grip on Harry and gave him a short, sharp nod. It was a thank-you of sorts, but he wasn't sure the guy would want to hear it out loud.

Despite it all, Tom was still his brother.

SARISI ISLAND

Effie was not at the Casa Delfino when Millie finally trudged back, but she already knew where to find her and headed straight up.

As she made her way to the old convent, knowing to take the faster route along the dusty road, Millie pulled out her mobile and finally made the call she'd been putting off all week. There was crying and screaming and plenty of recriminations but mostly there was relief. And she knew she owed them all so much, wondered if, yet again, they could ever forgive her, but she couldn't think about that now, her journey was not yet complete.

The hostel was empty when she got there, even Kostas was missing from his front perch, but that wasn't where she was headed. She walked through the reception area and across to the side, then unlatched the arched wooden doorway and stepped out to the small cemetery on the western side of the castle.

Effie was squatting on a windswept patch of grass in front of a tiny wooden cross.

"Your baby?" Millie asked softly, and Effie nodded, not looking around as she approached.

"Stillborn," Effie said. "Never even took a breath."

Millie reached towards her, but her back stiffened, so she just knelt on the grass beside her and waited. She glanced around and couldn't help smiling. They had spent many hours side by side like this, here in the cemetery swapping ghost stories or up in the dormitory or out on that Juliet balcony. And it wasn't all bleak.

There was some laughter, too, sometimes even dreaming. Despite the horror and indignity of it all, they had enjoyed their nine months together.

"Why didn't you tell me you lost your child?" Millie said at last and Effie sighed.

"I didn't tell anyone. Only the sisters knew. Oh and Zoe. Somehow the silly old witch had worked it out."

"Zoe's scary like that."

Effie smiled. "You have no idea."

"What about Nico? You never told him? He never twigged?"

She shook her head. "Although if Kostas hasn't worked it out by now he's thicker than he looks. I come here every month. Always leave something."

Millie glanced down, only now noticing the smattering of tiny, whitewashed shells and several faded plastic flowers, what looked like a silver charm bracelet.

"It's not that we meant to keep it secret. Is just the way it worked out." Effie hugged her knees to her chest, placing her head on them, looking across at Millie now. From that angle she looked sixteen again.

"He was like a gift from God, your boy. This is why I call him Theo. It was like fate or some of that crazy stuff you used to go on about." She smiled. "I no believe it until then. Until you left and my precious baby was taken from me, and your baby... he was just lying there in his crib, crying for his mother."

Now Millie stiffened and Effie reached a hand across and placed it on her knee.

She said, "I was crying so much too, Millie. I was so, so sad. I didn't think I could ever get over that terrible loss." She sniffed. "But then Aggie placed your boy in my arms and suddenly it all makes sense. Everything okay again. At least it was okay for me."

Then she reached her other hand over to grasp Millie's. "Please," she said, "you cannot take him away. I cannot lose another child. Maybe if you don't see him. Maybe is good you don't know him—"

"Effie..."

"You have no right." She whipped her hands back and hid her head in her knees.

Millie watched her sadly. She knew Effie wasn't talking legally— legally Millie probably could mount a pretty good case. She was young; nothing was signed; nothing was agreed. But she really meant ethically, morally, spiritually. And she was right. Millie told her so.

"But I'd like to get to know him a little, if that's okay."

The relief in Effie's eyes when she turned to look at Millie again was heartbreaking and she realised then that Effie, too, had been living in a kind of suspended universe, as terrified of Theo's face as Millie had been. Every time Effie looked at him did she see his biological mother? Every time the ferry arrived with a new batch of tourists, did she search for Millie's face among the crowd, fearful she'd return, demanding to see her child? Demanding to take him away.

No wonder she panicked when I finally showed up, Millie thought now. No wonder she fled on the first ferry out. No doubt she thanked God her boy was hidden away in Athens. *She wasn't to know that I would befriend Nico and end up in his apartment, staring at a photo that looked spookily like me.*

But she didn't think Effie minded her knowing, not really.

"Why didn't you tell me? Why didn't you just say?"

"I love him so much."

"Good! I'm glad." She reached for Effie's hand this time. "I *wanted* my boy to find a good home. I said that to Aggie! I'm so happy he found you, Effie, that you cared for him. But now…"

"Now?' Effie's voice was barely a whisper.

"Now I can't believe I ever thought the way I did. When I looked at that photo of Theo, yes, I saw a little of myself, but I also saw a little bit of him and it doesn't scare me anymore. He doesn't scare me now."

"Who?" Effie said and Millie took a deep breath.

She needed to say the name she had submerged for so many years, the name that had pulled her away from her child and thrown her asunder.

"My rapist," she said. "Theo's dad. He was a man on a ferry who pretended to be my friend. A man called Thomas Wilson."

For all their months together, alone in that convent, she had never told Effie the full story of what had happened and how it had unfolded, but it fell from her lips now. And finally she could not stay quiet.

It all started with a question, Millie told her. "A very foolish set of questions, in retrospect. What is love? What is it really? And can it be trusted?"

That morning, as the boat slapped against the Sarisi wharf, Millie watched that stranger give her the eye, invite her to follow, and like a fool, she accepted his invitation without thinking. Without considering anything or anyone.

"Hey, Millie, just chill," Monty had said. "We're not getting off yet."

She shook her head. "I am."

"What?" That was Angus, stunned and confused but not feeling the deep sense of betrayal that would rapidly grow inside his friend. A sense that would soon turn sinister.

"Sorry, but I need to go."

"I'll come—" said Angus, but she shook him off.

She wasn't being fair, she knew that, she had led him on, but how could she turn away now, how could she avoid her fate? And so she had shoved her foolish book into her pack and flung it across her shoulder, then whipped her ponytail from underneath and told Monty, "I'll catch up with you back in London."

"And if you don't?" Monty called after her.

"Then consider me happy and get on with your life!"

Monty had never remembered that part of the conversation, and Millie wished she had because it would have absolved her of all her guilt, guilt that was never hers to begin with.

Then she had laughed, full of exhilaration and promise, and done the unexpected. The thing her parents had always warned her against. She followed her heart instead of her head. She stepped off the boat and into its blinding consequences.

He was waiting for her on the wharf, her handsome Greek man, and told her his name was Akakios—"It's Greek for innocent, but everyone calls me Aki"—then he held out his hand and she took it without hesitation. She didn't think then, as she did so many times since: *What if I had just stayed on the ferry?*

Artemis found Millie three days later, half naked and bleeding, beneath an abandoned pontoon at the quiet end of Sarisi, just down from his *pension*. She had been brutalised, left for dead. At first he thought she *was* dead and reeled back when her eyes fluttered, rushing her to the nearest nurse, the only nurse, Sister Agnetha at the Sisters of Mercy Convent.

There, in a cold hard bed she slipped in and out of consciousness for weeks.

"What is your name?" she heard someone ask before the darkness swallowed her again.

And, "Where are you from?"

And, "Who are you?"

When she finally awoke, it was not the bruises or the bones that ached. It was her soul. Her heart. Her faith.

And when they asked again, "Who are you? Where are you from?" she did not answer because she did not want to know and so she turned towards the stone wall and refused to speak.

It was only when the bleeding stopped and the vomiting began that one question was finally answered.

Who was she?

She was a twenty-year-old woman with a baby growing inside her.

Millie first met Effie in that convent dormitory. She was from the neighbouring island of Paros, and pregnant, too, hiding like Millie, pretending it wasn't happening, although much more vocal about it. She had screamed and cried and lashed out the first few weeks and then eventually she had accepted her destiny, even embraced it.

The father was an older man, a friend of her parents, she told Millie one warm dark night, and they would kill him if they knew. That is if her brothers hadn't killed him first. That made Millie laugh out loud and finally, in the third month, she spoke.

"You're lucky you have brothers who love you," she croaked, and Effie's eyes had widened.

"You're Australian!" she cried. "I have cousins in Melbourne." She scrunched her thick eyebrows together and said, "Or Kiwi? You not Kiwi, are you?"

"Australian," she said, but that was all she would offer.

She was never going back.

But of course she did go back. By the eighth month she knew she must. And she knew she had to go alone. She didn't want this child. *His* child. The child of such brutality. And so she gave birth early one morning, in the same stiff bed, with Sister Agnetha at one end and Effie wide-eyed and still fat-bellied at the other.

And when that tiny child came into the world deathly quiet, Millie thought, *Thank God.* But then he cried and was thrust into her arms and she held him long enough to soothe him. Long enough to fall in love.

Two weeks later she was home, in the belly of her family and in a body she no longer wanted. There were no answers for her relieved family, no words for Monty who soon tracked her down at her parents' place, wanting to swap happy snaps, blissfully unaware that she had none, just a lingering memory of a man who took her hand and with it her faith in love.

"But that wasn't love," someone said, breaking through the monologue.

The two women looked around to find Nicholas standing behind them, his face deathly pale. He had heard everything.

"Don't you see," he persisted, stepping closer. "That guy on the ferry. It was just lust. Chemistry. It was nothing."

"*Nico*," Effie growled, warning him off.

Millie held up a shaky hand. "I know that now," she said and waved him over. "Don't you see that's why I'm here? That's why I've come back? Because the question still remains: What is love, really? And can it be trusted?"

For thirteen years she told herself no. She told herself never again. And yet the image of that tiny suckling child remained. Her love for him did not wither and die as she had hoped. It had only grown and intensified and left her angry and bitter and mean towards the people she should have been kind to—her parents, her *Eve* colleagues, especially Alex who had beloved children of her own.

She was here now, and she knew the answer to that question was very simple: Yes!

"I know that the love I had for that little boy, that was real, that could be trusted," she told them, "and I know nothing can change that love, Nico. Not the way he was conceived, not the way I left him, not the way his face would develop or the man he would become. And certainly not me hiding myself in my career, pretending it didn't happen or it didn't matter or some other bullshit. That was real! He was real, and that I know I can trust."

She turned to face Effie. "So please don't tell me I can't see him. Don't tell me he doesn't matter, that I shouldn't get to know him. I gave up everything for him. My body, my dignity, my trust. And now I just need to see him. To know it was all worth it. To know he's okay."

Effie nodded and grabbed Millie, holding her hard against her heart. "Of course you can see him," she whispered, "but I'm not the only one you must ask. I'm not the only one who loves him."

Then both women turned to look at Nicholas, and he smiled and said, "I think Theo is one very lucky child."

EVE MAGAZINE

Monty picked up the cardboard box and began placing her most precious items inside—her favourite issues, the awards they had won, the framed photos of herself, her team, some with company executives, some with A-list celebrities. She lingered over the picture of her and Amelia, dressed to the nines at a swanky film premiere and smiled. Despite their history, all the late nights and anguished moments, it had been an amazing ride, and she would have no regrets. She was looking forward to moving up two flights to the tenth floor, however, to *House & Feather*, to starting a new chapter.

To starting afresh.

She smiled, remembering the conversation she'd had with Millie late that night, while still at Ron and Beryl's house. How Ron had been speechless when at last his "baby girl" had called him back. For all his bluff, for all his bluster, he was so overcome he could barely speak and had fumbled the phone across, first to Beryl who assured Amelia everything was okay, then to Monty who burst into tears at the sound of her best friend's voice.

Amelia did sound amazing, a little weary but otherwise well, and it was such a blessed relief to hear she was safe. Monty didn't tell her about Tom's attack, not yet, but she did mention the book and how she knew what had happened all those years ago. Yet Amelia did not seem to care about that.

"It's not why I'm here," she told Monty over the scratchy line. "I can't give that monster any more of my time. I'm here for my son."

Monty knew the story—the truth about Millie's pregnancy and childbirth had come out eventually—and she understood that. "When will you be back?"

"I don't know. I haven't met him yet." Amelia sobbed a little then. "But I will, Monty. I will! I'm so, so close!"

Then she'd apologised again and hung up, leaving Monty and the Malones laughing and crying with relief, and Ron making firm promises that, once back, his daughter would never be let out of the house again.

"Monty?"

She turned around to find Hank leaning against the photo cabinet, staring at her with a worried expression.

She touched the bruises on her face and said, "You should see the other bloke."

He half smiled. The story had already circled the office, and she had made it clear she expected no sympathy, was determined to "get on", so he tried to ignore her battered body and said, "You heading up?"

She nodded. "*Eve's* all yours now, baby. I heard Gerry's already tapped you on the shoulder."

"It's not like he had much choice."

"Oh I think he had plenty of choices. You're a good designer, Hank. You'll be a fantastic art director."

He smiled. "I did have a fantastic mentor." Then he sighed wistfully and began walking away.

"Hank," she called after him, and he stopped and looked back. "Yesterday, you asked me out for a drink."

He took a step towards her. "Yes?"

"I'm just wondering, was that as a colleague or…"

She couldn't find the courage to finish the sentence and he smiled again and said:

"Or."

Then she smiled even wider.

SHEPPERDIN VILLAGE

Scarlett hugged Phil close to her chest and pushed the hair back from his big wet eyes.

"You'll be okay," she whispered, even though she wasn't sure he would be. And she felt her heart break for poor Amy as they watched her be buried for the second time.

But this time they were at the leafy Shepperdin cemetery and there was love all around her, and family and friends, and even a little laughter as they gathered afterwards at the Boot & Tucker to remember "adorable Amy" and swap stories of better times. When there was still happiness and hope.

Amy's parents hadn't stayed long, they were buckled over with grief, their expressions wretched, their bodies trembling, but they made it clear before they left that Phil was exactly where he needed to be—in the heart of Scarlett and Harry's large, happy clan. His relationship with his cousins was the only good thing to come out of all this.

Scarlett had only recently learned who Phil's biological father was, and she spied Angus Tower now at one end of the bar, flirting with a fashionably dressed woman with cherry-red hair who was rolling her eyes like she'd seen it all before and wasn't buying any of it, and she wondered if Angus would fight for custody but suspected he didn't have it in him.

Phil did though. He was a fighter, strong and resilient, and he would be okay. She believed it now as she watched him kicking a ball on the grass outside the pub, his cousins and friends gathered around him, his green eyes sparkling despite everything.

Phil had never belonged to Tom. He was always Amy's boy, and her death did not change that.

PART THREE

A few weeks later

EPILOGUE

The breeze is warming at last. The early tourists look a little less stunned and are leaving more layers in their backpacks, lingering longer on the beaches, smiling wider at the sharpening sun. I might linger a little longer too.

I feel welcome here. Apart from that one bleak night, I guess I always have.

I did get off that ferry, in case you haven't worked it out. I did follow my heart and get badly hurt and pull myself back from a very dark place.

A place that still occupies my dreams some nights.

I think about the years afterwards, after Thomas's brutal rape. How I swallowed down the truth and fled from it. I don't regret returning to Sydney and immersing myself in *Eve* magazine. The way I did it was harsh, unnecessary, at least for others. I know it was the only thing I could do; my floatation device. I behaved like a drowning man, grasping at my lifesavers, almost drowning them in the process.

I think of Monty and I'm so glad she did not drown. She has already booked her flight and will be coming to join me, to meet my boy, Effie's boy, and Nicholas's too. She gets two weeks' grace before throwing herself into the career she should have had years ago. Willow couldn't be happier; she's getting the best designer in the company. I'm not sure what will happen to the others. I've put in a good word for them all, especially Alex. She deserves the top job, but

Monty tells me she's not sure she wants it. Is considering her family. That would have shocked me once. Angered me even. Now I know what nonsense I spouted, how manipulative I have been. How smart Alex was all along. And how lucky she is to have such a devoted man like Tony to have her back, to have the courage to show up at my place one morning and stand up to a bully like me.

Oh, I'm not completely contrite. I did save the magazine. Gerry told me that over a boozy lunch several times. It was one more bad sales report away from being shut down. And I know I gave Alex the chance of a lifetime and kept Brianna on when the lazy slacker deserved to be sacked. But that's *why* I kept Brianna—because she had absolutely no ambition, and it made me feel safe.

And God I needed to feel safe back then.

But Monty had ambition and I do feel bad about that and about allowing her to take my guilt as her own. We might mock our naivety on the ferry that day, but we were grown-ups. Both twenty. Old enough to know better, old enough to own our own decisions. Even if she had jumped off the ferry and chased me down, I would have told her that. I would have laughed her away and kept walking towards my Greek guy.

The stranger who was less dangerous than the friend sitting across from me.

We only lasted two days, Aki and I, and then we realised our folly. We had so little in common, nothing to talk about. The lust was not enough to sustain us. So we smoked fake cigarettes in the early morning mist and shared one last kiss before I was to catch the red-eye on to Santorini.

We kissed. He smiled. He walked away.

I was getting back on the ferry. That's the irony! I was heading back to Monty and to Angus and ultimately to my rapist. But he came for me first. I think he would have hurt me no matter where I'd ended up.

I saw Thomas's eyes in his apartment that Friday before I left *Eve*. I saw the evil that Artemis speaks of, and so did Monty, and I am so dreadfully sorry. She told me about his assault during our last phone call, and it cut me to the core. If I had spoken up before I fled the country, if I had not been in such a stupid hurry, I might have spared her that.

I shiver and glance towards Nico, who is kicking a ball with Theo. My son. My beautiful, beautiful boy with his twinkling green eyes and floppy brown fringe and curiosity towards me, not anger or ill will. That, alone, fills me with hope. But I won't be performing any more coups, don't worry about that. It is not my place to march in and oust the old brigade. I have to tiptoe through their lives, hope to be involved, expect nothing.

I watch them for a while and wonder why I ever panicked. I no longer see any of Thomas in Theo. Sure, his hair has a reddish tinge, his shoulders already broadening, but he is so clearly his own person, fast evolving into his own man.

And I remember that question, the question that started all this: *What is love and can it be trusted?*

When it comes to my child I already know the answer. As for Nicholas Xydis? Time alone will tell. I don't yet know if *this* is love or lust or will even last the summer, but I also know it doesn't matter because finally I am asking. Finally I am moving past the bitterness and the cynicism and the fear.

I'm opening myself to love again, and isn't that what really matters?

Effie has offered me a job at the Delfy—she wants some time out—but I haven't accepted yet. I know my mother would be delighted—*she* wants me anywhere but *Eve*—but can I seriously downshift so dramatically? Switch smoothly from my publishing career to managing a hotel, bar and restaurant? Am I even capable of it? Again, time will tell and maybe Nico and Theo who are watching me now as I watch them, smiling, waving me across. Come, that wave says. Come play.

"Not a chance!" I yell back. I haven't played in a very long while.

Baby steps, boys, baby steps, please.

Later that evening, as I snuggle into Nico's chest, listening to him snore and marvelling at the beauty of watching someone you love sleep—no wonder Alex wanted to stay in bed on weekends!—I think about that day on the ferry, of the choices that I made.

And didn't make.

I wonder what would have happened if I had not followed the Greek stranger and had simply stayed on the deck, in Angus's lap. Would we have ended up together? Or would he have let me down like Thomas warned me he would that first night we met? I didn't realise it at the time, I thought he was just being a disloyal friend, but it wasn't Angus he was warning me about. It was himself.

"Chicks always fall for Angus first," he'd told us while his mate was fetching drinks in that smoky Roman bar. "But they soon learn, he's a flake. He never lasts the distance; always moving on to the next one. He only really cares about money."

He'd laughed and Monty had laughed along, calling him a jealous bastard, but when he spoke again it was my eyes he was beseeching.

"I'm in it for the long haul," he continued, his voice barely a whisper. "When I take a fancy to you, I'm in it for life."

I shiver at the memory and of what might have been, and for the first time in thirteen years I know that getting off the ferry was the right choice and it wasn't just because it created Theo.

Despite everything, I can't help thinking I made a lucky escape.

Then I snuggle deeper into my Greek man and I finally stop wondering, *What if?*

~The End~

ACKNOWLEDGEMENTS

Firstly, I'd like to thank my old school buddy Virginia Knight for strapping on her backpack and travelling through Europe with me all those years ago. It was during that journey—on a gusty Greek ferry—that the seeds for this story were first planted. While Sarisi Island is fictitious, along with Shepperdin Village and *Eve* magazine, there really was an Australian woman who jumped ship with a virtual stranger, and I've never forgotten the fear I felt for her, and the awe. I've often wondered what happened to that young backpacker, and hope she found the love she was rushing towards.

I'd also like to thank my twin sisters, Simone and Michelle, who read an early draft and advised so carefully and oh so kindly, as well as my editor and cheerleader Annie Sarac, my beloved reader Elaine Rivers, and family and friends who always have my back. Special thanks to Christian, Peter, Dianne, Michael, James, Debra, Antony, Morgana, Elaine, Lou, Steve, Tara, Nadine, Mandy, John, Louise, Bette, David and Poppy Jean. Thanks, too, to Sophie Hamley for setting me on this path.

And finally, thank you, dear readers, for your encouragement and support. Without you, my stories would never see the light.

For more news, views and exclusive giveaways:
calamer.com